"My name's Jer   "

"Do you know my master?" Impossibly, Wren looked *more* guarded.

"Yes. I do — did, rather. He didn't make it." Jere was silent for a moment, noticing the look of horror on the slave's face. "You did all you could — from what I heard from the lawyers, you were doing your best to pull him out, but the fire just got out of control. I'm sorry. For your loss."

Wren's face looked panicked for a moment, but he brought himself under control, breathing a sigh of relief. "Thank you, sir," he said carefully, still suspicious. "Are you a… a visiting doctor?"

Jere shook his head. "I'm Matthias's successor, I guess you could say. I inherited everything — his job, his house, his possessions."

Jere had rarely seen a projection respond so physically, but Wren's face went completely void of blood, his eyes widening in fear as he took a step back.

"Then you, you're my — "

"I own you now, yes." Jere struggled to keep the face of his own projection from going as white.

"Master, I, I apologize…."

"Wren, it's all right," Jere said, trying to be soothing. "You barely know what's going on. Just let me heal you. We can talk later."

Wren stayed where he was for another moment, frozen, still looking terrified. "Yes, master. As you wish." He walked toward Jere and dropped to his knees in front of him, head down.

Also recommended...

You may also enjoy these other ForbiddenFiction works:

Pathfinder by J.A. Jaken
Shai discovers he is a pathfinder and is desperate to find a genetically suitable partner to prevent his extrasensory talents from running amok. Unfortunately those talents make him a target for the brutal crime lords and other violent denizens who inhabit the city of Nhil-Rhar. Shai needs to learn how to use his pathfinder senses—no matter how much they terrify him—before he's trapped in a partnership that will enslave him for the rest of his life. (M/M)
http://forbiddenfiction.com/library/story/JAJ-1.000012

The House of Silence, Volume 1, by J.A. Jaken
The House of Silence is an elite male bordello catering to the obscenely rich. No matter how extreme or mundane the fantasy, the House of Silence is rumored to serve. Master Charon employs a group of versatile, beautiful young men–some lewd, some innocent, many with tragic pasts and hidden secrets of their own–who depend on him for safety. This volatile mix erupts when danger threatens. (M/M+)
http://forbiddenfiction.com/library/story/JAJ-1.000001

Inherent Gifts

Alicia Cameron

ForbiddenFiction
www.forbiddenfiction.com

an imprint of

Fantastic Fiction Publishing
www.fantasticfictionpublishing.com

INHERENT GIFTS
A Forbidden Fiction book

Fantastic Fiction Publishing
Hayward, California

CREDITS
Editor: Rylan Hunter
Cover Art: Adapted by Siolnatine from photo by Phil Date at Dreamstime.
Production Editor: Erika L Firanc
Proofreading: Kailin Morgan, JhP323

SKU: AC2-000068-01 FFP
ISBN: 978-1-62234-091-0

Published in the United States of America

DISCLAIMER

To everyone who read the early version of this book and begged for more. I started writing this for me, but your encouragement kept me going.

Contents

Chapter 1
A Healing Gift

The notification came by telegraph, a resurgent form of communication after The Fall, as well as by a speed messenger who never did bother to identify himself.

Jeremy Peters. Stop. Immediate presence requested at 141 North Meadow Lane Hojer. Stop. Medical property emergency and final will of Matthias C. Burghe attended on site. Stop.

Jere looked at the notification only briefly, feeling only the slightest pang of sadness at the loss of his one-time mentor. In all honesty, he had never really been able to call Matthias a friend — a fuckbuddy, a mentor, even somewhat of a father figure — but there had always been some sort of barrier between them. When they parted after Jere finished University, he was pleased to keep in touch with Matthias through the occasional letter and holiday card, but had never really counted on seeing him again.

"Sir?" The messenger said, raising an eyebrow. Speed messengers were not quite known for their patience.

"Of course." Jere's haze was broken. He walked to his desk and pulled out some money. "Pass this along, please: 'Leaving now.'"

The messenger rolled his eyes, as if slighted by the brief reply. Jere wasn't fazed; it wasn't as if the young, out-of-work doctor had a lot to spend after the county hospital had made his position "redundant" to allow an older doctor to resume his previous job. Redundant seemed to be a good way of describing much of his life at the moment. Begrudgingly, he handed over a decent tip, and at the last moment pressed a few extra bills into the messenger's hand.

"Under the table, could you set me up with a speed train to the address? I'd greatly appreciate it."

The messenger shrugged, then nodded. Side trips were excellent ways to make extra money, as there was no tracking system in place for messengers. Before Jere could say another word, the messenger had vanished.

Medical property emergency. Jere was a bit puzzled, wondering what had been lost in the telegraph system. He had heard that they often had accuracy problems. He thought briefly about the long-ago days when wireless communications had made tasks like sending messages as simple as picking up a device and speaking into it. It was more complicated than the psychic communications that had permanently shut down the wireless infrastructure, but psychic connections could only connect people who lived within a few miles of one another. Even telegraphs were only slowly starting to resurface, supposedly because the ancient technology was more stable and less likely to suffer from interference from psychic energy. Still, Jere trusted the mail system more than he did telegraphs, though he did appreciate the speed of the latter.

Not that he received telegraphs often. He hoped the error in the message was in the "medical" part, as he knew that Matthias had no family to speak of. Besides, Jere knew that his former acquaintance owned his home medical practice; presumably *that* was where the emergency had taken place. Buying the clinic and moving to Hojer was one of the reasons he and Jere had ended their relationship, if it even could have been called that.

He looked around his apartment, kicked aside a few *more* eviction notices, and packed some clothes hurriedly into a duffel bag along with a comb, toothpaste, and toothbrush. He briefly considered using the comb on the blond mess that he was passing off as a hairstyle these days, but figured the speed train ride would undo what little good it would be worth. Slinging the duffel over his shoulder, he grabbed his medical kit with his other hand, as it was the only thing in his apartment that was worth stealing, and headed off to the speed train station.

It was dark by the time Jere arrived. Fortunately, the end of summer was one of the few nice periods of weather, after the blistering heat had worn off and before the bitter cold started. It was a drought year, so there was no rain, and while the hike in food prices had been a burden, Jere was glad for the dry weather as he walked. He wondered if he should have written more in his telegraph, like his arrival time, or a request to be met at the train station and shown around. With no other recourse, he picked up a map from an information kiosk and started off toward the address mentioned in the telegraph.

He estimated that he had gotten about halfway to the house when he felt a searching presence in his mind, the way one would hear someone in the hall of an apartment building yelling around for a tenant whose room number he didn't know.

He dropped his guards a little so the searcher could identify him.

"*Mr. Peters?*" the voice inquired.

Jere nodded, purely from habit, and responded in kind. "*That's me. I'm close to the house — will we meet there?*"

"*Yes, sir, that will do just fine,*" the voice said. "*It would behoove you to hurry, Mr. Peters.*"

"*Will do.*" Jere cut off the communication. The man had been speaking to him as if he were dawdling. He picked up his pace anyway.

What Jere found at the address was a bit of a surprise. The combination home and medical clinic was rather large, although obviously of an older design. Matthias had mentioned that the place belonged to the town's previous doctor. One side of the building had been almost entirely rebuilt, within the last few days it seemed. A quick glance around the perimeter revealed scorch marks starting at the base of the house, extending for quite a few feet. A nearby tree had been cut down recently, but the stump was charred as much as the house must have been. A fire? It certainly explained the "emergency" nature of the telegraph.

A well-dressed man opened the door before Jere could knock, a mind gift habit that Jere found unnerving, despite growing up with the ability himself. He was equally unnerved by the enthusiastic handshake and the way the man half-dragged him through the doorway, making Jere feel weak despite the fact that he was taller and in considerably better shape than this man.

"We've had the structure restored, and some of the contents will be covered financially," the man said, ushering Jere inside. "The fire insurance covered it, fortunately for Dr. Burghe—well, fortunately for you, I should say. The grass will have to regrow itself though; no nature growers in a twelve county radius!"

Jere followed the man into the house. He didn't give a damn about the grass, he wasn't used to seeing grass anyway. The house was amazing, large and spacious and far beyond any place he would ever be able to afford in the next few years, even if he did find a job; not to mention significantly larger than any place any-one could afford in the city. Jere had heard rumors that rural areas hadn't suffered as much from overpopulation or the housing crisis, but a lot this large would fit his entire apartment back home—not to mention the thousands of people who lived in it. Was he really inheriting this house?

"Allow me to introduce myself; I'm Demlyn Montgomery, Dr. Burghe's lawyer. You'll be meeting my junior assistant, as well as our town notary."

Jere nodded, dumbstruck. Was this how everybody conducted business in these rural outlands? It was like they were waiting just for him. The false familiarity made him uncomfortable. "I'm Jere. As you know, of course."

The lawyer narrowed his eyes at him briefly. "Yes. Jeremy. Come, sit down and we'll discuss the details."

Jere found himself sitting on the guest side of what would soon become his desk, introduced to a Mr. Delgado, junior assistant, as well as a Ms. Young, town notary. The legalese and welcomes flew over his head almost without his notice as he tried to grasp the change that had come over his life in the past twelve hours.

"And so you see, Mr. Peters, this is why it is so important to us, to Hojer on the whole, that you agree to take over this position."

Jere was jerked back to reality. What had she just been saying?

His confused look hadn't given him away. "Oh, I know, it's a lot to take on all at once, especially for a young doctor. I mean, a whole town! In a new state! But Dr. Burghe had a lot of confidence in you, Mr. Peters. Said he wouldn't leave his community to anyone but you!"

"He did?" Jere asked, surprised. Matthias had always said that his skills were some of the best he had ever seen, but Jere always assumed it was just flattery.

"Oh yes," Ms. Young smiled at him. "We're often hesitant to hire outlanders, you know how it is, difficult to check references and everything, but you came so highly recommended."

"It's why he set up this arrangement," Mr. Montgomery continued, "and why the town is so eager to help. It's not easy these days to get a doctor, not a good one, to provide medical care for a whole town on his own, and in a town with the unique culture that you find in this state. For some reason, most young, promising kids at the start of their careers would rather starve to death in some overpriced apartment in the city with no hot water than come out here and live in comfort!"

Jere wondered briefly if this Montgomery had investigated his current living situation. The hot water had gone off two months ago, seemingly for good. He had heard others talking about moving out of the city, where the job crisis was terrible, but it had never been something he had considered. He had been scraping by on part-time gigs and disaster coverage for months now, and leaving Sonova had never seemed like a viable option. Plenty of other new healers were in the same position, and most would rather bide their time in the city where everything was familiar and convenient.

"Dr. Burghe left his position to you, and named you the sole inheritor of his estate, contingent upon your acceptance of the position. That means that this house, the clinic, any possessions or supplies or equipment—they're all yours. The settlement from the fire insurance will pay out to your account, and what remained in Dr. Burghe's bank account will go to you as well, after all necessary taxes and fees. I mean, you're practically guaranteed success here, Mr. Peters, not only from the inheritance, but also from the patient revenue. An entire town of potential customers, all yours!"

"An entire town?" They had mentioned that phrase a few times, but the idea was still daunting.

"Well, it's not a big town!" the notary hurried to say, casting a look at the lawyer. "Only about 3,000 residents, and maybe as many... others."

Others? What the hell did that mean? Tourism?

"And besides," Montgomery flashed his winning lawyer smile at him. "You'll have a slave! At least, I think he'll have a slave. Is he...?"

"Yes, he'll have a slave," the junior assistant supplied.

"A slave?" Jere felt as stupid as he must have sounded. Hojer was in a slave state? He knew they existed, but he had always thought they were rural, tiny, backwoods areas. Jere recalled the long, desolate walk through the dark streets of Hojer, the surprising lack of population or development. A glance toward the window reminded him of the lack of streetlights, but even in the daytime he would not be able to see the house of his closest neighbor from this distance. He realized with a sinking feeling that "rural, tiny, backwoods area" described Hojer perfectly. He returned his gaze to the others and repeated dumbly, "A slave?"

"Yes, you inherit him along with Dr. Burghe's other possessions. However, there is something you should be aware of," Ms. Young said hesitantly. "The slave is in pretty bad condition and would require medical attention rather quickly if you want to maintain usefulness. I doubt Mr. Burghe had him insured for very much, you know how young slaves are, and the rates and all."

"No. I don't."

Ms. Young laughed nervously. "Oh, no, I suppose you wouldn't, then, would you?"

"Well, anyway, the lad was pretty badly burned in the fire that killed my client," Mr. Montgomery continued, all business. "Sad thing, really. The fire chief says that it looks like he was trying to drag his master out when the fire caught him, too. It would be a shame to let a loyal slave like that expire."

"Expire?" Jere nearly needed his own hand to keep his jaw from dropping. "Right, right. Is he at a hospital, or...?"

Montgomery laughed, obviously unconcerned. "A hospital? Mr. Peters, *you* are coming here to be our doctor! Of course, if a resident had been seriously injured we could have placed them on a speed train to a city hospital, but even the closest veterinary would be too expensive to ship a slave, especially when it's so badly injured! And, with no master to sign for the treatment, well, who'd pay? No, we just hoped you'd be here in time to salvage what you could out of him."

Medical property emergency. That wasn't a bad translation, after all. What else would you call it when your property needed medical treatment?

"We've been checking in on him, as a courtesy to you. We managed to get him to keep some water down, but he's been pretty unresponsive most of today. You can look him over, he's just down the hall."

Jere looked at his watch. They had been discussing this "property arrangement" for forty-five minutes now. All the while, a human being had been excruciatingly burned and lying "just down the hall?" He took a breath to steady himself before he attempted to speak.

"I'll need to see to him immediately," he said stiffly, standing up.

"Now wait, wait, there's some legal business that needs finishing up before you can start that, I mean, technically, he's still a ward of the state until you accept—"

"Then let me sign what I need to sign and let me do my damn job!" Jere was very close to exploding at the casual indifference.

"Well, all right, all right, I can see you're eager—I'm assuming you're accepting the position, then? Can't be bad to have an eager doctor!"

Jere drew in a breath, reminding himself to be cautious in this new place. He could be patient and tactful when he needed to. "Yes, Mr. Montgomery, I would be thrilled to accept the position, and the house, and the slave. However, as I am not well-endowed, financially, I am quite eager to keep *all* of my property in good working order, and wish to see it attended to as quickly as possible."

The legal team of three smiled brightly as if he had just won the lottery, or as if there weren't someone dying in the next room, and the whirlwind of paper-signing began. Somewhere along the way it was explained to him that, in the event of his death or departure, he would need to select an incumbent, as he had been selected, and there was something about fees, and some sort of stipend from the state as an agreement to cover uninsured or financially distressed patients, and a partial healthcare reimbursement. Overall, the process seemed more laborious than necessary, all while someone lay dying in the next room.

Thirty minutes later, the paperwork was signed, sealed, and ready to be delivered, and Jere was hurrying to push the legal team out the door. As he left, his mind briefly reconnected a few dots, and he looked at Mr. Montgomery. "There was something about vacation time? I'll be needing that for the next two weeks in order to move and settle in. No visits this week, absolute emergencies only next week. Pass it on wherever things are passed on here. Pleasure meeting you."

He shut the door quickly, letting his head drop against it for the briefest second after he finished. He wondered what in hell he had just done.

Chapter 2
Forced Connection

Jere caught his breath and started walking through the house. He sent out a search presence similar to the one that had beckoned him here earlier. He felt, rather than heard a response, and it was chilling; pain, intense, awful pain and terror, coming in waves. Reaching out to someone psychically was intended to let one in on the other person's mental state, but usually not with this intensity. He blocked the connection somewhat, reducing the terror that seemed to spill over.

A door at the back of the kitchen joined the house to the medical clinic, and Jere was relieved to find that it was left unlocked. He easily found the room that the psychic noise was coming from; not an examination room, but a supply closet. He couldn't fathom why anyone would choose to put a patient there. What he saw nearly made his stomach churn.

The legal team had said that the slave was male, which was consistent with the rag thrown over his genitals, but not over where a woman's breasts would be. The burns were so awful that Jere wouldn't have been able to tell otherwise. The slave was stretched out on his back on a metal operating table, restrained by his arms and legs, with another folded rag under his head. Every inch of skin was burned, some red, some black, many parts cracked and oozing fluids. Worst of all were his hands, which were burned enough to expose bones through the thin skin. It looked as though someone had been placing wet rags on him, but the thrashing and shaking the slave had been doing had obviously displaced them.

Jere was unsure whether to move the slave or not. Why was

9

he not in a proper exam or surgery room? He brushed the thought aside, figuring that the fire that destroyed the house may have damaged some of the medical rooms as well. He preferred to treat patients in a familiar setting, but time was of the essence. Taking a deep breath and praying to a god he didn't quite believe in, he walked over and placed his fingers on the slave's neck, attempting to get a pulse without hurting him unnecessarily. He succeeded, finding a very weak but surprisingly steady heartbeat. The heartbeat allowed him some hope for the slave's survival.

The slave's eyelids flew open, revealing one blind, milky eye, damaged from the fire, the other a brilliant clear blue, disoriented and full of terror. The slave moaned, and both eyes rolled backward in his head.

Jere wanted nothing more than to dive right into the slave's mind, to start healing him, to ease his pain. His gift for healing ached to be put to use, but fortunately for his own well-being, he had also been gifted with a bit of common sense. Planning quickly, he returned to the kitchen, procuring a pitcher of water, some bread that hadn't yet gone off on one end, and some canned fish. After leaving them on a small table near his patient, he pulled in a comfortable desk chair from the meeting room, stepping out one last time to retrieve his medical kit. On the way back, he stepped into what seemed to be a bedroom, grabbing a few pillows and blankets off the bed.

He pulled the chair close to the slave, set the supplies nearby, and opened his medical bag to pull out a syringe and vial of liquid. As skilled as he was with psychic healing, nothing alleviated pain quite like an injection, and it took a great deal of the work out of the process for him as well. Had the slave been in better condition, he would have also sedated him, but given the circumstances, he was staying cautious. A heavy sedative might just silence that weak heartbeat.

He took the slave's outstretched arm, turned it slightly to better access the muscular part of his upper arm, and attempted to slide the needle in. His stomach churned as he was forced to press harder, forcing his way through layers of charred skin. He was relieved that he drew only the slightest moan of discomfort from the slave.

Jere waited a few minutes for the medication to take effect, breathing deeply and clearing his own mind while drinking some water. He needed to be prepared. After a few minutes, he slid close to the slave's head and placed both hands on him, one on each of his temples, with his fingers stretched down to his throat to feel his pulse. For the intense healing he needed to do, contact with the head would provide him the best psychic access. He closed his eyes and concentrated on the shallow breathing and weak pulse, carefully aligning them with his own as he opened his mind.

What he found was terrifying, although unsurprising. The slave's mind was mostly sparse, indicating his limited level of consciousness, even in his dream state. Even so, the atmosphere was intense. It felt warm, and Jere was aware of shadows of fire and beams falling all around him. He had encountered similar mind-settings before, enough to know that he had nothing to fear, no matter how real or terrifying the images were; they were simply projections from his patient. Who, it seemed, was now acknowledging him. A projection, a dream state image of the slave, was standing right in front of him.

"Hello," Jere said softly, waiting for a sign.

The slave looked at him, almost through him. He said nothing at first, but moaned in agony. Jere could hear the moaning inside and outside of his head at the same time.

"Am I dead?"

"No. Close, but not quite. You're very sick."

"They're torturing me. I want to die."

The boy — well, Jere assumed he was a boy, if his real body looked like his projection — spoke with almost no affect in his tone or on his face; as if he had given up on hope, pain, any feelings at all.

"I'm a mind-healer," Jere said softly, taking a step toward him. "I've come to help you."

The boy's eyes widened in fear. "Stay out of my mind! I'd rather die!"

Jere had been unprepared for this, but had encountered it plenty of times in feverish, near-death patients. The slave didn't seem to grasp that Jere was already *in* his mind, if he was in this state. He just wasn't in far enough. It explained the intensity and real feeling of the projections. This was reality for him.

He stepped back and held his hands up, indicating surrender. "I'm sorry, I was only trying to ease your pain. If I can't heal you, then can I at least get you some water? It's awfully hot in here...."

As he spoke, he carefully constructed a water pitcher and glass in his hands, the suggestion itself creating a gap in the slave's consciousness enough that Jere could insert his own projections into the dream state. They were no more real than the burning building or the clothes the boy had chosen.

The slave looked on longingly. "I would like some water, sir."

Jere made a show of pouring it slowly into the glass, while asking, nonchalantly, "What's your name?"

"Wren," the boy muttered absently, staring at the water which never seemed to stop pouring.

Jere stopped the flow, after allowing the glass to fill up. He stepped closer to the boy, holding the water out to him. "Wren, will you let me in?"

"Yes, sir, please!" He lunged for the water, which Jere gave to him.

At the same time, Jere placed both hands on the boy's head, exactly as he had done in real life, and shoved his way into the deeper parts of his mind.

Wren, to his credit, was attentive enough to realize what had happened at the last second, making a valiant attempt to resist. His efforts were futile, however, resulting only in a sharp burst of mental and physical pain. Jere absorbed a slightly less painful burst as he tried to cushion the bullheaded slave from the blow.

Jere hated to force mind connections. It was sloppy, painful and difficult, and he had been taught that it represented a certain lack of finesse on the healer's part. To be fair, the slave would most certainly have died before allowing Jere in. Clearly his injuries had left him too disoriented and traumatized to understand what was happening. Fortunately, Jere's healing capabilities had been ranked among the top in the state amongst his graduating class.

He settled immediately into work, first addressing the damage done to the internal organs. Nobody could explain exactly *how* mind-healing worked, but mind-healers seemed to possess some sort of ability to put the healing of another person into hyperdrive, as well as passing on some of their own health to the patient. Within minutes, Jere had cleared the boy's lungs of smoke damage, increasing the amount of available oxygen. He balanced out water and electrolyte levels as best he could, using his own body as a resource, nourishing dehydrated organs. He pressured the immune system to attack the infection that was coursing through the patient's body and detected the lack of infection quickly.

Under normal circumstances Jere would have stopped there, before exhausting himself, by taking a break, or even handing the patient over to another doctor. Neither was an option, so he prioritized, aware that his resources were depleting. Blindness was awful to treat, so he sent his energy to the boy's eye, repairing the damage, which, fortunately, was not nearly as complicated as it could have been. With all he had left, he started the healing on the boy's hands, knowing he would come nowhere near to finishing. The energy drain was simply too much. Feeling his own danger signs, Jere pulled away, more roughly than usual. The abrupt departure was accompanied by a sickening feeling of being sucked through a narrow tunnel. He found himself in roughly the same position in which he had started, only slumped down onto the boy's chest. Unable to pick himself up, he moved one hand to press against the boy's neck.

His pulse was stronger. Jere smiled weakly. He reached down and struggled to pick up the glass of water he had poured earlier, drinking the whole thing in a rather laborious expenditure of energy. He gave none to the boy — he didn't need to, he had let him leech almost all the liquid from his system during the mind-healing.

He felt the glass slip from his hands and drop to the floor, shattering. Satisfied that it was out of his way, Jere slumped onto the slave and promptly passed out.

Hours passed.

Or was it minutes?

It was hours.

It was light at some point.

Jere woke, and it was dark again. He had remained slumped

onto the slave's chest in a position not quite suitable for a professional. *That's why doctors usually have nurses*, he thought, struggling to sit up. He drank more water from the pitcher, as his glass was in shards around him, and chased it with the can of fish. He was pleased to discover that this was real, natural fish, not the synthetic "meat food product" that limited budgets and a faltering livestock supply forced people to eat. Salty, full of protein, and fairly easy to chew, the fish was just the thing he needed after an intense mind-healing.

He picked up the bread, dipped a corner into the water, and gently slid the drippy substance into the slave's mouth. Wren. That was his name. He was in a state of half-consciousness, sleeping more than anything, and Jere felt confident that he would be able to feed him without significant concerns of choking. Still, getting him to swallow the bread was a challenge, a careful process of ripping it into tiny pieces, coaxing it into his mouth, and massaging his throat until he swallowed it. More times than not, swallowing was accompanied by a low moan from Wren. Jere was careful and precise as he fed him, wiping any spills from his mouth before continuing, checking to make sure he was still breathing. He certainly wasn't going to go to all this work just to have the slave choke to death on a piece of bread.

The feeding process went slowly, but soon Jere was satisfied that he had provided the boy with at least *some* real nutrition. The second-hand nutrition that could be obtained during mind-healing just never seemed as effective. He felt himself growing less light-headed as the food sank into his system as well. Still weak, he struggled to his feet, legs aching from sleeping sitting up. Half-stumbling, Jere sought out a bathroom, relieved to find one in the room next to the supply closet he was working in. He returned, stretched his muscles, and checked the boy again. Seeing that he was stable, Jere placed a pillow under the slave's head and a blanket across his body. Dropping one of each on the floor for himself, away from the glass shards, he promptly curled up and fell asleep again. Beds were too far away, and he was too concerned about his patient's health.

Jere awoke again, feeling rested this time. He checked his watch, fortunate to have one with time *and* date on it. Three days had passed since he had arrived, and he only remembered minutes of it. Mind healing wasn't always an easy job, especially with a case this severe and little in the way of nutrition to restore himself.

He stood and went to his patient, checking his pulse and breathing again. Both had returned to almost normal, and the patient's skin had stopped oozing, starting to heal. Jere knew he needed to continue the mind-healing quickly in order to prevent horrible, disfiguring scars. Of course, even those could be removed with enough time and effort, but Jere wasn't quite up to time or effort at the moment. He trekked back to the kitchen and located some more canned goods, water, and crackers. The bread had turned a rather unpleasant shade of furry green.

After eating and drinking, he allowed himself a few minutes to explore the house — his house, he realized — hunting down the main bathroom this time, instead of using the tiny one in the clinic. He decided that showering would be worth his and his patient's while, and it took all his willpower to finish in a timely manner. Hot water was very, very pleasant. Clean, well-fed, and refreshed, he returned to his patient.

Once again, Jere began the healing process with a pain-killing injection. This completed, he attempted to enter the slave's mind, again only managing partial access. The landscape had changed; the fire and falling beams replaced by stark white walls, reminiscent of a hospital.

"That was a dirty trick." Wren glared at him across his own mind.

"Waiting for me?" Jere asked as if Wren hadn't spoken.

"I felt you come in."

Jere was surprised. Only people with strong mind gifts could usually feel others that way, and Jere could have sworn he remembered hearing something about the slave having some sort of accelerated physical gift, vision, speed, strength, something along those lines. Perhaps he had meant that he felt Jere's hands on him or something. He brushed the thought aside.

"I needed you to let me in last time, Wren," Jere said, matter-of-fact. "And you weren't about to. It was my responsibility to bring you back to health. I'm sorry about the way it had to happen, I know

15

it was unpleasant, but I tried to deflect it."

"I know. You shouldn't have. You should have left me alone." Wren gave him a dark look. "I just wish you would have let me die. You still could, it's not too late! It would be better."

Jere shook his head. Obviously, the kid had no idea what he was talking about. The pain he had been in must have been horrible.

The bitter resignation on Wren's face was matched only by the tone in his voice. "Who the hell are you, anyway?"

"My name's Jere. I'm a mind-healer."

"Do you know my master?" Impossibly, Wren looked *more* guarded.

"Yes. I do—did, rather. He didn't make it." Jere was silent for a moment, noticing the look of horror on the slave's face. "You did all you could—from what I heard from the lawyers, you were doing your best to pull him out, but the fire just got out of control. I'm sorry. For your loss."

Wren's face looked panicked for a moment, but he brought himself under control, breathing a sigh of relief. "Thank you, sir," he said carefully, still suspicious. "Are you a... a visiting doctor?"

Jere shook his head. "I'm Matthias's successor, I guess you could say. I inherited everything—his job, his house, his possessions."

Jere had rarely seen a projection respond so physically, but Wren's face went completely void of blood, his eyes widening in fear as he took a step back.

"Then you, you're my—"

"I own you now, yes." Jere struggled to keep the face of his own projection from going as white.

"Master, I, I apologize...."

"Wren, it's all right," Jere said, trying to be soothing. "You barely know what's going on. Just let me heal you. We can talk later."

Wren stayed where he was for another moment, frozen, still looking terrified. "Yes, master. As you wish." He walked toward Jere and dropped to his knees in front of him, head down.

Jere was startled by the sudden submission. He reached out a hand toward the boy, who cringed and flinched away, but moved himself back quickly, trembling. His eyes were wide, and he looked ready to dart away at any second, or start crying, or both. It was clear to see that Wren was barely holding himself together. Jere placed his hands lightly on the slave, not on his temples, but on his shoulders. He could feel the muscles of both the projection and Wren's real body tensing and shaking. He hesitated.

"Wren, I don't know what you think I'm going to do, but it's not going to hurt you," he said softly. "I can feel how tense you are on both planes. All I want to do is heal you. You've still got burns on almost every inch of your body. I know it was a little rough last time, but I swear, I'm better when I don't have to force my way into your mind. Just try and relax a little and I promise, I'll keep you as comfortable as possible."

Wren nodded, his breath a bit shaky. "Yes, master."

Jere waited, feeling him relax only the slightest.

"Wren, really—"

"I'm sorry, master, it's my fault. I can't relax, and if I can't do it, then..." he trembled as he continued "then you should hurt me with it. I want you to hurt me; I deserve it."

"Wren! I don't—"

"Please, master," Wren pleaded, his voice cracking, "Please, just don't make me wait for it any longer!"

Nothing in Jere's training had ever prepared him to deal with a patient begging to be punished, and he felt a wave of revulsion when he knew that in order to heal Wren, he would have to answer those pleas. He would hurt him when he healed him, but he was hurting him now, and it had to be done. With an overwhelming sense of regret, he gripped the slave's head in his hands and shoved his way in, finding only slightly less resistance than he had last time.

This deep in, he and Wren were uncommunicative. Perhaps, if he was lucky, Wren had simply passed out when Jere breached his mind that way. Regardless, Jere began the quick and thorough process of assessing the damage so that he could continue the healing.

The remaining burns were severe, but that was unsurprising. What Jere did find surprising, however, was the series of crisscrossed scars across the majority of Wren's back, legs, and stomach, and even a few snaking around onto his arms and chest. He dreaded to think of what had caused them, but sheer medical familiarity pointed fingers to at least a whip, a knife, and possibly a chain. Burn scars, not from the fire, but from something else, were interspersed as well. The oldest scar was maybe seven years old, the newest, well, the newest weren't scars at all, really. Fortunately, the skin-healing process didn't remember scars. The fire would actually give the kid a new chance at flawless skin. A meager benefit compared to so much pain.

Jere's work the second time around was less labor intensive and more detail oriented. He took longer, reconnecting skin fibers, redistributing blood and fluid, and promoting new skin growth. With Wren's hands, he needed to repair bones, muscles, and blood vessels before he could even attempt the skin. In order to heal it smoothly, he postponed the final parts of the healing, growing exhausted. He withdrew more gently this time, pleased to see that Wren was looking almost completely healthy. Jere untied Wren's arms and legs, horrified that he had been restrained so tightly over such bad burns. He forced himself and a dazed Wren to take some food before retreating to his little pile of pillows and blankets on the floor. The second he lay down, the world around him disappeared.

Chapter 3
Rules of a New Master

Wren awoke in the dark. A familiar feeling of panic and fear washed over him, strangely comforting. He lay perfectly still, as he had learned to years before. Quite simply, an early-morning rape was less probable if one didn't wake up the rapist sleeping next to you in the bed.

In the bed.

Wren's panic was quickly being chased by disorientation and he wondered if maybe he hadn't died after all. He doubted it, because if there was a sparkling afterlife to go to, he knew he wouldn't deserve it. It was more likely that he was sleeping, although pleasant dreams weren't very common in his world, either. Throwing caution to the wind as much as he ever did, Wren opened one eye, even twisting his head around a tiny bit to take in his surroundings. He was still in his master's home, but not in his usual place in the cellar — in fact, this was a bedroom. It looked an awful lot like the guest bedroom, but off, somehow.

Sitting up slightly, he looked at his own body, stunned that he was no longer injured. His hands were hard to move. He looked down and found them covered in bandages. Wren leaned back against the pillow and shut his eyes again, trying to piece together what had happened, how he had gotten here...

The fire. Of course. The room had been rebuilt from photographs. The walls were the wrong color, the bed was a different style, and that smell — that was smoke. There had been a horrible fire after....

Wren leaned over the edge of the bed and heaved, quickly

slamming his mind shut against any of those memories. Like a river flowing in, new ones took their place, fuzzy, confusing memories that he couldn't quite identify.

Hands. Hands on him, everywhere, pulling him. Putting water in his mouth. Hurting him. Touching his head. Fire whistles. More hands. The pain. God, the pain. A man, in his dreams. A pitcher of water and a glass. Was it a dream? Something that made the pain go away. The man again. Talking with the man. Being carried, too weak to protest, or even to open his eyes. The man... his master?

Wren's thoughts were interrupted by the sound of someone at the door.

"Wren, are you all right?"

The voice sounded gentle, but he knew better. He had made a mess, and here he was, lying around doing nothing! Wren struggled to sit up.

"Oh, good, glad to see—" Jere had been smiling, but it faded as quickly as his voice when he noticed the mess. "Damn. I did hope you'd be able to keep food down, but I think we might need to stick to liquids for a bit, hmm? The mind-healing can be rather draining."

Wren looked at the mess, and began to shake. He couldn't think right, couldn't respond, he had to clean it up before—

"And just where do you think you're going?"

Wren had, through his haze, been getting out of bed to clean.

"I—please, I'm sorry, master," he said miserably, feeling the room spin around him. Wren's stomach lurched again and he swallowed back the bile building at the back of his throat. "I'm sorry, I can clean it up. I'm sorry, I will, as soon—"

"Wren, stop!" Jere came closer and placed a firm hand on Wren's shoulder, guiding him back down to the bed. "I didn't heal you so that you could make things worse again."

The master didn't sound particularly angry. Perhaps he would only stop feeding him now, instead of beating him *and* starving him? Although he didn't need to hurt him physically, when he had such great mind control. Even better than his last master.... Wren shuddered at the thought. The line was thin between healing and hurting.

"Are you cold?" Jere asked, placing a hand on Wren's forehead. "No, you're pretty warm, but you don't seem to have a fever — guess that's one thing we've gotten clear of, huh? You kept having them for a few days."

Wren wasn't cold. He was frozen. It didn't make any sense for his new master to be talking to him like this, and there was nothing more dangerous than an unpredictable master. No orders, no cursing, no yelling — he was being talked to like his old master used to talk to his patients. Wren considered the possibility that his new master was just confused about how to talk to his slave that he had met first as a patient. If that was true, then it would only be a matter of time before normality slid back into place. Wren wasn't sure if the respite was good or bad, but he did know it wouldn't last.

His master came back into the room, holding a glass of something and a few towels. Wren felt a shiver of apprehension as he realized he had let his guard down, not even knowing that his master had left.

Wren's wide eyes followed him carefully as he tossed the towels over the pile of vomit, then pulled a wastebasket from behind a bedside table.

"If you can manage, in the future, could you use this?"

Wren nodded automatically. "Yes, master," he tacked on, almost an afterthought.

"All right." Jere nodded. He looked Wren over again, his lips tightening as if he were thinking very hard about something. "I want you to drink this. I'm sorry, it doesn't taste very good, but it should help to bring you back around and get you on your feet again. I've mixed something into it to keep you from throwing it back up again, I'm afraid that it doesn't help the taste any."

Jere handed over the thick, greenish looking liquid, and Wren trembled as he obediently began to drink it down. As promised, the taste was rather awful, but it all tasted like food, which certainly made it better than some other things Wren had been forced to put in his mouth. He focused on the sensation of warm liquid instead of the taste, and managed to down the entire glass without stopping or gagging once. Wren only hoped that if this was an experiment it would be over with soon.

"It's an awful, powdered mixture," Jere explained, oblivious to the sheer terror still in Wren's eyes. "Protein, dried seaweed — that's why it's green — vitamins, minerals, that sort of thing. A marvel, really, it's called Crucial Care. Hasn't caught on in most places, due to the taste. And awful enough that you can toss medications into it without making it taste much worse. But it's guaranteed to revive you a bit."

Wren handed the glass back. "Thank you, master," he managed, feeling instantly drowsy. The fear was still there, but his body could no longer hold on to the tension and his eyes blinked sleepily up at Jere.

Jere smiled. "I added a sedative too. You need the rest. We'll talk more when you wake up."

He slipped out of consciousness almost immediately.

Wren woke up and it was no longer dark. He lay there, silent again for a few minutes, trying to wrap his mind around what had just happened. Yes, there had been a fire. His hands still hurt; they must have been burned, badly. The rest of him must have been as well, but now, here he was, completely healed. Obviously this man — his master — was a powerful mind healer. Where had his old master even known him from? He hoped the new master was an old colleague, maybe a distant cousin. Someone who was distant enough from Burghe that he wasn't anything like him. That, or someone so much like him that he would end Wren's life without looking back.

The vile tasting drink had certainly worked its magic, because Wren noticed he no longer felt so fuzzy and exhausted. Not nearly so nauseous either, although his last memory of solid food coming *out* of him made him hesitant to try it again anytime soon. He realized, with a bit of surprise, that he was actually hungry. With dismay, he also felt an uncomfortable pressure in his bladder.

It had been something that the master — the *old* master, he corrected himself — would have made him ask for, beg for, if he was feeling particularly evil. The new master seemed a bit more practical. Wren debated for a few moments, considering the ferocity of the whippings he had gotten for soiling himself in the past. He decided that using the bathroom was the better choice either way. There had been a time when he would have felt something like this was his right, but those days were long since gone. He couldn't afford to think of himself as having rights and he couldn't allow himself to acknowledge his fury at losing them.

Wren stood up carefully, feeling an odd, tight sensation in his skin. There was a robe hanging on the back of the door: dare he wear it? He figured that the whipping he would get for being up and about and using the bathroom without permission would be bad enough; the pleasure he would feel from being wrapped up in one of those soft bathrobes wouldn't be able to make it worse. What was forty lashes compared to thirty? Slipping it on, he stepped out of the room, heading toward the bathroom and feeling vindicated when he reached his goal.

He hoped to slink back into the bedroom without being noticed. No such luck.

"Oh, Wren, I see you're up."

Wren felt the clench in his stomach that accompanied every bad decision he seemed to be intent on making. He could have waited. Could have coughed or something to catch the master's attention and asked if he could use the bathroom.

He dropped to his knees, face turned to the floor, where it was less likely to be hit. "I'm sorry, master, I apologize for my presumption. Please, forgive me."

"Presumption? Wearing the robe, or using the bathroom?"

The master sounded irritated. Wren cursed himself inwardly. Hadn't he been taught early on to list his misdeeds specifically so he could be punished for each one? He began again, "I'm sorry, please, master, forgive me, I — "

"Wren, stop! Stop!" Jere's voice was exasperated. "Just get up. For fuck's sake, get up and look at me!"

Wren stood up instantly, eyes wide with terror as he looked at his master. He hated being hit in the face; it almost always made him cry, and that brought more punishment.

Jere looked a little startled by what he saw. "Wren, you're not in trouble. I want you — I *need* you to take care of yourself. And if that means using the bathroom or keeping warm or whatever, then by all means do it! That's an order."

This, Wren understood. His master wanted him healthy so he didn't have to waste any more time or energy healing him. Wren breathed a small sigh of relief. The order to stand had been a small comfort; despite being taller than Wren, Jere didn't seem interested in towering over him as much as Burghe had. Then again, Burghe almost always ordered Wren to his knees, guaranteeing that Wren would feel as small and vulnerable as possible. Besides, this new master still had a bit of youthfulness about him, the soft face and somewhat lanky body in sharp contrast to the sturdy, uncompromising memories that Wren held of Burghe.

"Come to the dining room with me. We need to talk, and I want to give you a chance to eat and drink a little."

Wren followed immediately, stopping only when Jere did.

"Sit."

Wren began to drop to the floor where he was, thinking of all the times Burghe had had him sit at his feet while he was eating. How often he had hoped and prayed that a piece would fall to the floor.

"In a chair!" Jere exclaimed, sounding irritated again. He frowned at Wren and shook his head.

Wren jumped up, placing himself immediately into a chair and hating himself for not being able to get the simplest thing right. How was he supposed to know that the master had meant for him to sit in a chair? The master had disappeared around the corner, to the cooking area. Wren's thoughts began to spin out of control as he contemplated the various devices of torture that the new master might find in the kitchen. A knife? To cut him with? Something hot, off the stove, to burn him? Or, god, what if—

His thoughts were cut off as Jere returned, holding two mugs.

"Earl Grey or chamomile?"

Wren stared back at him, dumbstruck.

"I didn't know which one you liked, so I figured, I'd make both, and I'd have the other," Jere explained, as if it were the most natural thing in the world. "I like both."

"I, uh… Earl Grey, master."

Jere handed him the cup, keeping the other for himself. "There's no cream, haven't had the chance to get to the market, and sugar would probably just upset your stomach. Maybe tomorrow, though, if you take it that way."

Cream and sugar in his tea. Burghe had forced him to drink out of the toilet regularly enough that Wren kept it extra clean.

"Thank you, master."

Jere shifted uncomfortably. "Wren, I, well, I know this is a big adjustment to you, but I would rather you call me Jere. I don't mind. I'm actually, well, I'm uncomfortable being called master, and I really wish you wouldn't."

"Please, master. It isn't really appropriate for me to call you by your given name." Wren was hesitant to challenge his master, but not as hesitant as he would have been to use a free person's first name so casually. Was this a trap? "Please, let me address you at least somewhat respectfully?"

His master was quiet for a moment. Wren braced himself for what was coming next, the slap, the mind shock, the hot cup of tea thrown at his face.

"Well, I suppose that a compromise will have to do for now, then, won't it?" he said after a few minutes, with a note of resignation in his voice. Jere gave Wren a curious look. "And what about you, anything else you go by?"

Wren had often been referred to as "stupid slut," "useless trash," and other colorful euphemisms, but he would just as soon not suggest these to his new master. He went with the safe answer. "Whatever would please you, master."

Jere's face remained expressionless, except a slight frown at Wren's use of the word "master," which quickly disappeared as he moved on to other business. "Wren is just fine by me." He stirred his tea, avoiding eye contact. "Sir. Could you call me 'sir,' instead of master? Would that feel okay to you?"

"If you wish, sir." It didn't exactly feel "okay," but it did feel less terrifying. Except it was one more thing to remember.

"All right. It's settled then." Jere seemed pleased to have resolved the issue, though he still looked unsettled by the honorific. "I'll call you Wren, and you'll call me sir, and we'll both pretend not to be uncomfortable, and one day we'll have this discussion again."

"Thank you, sir." Wren cupped his tea with both hands, struggling to get a grip due to the bandages, and allowed himself a few sips. He couldn't remember the last time he had tasted tea.

"So...." His master was stirring his tea again. The nervous habit seemed out of place for an accomplished mind healer. "How old are you?"

"Nineteen, sir." Wren was comfortable in answering this. Nineteen, the prime of his life. Even for slaves, whose lifespans usually ran about half that of free people, nineteen was young. No worries about being sold away for being too old, experienced enough to know his way around. He only wished he wasn't tired of life already.

Jere nodded. "And how long were you with Matthias?"

"Since I was fifteen, sir. Four years. Since I left the training facility."

"How long were you there?"

"Two years, sir. Since my gift really started to emerge."

"And before that?"

"I lived with my parents, sir. My father had a mind gift, my mother was without."

Jere was silent for a moment. "You left home at thirteen?"

"I was... taken. At thirteen. Sir." Wren felt himself beginning to tear up, cursing himself for not being in better control of his emotions. He wished this man would just beat him if he wanted to hurt him, instead of torturing him like this.

"I'm sorry," Jere spoke gently. "That must have been horrible."

Wren didn't say anything, tried to focus on his breathing and not on memories of that day.

"Wren, I'm sorry if I upset you. I didn't know."

Wren glanced up at him only briefly. Any longer, and he was afraid that the hatred he felt would show.

"Wren, you must have guessed that I'm not from around here?" When he got no response, Jere continued. "I'm from Sonova. I grew up just outside of the city, went to University there, and was living in the heart of the city, well, until this week. I've traveled some, but I've never so much as passed through a slave state, as far as I know. And I don't know how the system works. It's never been something

I've wanted to think about at all."

The pieces of the puzzle clicked into place. This was why the master was being so kind and friendly and gentle. He didn't have the first clue of what to do with a slave! Wren let out a breath of relief. He could use this, *would* use this for sure. For as long as he could, anyway. Until his master learned all the things he was doing wrong. And it wasn't like it was Wren's place to tell him —

"I'd like it if, well, if you'd help me to navigate it."

The master's voice drew Wren's attention back sharply, despite his nonchalant tone.

"What I mean, is, well, I'm sure I'm prone to making plenty of social errors, and it would be nice to have some advice on how to, you know, make less. For a second, I almost didn't want to accept you, I mean, honestly, I don't *need* a slave."

Wren's heart pounded so hard he thought it might burst. He had almost resigned himself to the idea of being owned by this man, of staying here where it was familiar at least. He carefully smoothed out his voice before he spoke, hiding the fear and the anger that came with the idea of being disposed of so carelessly. "Yes, sir. Of course. There are plenty of avenues, if you wish, to sell a slave that you no longer want."

"What? No!" Jere shook his head vehemently. "I didn't mean that! I'm not selling you."

Wren relaxed slightly. "But, then?"

"Selling you — it would just be strange!" Jere made a face. "Like I said. I don't want to know more than I have to about slavery. But I guess, since you're here, you have to do *something*, so maybe you can try to help me learn my way around here. You must know more about how things go here in Hojer than I do. Oh, and I guess you could help out around here, chores and whatnot. I'm afraid I'm rather sloppy. I can manage on my own, of course, have been for years, but I suppose it could be nice to have help."

Wren was relieved that his new master wasn't going to sell him off immediately, but he couldn't help but wonder how long the arrangement would last, how long the man would keep a useless waste of space and resources. How long could it take to become familiar with Hojer? Wren hoped it could take a long time. He would have to be careful just how much he told his new master, but he could see this working out favorably for himself, at least until his master grew bored with him. "Of course, sir. I would be honored."

"Well, good!" Jere looked pleased, but the faraway look on his face indicated that he was thinking intently about something. "Maybe you could start by telling me about the slave system? How does it work here? I've picked up something from some of the paperwork I've signed that people with physical gifts are enslaved, surely something so arbitrary as one's gift can't be the deciding factor, can it?"

Wren sat silently for a moment, wondering what to say. He decided on the same bullshit explanation that his fifth grade teacher had told his class, nervous ten-year-olds giggling and thinking that they would never, *ever* be so unfortunate as to fall on the service end of the spectrum. He remembered her words, the descriptions he had read in textbooks, and the words he heard in the training facility. He channeled the cold, detached tone, the clinical descriptions of people like him, and forced the emotions he felt to stay hidden.

"When humans evolved, and the mind-body split became apparent, things were wonderful at first. Technology and healthcare had reached their zeniths, cities prospered, food and space were plentiful, and it didn't matter if some people were inferior to others. However, after The Fall, when the communication and banking systems went down and society as people knew it collapsed, a better system had to be developed. People's gifts had to be used for the greater good, like providing electricity, or trying to make crops grow, or figuring out ways to communicate once all the wireless networks went down for good. A system was needed that would allow the brightest and most promising to see to the interests of the state. The ruling bodies were concerned that those with physical gifts, who were naturally less bright and more prone to violence than those with mind gifts, would take over and destroy the fragile new society. As such, it was decided that every child who showed signs of a physical gift would be removed from society at his or her thirteenth birthday, the marker between adult and child. While many children show signs earlier, true indications of a mental or physical gift cannot be ascertained until this age."

Wren paused, drinking his tea as if it was his lifeline, trying to keep his hands steady. He remembered sitting in class and hearing this, his own physical gift already starting to show itself. He remembered feeling furious that he should be condemned to such a life, and trying to stamp that fury out before anyone noticed.

Jere shook his head. "And these are the same mind gift or physical gift distinctions used elsewhere, right? Physical being an enhanced normal ability, like speed or strength or one of the senses, mind being some sort of psychic gift not normally attributed to humans?"

"Yes, sir. At this age, a gift-identifier will have already marked the child, and usually warned the parents. The child is assigned a slave name, a... " Wren struggled to figure out the wording for this. There was no really tactful way to go about it, but he needed to let his master know, tactful or not. "A shortened form of their name, or a new name. Sir, slave names are all three- and four-letter names. Usually four. It helps to identify them." He waited for some indication that his master had made the connection.

"Huh." Jere nodded. "Well, that explains the looks I get. What the hell is that about?"

Wren shrugged. "It's just another distinction, sir. Some think that it has to do with associating slave names with four letter words — curse words — but honestly, all I've heard is that it helps for identification. Shortening one's name is not acceptable here."

Jere seemed to think about this for a moment before shaking his head again. "Well, go on then."

"Sir, some children are prepared for the removal. Others are not. Regardless, all are taken to training facilities, where they are taught the basic 'skills' of their new lives."

"Were you... prepared?"

"Yes. Sir." Wren's voice was sad and bitter. He blinked hard, forcing himself to continue. "At the training facility, they learn how to use their gifts for the purpose of pleasing their masters. Many slaves are unable to control the gifts at first, especially if they have acquired them suddenly. I developed mine gradually, which was helpful in adjusting. They teach them basic household skills, such as cleaning and cooking and how to be attentive to their master's needs. They teach them..."

Wren hesitated. He saw no reason to indicate to his master that part of the standard training package was sexual initiation and instruction.

" ...how to address free people appropriately, and basic rules of society that they must live by, although most children who grew up in a slave state understand the basic rules."

"Which are?"

"If you don't mind, sir, I'd suggest you check the full list at the city center," Wren said, blushing at his own inadequacy. There was no reason for him to know them all, but he wished he did, so he could answer this man's questions. "There are hundreds, and while I am aware of them all, I doubt I could recall them all. But the main ones, well, slaves are not allowed outside of their homes alone without a pass, slaves are prohibited from owning property or entering into contracts, required to obey any free person who gives a direct order, prohibited from assaulting any free person, prohibited from possessing weapons, prohibited from gambling or drinking—"

"So, you're considered children, under the law?"

Wren nodded, hating to agree despite the truthfulness. "Mostly, sir."

"Mostly?"

Wren immediately regretted his answer. Now he was stuck explaining, which opened up possibilities that he didn't want opened up. "Children have protections that slaves don't have, sir."

Jere looked at him expectantly, clearly not understanding.

"If you... if you beat a child, or... or harm it, or don't send it to school, there are things in place. To make sure that the child is safe. Agencies that check into these kinds of things. Slaves are viewed more like... like objects." *And you can do whatever you want to them*, he added on in his head, praying his master wouldn't make him elaborate.

Jere nodded, appearing to think about this. "Objects. Like a table. Or a pair of shoes."

"Yes, sir."

"And I imagine that many masters abuse this?"

"A master may use his slave in whatever manner he sees fit."

Wren's words were barely a whisper, his head down again.

Jere swallowed. "I see."

They sat there in silence for a moment more, until they were interrupted by a noise from Wren's stomach. He tried to cough, unconvincingly, to cover it.

"Good god, are you that hungry?" Jere exclaimed.

Wren reddened. There was no point in lying. "Yes, sir."

"Why didn't you say something?" Jere jumped to his feet, an irritated look on his face.

Wren cowered, silent in the face of the man looming over him. No reply would be adequate. He should have known better, should have been able to guess his new master's preferences better. Now the pain would come, and he would give in to it, because he couldn't fight it.

Jere stared at him for a second, then turned away. "Stay there, I'll be right back with something for you to eat."

Wren trembled in the chair. He tried to lift the mug of tea to his mouth, but between the shaking and the bandages, was mostly unsuccessful. How was he supposed to know? All of the rules were changing and nothing made sense. He *knew*, however, that previous requests for things like that had gotten him beaten, and certainly hadn't gotten him food. Complaining was never a good idea for a slave.

He reflected on his time with Burghe. If anything, he had eliminated a lot of these uncomfortable moments. Wren almost always knew what was expected of him with Burghe, because the orders were driven home with screaming and a slap or two, at least. There was never any guessing. He reflected on his time at the training facility, where they had taught him how to read his master's mood, in hopes of pleasing him more quickly. It had been such a long time since then, he wasn't sure how well he would still be able to do it, but he knew he'd better start, in case this complacency his master had wore off sooner, rather than later.

Jere returned with a somewhat forced smile on his face. "I found some bouillon cubes. Uh, there's quite a bit of protein powder in there as well, calories and strength and whatnot. There's some crackers here too, if you want."

"Thank you, sir," Wren looked hungrily at the soup-like thing in the bowl. "I... may I have some more tea, sir?"

"Of course!" Jere's smile seemed genuine this time. "Be right back."

Wren managed to lift a spoonful of the broth to his mouth, unsurprised to find it at perfect eating temperature. Asking for more tea had been a risk, but a calculated one. Maybe his new master liked taking care of him? There were worse things by far than a master who liked to pet and pamper his slave. Wren ran through a list of rules he had figured out so far: use the bathroom when you need it, stay warm, get healthy, ask for things, use "sir" instead of "master." Oh, and sit on chairs. The way the new rules were piling up, Wren wasn't sure he could keep track of them for long. Was that the point? Burghe had set him up to fail on more than one occasion, was this just another game? It would be a grand excuse to punish him.

Still, Wren wanted to cling to the pampering as long as he could. He knew better than to think he deserved it, or to think that it would last, but the temptation of this much comfort was just too enticing, even if the rules did go against everything he had known for the past six years. The only thing Wren was really uncomfortable with was the "master" issue, but it did help to differentiate his new master from Burghe. Perhaps this was why he had done it?

Jere returned with a fresh cup of tea, looking satisfied when he noticed Wren had eaten.

"It's pretty dense, so don't feel obligated to finish it all," he advised. "But if you're still hungry, let me know, and I can make you some more. Some people are starving after mind-healing."

"Thank you, sir." His master was right, it was indeed dense, despite the light feeling in his stomach.

"Now, I need to ask, and I do need you to be honest, so don't worry about offending me, but how are you feeling?" Jere asked, slipping into attentive doctor mode. "I've seen to your wounds, and they have obviously healed, the only thing I didn't do was regrow your hair, because, honestly, that's a waste of energy when there's so much else to do, but do you feel normal? Like you used to?"

Wren contemplated that for a moment. He felt *better* than he used to, to be quite honest. He wasn't aching from the most recent beating, he wasn't starving. He felt quite good. "I feel well, ma-sir." He had caught himself at the last second. He shuddered slightly. At this rate, he wouldn't stay feeling like this for long.

"Are you sure? Most people notice at least something different."

Wren considered how much his master seemed to like him to ask for things. He had to ask for something, just enough to show he could play along. "Well, uh, my skin does feel a little tight, I guess. Like if I stretch it, it will rip."

Jere nodded. "That's pretty normal. I had to stretch your cells to their limit to cover the burns. There's a cream that should help with it, I'll pick some up soon. Maybe, until then, just having a bath can help. I'll check the kitchen and see what might feel good to add."

"Thank you, sir. And... I mean, what about my hands, sir?"

"Of course. Those aren't finished yet — Wren, you had so much damage to your hands that I thought you might lose them," Jere said, calm in comparison to Wren's horror at the statement. "I did as much as I could, but I had to rebuild the basic structure — bones, blood vessels, muscles — and some things just don't mix well with mind-healing. I'm guessing it will be a few days before I can really heal the skin back around, and it might be uncomfortable until then. If it gets too bad, let me know. I can give you some pain medicine, but I'd rather not unless you really need it, because it slows your whole healing process down. Although, it has been amazingly rapid so far. May I ask, what is your gift?"

May I ask? Wren took a few seconds to recover from this. "Yes, sir, it's speed. I'm, um, I'm gifted with speed."

Jere nodded and smiled. "I was wondering. You know, people with a speed gift are often faster all the way throughout their bodies — metabolism and healing and everything. That could explain the high temperatures you've been showing."

"Yes, sir." Wren would rather not think about the reasons why he might have a higher temperature. Abnormalities were dangerous for a slave.

"While we're on the subject, what exactly did Matthias do with you?"

Wren froze. How much did he tell the new master? How many ideas could he live with giving him?

"I mean," Jere backtracked, "I don't mean to pry into his private life, or anything, I'm just trying to see the best ways that someone gifted in speed could be helpful to a doctor. You know, so I have a better idea of what you can do around here. I mean, you can't sit around and do nothing all day."

Wren had certainly never been allowed to "sit around" while Burghe owned him. But he was relieved by Jere's question—so naïve! All the things that one could do with a slave, and he was asking how he could help with his professional work!

"Well, sir, he would have me run errands for him. Pick up things from the pharmacy. Fetch water. Deliver messages. That sort of thing." *And he fucked me like I was a blow-up doll, and he beat me for fun, or when he was angry, or for no fucking reason at all. And he made me entertain his guests as they saw fit. And he played horrible, twisted games with me and sometimes —*

"That actually sounds quite useful."

Jere's thoughtful tone interrupted Wren's musings, and for a second, he was confused as to what his new master was talking about.

"Sir?"

"An assistant," Jere smiled at him. "I'd always hoped I'd be able to have one!"

"I... yes, sir." Wren was a little surprised. He had spent years following orders and hiding his resentment, but he had never thought of himself as something as normal as an assistant. "Whatever pleases you."

"Seeing you get better is pleasing me right now," Jere insisted. "You won't be of any use until you heal, and you need to rest for that to happen. You're looking a bit tired."

It was true. Wren had finished his meal, and was feeling the after-effects of a warm, full stomach. He also saw his chance to avoid further questions from this strange, strange outlander.

"Yes, sir. Perhaps I should go back to bed, maybe?" He added a yawn at the end, which started off as a ruse, but ended in an honest-to-god yawn.

"Of course." Jere stood and grabbed the dishes before Wren had a chance to consider doing so. "Do feel free to tell me to shut up whenever you'd like."

"Yes, sir," Wren said, halfheartedly. He was enjoying his current state of minimal pain too much to attempt something that stupid.

"Will you be all right if I go out while you rest?"

"Yes, sir."

Jere nodded. "Anything you need while I'm out?"

Wren shook his head. He wasn't stupid enough to fall for trick questions like that. Then again, the master did seem to like when he asked for things for his health. "Maybe that cream you talked about, sir?"

"Of course. And, Wren, take care of yourself while I'm out." Jere looked at him quite seriously. "I mean it, whatever you need, bathroom, food, water, extra blankets—please don't hesitate. I will be extremely displeased if I come home to find you in some sort of medical emergency again."

"Yes, sir." It was clear. Wren was an inconvenience, and being sick made him more so. His master wanted him back in service quickly, and even if it meant breaking some rules, Wren supposed his master's rules far superseded any he had learned at the training facility.

"All right then. I'm off." Jere looked at him for a moment, as if there was something more he had to say, then headed out the door.

Wren let out a breath he hadn't realized he had been holding. This new master was *strange*.

He got up and went to the guest bedroom, where he assumed he was to sleep, risking punishment to keep the soft robe wrapped around him. The master had said to keep himself warm, but Wren just liked the idea of being covered. Clothing, Burghe had insisted, was a privilege, and not one that he allowed his slave very often. Of course, Burghe had never spoken to him like this new master had, nor had he looked at him with such soft, grey eyes.

What the hell was he doing thinking about his master's damn *eyes*! They meant nothing, and it wasn't as if he were some innocent fifteen-year-old, fresh from a training facility, thinking that just because someone looked at him with some pity or treated him kindly that they would think twice about backhanding him across the room. But his eyes had looked so gentle....

Wren fell asleep, cradled in the robe, thinking of his master's eyes.

Chapter 4
Necessary Procedures

Jere had gotten some idea of the layout of the town the night he arrived, but it had been dark, and he had a mind presence to follow. Despite being mostly coherent, he hadn't had the energy or the desire to go out before now. Fortunately, it seemed that the town was small enough to guess at, and he quickly determined that he was headed in the right direction, passing a few houses that looked somewhat familiar.

He had been in Hojer just under a week. Long enough for two full-out mind-healings, followed by some heavy recovery time. The slave had slept through most of it, but Jere had revived enough to take a quick inventory of the house, making a mental note of all the food, medical supplies, and general items that he would have to purchase. A large portion of the house had obviously been lost in the fire; strangely, it seemed to have started in the master bedroom. The fire report listed the cause as "accidental-unknown," but there were speculations about a dropped cigarette or improperly extinguished candle. Last Jere knew, Matthias had never smoked, and he hated the smell of candles.

Regardless, the fire insurance had been quick to pay out, and Jere was certain that he would have plenty to cover his start-up costs. In the hours he spent waiting for Wren to recover, Jere found some time to look over the details of his employment in Hojer. As he vaguely recalled hearing the legal team explain to him, he was partly employed by the state. The citizens of Hojer were covered by a tax-supported healthcare arrangement that provided them with subsidized medical care. The same arrangement provided the town's doctor with a healthy monthly stipend and benefits of his own. Even before The Fall, arrangements like this had become common, even necessary, as overpopulation led to rapid spread of diseases. In the resulting chaos after The Fall, easily treatable yet highly contagious diseases threatened to take down major cities left and right, and with the banks collapsing, few people had the funds to pay for treatment. States of emergency were declared, and almost every government agreed that public health concerns were vital not only for quality of life, but for the very existence of the human race. Healthcare providers became state employees, especially in rural areas. Landing a position as the sole provider for such a large population was rare, but extremely lucrative. Jere was amazed at his good fortune.

And then there was Wren. He was a rather skittish kid, although Jere figured anyone would be after having been so close to dying. But that didn't explain the marks on him. Someone had hurt that kid pretty badly, and Jere was certain that his old buddy wasn't entirely innocent. He didn't even know what to make of that. Sure, Matthias liked to play rough sometimes, but that was.... Jere decided he'd rather not think about it now. It was enough of a shock to reconcile his mentor's death, not to mention trying to figure out everything he needed to know for his new job, and where things were around town. Once patients started coming in, he was sure he'd be swamped.

He intended to go straight to the pharmacy, then the grocery, then head home, but he spotted a library first. He stepped inside and was greeted with the familiar smell of books and dust and library things. Despite the reported decline of libraries and books in the years before The Fall, their popularity had surged exponentially after all the communications systems had gone down. Sometimes, simpler was better. He wandered up to the counter and tapped on a bell that sat there, looking around at the nearly deserted building.

A frazzled, middle-aged woman came out from behind a door, carrying an armload of books. She appraised him quickly as she sat the books down on a counter.

"New doctor, am I right?" she asked.

"I... yes." Jere was a bit startled. So that's how the town

worked.

"Good thing you're out and about. Heard you were a bit un-common, and you haven't come out of that house since you got here. Locked up in that house with the slave-boy, eh?"

The woman's disapproving look was the exact same one his grandmother had given him when he had decided, at age eight, that he wanted to be an acrobat.

"Uh, no, I—" Jere, remembering the conversation he had just had about slaves with the "slave-boy," decided he didn't have to answer that question. "I actually came in here today looking for some books on slavery, ma'am. I'm guessing you've heard, but—"

"But you're from a much more progressive area where there are no slaves, and now you're stuck with one?"

The woman reached under the counter and pulled out a stack of books. "And don't worry, Dr. Peters, I'm not a mind-reader. I'm a *dular*, actually, no gift to speak of, mental or physical. No, Mr. Montgomery has sent a slave over with a message—twice now, to warn me."

To call someone a *dular* was often derogatory, but in this soci-ety, at least, it seemed it was better than being a slave. Jere decided not to comment.

Instead, he looked at the books she had pushed toward him. *To Train Up A Slave, Curbing Disobedience, Top Tips for New Masters (6th edition), 101 Highly Effective Training Tips,* and *Slave Training for the Delicate Soul.* They looked like a twisted amalgam of child-rear-ing and business management. He opened the top one and flicked through it, startling visibly once he saw the pictures that could best be described as torture. He slammed the book shut, trying not to look too shocked.

"You'll want to start with the bottom one, Dr. Peters," the li-brarian indicated *Slave Training for the Delicate Soul.*

"I'm sure," Jere said dryly. He had no intention of looking through any books on slavery, but didn't know how to reject them outright without seeming rude. "Actually, what I wanted was a little different. First off, do you have a list of medical journals that you carry? I try to stay up-to-date on research. And I'm a bit curious about Hojer? Is there anything about current events or laws?"

The librarian's eyebrows rose, but she looked pleased. "Well, well, aren't you the hard worker, Dr. Peters. Let me grab those for you."

She returned, moments later, with the list of medical journals, some books and pamphlets on Hojer, and a paperback mystery novel. "Dr. Burghe always used to come in on Fridays to read the latest medical journals, and sometimes he'd bring that boy of his and let him read as well. Always straight to the mystery section, that one. I thought it might be something to help him pass the time while he heals up."

"Yes, I'm sure it will," Jere mumbled, glancing down at the stack of books in front of him. "Do you know — Dr. Burghe, do you know if he treated the boy unusually or...." What was he even asking? He couldn't shake the image of the scars that he had healed. He wanted some sort of proof that his old mentor had nothing to do with it.

The librarian smiled at him, shaking her head a little as she did. "It isn't my place to judge, being a *dular* and all, but Dr. Burghe was certainly a very strict master."

Jere waited, hoping for something to solve this puzzle and allow him to dismiss it entirely.

"He wouldn't have been taking advice from the *Delicate Soul* book," she hinted, more pointedly. "I hope a nice young man such as yourself will be a bit more progressive. He's a good boy. And smart, too."

Jere smiled. "Thank you, Ms. —"

"Call me Imelda," she said, stuffing his books into a bag. "I'm happily turning into an old spinster, but I'd rather not be reminded every time you call me by my family name. Do tell the boy I said hello."

Jere walked out of the library, stunned. He was greeted with similar familiarity at both the pharmacy and the grocery, where he was informed that his purchases would be applied to his line of credit, which he could settle at the end of the month. Back home, he wouldn't have been able to get credit to hold him until his paycheck came at the end of the week — when he was getting a paycheck. Now, if he recalled correctly, he had an accountant on retainer, and a healthy sum of money to spend, in addition to the income he would soon start to receive.

After stopping briefly at a post office, Jere sent off a letter to his former landlady to settle his affairs back home. After all, he was going to be in Hojer for some time, no sense having someone try to track him down for rent money. He hoped she'd ship his belongings. This taken care of, he made the dull trip home, regretting buying as many supplies as he had as his arms grew tired over the distance.

After the groceries and other supplies were put away, Jere decided to make at least some use of the office he had inherited. Besides, it kept him closer to the slave he had inherited as well, so he could make sure the poor kid was using the bathroom or whatever he needed to do. Who didn't use the bathroom when they needed it? Jere was uncomfortable at the thought. Hojer was weird. Slavery was weird. He perused the list of medical journals, marking off the ones he would like to make sure to read. *This* he was familiar with.

He felt Wren wake up; for someone with a physical gift, he had a very strong mental presence. Jere picked up the mystery book that the librarian had gifted him in one hand, the jar of skin cream in the other. Carrying both, he stepped out of the office and knocked on the half-open door of the guest room that Wren was staying in.

"Yes, sir?" a quiet voice answered.

"Can I come in?"

"Of course, sir."

Jere came in to find Wren curled up in a corner of the bed, still wrapped in the robe he'd found earlier. Jere wondered if the kid *had* any clothes.

"I brought you this," he held up the cream, "and the librarian thought you might like this."

Wren's solemn face betrayed him with a smile for the briefest second before carefully slipping back into its blank mask. "That was very kind of her, sir."

"Well, would you like it?"

Wren hesitated. "I, if I may, sir. Yes."

Jere couldn't help but frown. The slave acted as if Jere had asked just to torment him. "Of course you can. Might be a challenge to read with your hands all covered in bandages, but I'll have you fixed up pretty soon."

"Thank you, sir." Wren's voice was small and almost guilty, but the look he gave Jere was enough to make him forget about that.

So damn grateful for a fucking library book, Jere thought. "Speaking of healing, why don't you go ahead and take that robe off for me, see what we've got."

At "take that robe off," Wren had drawn in a sharp breath and stiffened up. "Yes, sir," he forced out, bandaged hands shaking as he started to try to untie the belt holding the robe together. "I... I'm sorry."

Jere was confused and more than a little frustrated. Everything was so strange here. He was performing a medical procedure, not subjecting him to some terrible sort of torture. He took a breath and reminded himself to go slow. "Wren. Wren, stop, look at me."

He froze, head down, and looked up at Jere from beneath his eyelashes. "Yes, sir," he whispered.

"Listen, you didn't do anything wrong, okay? I'm not angry at you," Jere tried to be convincing without being too overpowering. "Whatever you're thinking you did wrong, well, you didn't, and I'm not going to punish you, or hurt you, or whatever, okay? I won't do that. Or... or anything else."

Wren was still frozen and white as a ghost, but he had at least started to breathe again.

"Now listen, I just want to get a look at how you're healing, and put this cream on, all right? No big deal."

"I can put it on myself, master." Wren cringed as soon as he said it, as if he was expecting Jere to hit him.

"You can't reach everywhere, your hands are covered in bandages, and I need to have a look at you anyway," Jere said, matter-of-factly. "I'm a doctor. It's not as if I haven't seen you naked — hell, I carried you in here naked, if you don't remember — and if you'd like, you don't have to take that damn robe off ever again, but only once you're healed. Got it?"

"Yes, sir," Wren acquiesced, fumbling with the robe again, this time without shaking as much.

Jere waited, mostly patiently, until the boy had taken the robe off. He sat on the edge of the bed, bandaged hands in front of his penis, as if it didn't exist if nobody saw it. Jere tried to brush off the uncomfortable feeling spreading through the room. "Front or back first?"

"Front, please, sir." The words were barely audible.

"Lie down on your back," Jere said gently. He had brought a towel with him, in case any spilled, but decided he had a better use for it. He spread it across Wren's groin area, like one would at a massage parlor. "Better?"

"Yes, sir."

"Pay attention to what I'm doing. I'll help you apply it for the next few days, since your hands are bandaged up, but after that, I suppose you'll be able to get to it on your own. I'll keep doing the places you can't reach." Jere couldn't help but notice how uncomfortable the boy was, stiff and still on the bed, barely breathing. He almost wished that Wren was still unconscious, just so he could do his job more easily.

Jere started at Wren's feet, moving quickly and efficiently, explaining as he went along. "You'll need this for at least three or four days. Make sure you really rub it in, but don't be too rough. Your skin *can* tear, and what's the damn point in that? I should have taken pictures of you last week, you looked like burnt toast."

"Yes, sir." Wren mumbled. His eyes were open, fixated on the ceiling. Jere wasn't sure if that was better or worse than making eye contact. He had always been uncomfortable with extended care of anxious patients.

Finished with most of Wren's front, Jere pulled the towel away briskly, revealing his genitals. He pretended not to hear the sudden intake of breath, and busied himself squeezing more healing cream from the tube.

"Please, sir," Wren's words were barely audible.

Jere didn't have to look at his face to see that his jaw was clenched, nor did he want to. "It's skin," he stated, his tone perfunctory. "It will be quick."

"Please, sir, I won't complain, or say that it hurts, ever, just don't. I can do it."

"No." Jere tried to shake the feeling that he was doing something awful. "It's my job. This part of your body has delicate skin just as much as the rest does, and it's not like it's something I haven't seen

43

before. I healed you, and I'm not about to let you damage yourself by being stubborn about this. Don't make such a big deal out of it."

Wren didn't reply, but Jere could see his hands clenching into fists at his sides.

"Hold still," he ordered, placing his hands firmly on his patient's penis as he did. He ignored the short, ragged breaths he heard as he carefully applied the cream that would facilitate the rest of the healing. It was just a medical procedure, after all.

Jere leaned back once he finished. Wren was silent again, but his body was still tense, and he didn't look away from the ceiling, even once he must have realized Jere was finished with the front. "Flip over."

Wordlessly, Wren did as he was asked, pressing his face down into the pillow, arms clutched beneath him as though he thought they'd get lost.

Again, Jere started from the bottoms of his legs and worked his way up, hesitating when he reached the boy's ass, and then going for it, working both hands around the soft skin and trying to be quick and thorough about it. He felt the unmistakable motion of the damn kid sobbing.

Against his own better judgment, he stopped. "Wren…."

"I'm sorry, sir. I'm sorry, please keep going. I'm sorry, I'll stay still. Please, sir…."

"Wren…." What was he supposed to do now? Telling him to stop begging seemed cruel and useless, touching him would certainly not be comforting. When he worked with scared children, there was always someone else there, a parent, a nanny, someone they trusted. Someone who wasn't him, but right now, he was the only person available.

"Wren, listen." Jere forced his voice to sound calm and assertive, but still kind. "I'm going to keep applying the cream, and I'm also going to check around the entry to your anus for damage. There was some tearing — yes, I found it, it's my job — and I need to make sure it healed. I'm going to go very slowly and I'm not going to hurt you, but I need to do this to make sure you're healthy. I want you to stay with me and be brave, but it's okay if you're scared, and it's okay if you cry, and if you really don't think you can handle it anymore, I want you to tell me and we'll figure something else out, all right? I won't be angry, no matter what happens."

This was the same speech that he gave terrified kids before their first mind-healing. Well, the last part, anyway. Fortunately, he had never told a child about anal tearing. It almost always worked, and if not, bribing them with candy afterward did. Jere didn't have any candy.

Wren tried to compose himself. "Yes, sir. I, I'll try to... I'll try."

Jere nodded, placing his hands back where they were, rubbing the lotion in and making sure he had some on his fingers as well. "Go ahead and take a deep breath for me. Okay, now let it out."

As Wren exhaled, his body relaxed the tiniest bit, allowing Jere to slip one slim, gloved finger about an inch inside of him. Jere felt awful as he heard the poor boy whimper, but held him steady with his other hand, while his finger moved around expertly, feeling for any irregularities.

"It's okay, Wren, you're doing just fine. I know this is uncomfortable, but you're almost done, and it's looking like you're healthy, and I won't have to do *this* again. I'm sorry."

He finished and withdrew his finger, discarding the glove. The tearing had healed, and the skin inside was stretching and working as it was supposed to. Given the way it had looked before, Jere wondered how the boy even managed to clear his bowels.

"I want you to drink more fluids. You seem to be getting a fever again, but it's not that bad." It was so much easier to focus on medical needs.

He moved carefully up Wren's back, rubbing the cream in evenly. He felt him weeping still, ever so slightly, and as he finished applying the cream he whispered, "I'm so sorry. Whoever... I'm so sorry."

Wren said nothing.

Jere took his hands off the slave and stood up. He picked up the robe from the end of the bed where they had left it, and turned to face Wren, who was still hiding his face in a pillow. He spread the robe over him, tucking it in around the edges of his body on pure instinct. "Thank you for letting me do that," he said, stepping away. "I'll be in the office if you need anything."

Jere retreated to his office. The boy unsettled him. Jere hoped he would calm down in a few days, maybe once he was finished healing, and then perhaps things would start feeling a little more normal around here. Deciding to focus on more pressing matters, he carefully began reviewing the stack of papers and contracts he had signed the night he arrived, immersing himself in familiar territory.

Chapter 5
New Beginnings

It hadn't been painful. Or rough. The master hadn't even gotten angry at him.

The simple act of kindness, of reassurance, of gentleness was what broke Wren at that moment. He held himself together, mostly, until his master left the room, and then began to sob silently, a skill he had learned years ago, as if his heart would break. It was the first time since he had been taken as a slave that anyone had laid a hand on him that didn't result in pain or torture.

Somewhere along the way, touch had become something to be feared, dreaded even. From the moment he had been taken from his parents' house by two rough-handed guards, touch had been something that dragged him to new places of misery, hurt him, violated him in countless ways. Even touch that should have felt good — might have felt good in any other situation for any other person — even those touches felt awful, dredging up memories of pain and abuse. He had rarely been allowed to touch himself, and even when he did, he still failed more often than not to escape the memories his body had of other people's hands on him. His own body betrayed him by keeping him alive for so long, and he could barely stand to touch it more than was absolutely necessary to keep himself clean and presentable.

He recoiled from others and he felt physically ill when he touched himself, and yet this outlander had just put his hands all over him and none of it had hurt, even the most intimate and embarrassing parts, and he hated that a part of him liked it just a tiny bit. Even worse, he hated to think of what it would be like when it ended.

So he sobbed, silently, into his pillow, crying himself to sleep.

This is what you think life is like, huh? Playing the scared little pretty boy while the good doctor dotes on you? You thought you hurt before, you have no idea!

The whip cracked down on his skin again and again, searing lines across his flesh that split and bled and ached and burned until they caught on fire, actual flames, leaping in front of him and behind him and consuming and he was stupid, so fucking stupid for not stopping it faster. You're a speed slave Wren, what the hell is wrong with you Wren, WREN, why can't you do anything right, Wren —

"Wren!"

His eyes opened to find his master standing in his doorway, wearing, it seemed, nothing more than a pair of shorts.

"Sir?" Wren was still a bit disoriented, the imagined pain subsiding rapidly as he woke up.

"You were having a nightmare," Jere told him, sounding sleepy. "God, I heard you clear across the house—not to mention the projections. Can you always project your feelings so strongly?"

"I, I'm sorry, sir," Wren didn't know what else to say. He had never really noticed that he projected anything at all, although his masters were constantly on him to keep his emotions in check. Is that what they meant?

"It's okay, I just—I couldn't take it anymore. And you didn't sound like you were having such a great time of it either. Do you need anything?"

"No, sir. I'm sorry for waking you."

"It's all right. Just...." The master's voice was hesitant, as if he were about to say something. "Just get some rest."

"Yes, sir. Thank you for waking me, sir."

Jere left, and Wren stared at the ceiling, slightly illuminated by the moon that continued to show itself years after the stars had disappeared. Wren remembered his grandpa's stories of the stars that shone when he was a child, and his hopes that they would show up again one day, now that The Fall had eliminated most of the pollution that had filled the world before. In a way, the old man had explained, the economic crash and resource crisis that resulted had been a blessing in disguise, forcing people to live cleaner, simpler lives and abandon old methods of production in favor of newer, cleaner ones. While the newer resources were more difficult to harness and significantly more costly, they were all Wren had ever known. Wren wasn't sure what to think about stars, but he did appreciate the moon on dark nights.

This was surreal. Everything was surreal. He shouldn't be alive. His master shouldn't be treating him so well. He shouldn't be lying in this room with light blue walls that should have been brown, in a twin bed that should have had round knobs instead of square. He shouldn't be thinking about the moon. He wasn't really tired anymore, but he lay there quietly, resting as his master had ordered, and dozing off now and then. Mostly he wondered what his strange new master was thinking about down the hall, if he was even awake at all.

Wren was surprised to wake up the next day when he heard a door shut. He stayed in his room, listening through the walls, where he could hear voices from the clinic. Mrs. Jennings was in for another "accident" that required emergency attention. The master probably had no idea, but Wren was certain that Mr. Jennings, whom he had never met, beat his wife. Wren couldn't bring himself to care. She was a free woman. She could leave if she wanted to. He never felt anything but resentment toward free people who let themselves be hurt. Most days, he felt nothing but resentment toward free people as a whole.

If there were clients, that meant that the master was working, which meant he didn't require Wren's presence. Wren pulled the robe around him happily, picked up the mystery novel, and began to read, although turning the pages was a bit of a struggle. For once, he was happy to be so talented with his tongue.

A tapping at his door some time later made him realize he had lost track of time.

"Morning, Wren," Jere said, as he walked in the door. "First day back in business and here you are in bed, still?"

Wren's whole body grew hot, almost feverish with his anxiety. He hadn't expected his master to come and check on him, and certainly not this early in the day. Of course, he should have known, this man seemed like the type to linger and watch his every movement. How could he forget so quickly, how could he make mistakes so quickly? He dreaded the punishment that would come for this. Surreptitiously, he tucked the book under his pillow in hopes that his master would forget about it, that it wouldn't get taken away along with whatever else would happen.

"I'm sorry, sir, I should have—"

"Bullshit." The master's voice held a tone of finality. "I wanted you rested."

This couldn't be good. Masters never wanted you rested, unless they had some unpleasant, laborious task, or punishment, or fucking—actually Wren failed to see how those three were different from one another.

"We have some things to talk about today, planning and laying down house rules and figuring out how things will go for the two of us."

Jere's eyes were clear and calm as he spoke, although the light in them seemed to die down a bit as he took in Wren's reaction. Wren knew he must have gotten all pale and scared again.

"Come out and have something to eat—I know you haven't, by the way, are you trying to starve yourself? I thought I told you to eat. So we can talk while we eat, okay?"

Wren nodded. As if he had a choice. "Yes, sir." He followed Jere quickly to the dining room.

As he walked, Jere narrowed his eyes at him. "I've been all through this house and I haven't found any clothes for you."

Wren panicked for a fraction of a second. Of course he hadn't. Burghe had only allowed him to wear clothing on special occasions, and they were down in the cellar, where Wren was probably *supposed* to be sleeping, except the new master didn't know there was a cellar yet, and Wren wasn't particularly looking forward to going back down into it. He could lie about it now, and when he was forced back into the cellar, he could hide the clothes before they were noticed. His speed gift would make him fast enough. "I, uh, I suppose they were lost in the fire, sir. They might not have been inventoried. Slave clothing isn't that valuable."

Jere nodded. "Right, right. Well, what sort of thing did you usually wear?"

They had settled at the table by now, and Wren dropped into a chair, staring down at the deep, dark wood that was almost an exact replica of the old one. He tried to think of the best answer. He was pretty sure he couldn't get away with lying about this.

"I, sir, I generally wore... I wore scrubs, when I helped in the medical area." That wasn't a lie.

"Of course, that makes sense. But around the house?"

"Well, sir, I—I usually only wore a, a kind of loincloth thing. Sir." It had really been little more than a rag. And that was only on the rare occasions when he had been granted such a privilege.

Jere studied him. "You don't strike me as much of a nudist, kid."

Wren dropped his eyes. He certainly wasn't, but it wasn't ever his decision. "If it pleases you, master."

Jere nodded. "All right then. As much as I see you like that robe, perhaps a different wardrobe is needed, hmm?"

Wren didn't understand. He clutched the edges of the robe, unwilling to let it go. Wasn't it enough that he could be stripped naked at any moment?

"I see that someone thought it was a good idea to drop by a few photo catalogs in the mail—did you know we had a mailbox? Of course you did, you live here—but anyway, it seems that my threadbare sweaters aren't exactly in fashion for the town's new doctor, and they want to make sure I don't look like some poor city street urchin. And so, I thought, you know, you could pick some out too. For yourself? I mean, I'd just as soon not have you in a loincloth...."

Wren relaxed a little. So maybe his master wasn't interested in boys then? That would be a relief. And he certainly wouldn't want his slave looking like some sort of trash.

"Yes, sir, thank you!"

Jere smiled, and handed over the books and a pen. "Here, you pick out what you want, I'll find food. Think you're ready for something solid?"

Wren was actually quite hungry, but the thought of going back to the synthetic cloned food product was enough to make his stomach turn. "I, if I could sir, I would love some more of the broth you gave me yesterday?" He tried to look as innocent and hungry as possible. "I just don't want to get sick again."

Jere smiled. "Sure thing. But can you at least try and eat a piece of toast for me? I promise, it will make you feel better to have at least a little something solid in your stomach. You don't have to have anything on it even, although I might try to tempt you with a bit of peanut butter or cinnamon or—"

"Strawberry jam," Wren said without thinking, so caught up in the food that Jere was describing. His eyes widened with fear the second he realized he had spoken out loud.

Jere shrugged as if the request was nothing unusual. "Strawberry jam it is, then. Glad I could wake your appetite up!" He headed off to prepare the food.

Wren cursed himself inwardly. He had let himself grow stupid and careless, and he couldn't afford to keep doing that. The master was still in the mood to take care of him and indulge him now, but just because he wasn't being thrown around didn't mean he could let himself get into such horrible habits. Interrupting, speaking when he wasn't spoken to, not addressing his master properly—or at all—asking for something as if he deserved it—

"Finding anything you like?" Jere's voice came from the kitchen, accompanied by the smell of food.

"Uh, still looking, sir," Wren scrambled to find something in the catalog. Another thing he was doing wrong—getting lost in his thoughts.

"Take your time." A clatter of pans. "Dammit." The sound of running water. "Nobody said we have to order today. I have my lab coat, damned if I need anything else in a hurry."

"Yes, sir." Wren smiled, relaxing a bit in spite of himself. Perhaps he would be doing the cooking in the future.

A few minutes later, Jere came out with a bowl of broth, a jar of jam, and six pieces of toast.

Wren's eyes widened.

"The toast is for me, too. There were other things, but they didn't work out." Jere pushed a piece toward Wren. "Here, have at it."

Wren hesitated. He had been hoping that his master would

have put the jam on it. What if it was some sort of trap? If he took too much, he'd be greedy and wasteful, and if he took too little, then maybe he didn't really like it, and why did he ask for it, and—

"Sir, could you...? I don't think I can, with my hands like this."

"I forgot, your hands aren't good for much of anything at the moment." Jere put his own toast down on a plate and took the piece from Wren. "How much do you want?"

There seemed to be no end to all the possible ways that Wren might find himself backed into a corner. "Uh, as much as you'd like me to have, sir."

There was that frown again. Wren tried to stay calm, knowing that his master got irritated when he started trembling. He didn't say it out loud, but his body and his face and his tone said it.

"I'd like you to have as much as you want. I'm not really in the mood to play guessing games."

"Two spoonfuls, sir?" Wren couldn't resist wincing. Two was probably too many. One would have been better. Definitely one. Why hadn't he said one?

Jere spread two spoonfuls across the toast, scraped the spoon off on the edge, and looked at it disapprovingly. He added one more heaping spoonful, much to Wren's poorly hidden delight.

"I decided you should have three." Jere's tone was deadpan, but the smirk at the edge of his mouth made Wren smile as well. "So, what did you find?"

Jere slid the tiniest bit closer to Wren, just enough to make him tense up and watch his master's hands warily.

"Well, sir, slaves wear things that are a bit more simple," Wren tried to explain. It was so hard to think with the sugar and the fruit exploding on his tongue. It had been so long since he had eaten real food and his hand shook as he tried not to shove the warm bread into his mouth. "Um, it's not a law or anything, but everybody does it."

"And I should too, if I don't want to look like the village idiot." Jere grabbed another piece of toast for himself. "Okay, so could you find anything like that in here?"

Wren nodded. He saw no reason to point out that "simple" clothing usually meant cheap and easy to be ripped off or pulled down, without the hassle of buttons. "See, like this here, sir."

At Jere's urging, Wren picked out a number of simple, appropriate outfits for himself, and even a few casual things to lounge around or sleep in. "In case you ever decide to abandon the robe," Jere had teased.

Wren was speechless, for once out of cautious pleasure instead of terror, as he alternated between toast with jam, broth with real chicken flavor, and the thought of actual clothes that were clean and fit well and covered him.

"Now for the real challenge."

Wren almost choked, thankful that he had years of practice suppressing his gag reflex as a piece of toast slithered, unchewed, down his throat. "Sir?" he managed, his eyes watering. He should have known something awful was coming.

"It's better if you chew it," Jere advised, handing him a glass of water. "What I mean is, well, I don't quite know what's proper here. Actually, I probably don't know what's proper anywhere. It's rather embarrassing, but my clothes have largely been gifted to me by my mother, who insists that she wants me to look like a real adult instead of… whatever it is she thinks I look like. And so, as I start this 'real adult' thing, well, I was thinking that maybe you had helped Matthias pick out clothes in the past? Or at least paid attention to that sort of thing?"

Wren just stared at him. His master wanted a slave picking out his clothes?

"Just, I don't know. Make me look professional. But not like an uptight twat, like that lawyer."

"Mr. Montgomery?" Wren checked, agreeing with his master.

"You've met him, I see," Jere noted.

Wren panicked for a moment. What was wrong with him, suggesting that about a free person, and someone whom his master might respect, might even like! "I, uh, he's the only lawyer whom Mr. Burghe had on retainer, sir, I just thought, you said—"

Jere shook his head. "It's fine, Wren. I know what you meant. And besides, I was the one who called him that, not you."

Wren forced himself to appear calm, despite the fact that his heart still raced at the near-disaster. He flipped to the less casual section of the catalog. "Here, sir," he pointed. "This is, well, this is the sort of thing that a lot of well-dressed men wear."

Jere nodded. "I could see myself in that. Minimal, classic. Now, what about the colors? I kind of like this one."

Wren glanced at the atrocity Jere was pointing at, and understood why his mother still picked his clothes out for him. "Uh, sir, I think solid prints are a bit more suitable for you. The darker ones, like this one here. It would really bring out your eyes."

Jere was quiet for a moment, and Wren started to get nervous. He had done the right thing, hadn't he? Of course not; Wren realized his mistake right away. He should have known that his master only wanted him to nod and agree with whatever he picked. He held his breath and turned his head away ever so slightly, hoping to place his teeth out of the way of his master's hand when he hit him.

"Damned if you're not right," Jere said. "I suppose I should let my mouth talk louder than my clothes, huh?"

Wren just barely heard his master's voice over the pounding of his own heart. "As you wish, sir," he managed, automatically.

Jere pushed the pen at him. "Here, pick out the ones you think would be best on me."

Chapter 6
Old Patterns

Wren found himself flipping through the pages of the catalog, glancing back and forth between the images and looking at his master, circling a shirt here, some pants there, picking out a few complementary colors to put together a solid outfit as he went along. He stuck to mostly dark colors, which would contrast nicely with his light hair. Jere commented on a few of them, but mostly looked pleased to have someone to take this seemingly onerous task out of his hands. Wren was halfway through his second piece of toast when he nearly choked again, realizing that he was eating his *second* piece of toast. His master had nonchalantly spread some jam on it and placed it in his hand at some point when the other one disappeared. Thinking better of it, Wren ate the remainder very quickly as he finished picking out his master's wardrobe.

"Well, now that we have some reasonable assurance that we won't be strolling around naked, let's talk about what things around here are going to look like, okay?"

The master's tone made it perfectly clear that this was not a question, but an order. "Yes, sir."

"Okay. So, we're already to starting to get patients in, despite the fact that I'm technically still half-time on vacation. I'm guessing that means I'll be pretty busy."

Wren nodded. Was he supposed to say something?

"Now, I'm fine taking care of things around here for now, because under *no* circumstances do I want you damaging your hands any further—I will not be thrilled if I have to repair them. But, hopefully by the end of the week I'll have a chance to get in there and heal them up the rest of the way, and then I'll need your help."

Well, then, it's good that I'm a slave, Wren thought, feeling guilty the moment he did. But he would rather pretend that he was irritated with his master than try to deal with the fear that was threatening to eat him alive at the moment.

"I was thinking, well, I mean, I'll help out as much as I can, but you're probably better at it anyway," Jere fumbled. "You know, household stuff. Like, if you could keep it picked up in here? Maybe take care of the cooking? I mean, toast is delicious, but it's sort of my specialty. As in, it's the one thing that I can successfully cook without burning or making too salty or whatever. You said they taught you about it at the training facility?"

"Yes, sir."

"Good, so if you could do that, that would be great." Jere looked at him expectantly.

"Yes, sir."

"Once things start picking up I'll let you know when I need help in the clinic. I mean, emergencies are always in need of speed, and sometimes it's just nice to have an extra set of hands. So I do expect, well, I mean, I hope, that if I call you, you'll come?"

Wren tried not to laugh at the absurdity of that. What else would he be doing that was more important? The only way he wouldn't come was if he had been beaten too badly, but Wren was trying to avoid thinking about that. Everything Jere said felt like a test and Wren never knew when he would fail or even if he already had.

"Yes, sir. I should be able to hear if you call me from anywhere in the house or the clinic."

"Good, good." Jere nodded. He paused a moment before speaking again. "You say your gift is speed, but I've never seen you use it."

Wren had been taught from the first moment he arrived in the training facility that gifts were to be used solely for the purposes of the master. Before his new master had healed him, he used to be able to pick out some of the first scars he ever received for forgetting that rule. He decided to alter the truth a bit. "Sir, I, I can't use it without your permission, sir...." Apparently the alteration was a bit too close to a lie for his comfort, as he stumbled over his words.

"Oh." Jere seemed to be considering something. "Well, that certainly isn't a law or anything."

"Not a written law, sir."

"Like with the clothes," Jere shook his head, as if the idea was just that strange to him. "Well, then, you have my permission to use it whenever you'd like, for whatever you need it for."

"Thank you, sir." Wren doubted that his master really meant this. He just didn't know how much it could be taken advantage of.

"I guess that's pretty much all I expect from you," Jere said, obviously trying to force himself to sound nonchalant. He sounded awkward and almost as nervous as Wren felt. "What do you need from me?"

Wren didn't fall for it. "Serving you is enough for me, sir."

"Surely you must have questions or something?" Jere stared at him expectantly. "Something you want to know, or wonder about me, or... anything?"

Wren felt pressured to ask something, and he figured an upfront discussion of what punishments he should expect couldn't hurt too much. "Well, sir, if I, if I make a mistake, or if I should... shirk my duties?" Just contemplating it was making him shudder. "What will happen then?"

"Well, I suppose I'll chat with you and figure out what happened, and see what we can do to make it different in the future." Jere smiled back at him, looking innocent to the point of naïveté again.

"Or what if I break something, sir?" Wren tried. Burghe had instituted a policy that every broken cup, plate, or bowl got repaid with a broken bone. Wren hoped that his new master wasn't that creative.

"Well, I'll certainly have you clean it up...." Jere let his voice trail off.

"Sir, what happens if I don't perform a chore quickly enough?"

"You have a speed gift. You'll certainly do better than I ever would. What do you think would happen?"

Wren just stared at him. His old master could have listed a thousand detailed tortures for each of those things. At that moment,

Wren hated the man sitting in front of him, hated everything he and the other free people like him stood for. All the games, and tricks, and manipulations. The fake friendly face his master had now, that he would have until he realized the kinds of abuse he could heap on his slave without repercussions. Wren couldn't speak.

"Wren, if you think I'm going to punish you for those sorts of things, I'm not." Jere spoke quietly, looking down at the table. "I see no reason to punish you at all. I know what happened to you; at least, I know the end result of it. I know about the scars you had, I saw them all when I healed you. I saw them from the inside. And I just want you to know, whatever the reason was, it wasn't good enough. You shouldn't be beat up like that for anything."

Wren was silent for a moment. He knew his master had healed the scars, but he didn't realize... he certainly hadn't thought that he had put the things together to figure out why. His master would know what an awful slave he had been. He trembled as he spoke. "Thank you for saying those things, sir, but I have made mistakes in the past. I was punished as my masters saw fit."

"Of course you made mistakes!" Jere said, sounding exasperated. "And I'm sure you will again. You're human, and it happens. No damn reason to punish you because of it."

Wren only sat there. What could he say? A part of him agreed, knew and had always known that the abuse he had taken was just that — abuse. But the other part, the part that kept him in check, the part that got him through to see the next day alive, that part was terrified to even be thinking such an offensive thing. Masters deserved to treat their slaves as they saw fit, and as a slave, he was deficient for ever questioning this. He had to ensure that Jere never saw this part of him.

"Look, Wren. Here's the thing — I'm not here to hurt you, or punish you, or beat you or burn you or — or whatever the hell else it was that anyone else has ever done to you. I don't really care what it is you do — short of you trying to kill me, you can pretty much lay bets on me not laying a hand on you, is that clear?"

His master's words were very clear, but the tension in his body, the way his eyes had narrowed and his voice had gotten louder and deeper, indicated obvious anger. What the hell kind of cruel trick *was* this? His master obviously knew things and now he was toying with him, but Wren knew better than to be drawn in. Wren resisted the urge to shudder, and slowly forced himself to nod. "Yes, sir."

Jere ran a hand through his rather unruly hair and sighed. "Look, I don't know how to convince you, but it doesn't matter much, does it? You'll just keep doing what you do, I'll keep doing what I do, and maybe we can just coexist, you know? Not make such a big deal out of things. Or something."

"Yes, sir." Wren had no idea what to make of his master's request to "coexist," but dared not ask.

They stared awkwardly at each other for a few moments.

"I'm going into town to run some errands," Jere announced suddenly, standing up. "I'll be back later."

Wren watched his master grab his keys and jacket. He avoided even looking in Wren's direction, much less making eye contact. He struggled with the door and headed out, fleeing as if a pack of wolves was on his heels. Wren breathed calmly again once he was alone, the pressure of uncertainty finally escaping him.

With a bit of mischievous glee, he flitted to his room and back a few times, exercising the speed gift that he had so often been forbidden from using. The house was large, and the distance between the kitchen and the bedroom was enough to get his heart beating after a few quick laps. Remembering that he and the master had left quite a mess on the table, he cleaned it up as best he could with bandaged hands and retreated to his room in record time. He did so miss using his gift.

Chapter 7
Coexisting

Jere came back from town later than he had originally planned. After visiting the limited selection of businesses in town, he decided to go for a walk. He had never been much of a nature enthusiast, in part because there was so little of it in Sonova, similar to most of the heavily populated areas in the world. With so many people needing housing, a patch of trees or grass seemed ludicrous. Despite the millions who had died during the riots after The Fall, population was on an upswing again, with people living nearly twice as long as they had centuries ago. Jere smiled at the thought of overpopulation—in a place like Hojer, one would never know it was a problem. He couldn't recall the last time he had been alone for so long outside of his own home. Then again, he wasn't alone in his new home, if he could call it that. He'd rather not, in fact, he'd rather not think about that at all. Instead, he looked the rivers, nearly devoid of water, and tried to count all the trees he could see without turning his head. Generally, he avoided going home. The truth was, the kid made him uncomfortable as hell. He knew that Wren had been pretty roughed up, but every move Jere made had him flinching as if Jere had slapped him.

The very thought of it irritated him. But not as much as it sickened him.

Jere had met Matthias in university. Jere was a typical first-year student, ambitious and idealistic and not so bright. Sure, he was good in his classes, excelling to the top of most of them, and quick to learn from books. However, he lacked the certain life experience that he would have had five years later.

So, when his visiting professor, nearly twice his age, asked him out to coffee to talk about "assignments," he actually brought a book bag.

Matthias had brought a duffel bag of various sex toys.

They used most of them that night. They used all of them and more in the next few months.

And that's how it began. Coffee turned into dinner turned into drinks at Matthias's apartment turned into fucking turned into not-dating. Not-dating meant that anyone who dared ask such a stupid question as "Are you dating the professor?" would get shot down with a glare. Not-dating meant they introduced themselves as friends or as a professor and a student, but never as anything else. Not-dating meant they said "I liked that thing you did" or "I'm free tonight," but never "I love you" or "Do you want to meet my parents?"

They both liked it that way, and Jere had been thoroughly smitten with the middle-aged man. In between fucking him into the mattress and teaching him the finer points of sucking cock, Matthias had given him career tips and set him up to meet with hospital directors in hopes of finding him a job. Jere was young, inexperienced, and needed any opportunity he could get. If his beloved mentor asked that he try out some new and different things in bed later that night, who was he to complain? He even liked some of them.

Of course, Matthias had never been cruel. Not with Jere. He would push and cajole and, once, almost even beg, but he had never been forceful. He was calm and gentle enough that he could lull the then-new medical student into his first gang-bang, a series of complicated ropes tied tight enough that he couldn't move, even an interesting time with a very sharp series of knives. That hadn't gone over as well, despite the coaxing on Matthias's part, but when all was said and done and healed, the sheets tossed into a bucket with some bleach to take out the bloodstains, Jere had been able to admit that it was exciting. And Matthias had promised never to do it with him again.

So Jere had started to get some idea of what Matthias was about, but in large parts, the man remained a mystery. Jere knew that he had ties to some rural outland, but didn't know which one, and Matthias never rushed to volunteer that information. Jere had guessed that he was accepting of slavery, as he scorned the activists that paraded around campus, despite there being no slaves in the state. Jere, focused as he was on his own life, couldn't care much either way. The flyers ended up in a drawer with those for saving starving children and resurrecting the internet and whatever other flighty cause was hot that week. They made good rolling papers, thin and small as they were.

When Matthias left it had been rather uneventful. They had gotten coffee, real coffee, as Matthias always had the money to supply it. As they finished, he casually mentioned that he would be moving and not returning. Jere was somewhat surprised, but he would be leaving the university in the next few years anyway, and neither of them had ever expected to continue their relationship, whatever it was. They exchanged addresses, wrote occasionally at first and then on holidays, and that was it.

Jere had no idea that the man had really thought of him much since then. He would have been surprised to get a tip-off for a new job in Sonova after this much time, Although he had gotten a few of those at first, this was something he would never have expected. He didn't even know if he would have agreed to it, had the conditions been specified in advance. This place wasn't his style at all; he preferred the city life, the bustle and excitement, the convenience and anonymity that tens of thousands of people provided. As it was, he only planned to work here for a while. He could build his income, gain experience and age and credibility that would make him more marketable into the future, but he couldn't imagine being stuck here more than a few years.

He regretted how little of Matthias's life had been left behind for him to peruse. Since the fire had started in the master bedroom, it took with it almost all personal effects and indications of his life-style. The design of the house had left only the kitchen intact, and the medical clinic, which was fortunately separated from the rest of the house by a thick wall that had stood up to the fire and smoke. All that was left of Matthias's possessions was medical equipment, a tiny bit of food, and the slave. All Jere could really gather from this was that Matthias had been quite well-off, not particularly adept at feeding himself, and, well, the slave.

Jere had never really cared about slavery, it was more his sister's thing, a girl thing, caring about everyone. He knew that there were different reasons that different states had adopted slavery, different ways in which they carried it out, and different laws; it was little wonder he knew nothing substantial about it. Learning medicine was difficult enough without mixing in social issues. Sonova didn't have slaves, so he didn't have to know about them. Besides, he only saw Jen on holidays, and even then, his sister's rather hectic travel and work schedule had kept them from visiting for a few years. Jere's mum had always forbidden everyone from discussing politics on the grounds that it was too disruptive, and Jere liked it that way. Now, though, he wished he had some idea of just what he was facing. It might have helped him navigate situations like the one he created when he arrived home.

Jere had come in late, trying to avoid Wren and conversation and everything, really, and caught the kid speeding across the house for something. Jere was a bit startled, but beyond that he didn't care. Back home there were speed messengers all over town, he had just never lived with one. But Wren had gone dead white and started mumbling some sort of terrified apology as if Jere had walked in on him doing something unthinkable, like decapitating a patient.

Jere, of course, hadn't helped the situation by snapping at him to calm the fuck down, and storming into the bedroom, where he was now, awkwardly staring at the ceiling. Truth be told, he would have preferred the aggressive kid he met in the projection, telling him off and getting angry at him. That, he knew what to do with. This... he was trying to be nice, to act like things were okay, to figure out what spooked the kid so much, but it seemed futile. He was constantly, mindlessly terrified, and Jere couldn't even begin to predict what would make it better or worse, except leaving him alone completely. It was too bad, because Jere saw flashes, here and there, of intelligence in Wren. Someone he could talk to and ask questions of and sit around at night drinking tea or hot chocolate or maybe even a few cocktails or a nightcap or....

Jere was startled awake by muffled screams again. He had been dreaming about Wren? He had been dreaming about drinking cocktails with a slave who hated him and was probably having night-mares about him right now? He pondered a variety of causes for such temporary insanity, decided that stress and a lack of restful sleep was certainly the cause.

Jere got up wearily, trudging across the house and cursing it for its spaciousness, until he arrived at the slave's room. He wondered, hazily, if this had been his room in the past. He reminded himself to check at some point as he pushed open the door. Three nights in a row, these dreams.

He walked over to the bed and put a hand on the kid's shoulder. "Wren," he shook him a little.

His eyes flew open in a panic, and he curled into a ball, protecting his head, which was just now starting to grow a faint covering of dark hair.

"Jesus." Jere pulled his hand back as if he'd been burned. "I was just waking you up. Again. Didn't mean to scare you."

Huddled against the wall, Wren began to whimper as he trembled.

"Listen, I, fuck. Are you okay?" Jere asked, feeling useless. He asked every night, and had no idea what else he was expecting.

Never taking his eyes off of Jere, Wren nodded. "Y-yes, sir. I'm sorry, sir. I didn't mean to—"

"I know." Jere cut him off, too exhausted to listen to the painful-ly sincere apologies again. "I'm not angry at you for having dreams. I just want us both to be able to sleep. So I'm going to do exactly that."

"Yes, sir. Thank you." Wren's eyes were still fixed on him, wait-ing for his next move.

Jere didn't say anything. Nothing he said mattered anyway, so he just went on back to bed.

He lay there, casting angry glares at the ceiling. His former men-tor had been a psychopath. He was terrifying a slave without trying. He knew nobody here, couldn't get a single night's sleep without being woken up with screams, and on top of it all he had suddenly developed insomnia.

He debated getting up, but that would only further the prob-lem. He wished for a drink, but it was only a few hours before he would be waking up to work in the clinic like a responsible adult. He cursed quietly, and flopped onto his side, only to roll back onto his back.

He was too tense, he realized. Relaxing would help. Relaxing always helped, and there was a tried and true method of relaxation right at his fingertips....

He grinned, kicking off his boxer shorts and grabbing his cock. There. Now it was *really* at his fingertips.

He settled back, starting with light, soft strokes that went from base to tip, just working himself up. How many times had this gotten him through tense exam nights in university? It never failed. He twisted as he stroked, smiling as he was able to focus all of his nerves and tension on this one particular body part, chasing away the rest of his worries. So what if the kid didn't like him—did it matter? Maybe Wren did like him, Jere wasn't sure. He was hard to read. Hell, maybe he was lying in bed down the hall jerking off and thinking about him, too.

Jere smiled at that idea, half because it was ridiculous, and half because it was kind of hot. It was right up there with his ridiculous idea of having cocktails and casual conversation with the kid in the ranks of things that were never going to happen.

Jere figured he was probably more tired than he initially realized, if he was getting turned on thinking about impossible things. He readjusted himself, leaning further back, and raised his hips, working his cock a little harder. He let his mind wander, thinking about the pretty boy he had hooked up with in Sonova, just a few days before he left. God, it was so long ago, now!

But he could still remember the boy's eyes, the way they flashed up at him as he smiled, coy and cute, the bright blue not unlike a certain someone. The shock of bright green hair, artfully dyed, which Jere enjoyed running his fingers through, despite the green tinge he found the next day. He had introduced himself as "Envy," a play on the color of his hair. Jere doubted it was his real name, but hadn't been concerned with that then.

Envy and Jere had both been kicked out of a club at the same time, on the grounds that neither had nor were planning to get any money, and they had decided to make the best out of their situation and go home together. Jere missed nights like that. They went back to his place, unkempt as it was, but it didn't matter, because they had gone straight to the bed, where Jere found himself pinned to the mattress seconds later.

Jere's grip on his cock tightened at the memory. He wanted that so badly, someone to throw him down and take him like that again. Were there people here that he would even be interested in? Could he connect with anyone here long enough to have a good, hard night of fucking, even if that's all it ended up being? The only other person he ever even talked to here was Wren, and he didn't seem like the type for a casual roll in the hay.

That night had been great; Jere ended up sucking the other boy off and getting him worked up, allowing Envy to pin his arms above his head and hold Jere in place as he fucked him, pounding into him with a carefree smile on his face as Jere rocked back against his cock like they were waging battle.

Jere thrust harder into his hand, thinking about the way it felt, how nice it had been to ride that hard cock all night. He put a finger in his mouth with a grin, thinking of how Envy's cock had tasted, sucking in the same way as he had that night. After a few moments, he took the finger from his mouth and moved it between his legs as well, teasing his ass as he temporarily slowed down the hand on his cock. Yes, that had been a night to remember.

His thoughts jumped to Wren again, and he knew he shouldn't, knew it wasn't right or respectful or whatever, but it was just thoughts, a sexy daydream, and besides, Envy from Sonova looked enough like Wren that Jere could convince himself that he was thinking of him instead. He pictured the slim, slightly shorter body stretched out on top of him, and he bit his lip to keep from crying out as he worked his finger inside of himself, just barely too fast, just barely making it hurt. He imagined it was a cock, and he closed his eyes, picturing the person on top of him doing it.

It felt so good, having someone inside of him like this, and he thrust back, pressing himself down onto his own finger. He could have taken more, but he didn't feel like reaching for lube, and he knew his own body quite well enough to work with just the one. The fantasy man who was fucking him in his imagination did as well, and soon he felt the familiar tightening. His breath grew shallow and rapid, and he worked the hand on his cock harder and faster. Jere bit down on his lip again, harder this time, making it hurt, and as it hurt, he groaned and worked his finger in and out of his ass again. He pictured the face that the person fucking him would have; he would be so excited, feeling so good as Jere tightened around his cock. He thrust a few more times, holding on to that image, before he finally came, clenching his teeth together in order to keep himself quiet.

Jere lay there, feeling the tension draining out of his body. No, nothing he did or didn't do seemed to matter to Wren, but at least his fantasy had put him in a better mood. He settled into sleep, sated and rather exhausted now. Perhaps, if he was lucky, he would forget his guilty fantasy by tomorrow morning.

Chapter 8
Healing

The next few days went similarly. Jere and Wren tried to avoid each other, Jere woke Wren up from screaming nightmares more often than not, and both were generally uncomfortable in each other's company. Jere was happy to be kept busy enough with medical visits to occupy himself most days, but not so busy that he needed help yet. So they ate together, when Jere couldn't find an excuse to work while he was eating. He was pretty sure that they were both looking forward to the day when Wren would be able to prepare food for them, as Jere's skill set of toast and soup and sandwiches had grown rather dull.

Which brought them to Sunday. Jere discovered that Matthias had regularly worked half-days on Sundays, which meant that Sunday morning was a mess as Jere struggled to process through all the patients who strolled through his door "before he closed." He wouldn't begrudge anyone an emergency, but more considerate planning from non-emergency patients would have been much appreciated.

Never one to look a gift horse in the mouth, Jere decided that he too would stop work early. He tidied up the clinic a bit, stepping into the house to find Wren hiding out in his room again. His door was open, as usual, but Jere knocked on it anyway.

"Yes, sir?" Wren stood up immediately, looking nervous and guilty. The book he was reading, another mystery novel that the librarian had forced upon Jere, effectively disappeared.

"I, uh, I seem to have the rest of the afternoon off." *And I thought I'd stand here being awkward.* Jere tried to summon up the confidence he had with his patients. "I thought I might have a look at your hands today."

Wren nodded. "Where would you like me, sir? An exam room in the clinic?"

Jere shrugged. "Actually, you may as well be comfortable. We can do it here, if that's okay?" The clinic was cleaned up for the day already.

"Yes, sir."

Jere motioned for him to sit down on the bed, and he pulled a chair up next to it. "Now, unlike the last two times, you'll actually be conscious for this one. Do you want a painkiller injection?"

Wren shook his head quickly. "No, please, sir." His tone bordered on panic.

"All right." Jere settled down next to him. He wondered if Wren was afraid of needles. "Now, I'll take off the bandages first, it might sting a little bit, so be prepared, okay?"

"Yes, sir." Wren squeezed his eyes shut and held out his hands, allowing Jere to remove the bandages as quickly and gently as he could. Wren stayed completely silent.

"Good, you're doing just fine," Jere said softly. "Now, go ahead and rest your hands in mine and relax. I won't be in your head quite the way I was before, but I do need you to let me in a bit so I can heal you, all right? I'm sure you've done this before."

"Yes, sir," Wren mumbled, but showed no indications of relaxing or letting himself be healed. His breathing grew shallower and quicker.

"Wren—"

"I'm sorry sir, please, just go ahead and do it! I'll try to be quiet!"

Jere let the boy's hands rest on his lap. "Wren. Open your eyes and look at me."

Obediently, he did, his wide blue eyes betraying him with angry tears.

Jere held himself back from cursing. "Wren, this isn't going to hurt. Okay? Have you never had someone heal you properly, for fuck's sake?"

Wren's eyes dropped to the floor. "I- I'm resistant, sir. And so, if it hurts, I deserve it."

"Bullshit."

Wren flinched at the tiny increase in Jere's volume.

"Look, if you're resistant, that just means that your healer isn't doing a very damn good job." Jere actually believed this; he had yet to meet a conscious patient whom he could not ease his way into healing gently. "And it just so happens that I'm awful fucking good at my job. Now tell me, have you ever had a good experience with a healer?"

Wren was quiet for a moment, then he nodded. "Yes, sir."

Jere bit the inside of his mouth to keep himself from screaming at the boy's hesitation. "And that was?"

"When I was a little boy, sir," Wren said quietly. "Before...."

"Before you found out you were a slave?"

Wren nodded. "Yes, sir. And before my gift showed. The gift, it makes it hurt."

What kinds of lies had been fed to this kid? "Wren, it can be a little more challenging to mind-heal someone with a physical gift, but it's certainly not impossible! The healer just has to try a little harder, because the channels that exist between people with mind gifts aren't as strong. But we've got time, and like I said, I'm good at my job."

"Yes, sir."

Jere couldn't help but grin. "Now, I can tell you don't fucking believe me, and that's okay, too, but I want you to try something, okay? Someone might have used this when you were a kid, or maybe not, hell, what do I know about how anything is done here? But it works with kids, and it works with adults, too, so will you give it a chance?"

"Yes, sir."

Jere waited for a moment, expecting more. "Okay. Think of a piece of paper for me? Really focus in on it, what it looks like, what it feels like, what color it is. Can you do that?"

"Yes, sir."

"Good. Keep thinking about it. Now, while you're doing that, you'll feel me enter your mind a little—no, don't stop thinking about it, and don't pull away, trust me, all I'm going to do right now is make the connection, okay? You just worry about what that piece of paper looks like. Now I want you to draw something on it. Imagine what it would be—and make it something simple, okay? Keep focusing on it and ignore me."

They were silent a moment, both concentrating on their tasks. As he had pointed out earlier, Jere didn't have to be in Wren's head quite the way he had before—with a conscious patient, he only sought access to the very surface of his mind, seeing what that person saw, through their eyes, glimpsing their thoughts and occasional memories in a straightforward, coherent way. Focusing attention on one thing was an ideal way to make this happen.

Jere spoke softly, keeping the energy level in the room as low as possible. "Is it a star?"

"Yes, sir," Wren replied, sounding shocked.

"Good," Jere smiled. "Keep focusing on the paper. You're halfway there. Now I'm going to add something too, and I want you to concentrate on what it is. Tell me when you have it figured out."

More time passed, and Jere concentrated on the image of a fish, picturing it drawn onto the paper. He sent out his projection carefully, so as not to overwhelm the boy.

"Is it... is it a fish, sir?" Wren asked tentatively.

Jere smiled. It was fun to show someone how to do this. "Yes. Good! Congratulations, we've just made that connection that you were so damn afraid of. No resistance at all, was there?"

"No, sir," Wren said, a little shy.

"Okay, now I'm going to go ahead and heal you up—it shouldn't be painful, but it might be a little bit uncomfortable, all right? You didn't want a painkiller injection, and that's fine, I'll block most of the sensation, but it means you'll still feel part of what happens. Just hold still, and if it gets too much, tell me, all right?"

"Yes, sir." Wren held out his hands in anticipation.

Jere took them in his own, needing the physical connection to facilitate the mind-healing process. Wren's mind seemed almost intentionally blank, except for the remaining image of the paper and the star and the fish. Jere worked slowly, trying not to scare his still terrified patient, and was pleased to find that the he was healing pretty well already. He repaired the skin to cover the raw flesh, felt some tiny blood vessels spring back into life, and even summoned up a bit of extra energy to grow fingernails. It wasn't a long process, but time passed differently during mind-healing. Jere guessed that nearly an hour had passed before he had completed the boy's hands to his satisfaction.

"All right, now I want you to do one more thing for me," Jere said, once again allowing Wren to rest his hands on his lap.

"Yes, sir," Wren said, much more at ease than he had been.

"That paper I had you think of—I want you to think of it again, just as it was." Jere waited, feeling with his mind until he was certain the kid had done as he had asked. "Now, I want you to think of erasing the misshapen little fish I drew, taking it right out."

Wren hesitated for a moment, then did as he was asked. Jere felt himself being pushed out of his mind bit by bit as the image was erased.

"Look at your hands," Jere instructed, grinning a bit. Wren had kept his eyes closed almost the whole time Jere was healing him.

"Thank you, sir," Wren looked up at his face for a minute, then quickly looked back down again. "They, they're better than they were. Before the fire."

"I told you I was good." Jere couldn't resist smirking. "Now, you'll need to put that cream on them, like you did everything else—but more, because hands are always drying out and stretching and being washed—put it on six or eight times a day. The more you put it on, the better they'll heal. Are you feeling all right?"

"Yes, sir." Wren responded, then hesitated a moment. "Sir, I, uh, how did I, I mean, how did you get me to...."

"Are you wondering why it didn't hurt to do the mind-healing?" Jere couldn't stop himself from interrupting; the boy's stammering was just too painful to continue.

"Yes, sir. And, I mean, you could have done it the other way, like...."

Jere sighed. "Like I said, any good healer can do it without causing pain. But I'm guessing that you've had it done painfully a lot of times before?"

"Yes, sir. Um, I was told that after the gift shows, that it makes it hurt, and that it's worse if you resist, but I could never stop resisting." Wren looked down, ashamed.

"Well, you've had shitty treatment." Jere spoke with a tone of finality. "I'll see to it that it doesn't happen again."

"Thank you, sir."

"Has anyone ever…" Jere struggled with how to phrase his next question. "Has anyone ever used it as punishment on you?"

Wren went still, his breath catching a little as he spoke. "Yes, sir. My last master used to use it quite often."

Jere was quiet for a moment, trying to keep his rage under check. Using a healing gift that way was unethical and wrong. "I'll see to it that that doesn't happen again either."

Wren looked up at him then, almost doubtful, certainly shocked. "Thank you, sir."

For once, he actually seemed to mean it.

Chapter 9
Learning

Wren sat in bed after his master left, stretching and flexing his hands, marveling at how smooth and soft they felt, and at how much they didn't hurt. He ran them across the clean cotton sheets, gripped one of the square wooden knobs on the bed, even blew some warm air over them. No pain. The pain over the last few days hadn't been awful, but it had always been there. For the first time in longer than Wren could remember, he was in no pain at all. He wanted to cherish the feeling as long as he could. Everything was too good, too nice, and it would all burn out too soon, Wren was certain.

He had, as had become his habit, declined afternoon tea with the master. While he longed for a sweet, warm cup, he wasn't up to the discomfort that he felt when he they were together. He struggled to keep up much of an appetite, anyway, and the thought of sharing yet another meal was too much. Even though Jere had been quite giving, Wren doubted he'd let him take food back to his room to eat or drink alone, especially now that he wasn't sick anymore. He realized that since he was no longer incapacitated, he needed to start cooking and cleaning and assisting the master with his medical work. Anything to prove himself useful.

For the moment, he retrieved his book. He had already read it, but he liked going back to look for clues that he missed the first time around. He thought the mystery novels were amazing—just like slaves, the detectives had to always be alert, watching for clues, moods, subtle changes in tone—all that. But unlike himself, the detectives always noticed. Even if they didn't, they could always fix things and catch the criminals later. It was just another chance for them to shine. For a slave, not catching things meant you got beaten later, or didn't get dinner, or... there were a lot of pretty awful things that a slave risked. Wren decided he'd rather not think about those right now.

A few hours later he could no longer ignore his hunger, and decided it might impress his master if he offered to make dinner. He left his room and walked somewhat reluctantly to the room next door, where his master was sitting in his office, looking deeply engaged in something he was reading. Wren hesitated silently in the doorway for a while, uncertain whether interrupting him was advisable or not.

In his nervousness, he more or less forgot to breathe, and compensated by gasping for air, enough to draw Jere's attention.

"Wren?" the master looked up at him expectantly.

"Yes, sir." Wren was starting to reconsider this decision. Why had he wanted to disrupt his master anyway? "Sir, I was wondering, would it please you if I made dinner?"

Jere smiled. "It would, yes. Neither one of us wants to keep suffering from my ridiculous attempts to feed us, do we?"

Wren hoped that avoidance would be an acceptable way to address this question. "Sir, what shall I make for you?"

Jere shrugged. "I eat pretty much anything. Just make whatever you'd make yourself."

Wren hesitated. Usually, if he made something for himself, it was the horrible synthetic food product that was reserved strictly for slaves, and he certainly couldn't feed his master *that*, could he?

"Do you have some sort of strange eating habits I don't know about?" Jere asked, raising an eyebrow.

Wren sighed. He couldn't tell if his master was simply unaware of the customs here, or if he was purposely trying to set him up to fail. He yearned for a clear order. "Do you like pasta, sir?"

"Sounds great. Thank you." Jere went back to reading, shaking his head in a way Wren couldn't understand.

Wren backed out of the room quickly, heading to the kitchen. There was no use in telling his master *why* his eating habits were strange. If the master thought it was normal for a slave to eat real food sometimes, like when he was sick, or maybe even at holidays, who was he to disabuse him of the notion? He wouldn't go so far as to tell his master that slaves were always restricted to synthetic food product, but he wasn't about to lie to him outright, either, and act like all this good food was normal. Perhaps if he just ate the synthetic food sometimes, it would go unnoticed when he snuck some real food here and there.

About an hour later, Jere strolled out into the kitchen. "Something smells good."

"Thank you, sir. It's almost finished."

Jere deposited himself at the small table in the kitchen.

"Sir, if you'd like, I'll bring the food into the dining room when it's ready," Wren said somewhat hesitantly. He didn't want to be watched.

Jere stood up, making Wren back up against the stove and away from him. "Well, then, I'll leave and stop disturbing the chef. Is there anything I can help with, setting the table or anything?"

The heat against Wren's back was nothing compared to his desire to put distance between himself and his master. He forced his voice to stay steady. "No, sir, that's been taken care of."

"Right, right. Speed gift. Well, then, I'll get out of your way."

Wren relaxed once he walked out of the room. Having his master around had always made him nervous, more likely to drop or break or burn things, and then, the price to pay for that....

His thoughts were interrupted by a timer going off. He flipped and scooped and poured and plated, and moments later, an appetizing plate of pasta, complete with sauce and meatballs and bread, was sitting in front of Jere. Wren sat down to a warmed up bowl of synthetic "meat" protein matter, with a grayish pink color.

Jere stared at the food. "Just what the hell is that?" he demanded.

Wren's heart started to pound. "Sir?"

"That. What you have in that bowl."

Wren realized that Jere wasn't talking about his own mouthwatering plate of goodness, but rather about Wren's shapeless, flavorless glob. He relaxed ever so slightly.

"It's... it's synthetic meat, sir."

Jere stared at him.

"Syn-synthetic food product. It doesn't resemble a specific

meat, sir."

Still no reply.

"It's what—slaves eat it, sir. It has all the necessary vitamins and minerals and stuff. And no added flavors or colors or sugar or anything unhealthy or expensive or—"

"Do you like it?" Jere's nose was turned up in disgust.

"I...." Wren was at a loss. Of course he didn't like it. Nobody ate synthetic food because they liked it, they ate it because it was preferable to starving, and starving was the only other option. "Sir, I—"

"Christ." Jere grabbed his fork and moved in Wren's direction.

Wren dropped under the table, terror bitter in his mouth. He knew that he was supposed to stay still for punishments. He had taken quite a few beatings to get this lesson instilled in his head properly, and he was usually stoic about it, but something about a fork coming at him had crossed a line. He waited for the repercussion.

He heard the unmistakable sound of a fork scraping across a bowl.

"You can't possibly enjoy this." Jere's voice was calm, almost amused, above Wren's head. He heard something being spat out. "I mean, I've eaten some pretty low-grade stuff when money was tight, but they at least tried to cover up that synthetic flavor. This is... this is just awful."

Wren said nothing. What was he supposed to say? He was huddled under the dining room table, where he had *hidden*, like a child, from a punishment that apparently existed only in his imagination. He had made himself a bowl of "awful" synthetic stuff that his master seemed offended to even have on his table, and now he was distracting this same master from eating his dinner, which Wren knew damn well would be perfect. Clearly, if he had any hopes of reading his new master, he should give up now, because he had failed at every attempt. He shuddered as he thought of the punishment that would befall him for tonight's mess, the least of which would be being forced to eat the synthetic food.

"If you're finished inspecting the floor, I'd really appreciate it if you'd join me."

Wren drew in a breath. That was an order, no questions asked. He crept back up into his chair, looking down in shame and trying to hide his terror.

"You can pretty much bet that I'm never going to stab you with a fork at the dinner table." Jere put his own head down to catch Wren's eye. "Or anywhere else, for that matter."

"Yes, sir, sorry I misjudged that, sir."

"Now, about this food...." Jere poked at the synthetic blob that he had pulled toward himself while Wren was under the table. "Go, toss it out. And the rest of it, too. It's awful, and synthetic food isn't exactly the healthiest thing anyway. I don't want anyone in this house eating it."

Wren nodded, standing quickly. How was he supposed to know? The injustice burned through him, warring with the pangs in his stomach from the appetite he had stupidly let build up.

"Is there more of this?" Jere indicated his own plate.

"A little, sir. I wasn't sure how hungry you were."

Jere nodded. "All right, well, when you come back, put it on a plate and bring it with you."

Wren nodded. "Yes, sir." He sped out and was back in seconds, a much smaller portion of food on another plate. He handed it to Jere. "Shall I go back to my room now, sir?"

Jere narrowed his eyes. "No, you should sit down and eat dinner. I said you weren't eating that shit anymore, not that I wasn't ever going to feed you again! Here."

He dumped some of his own food onto the second plate, ripped the garlic bread in half, and pushed it over toward Wren, who was sitting, mouth open in shock.

"Wren, dammit." Jere said, and for a moment, Wren thought he was just going to leave it at that cryptic, nerve-wracking statement. He continued, "Look, I've said this before, but I'm not going to hurt you. I'm not going to stab you, or get angry at you for stupid shit like not knowing what to make for dinner, or not feed you or feed you that shit."

"Yes, sir." Wren said, reflexively.

Jere looked like he wanted to say more, but shook his head and stuck his fork into a meatball instead. "This is delicious, by the way," he mumbled, mouth half full of meatball. "I'd really suggest eating it before it gets cold."

Wren opened his mouth to say something. Closed it. Opened it again, and popped a forkful of food into it. It really was delicious. He didn't deserve it, he knew that, but just this once, he could indulge. He hadn't been able to comfortably eat real, good food in years, just stolen bites here or there. Occasionally, the master's guests were amused by hand-feeding him table scraps like one would a puppy. But usually, it was the synthetic food, and that was always awful.

"Surely they didn't teach you all this at the training facility?" Jere asked, starting on the bread.

Wren shook his head, finishing his mouthful of food before speaking. "No, sir. I mean, they taught us the basics, but actually, my mother used to cook a lot, and I'd help her."

Jere smiled. "Well then, thank you to your mother."

Wren just nodded, eating quickly, in case his master should return to his senses and decide to take the food away before he could finish.

"What were they like?" Jere asked, out of the blue. "Your parents. Were you close?"

Wren almost choked. He had never been asked a question like that. It was almost a given that you didn't talk about a slave's previous life—his childhood, as a not-slave. But of course, this odd, odd outlander would love to poke and pry at him when he least expected it. "We... somewhat, sir. We were a typical family, sir. My mother and I did some things together."

"What changed?"

"I, well, my gift came, sir." Wren tried as hard as he could to keep the bitterness out of his voice. "My father, he was, he was very disappointed. He blamed my mother, she didn't have a gift, you see, and he thought that it was her genes that were defective."

Jere said nothing, but Wren noticed his hand tightening around his fork again. Despite his earlier promise, Wren had to fight with himself not to cringe away from the evident threat.

"I don't think about them much now, sir." Was he trying to make his master feel better?

Jere cursed under his breath. "I'm sorry. It must have been awful. To leave them."

Wren shrugged, wishing he could just will this conversation away. He wished he could believe that his master was punishing him with it, but he seemed to have no idea what effect it had on Wren, and Wren preferred it that way. He couldn't let on how much it hurt him to talk about his family, it would just be ammunition for his master to use against him in the future. "Not too bad, really, sir. By the time they came for me, I wanted to go. To stop being such a shame to my family."

"Whatever gave you that idea?"

Wren looked away. He didn't want his eyes to give away the pain these memories caused him. "Sir, when I was identified, my father had already known for a week or two. He had told me everything that would happen, in excruciating detail. I tried...." Wren had no idea why he was saying this. It was so hard, and so painful to think about. "I tried to run away from home, sir. A stupid twelve-year-old boy with no idea what was further than the edge of town, I tried to run away. And of course I was caught, and he—my father—he gave me my first real beating. For shaming the family. Having a *useless* gift that burdened society." Wren paused, refusing to blink and succumb to tears. "It wasn't even a week later that I was taken."

Jere had gone a little pale during the story. "There is *nothing* wrong with a speed gift. Any physical gift, for that matter."

Wren was quiet again. That was something he didn't dare allow himself to think about. He would never correct his master, but he knew that Jere was wrong.

"How could a person do that?" Jere wondered aloud. "Just turn on their own child, just because of their gift? All the years you've spent raising them?"

Wren had never considered it that way. "Sir, people here don't really get too close with their children, not when they're young. You raise them, and you teach them, and if they have a mind gift, then they're worthy of love, and if not, well, you wouldn't consider a slave to be your child. It's such a disgrace."

"Do you know what people with physical gifts do in Sonova?" Jere asked, shoving some food in his mouth as if chewing it would fix the world's problems.

"No, sir." Wren hoped it wasn't something terrible.

"They have careers," Jere said quietly. "They work as messengers, therapists, accountants. They do the same thing as I do, and they often get paid better, especially since the mind gift bursts started and we're all over the goddamn world. They have homes and families and pets and debt, just like the rest of us."

Wren sat there silently for a moment. Was it true? It would make his situation seem worse, if it was. Could he really be treated normally outside of the slave states? "But, there's more than one slave state—" Wren clapped a hand over his mouth the second he realized he had spoken out loud.

"Well of course there is," Jere said, as if nothing had happened. As if Wren hadn't just spoken out of turn, and possibly tried to contradict him as well. "I'm guessing that there's interstate slave trade; keeps people away from the communities they grew up in, am I right?"

"Yes, sir."

"How they get people across non-slave states I'll never know, although, hmm, maybe freight trains? I mean, really, you can't even tell what's in them, and who even knows what happens if a slave tries to cross into a non-slave state, or god forbid, someone with a physical gift would try to come to a slave state like this one, but..." Jere seemed to lose his train of thought. "But it certainly doesn't mean there is anything wrong with a physical gift, or a speed gift, or you. Wren, of all the things I've inherited from Matthias, you are probably the most valuable thing I could have gotten."

Wren sat there, stunned. He hadn't realized his master considered him anything other than an annoyance. "Yes, sir?"

Jere shook his head. "And you don't even realize it. Don't you see—the amount of money I'll be saving in hiring an assistant, maybe even two; the time I'd save, having you run out for supplies or cook dinner or something—doctors back in the city would *kill* for someone with a speed gift as an assistant. Plenty of the nurses in the hospitals were speed gifted, and they made nearly as much money as the doctors. And they didn't get laid off when the older crowd wanted to come out of retirement."

Wren lay in bed that night, going over the almost surreal conversation he had had with his master at dinner. After their conversation about gifts and slavery, they had been mostly silent, finishing up the meal somewhat amicably. Jere even brought out some pastry he had bought for dessert, as he said, to make up the space in their stomachs from the smaller dinner.

Wren still wasn't entirely sure what to make of his master, but he did seem to be a decent guy. He was superbly nice and pleasant and kind, but Wren knew better than to expect this for the future. Slave-owning seemed to have a way of drawing out people's darker sides, and Wren knew he could only keep up his façade of scared, perfect slave for so long before his master started to catch on to the type of slave he really was. Regardless, he had finally made peace with accepting it for as long as it would last.

He reminded himself once again that the man was an outlander, a city-man, and also young. Burghe had grown up in a slave state, lived in them on and off, and was from an older generation. A generation that was much more fond of its fists than of talking, which Jere almost never seemed to tire of. While the day would certainly come when Wren would anger him enough to warrant punishment, each and every day that it could be pushed back would be a good one. And in the meantime… well, the master was actually rather pleasant to be around.

Chapter 10
Sleeping Arrangements

Wren's first few days assisting in the clinic had been rather challenging. Jere could acknowledge, logically, that they must have been a challenge for the kid as well, but he found himself wanting to pull his hair out more often than not as Wren continued to cringe, flinch, and radiate terror whenever anything was not done perfectly. All the same, there were the rare occasions when Wren would look angry, just for a second, before the scowl was wiped clean with a blank expression that left Jere wondering exactly what he might have done to be offensive. Jere was kind of at a loss. Reassurance failed, promises failed, and he wasn't about to consider threatening the kid. For the most part, he tried to leave him alone as much as possible, avoiding him except at work and sometimes at mealtimes, although Wren had taken to eating in his room most of the time, once Jere assured him it was okay. Jere figured Wren was just as tired of their awkward interactions as he was.

The extra set of hands was nice, at least. It would have been better if the extra set of hands and the speed gift hadn't come attached to an anxious, flinching slave, but Jere had to admit that having the help was better than not, and Wren did seem to enjoy being useful. Actually, it was the only time that he seemed even remotely calm. Jere wondered if there was anything else he could ask him to do to keep him busy and, more importantly, out of his way. They both seemed more comfortable when they were in separate rooms.

Jere cursed as he tipped over a tray of supplies. "Wren, come here," Jere ordered, exasperated. He was still struggling to get used to his new surroundings.

Wren rushed into the room eagerly, nearly in a panic. It was his usual manner of entering, and Jere couldn't help but be aggravated by the eagerness and anxiety. "Yes, master?"

Jere hated that he sometimes called him master in the clinic, even if it was supposedly politically correct. He didn't want to be reminded that he owned a slave, and he didn't want to be reminded that the slave seemed terrorized not only by Jere's old friend, but by Jere as well. "Clean this up," he scowled, wanting nothing more than go back to pretending he was back in Sonova like he had been doing all morning.

Wren froze, looking up at him apprehensively. Jere turned away so it wouldn't be as obvious that he was rolling his eyes. He was doing his best to make his "assistant" as comfortable as possible — explaining things, giving him food, letting him take breaks — what else was he supposed to do? If Wren made some requests, Jere would have been happy to grant them, but he wasn't a mind reader.

He glanced back to see Wren still standing there. "Today, please?" Jere finally relaxed as he left the room and left Wren to clean up the mess.

In some areas, at least, Wren was starting to take initiative to take care of things on his own. Tasks were completed quickly, dirty things were cleaned meticulously, and Jere didn't have to make an effort to thank him for the food he prepared each day. With that in mind, Jere found it impossible to understand why Wren couldn't seem to do the simplest of things when he was around.

Later that evening, Jere brought out the list that Wren had made, carefully accounting for any items that were needed or missing from the house that they would need to purchase or have replaced by the fire insurance. It was a thorough list, which was no surprise, but Wren had practically begged Jere to review it. Wren responded well to praise, so Jere hoped it would encourage him to be a little more assertive about things around the house. Jere realized he had never found out what the living situation and sleeping arrangements had looked like before.

"By the way, Wren, I've been meaning to ask you, which room were you in before the fire?" Jere smiled as he asked, hoping that the kid wouldn't be too polite or scared or whatever he was to actually tell him. He really did want him to be comfortable.

"I, uh, I didn't quite have a room, sir."

"Oh." Maybe he had slept solely in Matthias's room? It seemed so unlikely. He wasn't really sure he wanted more details on the subject, but he felt pressed to ask. "Well, where did you sleep?"

Wren's eyes darted sideways, toward the kitchen, for just a second. "I, uh..." he took a breath, seeming to steady himself. "I slept in the cellar, sir."

"There's a cellar?"

Wren nodded slowly, his entire body tensing up as if anticipating something. Jere had no idea what caused the reaction. Had he asked something wrong? Should he have known more about the house? Well, he probably should have, he realized, as the owner of the house, but he was just busy with other things—preventing this kid from dying, for starters—and hadn't looked over the floor plan much at all.

"Well, I'm sorry to have taken you out of your space, then," Jere said. "I mean, I never meant to presume. I just figured that whichever room you had been staying in had been destroyed in the fire. You could have said something."

"I appreciate the room you gave me, sir." Wren was looking away again, nervous. "Of course, if you want me to return to the cellar now...."

Jere looked at the kid. He was clearly afraid of something, now what the hell was it? Knowing him, it could be anything from wanting to move, to not wanting to move, to having forgotten to dust behind the trashcan earlier. Jere shifted uncomfortably. "Mind showing me where it is? I'd like to see this secret part of the house."

Wren drew a shaky breath. "Yes, sir."

Without another word, Wren led them through the kitchen, around the back door, the one to the backside of the clinic. He kicked aside a rug that Jere had never paid much attention to, revealing a simple wooden door with a neatly sanded hole cut out of it for a handle. Bending slightly, he pulled the door open, revealing a dark set of stairs.

Jere peered over at it. "Is there... light down there?"

"The bulb was out last time I was down there, sir." Wren's voice was carefully stripped of emotion.

"Well, go grab one, and a flashlight." *And some holy water and a can of pepper spray*, Jere added, to himself.

Wren returned a few seconds later with the requested items, handing the flashlight over to Jere. He lit the way as they descended, and held the flashlight as Wren put in the lightbulb. Clearly, by "out," he had meant "nonexistent," not "burned out" as Jere had thought.

The light made the place more visible, but not much less creepy. The floors were dirt, and seemed inexplicably better suited to a twenty-first century horror film than a modern home. The ceiling was low, with exposed pipes and wires and wood from the house above. Some of the piping and support beams extended down, and between them there were lopsided shelves, threatening to tip their contents. The shelves were filled with an assortment of things, and there seemed to be little organization to the mess. Further back, Jere noticed a few cases of canned goods, including some synth food, which he struggled not to turn his nose up at. One side of the room contained old and broken furniture, the likes of which Jere couldn't imagine in any part of the house. As anticipated, there were some cobwebs, but they looked relatively new.

"You slept here?" Jere tried unsuccessfully to keep the disbelief out of his voice.

"No, sir." Wren had his arms wrapped around himself despite the fact that it was comfortably warm, given the late summer temperatures. Despite the nice weather now, Jere knew that in a few months, winter would arrive, bringing below-freezing temperatures on a regular basis.

"I slept back here, sir."

With that, Jere followed him further back, through a sort of doorway. They emerged into a sub-cellar, lower than the rest of the cellar, and even less inviting. In the center was a beam of some sort; Jere could only assume it was part of the structure of the house. Connected to that beam was a metal ring on a thick chain, and Jere realized it was a collar of some sort. Surrounding the beam was an assortment of fabric that Jere assumed had once been blankets or clothes. The majority was the suspicious, dark brown color of dried blood, and Jere realized with a bit of a stomach lurch that the dirt floor was stained with it as well. A bucket sat in the corner, and he had absolutely no desire to find out whether anything was inside it.

"Wren..." he started, and realized he had no idea what to say to this. That anyone could keep another human in these conditions; that Matthias, who brought his own silk sheets and super-thick towels to hotels, could keep a boy in these conditions. Jere was slightly disgusted with himself at being involved with someone who could do such a thing.

Wren kept his head down, but looked up at him with dead eyes. "I, if you want, sir, I can, I can sleep down here again and — "

"No!" Jere protested a little too forcefully, horrified at the very thought. "I mean, no, you don't have to! Christ, I would never ask that of you. Ever. Okay? I wouldn't do that to anyone."

Wren had winced at first, but seemed relieved that Jere wouldn't actually force him to come down here. "Thank you, sir. I'll serve you better by having a room closer to your own, sir."

"Fuck, it isn't that," Jere muttered. "Why is there...? Did he...? Why did he chain you up?"

Again, Wren looked away. "When I had displeased my master, he disciplined me in a variety of ways, sir. Restraints were one of the ways, or being locked down here for long periods of time so I would learn better."

"What would you do that was so horrible that he'd put you down *here*?" Jere demanded. It was wrong, cruel, and evil. There were bugs and probably mice and whatever diseases they might carry. It would be freezing in the wintertime, literally, enough to be dangerous. The cellar did not appear to have heat of any sort, which meant that, in addition to being painful and unpleasant, it was potentially dangerous to keep a human being down here for any length of time. That anyone could do this to another person was appalling.

"Talking back, sir," Wren answered, nearly whispering. "Failing to obey orders. Sometimes, I didn't even know."

"And he'd leave you down here for how long?"

"Hours, sir. Days, sometimes."

"That's disgusting!" Jere snapped. He wished he could confront Matthias and ask him just what the hell he thought he was doing. "This whole place is disgusting. Get upstairs!"

Jere was startled when he realized Wren had sped upstairs immediately. He supposed that Wren didn't want to stay down here any longer than necessary. He followed him up and found him standing in the dining room, trembling. Jere sat down, wondering what had set the kid off this time. After a few minutes of silence, Wren sat as well, on the edge of his chair.

"What the hell were you supposed to learn by being down there?" Jere wondered, unable to let go of the thought of locking someone up down there. "Apparently it didn't work if you were down there that often!"

"I was supposed to learn how to be more obedient, sir." Wren's voice shook as he said it. "I'm sorry."

"What are you sorry for?" Jere demanded. "I'm sure you didn't ask him to lock you up down there!"

"I disobeyed, sir. I didn't learn fast enough, I—"

"It was supposed to be a rhetorical question." Jere resisted the urge to throw up his hands and walk out. Every time he tried to have a conversation, every time he asked a question, Wren was too busy apologizing or begging or blaming himself for something to do so. Jere's nerves were thin enough from the chaos of the clinic; the lack of rational conversation was about to push him over the edge.

They sat in silence for a while as Jere tried to focus on something else, to direct the conversation to a more neutral topic. "Do you know what it was used for before he made you stay down there?"

"I believe it was simply extra storage space, sir," Wren supplied. "I'm not quite sure, but I remember when I was first purchased, it was storage for furniture or extra food. It *can* be rather nice to have extra food, sometimes these parts of the country have shortages of things."

"Shortages?" Jere was surprised. While plenty of things were exorbitantly expensive back home, everything imaginable was available.

"Yes, sir. Coffee. Spices. Fruits. That sort of thing." Wren explained. "It's not like in more affluent areas, where a nature grower can just use their gifts to grow crops. From what I know, most of the luxury items here come all the way from Sonova, and that's if the speed train doesn't run out of fuel or freeze on the tracks or the food doesn't go bad. And if the prices are too high, merchants here won't bother to stock it, because almost nobody would buy it anyway. My old master used to special order coffee by the case and store it in the cellar. It stayed very fresh in the winter."

"Right, right." Jere shuddered at the thought of eating anything from that area. "Well, I'm sure you have everything we need on the list, you know more about what's available here and what's not. Let's keep it in the pantry upstairs, though? As far as the cellar, maybe one day I'll think of a use for it."

Wren paled.

"No, no, not that!" Jere rushed to correct himself. "Seriously, Wren, the thought of putting a person down there is horrifying. There is nothing you could do that would ever possess me to put you down there, I promise!"

"Thank you, sir." Wren breathed a little more easily.

"I just, I still have a hard time understanding how he could have done that. How anyone could have done that. Fuck." Jere shook his head. No wonder the kid had nightmares.

"He said it made me more obedient, sir," Wren spoke quietly, looking down at the floor. "That I deserved to suffer when I misbehaved."

"I won't ever put you down there," Jere repeated.

Wren took it as dismissal, which was fine, because Jere needed a moment to process what he had just witnessed. He would never have expected his former playmate to be cuddly or indulgent, but this was sick, depraved even. It just didn't fit with what he knew of Matthias. It didn't.

Did it?

There had been a few times that his mentor had been bossy with him, but he was older, Jere always dismissed it as that. Older, wiser, more worldly. Jere didn't think too much of it, and besides, whenever he called him on it, Matthias backed down and made a joke about how he was stuck in "professor mode," treating everyone like he treated his students.

Jere figured it was only fair, since he *was* his student when it all started.

There were those interactions, though, here and there, that had seemed off when they were together. Besides his obvious scorn for peace protesters and anti-slavery activists, the older man routinely mocked homeless people as they begged for spare change or food, and refused to ever heal them or even speak kindly to them. Jere had always brushed it off as being wealthy and spoiled. After all, Matthias treated him quite well.

One interaction stuck out above the others, though, one that Jere hadn't thought of in years. They had been heading into one of the hospitals, just a few weeks before Matthias announced that he was leaving, and as they did, a team of people rushed by. A young man, probably a student at Sonova University, had tried to kill himself by jumping off of one of the taller buildings on campus. He succeeded, Jere found out later, but at the time they saw him, he was alive, his arms and legs mangled, his face bleeding from a large laceration on his cheek. He was terribly alive, screaming and moaning and writhing on the stretcher as they wheeled him into the intensive healing area.

Matthias had put a hand on Jere's shoulder, pausing them both there for a moment as the team went by, and when they disappeared behind a set of swinging doors, he turned Jere to face him.

"Isn't he beautiful?" he asked, his voice dreamy, a slight smile on his face.

Jere remembered he had jerked away, disturbed. "He's going to die!" he replied, feeling a bit ill at the knowledge. "He's in so much pain!"

For one breath, maybe two, Matthias's face reflected blissful appreciation.

As suddenly as it appeared, the expression was wiped away, his usual more serious expression replacing it instead.

"Oh, come now, Jere, I didn't mean it like that," he said, the chastising, patronizing tone he sometimes took undercutting his words. "I just meant he was a nice-looking boy, and besides, he's probably out of pain by now already."

He kept going, kept making excuses and saying things about peace and things like that, but Jere couldn't figure out what to do with the look he had seen on his face. What kind of person found such agony beautiful?

Back then, it had been easy to dismiss the horrifying thought that Matthias did enjoy watching the boy suffer. Matthias was a healer, a professor, a friend, not some sort of scary monster that took pleasure in others' suffering. Not the kind of man who would lock up a slave in a dark, cold basement, or chain him up. Jere didn't like to think about it, if it was true, but it explained a lot. If Wren had grown used to treatment like that, it made sense that he flinched and cowered. Jere just wished he knew how to make him stop.

Chapter 11
Upsetting Patients

Jere had been in Hojer for a month. Wren had worked with him for most of the day during the past few weeks, and both master and slave were surprised by how efficiently they worked together. Initially, Wren had been nervous as his master showed him how to do things, because learning new tasks often meant making mistakes, and mistakes required correction. Jere's correction was gentle, helpful, and entirely pain-free, unlike most of the correction Wren had received from everyone else in his life since he had been a slave. When Jere had finally grown fed up with Wren tensing up or trembling, he made him look him in the face and firmly ordered him to calm down, insisting that mistakes happened when someone learned new things. He even promised that nothing bad would happen when he did. It was a direct order, and Wren had no choice but to obey. It was somewhat comforting.

Still, those weeks had been rough. Jere was unpredictable; friendly one minute, snapping and dismissive the next. Wren wanted to find out how he was causing it, wanted to find some way to fix it, but the more he tried, the more irritated Jere became. Some days, his master seemed to be avoiding him all together. Wren was terrified that Jere would become too fed up and sell him, and did everything he could to make himself useful, to be noticed. Even being criticized would be better than being ignored and left to wonder.

The work that Jere had him doing was simple enough, most of it not too different from what Burghe had ordered him to do. Jere allowed him to do much more, preparing medications and supplies and getting injections ready, which terrified Wren at first. His master assured him that he would do fine, and that even if there was a mistake, nothing they used would be toxic to a patient. Wren wondered, however, what the toxic level was for a slave making a mistake on a free person.

The largest task that Jere had Wren do, that Burghe hadn't, was deal with the patients, setting up a check-in system, greeting them, receptionist-type things. Wren was horribly uncomfortable around free people, but Jere didn't seem especially comfortable around most of the citizens of Hojer, either. The master was good at his job, and actually quite good with patients, but Wren had noticed that he didn't particularly enjoy the company of most of them, which left Wren to the undesirable task. For the most part, this had gone well; Wren had been taught to be careful and polite and respectful, and the patients were too eager to see the doctor to torment him like a guest might. Plus, he always had the excuse of needing to help his master to fall back on if someone got too demanding.

Of course, some people took demanding to new levels.

Wren was taking care of some filing, something that he had very, *very* hesitantly suggested to his master only the day before. Jere seemed to have no record-keeping system whatsoever, and Burghe's system had never made sense to Wren, and seemed incomplete anyway. Jere had been thrilled with the idea, and dumped the entire project in Wren's hands, encouraging him to let him know if he needed anything else for the task.

"Boy!" The shrill voice interrupted him at the same time as he heard the door open.

Wren jumped, startled, then quickly put the filing down and turned to address the speaker. "Yes, miss, how may I help you?"

"How the hell do you *think* you can help me, you stupid slave? I need to see a doctor!" The woman was clutching her left hand, which was poorly wrapped in a dishtowel. "My little Precious-Poo-ki-Kins bit me!"

Wren assumed that the woman was talking about a dog, and not one of her own demon spawn. "All right, ma'am, my master is engaged in mind-healing right now, and will be with you as soon as possible. I'll let him know that you're here."

"As soon as possible?" the woman screeched. "You get him out here now, boy!"

"Yes, ma'am." Wren said, trying to be placating. He stepped through the door to the back of the clinic, where he and Jere had devised a list to indicate who was next to be seen. They had come up with a rating system, designating ultimate emergencies as things to be dealt with immediately, even if Jere was healing someone else at the time. These included severe head trauma, severed limbs, or massive blood loss. Common things, like a cold, a broken bone, or a rash, were given the lowest priority, aside from wellness checks, which only required a healer to scan one's body for complications. Everything else fell somewhere in the middle, and Wren guessed that this woman's dog bite fell toward the lower end, as there was only slowly dripping blood. He made a note to the list, wondering if he should put anything on it to indicate that the woman was somewhat agitated.

Jere stepped out of an exam room in a hurry, rushing toward the supply closet, and Wren thought he could do better by letting him know firsthand. He stood in the doorway while his master looked through the supplies.

"There's a woman with a dog bite in the waiting room and — "

"I'll get to her when I have a chance!" Jere cut him off. "Can't you see I'm busy? Put it on the list."

Wren burned with shame. Of course, that was the plan they had devised. He was stupid to overstep his boundaries. "I have, master, I just — "

"I thought we were going with 'doctor' in here?" Jere grabbed what he was looking for and rushed back into the exam room he had been in before Wren had a chance to say anything else.

He shouldn't have tried in the first place. Biting his lip and trying to keep himself from showing any of his inappropriate emotions, Wren went back into the reception area and tried to focus on his work.

The woman approached his desk. "My name is Selvia Mulner!"

Wren didn't know or care why this woman was telling him this; he had been planning on having her fill out an information sheet after she had been seen. It would reduce the chance of her dripping blood on his paperwork.

"All right, Miss Mulner, the doctor will be with you as soon as he's finished with his current patient."

"I told you to get him now!"

Wren resisted the urge to drop to his knees. This woman had no authority over him, well, no more than any free person. And his master's orders superseded any she would give him.

"Ma'am, I'm sorry, but he is with another patient. He will be with you as soon as he is finished. There is no one else waiting but you."

The woman slammed her non-bloodied hand down on the desk. "Don't you *dare* get smart with me, boy! Now, I'm going back there, and you'd better get that master of yours to come out and treat me like I goddamn well deserve!"

"Ma'am, please sit down," Wren struggled to keep his voice steady. "He will be out —"

"Don't you fucking try to placate me, you whiny little shit!" Another bang on the table. "I need to see the damn doctor, and I need to see him now! And I will not tolerate some fucking *lackler* telling me I need to wait!"

Wren flinched. *Lackler*, the derogatory term for someone without a mind gift, was a word not often heard in polite company. Of course, this woman was far from polite. "Ma'am, I'm sorry if I —"

Wren's words were cut short as the woman slapped him hard, sending him reeling to the floor. Unable to do anything else, Wren curled himself into a protective ball as the woman continued to scream at him. He heard her storming around the desk, and he tried to roll underneath it without seeming too noticeable. He braced himself for the kick.

It never came.

"What in the hell is going on out here?"

Wren started to shake in earnest as he heard his master's voice thunder angrily from the doorway.

"What's going on is your stupid little slave thinks I should just sit here and bleed to death because he's too lazy to go and tell you I'm here!" Miss Mulner snapped, still as angry as she had been. "And then he started getting smart with me, so I cuffed him!"

Wren would hardly call what the woman did to him a "cuff," but he said nothing, still huddling on the floor. Moving only brought worse pain.

Jere was silent for a moment, his strained breathing the only sound that could be heard in the room. He finally spoke, his voice low and even and dangerous. "Ma'am, you will go across this room and sit in a waiting chair. I will deal with you when I am ready. And you will keep the screaming and yelling to a minimum. If you are in that much pain, I can sedate you."

Wren heard the footsteps retreating, and a chair squeaking slightly as the woman deposited herself in it. He heard his master approaching and he prayed for quick unconsciousness.

"Wren." The master's voice was slightly calmer. "Get up. Go inside and wait for me in my office."

Reluctantly, Wren stood up, looking questioningly into his master's face. When he saw nothing there, he fled. He used his speed gift to its fullest, needing to escape from this mess even if just for a minute.

He went into the office, a place where he never went unbidden, except sometimes to clean, and wondered briefly how his master would want him. He knew the honeymoon period was over. He had finally managed to anger his master enough that he would punish him. Of all the things he could have done wrong, upsetting a patient was probably at the top of the list, and he berated himself for not doing better. He could have been more placating, he could have done... there had to have been something he could have done, some way he could have redeemed himself. And now the woman was angry, and she had told the master that he had been smart with her, which he really didn't think he had. He knew that what he thought didn't matter, because the master would never believe him over a free woman.

Wren looked at the chairs, wishing he felt like he could sit in them. Wishing he deserved to sit in them. Instead, he knelt down in the middle of the room, then leaned forward to touch his forehead to the floor. He couldn't think of a more submissive position, and he hoped that the master's shock at seeing it would distract him somewhat from the punishment he was going to deliver, whatever it would be. It also displayed his back and ass most prominently, which might encourage the master to hit him there instead of other, more delicate places. He debated stripping off his clothing as well, to give the master easier access, but Jere had never indicated any interest in seeing Wren naked, and so he hoped that he might allow him to keep his clothing on. Even the little reprieve that the thin cotton scrubs would afford him would be worth his while.

Jere had been finishing up with his last patient, a rather pleasant, if somewhat absent, older man who smiled blankly at him and called him "son." Having sedated the gentleman to allow him to rest for a bit, Jere stepped out into the prep room, when he heard a raised voice. Sensing the potential for upset, he was walking toward the reception area when he heard the unmistakable sound of a hand striking flesh, and rushed out to see his "assistant" huddled on the floor in terror. His rage had barely subsided since that moment.

Jere forced himself to glance down at the list he had grabbed on the way up front before addressing the rather vile woman sitting across the room from him. "Miss Mulner?" he glanced in her direction.

"That's me, and—" she began.

"Dog bite?" Jere cut her off abruptly. He didn't want to hear her talk.

She nodded. "Yes, and let me just tell you—"

"Give me your hand." Jere had walked over to her, and was holding out his hand impatiently.

"Well—"

Jere took her hand when she offered it, tugging it none-too-gently toward himself, and shoving his way into her mind as forcefully as he dared without causing himself pain as well.

Miss Mulner gasped from the physical and psychic pain, but wisely held still.

A few minutes later, the healing was completed, and Jere let her arm drop unceremoniously. Without another word, he walked over to the desk, jotted something on a piece of paper, and handed it to her.

"Pick this up at the pharmacy on the way home and apply it three times a day," he said curtly. "Forty-five denn for the copayment."

"Well, *I* heard you were gentle!" she exclaimed, sounding offended.

Jere glared at her, his eyes cold and dark. "And *I* heard it was impolite to lay your hands on someone else's property."

"Well, I...." Disgusted, she fumbled around in her purse for the money. "Dr. Burghe would *never* have tolerated this!"

Jere didn't know whether she was talking about something Wren had done, or the purposefully rough treatment he had given her. Nor did he care. "There are different things that one will and will not tolerate, Miss Mulner. I'd keep that in mind if you return here again."

With an overly dramatic sigh, she dropped the money into his hand and stormed out. Jere walked over to the sign-in sheet and put a star next to her name. He and Wren would have to think of some sort of system for difficult patients. After a second's consideration, he crossed out the star and drew in a little pitchfork instead. It seemed much more fitting.

After checking on his sedated patient, Jere went to check on Wren. The poor kid had been terrified; he needed to make sure that he was all right, that the horrid bitch hadn't actually harmed him. He was startled and somewhat sickened to find his slave prostrating himself in the middle of the office, shaking like a leaf.

Wren heard his master's footsteps approaching the room and felt his heart speed up. His muscles ached from the stressful position; clearly, he hadn't been holding it enough, he had gotten out of practice. He used to be able to hold this position for *hours* without shaking, even when he was this terrified. Try as he might, he couldn't keep himself under control. This was it. This was the final straw. This was the mistake that couldn't be brushed under the rug, that wouldn't be okay, that couldn't be a "learning experience." This was the moment that he found out how much his master really could hurt him.

The footsteps stopped momentarily in the doorway. Was he thinking of how best to punish him? Had he forgotten some implement of torture and pain that he would need to get? Would he send Wren to get it instead? Wren shuddered at the thought of having to keep himself upright long enough to fetch something to be beaten with. He listened for any clues, the sound of a belt being unbuckled, a whip uncoiling. Did they even have a whip anymore?

Then the footsteps came closer, and Wren could tell that his master was standing directly in front of him. He kept his head down, secretly wishing he would pass out from fear now instead of from pain later.

"Wren?" His master's voice was soft, calmer than it had been. An edge of that anger was still there, but Wren heard something else in his voice that he couldn't quite place. "Look at me, please."

Not wanting to be any more disobedient than he already had been, Wren turned his head up quickly. He saw Jere kneeling in front of him, in a position not so different from his own, a distressed look on his face. He waited for the yelling to start.

"Are you all right?"

Concern. That was what Wren had heard. But why would he be concerned? "Yes, sir." Wren said, resisting the urge to look back down at the floor. He debated for half a second between holding his tongue and expressing his contrition. He chose the latter. "Sir, I apologize, I never should have—"

"Don't be ridiculous!" The words had a harsh feel to them, but were spoken softly. "Hold still."

Wren's stomach clenched in fear as his master's hand approached his face. This was it, then, the master would punish him with mind pain. Of course, it was his gift. Much more effective than other things, especially if he was squeamish. He had said before that he wouldn't, but that was before, when Wren was behaving perfectly, when he wasn't upsetting patients. He braced himself and closed his eyes, letting himself go slack physically and mentally in preparation.

He felt the master's hand brush softly across the place where

Miss Mulner had slapped him. A small prick of pain started to form at the edge of his awareness, but was banished as soon as he noticed it. He felt the familiar warm sensation of healing, and a moment later Jere pulled his hand away and sat back on his heels.

"You're warm," Jere observed, distracted for a moment. "Are you feeling well?"

Wren wished he could pull further away, hide his warmth and injuries and mistakes and deal with them on his own. Like he tried to deal with them before. Realizing his master was looking expectantly at him, he shrugged, hoping it looked less like a wince than it felt.

"I'm sorry," Jere said, almost looking through Wren. "This won't happen again."

Wren remained frozen in position. This was it? The master was going to heal him and apologize for whatever he was even apologizing for? Surely it must be some sort of trick.

"Please sir, I'm sorry I upset her, and made her hit me, and that I was smart with her." Wren carefully listed his misdeeds. Were there more? There were always more. The master would tell him in a minute what more he had done.

"Wren," Jere's voice sounded pained, but it still held an edge of anger that Wren couldn't quite place. Wren felt a hand clasp his shoulder very, very lightly. "I'm sure there was nothing you could have done. Get dinner ready, we'll talk more about this later."

Wren felt the hand leave his shoulder, and heard Jere stand up. He heard his master start walking toward the door, pausing just before he left the room.

"I'm not angry with you, Wren. Please know that you will not be punished in any way for this. There's no reason to worry yourself. And if you're not up to making dinner, you don't have to, I'm pretty sure I can summon something up out of a can or a box or something. You're doing a great job." He stood there another minute before walking out briskly.

Wren waited until he heard Jere's footsteps disappearing down the hall before he collapsed in a heap on the floor. Almost without thinking, his hand came up to rest on his shoulder where Jere had touched him. The master never touched him, not unless he had to, like when he was healing him, or applying the cream, or the few times he had instructed him on how to prepare some sort of medicine. His hand had been so warm and gentle, barely there, but heavy enough to feel something. Wren struggled to place the feeling. Comfort. That had been the feeling that he had gotten from his master. But why would he want to comfort such a mess of a slave?

Wren realized he was crying again; silent, warm tears falling down his face. He hadn't even been punished, what the hell was wrong with him! He curled up in a ball on the floor, where he deserved to be, and cried until he fell asleep. A part of him wished the master would come back in and punish him properly for acting like such a whiny little bitch. A bigger part of him wished the master would come back in and put his hand on his shoulder again, and tell him that everything was all right.

Chapter 12
Deeper Connection

Jere returned to the clinic, as eager to get out of the house as he was to return to his patients. Patients, he knew what to do with. Slaves, on the other hand....

He felt stupid, careless. How could he not have seen this coming? He knew what Matthias had done to Wren, and he saw how the free patients treated the slaves they sometimes brought in with them. Why did he think that Wren would be treated any differently just because he was working at the clinic?

He was furious, both with that woman and with himself. She had no right to touch his assistant, or his slave, or whatever, but he hadn't even considered it as a possibility. Never even considered telling Wren that he could come and interrupt if he felt like he was in danger, because that wasn't something a person should need permission to do in the first place. Jere figured there had to be a law against such treatment; after all, it shouldn't be his responsibility to watch for that all the time.

He tried not to think about the fact that Wren *had* tried to tell him something, but he was too busy with his patient and too busy obsessing over Wren calling him "master" to notice.

He burned off the rest of his angry energy healing patients, glad he could channel it into something positive. In between, he tried to think of solutions to the problem of Wren's safety.

By the time Jere finished in the clinic, Wren had finished dinner, if the smell was any indication. Jere strolled through the door, relieved to find that the kid at least *looked* a little calmer than he had earlier. Jere grinned as he looked at him.

"Smells good in here!" he said, enthusiastically.

"Thank you, sir," Wren mumbled, a bit shy. He sped off and returned with dinner seconds later. "Gnocchi with parsley and roasted chicken, sir. I hope it pleases you."

"I'm sure it will," Jere gave it an appraising look. He sat at the table, and looked at Wren expectantly, nodding and smiling when he sat down as well.

"This is amazing. Really. I had no idea my new life would come with such great food!"

"Thank you, sir."

They sat there quietly for a while after that, sharing each other's company without much to say. Jere wanted to talk more about what had happened earlier, but they were both enjoying dinner. Seeing the kid for once not trembling or begging his forgiveness was almost too good to interrupt.

When they were both nearly finished, Jere decided to make his move. Wren had an uncanny knack for escaping the very moment the last bite of food had been eaten, first to clean up, then to do whatever he did when he was alone. At least the majority of the meal had been enjoyable.

"I was thinking...." Well, that wasn't the best of starts. "Wren, have you had a direct mind connection opened with someone before?"

Wren nodded. "Yes, sir. When I was very young, I had one with my father, and then my trainer at the training facility, and my last master had one with me as well."

Jere was pleased, though not surprised. Those with physical gifts often had considerable difficulty communicating mentally like those with mind gifts could. A direct connection, usually reserved for very close family and lovers, could also be very beneficial in communicating with people who had physical gifts or no gift at all. In addition to allowing those who were connected to speak directly and privately to one another, it allowed both partners better access to each other's emotional state.

"Good, so, you're familiar with how they work and everything?"

Wren hesitated a moment before he spoke. "Yes, sir."

"Because, I was thinking, it would be helpful. For us. If you and I had one." Jere wondered if it was possible for him to sound any more awkward. He doubted it.

"As you wish, sir." Wren had stopped eating, simply pushing the remainder of the food around on his plate, keeping his eyes on it.

Jere struggled to find the right way to ask the next question. He knew that if he asked it the wrong way, the kid would get scared again. Of course, even if he asked it the right way, the result wouldn't be much different. Or he wouldn't answer at all. He tried for an open-ended question in hopes that he would at least say *something.* "What were your other mind connections like?"

"They were fine, sir."

Fine. What a useless fucking word! Jere tried again, a bit more directly. "If they were fine, why are you so nervous all of a sudden?"

Wren froze, still staring down at his plate. "It's no problem, sir. You can initiate a mind connection with me easily. I won't resist you."

Jere drummed his fingers on the table as he tried to rephrase the question he had asked twice already. "Wren, has someone hurt you with the mind connection before?"

Wren hesitated again. "When I have deserved it, sir."

Jere resisted the urge to throw something. "That's *not* the way mind connections should be used."

Wren said nothing, but did seem to shrink back from Jere's growl.

"Here's the thing, kid," Jere made a pointed effort to soften his voice, and even to loosen his death grip on his fork, which had somehow become the vessel for his frustration. "What I want is a way to communicate with you if anything goes wrong, if you're in danger, if I'm not reachable otherwise and you need something. Like today. I feel responsible for you, and I think that if we have the connection open, you can ask me for help, or I can find out how you're doing, or... whatever."

Wren nodded, looking very serious. "Yes, sir."

Even without the connection being established, Jere could still feel the terror emanating from Wren. Aside from the gift, he could see how pale he had gotten at the suggestion. "You can shut down the connection whenever you want. I mean, I'd rather you not take it down permanently, but if you want to block me, suit yourself."

Wren looked at him, confused.

"Have you never been shown how to shut down a connection?" Jere was surprised.

"Sir, I would never have been allowed to do so."

"Didn't you learning blocking skills as a child?" Jere asked. "It was part of our skills that we learned along with counting and spelling and tying shoes."

Wren shook his head. "No sir. Those things are learned here as part of high school education. You see, they... they don't want anyone with a physical gift to know how to do it. A slave shouldn't be able to deny his master access to any part of him. So children, as a whole, are prohibited from learning it."

Jere was shocked. How the hell did this society function? "But what if the child has secrets or something — family secrets — that someone else is trying to invade upon?"

"That's why the child has a direct mind connection with its parent, sir," Wren explained. "The additional connection provides that extra protection. Most slaves who are in charge of any sort of confidential information will have the same sort of connection with their masters."

"That's just..." Jere didn't quite know what to call this. "Stupid" came to mind, along with "cruel." "Well, I suppose it makes sense. But you'll learn at least some basic blocking skills. It's just, it's fundamental. And I'll admit, I might not always be the best person to be connected to. I'll show you some different levels of blocking too — it's the difference between having a door shut and a door locked, more or less."

Wren looked puzzled. "Yes, sir. As you wish."

Jere shook his head and changed the subject somewhat. "So what exactly happened today?"

Wren stiffened, but kept his voice level. "Sir, Miss Mulner came in and was very upset that I did not get you quickly enough to please her. I did go and write a note for you. I didn't assess that she was in danger enough to interrupt you. And then she continued to get angry, and I was smart with her, forgive me, sir, and she struck me."

Jere narrowed his eyes. This kid, smart with anyone? It irritated him that anyone would dare to think that. "What did you say to her?"

Wren began to tremble. "Please, sir, I don't know. I kept asking her to sit and wait, and telling her that you would be out shortly, and apologizing. I don't know what I did wrong. I understand if you... if I should be corrected."

"Wren, you did *nothing* wrong. She was just as belligerent with me," Jere said firmly. He honestly didn't believe that it was even *possible* for Wren to have done anything wrong, he was such a perfectionist. No, he was pretty sure that the uncomfortable blame fell on him. "I just want to know, would it have been helpful if I were out there earlier?"

Wren almost nodded, then seemed to think the better of it. "It is as you wish, sir."

Jere held in his frustration. "Fine then, I wish I had been out there earlier. Was there a point where you would have liked me there?"

"Yes, sir. When she started getting very upset and yelling and pounding on the desk, having you there would have possibly diffused the situation."

"Okay. I'll be there in the future. And Wren, you have my express permission to interrupt me, regardless of what I'm doing, if someone is threatening you or hurting you. That's not acceptable for anyone to do, and you shouldn't let them do it."

"Yes, sir. Thank you, sir."

Jere nodded. He decided to keep the conversation to a minimum for the rest of the night. He and Wren worked well enough together, and could even enjoy passably comfortable silence, but conversation was full of awkward tension. Having no idea how to counteract this, silence was usually the best alternative.

After dinner was cleaned up, Jere went ahead and led Wren through the steps to establish a mind connection. He developed it almost instantly, putting up no resistance to the intrusion into his thoughts, unlike the previous resistance he had shown while Jere was healing him. Jere showed him blocking skills, as promised, and was pleasantly surprised by the facility with which the slave picked them up, having never had instruction in the area before. He explained that having an open connection of the type he had set up would allow them to communicate back and forth between each other, but not to "overhear" thoughts that weren't actively broadcast. He also explained that they might have a little bit of an overlap of emotions, especially strong ones.

Jere was pleased to realize that this meant he would be able to help Wren rein in his emotional projections at times. This would be especially helpful at night, when he still occasionally woke up screaming and sending off waves of terror. The connection wouldn't allow their dreams to connect, but the heightened awareness of each other's emotional states and the ability to influence them would allow Jere to help keep some of the panic and terror at bay. Wren, true to form, nodded complacently and agreed with whatever his master was teaching, showing, or telling him, to the point of near-frustration on Jere's part.

Having the mind connection was helpful. Wren was able to use it, however hesitantly, to get Jere's attention when he was working, making patient management smoother and more efficient with each passing day. Jere felt better knowing he was preventing another irate patient from smacking the kid around again. Further, they managed to develop a sort of comfortable shared space, something they had not been able to attain in any other setting. The mind connection provided a calm, contained environment through which they were both able to express their wants and needs. Wren almost never initiated the conversation, doing so only when it was strictly work-related, or if Jere asked him to. For Jere, this was a familiar method of communication, albeit one that was very rarely initiated between two such emotionally distant people.

Chapter 13
Detained

Three months had passed since Jere arrived in Hojer. Since he pulled Wren back from death, healed him, turned his body into an unscarred, pain-free thing that Wren didn't even recognize. Wren couldn't help but wonder what the point of it was, of saving him. As far as he could tell, his master had done it simply because it was his duty, as he seemed to feel that it was his duty to keep Wren and to not actively harm him.

In the grand scheme of things, Wren supposed, he should be happy with this life. Wasn't this what he wanted? When he thought back to his days at the training facility, when he still had some modicum of hope left, yes, it was. Someone who wouldn't hurt him for frivolous reasons, someone who didn't rape him, someone who would let him eat and wear clothes and pretend to act like a normal person.

He had all these things, and yet he still wished on most days that the fire had taken him before this new master reached him. It had been so close, death, just beyond his reach. Tantalizing, almost, and it beckoned him back. He had all these things that he used to want, but they weren't enough, he still wasn't at peace. Perhaps he had been right, thinking that death would be the only way he could find it.

Besides, physical pain wasn't the only thing that could hurt. Jere's abrupt dismissals and constant irritation and snapping wore on Wren's nerves in ways that he couldn't reconcile. Sometimes Jere glared at him and demanded, "What!" like Wren was supposed to complain to him or ask for things to be different, but he couldn't, and he couldn't explain it to the man. Wren knew better than to ask for things to change, because he was already being treated ten times better than he deserved to be. At times he was tempted to push back, to create problems, to provide his master with a valid reason to punish him or yell at him or hurt him, but the tiniest flicker of self-preservation prevented him from doing so. Besides, he knew Jere didn't deserve that sort of trouble any more than he deserved to be stuck with Wren.

He wanted to hate his master, like he had hated his last master, and his trainers, and everyone who had ever laid a hand on him since he was taken as a slave. But he couldn't. Jere was too noble and kind to hate, even when Wren was feeling the brunt of his irritation. Wren knew he had nobody to blame for his situation but himself. From as far back as he could remember, his parents, his teachers, everyone around had made it clear that people got what they deserved, that everyone had to be accountable for their actions and thoughts and gifts and everything else. Respect and productivity had been drilled into his mind well before he was taken as a slave, and no matter how low he sunk, he couldn't rid himself of these old ideals.

He tried his best to be unobtrusive, to ignore and avoid his master as much as possible while still trying to be as useful as possible. To stay needed. As much as he wished he had died, he would still rather be here than be sold, and the possibility terrified him much more than any threat of punishment, although his master never made those. Wren assumed it was because he couldn't be bothered to waste his time on such a task; if he became too much of a challenge, his master would probably just sell him, without threatening or warning. He seemed happier alone, anyway. Most of the time, he didn't even seem to notice Wren.

The mind connection helped somewhat, in that they didn't have to talk as much, and that was always positive. Wren was still uncomfortable with it, despite the blocking skills Jere had taught him. Jere had rambled on and on about "privacy," as if it were some sort of right, and all Wren had been able to do was stare back silently and nod his head as though he agreed. Perhaps privacy was valued in non-slave-states, but in Wren's experience, free adults were the only ones fortunate enough to benefit from such a lofty concept. Privacy was a stepping-stone to secrets, and secrets undermined obedience and control. Privacy had no place in a slave state. He dreaded the day his master would decide to push past those barriers and invade his mind as he had every right to do. What secrets would he come across first? Wren dreaded the horrible things that could be found out. It was only a matter of time, but Jere would figure him out, figure out how terrible he was as a slave, as a person, even. Wren thought again about the allure of flames engulfing him.

It was mid-November, and the weather had turned cold overnight. While the cold wasn't surprising, the rapid change was, even given the severe weather that struck every year. Three feet of snow and ice had fallen in the past twelve hours, and Jere was bombarded with requests for frostbite treatment, hypothermia evaluations, and broken bones from slip and fall accidents. It was the end of the day, but nowhere near the end of the workday, and Wren wished for nothing more than these stupid assholes to stay *home, inside* where it was safe. He kept his master supplied with coffee, glad to be of some use.

Jere drank it without comment as usual. Wren, also as usual, poured himself a cup that he would not drink. His master seemed to like seeing him eat or drink or whatever, but Wren found it to be too much effort. He ate when Jere was watching him, at least enough so that he wouldn't question him about why he wasn't eating, but for the most part, he took meals in his room, or lied and said he had eaten them earlier. It was strange to realize, but it was much easier to eat when he was starving. He had lost some weight, but it didn't matter; nobody was looking at his body anymore anyway.

Wren was standing at the counter, gazing out at the snow, when a small group burst into the room.

"My father!" the woman screamed, rushing up to Wren with a pleading look in her eyes. "Please, quickly, get the doctor!"

Wren was shaken out of his stupor. "What happened, ma'am?" he asked, feeling his heart rate go up despite his exhaustion.

"He's had a heart attack, he's not breathing!" the woman provided.

"Pulse?" Wren glanced at the slave who was carrying the older man. He shook his head.

"I'll be right back," he promised, the urgency forcing him to run. He hesitated for only a fraction of a second at the door to the exam room that Jere was in, hating to bother him.

He burst through the door. "Sir!"

Jere frowned as he spun about. "Wren, honestly, could you—"

"Sir, please, we've had someone with a heart attack," Wren dared to cut him off, paling as he did. Jere had ordered him to interrupt in any way necessary for absolute emergencies, but it was still so uncomfortable. "Please, sir, he's not breathing, and he has no pulse!"

Jere dropped the cast he was working on. "Stay here," he ordered his current patient. "I'll be back as soon as I can."

Wren rushed back to the waiting room, Jere running behind him.

"Wren, help me get him to the exam room." Jere sounded panicked, concerned over this stranger's welfare. Wren didn't really share the sentiment, except that his master was concerned.

He smiled at the woman who had brought her father in, keeping his voice calm so as not to upset her further. "Miss, I'll be right back, we need to get your father to our exam room."

Wren quickly moved to support the man's legs while Jere took his arms. They took him back, shutting the door behind them to prevent the woman and slave from following. Placing him on the table, Wren looked at his master for instructions.

"Stay." Jere said curtly. "I'll probably need you with this."

Unceremoniously, Jere began assessing the damage. Wren waited, wishing there was something for him to do. This was the way it always went; Jere worked, Wren sat, useless.

"Wren. Substance 48, quickly!" Wren jumped at the urgency of the order. He darted to the supply room, in search of the substance that could be used for organ regeneration.

He found a nearly empty bottle and felt his palms begin to sweat. He rushed back to the exam room anyway, where Jere stood with his hand held out expectantly.

"We're out, sir." Wren's eyes were wide. He held the requested bottle in one hand. "There's barely a drop in here!"

"Go to the pharmacy and get some! Now!"

"Yes, sir. If you'd write me a pass—"

"Wren, he's dying! Just go, for fuck's sake, now!"

Wren hesitated for half a second, but at the direct order, sped away fast enough that he stirred up a breeze.

The trip into town could only have taken a minute, but the terror Wren felt at being out without a pass made it feel like hours. It hadn't been his fault that they were out of the product, Jere made the inventory lists for things like that! And a pass, if his master had just spent ten seconds giving him a pass, none of this would be a problem, he wouldn't be shaking and sweating and terrified and getting strange looks in the store.

He forced himself to select the product, checking to make sure it was the right one, and he took it to be rung up. He tried to act normal, tried not to stand out. He almost wished he didn't have a speed gift, because it was so obvious, and it would make it so easy for him to be identified as a slave. But maybe his speed gift would allow him to get home before he was caught?

"Hey! I said, how are you paying for this?" the cashier's voice cut through his panicked thoughts.

"I, my master, sir, Jeremy Peters, he has an account," Wren mumbled, signing the slip that was handed to him and feeling his stomach drop as the man took forever wrapping the product up and placing it in a bag.

He didn't hear the man's next words as he handed the bag over to him, because he felt a firm hand on his shoulder instead.

"Your pass, please?" the officer demanded.

Wren could feel the scrutinizing gaze that the woman gave him, probably taking in his red face, shortness of breath—not to mention the very expensive product he had just purchased. "I, I don't have one, ma'am." The words seemed to get stuck in his throat.

The officer was silent for a moment, and Wren knew she was communicating with someone through mindspeak. A few seconds later, a burly slave came and put his hand on Wren's other shoulder. He wasn't forceful, but his size alone was enough of a threat that Wren knew better than to run off. He started trembling and held the package tight, willing himself not to drop it.

"Let's get you down to the station, then," the officer said, directing him.

Wren knew better than to beg or plead or resist. It wouldn't work anyway, and his punishment would be worse. He did the only thing he could think of.

"*Master*," he said hesitantly through the mindspeak, absolutely terrified. "*I've been detained.*"

Chapter 14
Unfinished Business

Jere, somewhat preoccupied with the task at hand, was a bit brus-quer than he would have been otherwise. *"What!"*

"Please, please sir, I'm on my way to the police post, sir, I, I won't be able to make it back unless you come and claim me. I didn't have a pass, sir."

Jere cursed, out loud, so the slave wouldn't hear it through the mindspeak. Of course, he hadn't had a pass because Jere had been too fucking hurried and impatient to give him one. What the hell had he been thinking, anyway? Now the kid was at the fucking po-lice station?

"Wren," he said calmly, trying to keep any more irritation out of his voice. *"When you get there, have someone contact me mentally – tell them my name and they should be able to search me out. Everything will be fine."*

"Yes, sir. Thank you, sir."

Jere swore again, cursing himself for being such a fucking idiot. This was the exact opposite of what he needed right now.

"Mr. Peters?" Jere felt the searching mindspeak just minutes later. *"This is Officer Dobson –"*

"Doctor Peters," Jere clarified, cutting her off. *"I'm in the middle of surgery and I need my slave back here* immediately *with the product he was sent to purchase."*

"Yes, sir, I understand, but you see, he was out without a pass –"

"I need that product now or a man will die!"

"Yes, doctor, and we'll certainly send one of our speed slaves over with –"

"*That is a valuable, vital medical product, my patient will die if he doesn't get it in* perfect *condition! I don't want any goddamn slave bringing it over here, I want* my *boy, with the product in hand, and I want him here right fucking now! This could be your father on my healing table!*" Jere had managed to raise his mindspeak voice to a level of uncomfortable yelling, enough that he could feel the officer pulling away from the connection to dampen it a bit. He wasn't exactly sure what would be necessary to bring Wren home, but he was willing to bet that being an entitled, self-important twat would work. It usually did, for someone who had the right amount of money and prestige to back up the attitude.

"*Well, you'd have to come by later and fill out some paperwork and such....*" The officer sounded inconvenienced. "*Our policy is to deal with this immediately unless there is a very compelling reason to postpone it.*"

"*Ma'am, I would be happy to spend all night at the station doing whatever is necessary, after I save this man from dying. Put out a warrant for my arrest if I don't show up, I'll be there, just send the slave back here so I can do my job!*"

"*All right then, but really, as soon as possible, Dr. Peters.*"

Jere shut down the connection with her, shifting his focus to Wren. "*Home. Now. Quickly.*"

Barely a moment had passed before Wren shot in the door, still looking pale and breathless. He handed the bottle over to Jere and dropped to his knees. "Thank you, sir —"

"Thank me later!" Jere opened the bottle and began to prepare it. "Get up! I need your help now."

Jere's skilled hands moved nearly as quickly as Wren's. They worked together wordlessly, with Jere occasionally directing Wren's actions via mindspeak. Full sentences and words became unnecessary, and Jere could send instructions such as "to the right" or "a little more" without actually speaking them. The man's heart was removed, and the substance, mixed with a little of the man's own blood and a tiny bit of the damaged heart tissue, was poured into the cavity. All the while, Jere was struggling to maintain as close of a mind connection as was possible, healing him from the inside and forcing his blood to re-route to the new substance, molding it into the heart the man was supposed to have. The process was long, complicated, and risky. While organ growth had revitalized medicine and extended human life by decades, the procedure had many risks, and only half of attempted re-growths worked. Jere was even more concerned by the amount of time that he had been forced to wait for the substance.

The new heart finally began to beat, and Jere felt himself weakening from the struggle. Ascertaining that the patient was stable, he pulled back from the connection and felt his legs begin to give way beneath him. He looked at Wren helplessly and felt himself being guided to the floor as he lost consciousness.

"Sir?"

Jere felt a brief pull at the mind connection. He was so tired.

"Sir?"

Now something was being pressed to his lips. Unwillingly, his mouth opened, and he felt the thick, foul-tasting liquid dump into his mouth with a taste of... was that honey? He gave in and swallowed, rewarded by more liquid pouring in.

About half the glass had made its way into his unwilling stomach when he found the mind connection with Wren. *"Enough. Enough. Thank you."*

Jere felt the glass pulling away. He opened his eyes to see Wren hovering above him, green liquid-filled glass in his hand.

"Sir, I hope I did as I was supposed to, I tried to remember what you told me—"

Jere held a hand up, halting him. "Thank you, Wren. You did just fine. Help me up?"

"Yes, sir." Wren looked relieved, holding out a hand to pull Jere to his feet.

"Go out front and see if you can make heads or tails of the mess that I'm sure is out there, all right?" Jere stood up wearily, looking at his wristwatch. Only about fifteen minutes had passed. He had pushed himself too far, but not that much. "And put the closed sign up, it's certainly past time. If there are emergencies, they can take a fucking speed train to the emergency center in the city."

"Yes, sir," Wren looked at him hesitantly. "Sir, I was wondering—"

"Can't it wait?" Jere immediately felt like an asshole, but his head was honestly *pounding*, and he had patients to see, regardless.

"Yes, sir. I apologize." Wren's wide eyes betrayed his calm tone of voice, and he was looking at the floor as he hurried off.

"Well, shit." Jere muttered to no one in particular. He hadn't seen the kid this jumpy in months.

Jere checked his heart patient, made a few adjustments, forced himself to down the rest of the horrid liquid, reapplied the cast on the now furious man who had fidgeted his way out of most of it, and then back to something else he had started earlier, and then....

It was nearly three hours later, four and a half hours after closing time, when Jere shoved the last and final patient through the door. He told the young woman whose father's heart had been replaced that she could come back to collect him in the morning. This had produced nearly unlimited screeching and complaining, as if Jere really *wanted* a grouchy old man staying in his clinic overnight. He wandered into the dining room and dropped down at the table, letting his head rest on his hands and closing his eyes for a minute.

He heard Wren approaching, tentatively sitting down. Jere had given him the okay to sit months ago, but the kid still seemed to have trouble believing this to be true. At the moment, Jere was exhausted by the mere thought of standing up.

He raised his head, and saw the boy looking at him, almost waiting for something, and trembling just a little.

"Wren, look, kid, I'm sorry I snapped at you earlier." That was a bit of an understatement. "Okay, I'm sorry about *all* the times I snapped at you earlier. I can be a real prick when I'm this tired, and I know it's not right to take it out on someone, but I've always done it. Like I said, prick."

Jere watched as Wren took a small breath before speaking. He still looked just as nervous.

"It's okay, sir. It's your right to treat me as you see fit. I'm sorry if I seemed bothered."

Jere let his head drop back down on his hands again. He was too tired to make a logical argument about this.

"Sir, if I may?"

Wren waited until Jere nodded. Nodding took a lot of effort.

"The police post, sir. They'll be expecting us. I know you've asked me to explain cultural things before. Sir. And, um, this is one of those things. If you don't show up soon, it will be unpleasant."

For someone with a speed-gift, the kid sure spoke slowly! Every word was labored, like he was hunting it down, or waiting for permission to continue speaking. Jere nodded. "Of course. Of course they will. Because eleven o'-fucking-clock at night is exactly the time that a reasonable person would go attend some petty formality. All right. Do we change out of these, or go as we are?"

Wren blushed, as he often did when Jere asked his advice. "Um, we should look like we've come straight from the clinic, sir."

Jere dragged himself up. "All right. Let's get this done, then."

Chapter 15
Punishment and Responsibility

Wren could barely keep his heart from pounding as they entered the police post. While his master didn't seem to care about the law, Wren knew exactly what awaited him as a slave for breaking it, and he wasn't looking forward to it.

Jere was standing next to him at the desk, speaking with the same officer who had communicated with him earlier. Wren barely heard either of them as the officer explained the law, and why it existed, and on and on and on. He wasn't exactly in a betting mood right now, but if he had been, he would have put money on Jere having no idea what the woman was talking about either. At least his master had admitted that he had told him to go without a pass, which cleared up any misconceptions that Wren may have been making a runaway attempt. Wren realized he should have briefed his master on this before, but he had never thought of this coming up. Jere grumbled a bit, but paid the administrative fee for the offense without complaint.

"All right, Dr. Peters, everything is all taken care of, sorry about the disruption," the officer said with a smile. "Just one more thing and you'll be all set to go home!"

Wren squeezed his eyes shut for a moment and tried to force himself to relax. Here it was, then.

"Andy, take the boy in back, strip him and give him the thirty lashes, then they're free to go."

Wren gasped, involuntarily, but didn't move. He couldn't — any movement would be considered resistance, and he couldn't resist. At one point, thirty lashes would barely have been anything, but this new master had spoiled him, had lulled him into feeling safe and secure, and certainly out of the habit of being beaten. He hadn't felt this terrified since he was a new slave, and his skin was so soft and unmarked.

Andy was a slave, probably strength gifted, and rather burly to add to it. Wren wanted to be sick at how badly this would hurt him. He saw a beefy arm reaching toward his shoulder, and tried not to think of —

Two small, strong hands gripped his shoulders, pulling him aside, to the other side of his master.

"Don't you *dare* touch my property."

The police department's slave, caught between a direct order from his mistress and a much more threatening direct order from a frazzled looking free man, glanced at the officer before moving.

"Dr. Peters, what is the problem?"

"This is entirely unnecessary. I don't want the boy whipped." Jere's left arm stayed tightly around Wren's shoulders.

"Sir, this is protocol. A slave who is found out without a pass is subject to —"

"It was my damn fault! *I* was the one who sent the kid out for fuck's sake! Someone's life was at stake!"

The officer smiled in what Wren assumed was supposed to be a placating way. He did placating looks much better. "Sir, regardless of who did or did not order the slave to go out, all slaves are taught in their training facilities the necessity of having a pass, and the punishment for not getting one. The responsibility falls on the slave, and so does the punishment!"

"He's my goddamn slave, and if there's going to be anyone whipping him, it's going be me!" Jere's voice had gone cool and calm.

"Sir, this is our procedure," the officer said firmly.

"Too fucking bad!" Jere snarled back.

Wren had started to tremble again. He had never heard his master this angry, and wasn't quite sure how this police officer wasn't intimidated. Although, she had the law behind her, not to mention her gun. Wren tentatively pushed at his master's mind, *"It's okay, sir, I'll be all right."*

"No. It's not fucking okay." Jere looked at him strangely, not angry, but not in his usual calm way, either. "Look, this isn't just some useless slave that I keep around to look pretty—I need him for medical assistance. You wouldn't take away my surgical tools, you shouldn't incapacitate my slave."

The officer seemed to stifle a laugh. "Dr. Peters, thirty lashes will hardly incapacitate the boy, regardless of what you may think. Honestly, slaves are pretty sturdy—and besides, you're free to heal him up once you get home."

Wren saw his master clench his jaw. "That's *not* the fucking point. You're not—give me a minute to think about this."

"Take your time, I'm here all night."

Jere took a few steps away from the desk, pulling Wren with him, arm still wrapped around his shoulders. It was oddly comforting, despite how angry his master obviously was with everything. With everything that Wren had caused. Almost without thinking, he let his head drop down onto his master's shoulder, the tiniest whimper escaping his lips as he did so. What the hell?

Jere just stood there for a few minutes, Wren frozen on his arm. Wren felt a slight squeeze—was that a hug? Jere turned them both around and walked back to the desk. "Officer Dobson, am I correct?"

"Yes. Have you collected yourself?"

Jere flashed a winning smile at her, managing to look sheepish and convincing at the same time. "Yes, officer, I sure have. I want to apologize. It's been a rough day."

"It happens, Doctor."

"I was just thinking—no, don't interrupt, hear me out. I was just thinking that *all* laws like this have exceptions, somewhere, deep in the law books. But certainly, someone as busy as you, in a police post with so many more *important* things to do, well, you wouldn't have time to go looking up things like that, would you? I mean, I know, resources are scarce, I mean, they're scarce all over! But sometimes, if someone can help, say, with resources, well, things like this can be found. Arrangements can be made."

Wren was pretty sure he was hallucinating at this point. Was his master trying to bribe an officer to save him from punishment?

It was wrong, all wrong. *"Please, sir, please don't! Just let them do it, it's okay, it was my fault!"*

"It was not!" Jere protested. *"Let me try to find a way out of this!"*

"The only 'arrangement' you will be making at this point is deciding whether you'd prefer to watch or to wait out here," the officer pointed out, her face impassive. "Unless, of course, you'd like to turn the boy over to our custody until you can obtain legal counsel, who would most certainly tell you that you are wasting your time. My slave can ready the restraints and the holding cell, if you'd prefer that?"

Wren started to tremble. His mind flashed to the nights he spent locked in the cellar, chained up, starving and cold. He doubted the accommodations here would be more comfortable, and he didn't know if he could survive that again. *"Please, sir, it will only make it worse! You can't fight it! Don't leave me alone, here, please don't leave me!"*

Jere looked back and forth between Wren and the officer. Wren hoped that he would keep his mouth shut, go along with the officer's demands, whatever was necessary to comply. It was all they could do at this point; didn't his master see that? He wished Jere would just listen to him, just trust that Wren knew better about how to deal with things in a slave state. But his master barely ever noticed him when he was behaving perfectly, why would he pay him any mind now that he was messing up? If they had complied with the laws in the first place, none of this would ever have happened, and Wren wouldn't be causing so much disruption.

"I—no. I wouldn't prefer that," Jere mumbled, looking defeated. "I apologize, I just thought... I'm just used to things being done differently."

"I'm sure." The officer rolled her eyes. "Now, let's try this again. Andy, we're ready for you, now. Will you be watching, Dr. Peters?"

Wren cast a glance at his master, pleading with his eyes. *"Please, don't let them take me back there alone."* The official punishment was a slap on the wrist, but slaves had no recourse to unofficial abuse. As much as he knew his master wouldn't want to be bothered, Wren needed protection. He would willingly accept any additional punishment once they got home, just as long as he wasn't hurt too badly here.

"Yes," Jere said, looking as scared as Wren felt.

Jere was floored. He knew this place was backwards, but this — this was something out of an ancient history book. The law was something to keep people safe, not to hurt them. People deserved trials, humane treatment, reasonable consequences, not to be beaten like animals.

But, hadn't Wren indicated that slaves were treated worse than animals?

Jere followed as the boy he had grown so used to having around was led by the arm into a back room by the slave, followed by the officer. The room was sparse, narrow, and fitted with a pole in the middle that Jere realized could only be used for tying things — or people — to.

"Clothes off and placed on the chair," she ordered Wren, then turned to Jere. "Will he need to be restrained?"

Jere resisted the urge to tell her to ask Wren for herself, he wasn't stupid, he could speak! He heard Wren's voice supplying the answer immediately in his head.

"*I can stay still, sir, please ask her not to tie me.*"

"Don't tie him," Jere choked out, feeling complicit in this.

The officer nodded, glancing at Wren as he stood frozen in the middle of the room. "If he's not getting his clothes off, you can strip him."

Jere knew the woman was talking to her slave, the big one with the muscles, but he pretended to misunderstand. "Of course," he said, forcing a smile as he jumped to Wren's side, all but bumping into the police department's slave on the way. He locked eyes with Wren as he stood in front of him, fingers barely touching the hem of his shirt. "*I'm right here,*" he promised. "*I won't leave you.*"

He pulled Wren's shirt over his head as Wren removed his pants with shaking hands. Jere felt sick as he took the pile of clothes in his arms and dumped them unceremoniously onto the chair.

"Dr. Peters, if you're staying, you need to be back here with us or in front of the slave," the officer informed him curtly. "This department wants nothing to do with the liability of you getting hit by a stray lash."

Jere said nothing, too furious at the thought of them caring about his safety when they were purposely hurting someone else. He moved in front of Wren, taking a few steps back until he hit the wall behind him. It was probably safer for the officer that he was on the other side of the room from her anyway.

"For appearing in a public area without a pass, the penalty of thirty lashes, to be delivered upon bare skin with a regulation grade whip," the officer recited, sounding bored. "Slave, you may hold on to the beam for support, any attempt to resist or evade lashes will be considered an escape attempt and will be punished by up to an additional one hundred lashes. Andy, you may begin."

Jere didn't have time to process the short speech or the associated threats. He was too busy being furious, angry at the officer, at himself and at the entire town of Hojer. He wanted to hit someone, and it wasn't fair that the only person being hit was the last person who deserved it.

"I'm so sorry, sir, I'm so sorry I got into trouble! Please, I'll make it up to you, I'll do better, I'll do anything you want me to!"

Jere could barely focus on the voice in his head, he was too horrified by the sound of leather brutally striking flesh, and the strained moans and gasps that Wren was making out loud.

"Dammit, Wren, this is fucking bullshit!" Jere snapped, consumed with rage and helplessness.

"Please, sir, I'm so sorry, I inconvenienced you, it's my fault, I never should have, I'll never get in trouble again, sir! Please, don't be angry! It's my fault!"

"How can I not be angry!" Jere raged. *"We're at a goddamn police station and you're being whipped! I give you one order in this piece of shit town and this is what happens?"*

"I'm sorry, sir, I shouldn't have asked you to come. It's not a big deal, being whipped, it's not that bad, I promise, I'll still be able to work and everything and you don't have to heal me if you don't want to. I shouldn't have gotten you in trouble. I shouldn't have gotten caught, sir, please, I'm

sorry!"

Jere was struck by the horrible realization that Wren really didn't seem too bothered by the whipping, aside from the unavoidable pain, but he was still terrified. Jere realized that *he* was what Wren was terrified of.

"*This is not your fault,*" he insisted, forcing the anger out of his voice. He blocked his end of the connection carefully, masking the anger and letting the concern and fear come through. How could he have missed this? He was raging, terrifying the kid, but all he could pay attention to was his own anger and culture shock? Wren didn't need any of that. He needed support, like any decent human being would have noticed well before the whipping ever started.

"*This is not your fault,*" he repeated. "*It's mine. You don't deserve this.*" How did he convince Wren of that? He had been nice enough to him, hadn't he? He was a healer, he healed bodies, not minds! The thought jerked him back to what was happening, the abuse being piled on Wren's body. The whip seemed to keep coming down, hard and fast, whistling as it cut through the air and the skin beneath it. Jere itched to use his healing gift, *now,* and end the pain, but he couldn't, not yet.

He watched Wren clutch the beam in the middle of the room, his knuckles white with effort, his lower lip bleeding as he held back screams. Jere doubted he would have stayed so silent under such treatment. He couldn't help but notice how thin the boy had become, skeletal, almost as thin as he was when Jere first arrived. He had put on weight before, hadn't he? Surely he had been eating?

Jere couldn't delude himself for more than half a second, though. Clearly he *hadn't* been eating, if the spindly arms and prominent ribs were any indication. His cheeks were sunken in, the pallor most noticeable there. How had he not seen this before? He knew that Wren had recovered well, eaten regularly, started looking healthy and put together. And he had been providing everything that Wren could need — food, clothing, medical care. Jere was bothered by slavery, every time he interacted with Wren he was reminded of the fact. What else was he supposed to do?

The answer was as clear as the state that Wren was in. Wren needed attention, care, some sort of acknowledgment that he was valued. Because Jere did value him, as an assistant, not to mention as another human being. How could he let it come to this? Had he really not looked at the boy in that long? He saw him every day. But it was easier to pretend that he didn't.

Jere was dimly aware that the sound of the whip had stopped. He stayed, frozen, staring into Wren's eyes, willing his own not to well up with matching tears. "*I'm sorry,*" he said, knowing it wasn't enough. He should have been the one up there, for being so thoughtless. Wren just stared back at him, looking defeated.

"See, not so horrible, was it?" the officer said. "You're free to go."

Jere didn't move. He heard a door shut, and he realized he and Wren were alone. "I'm sorry," he repeated, out loud, as if it would matter more that way.

Wren sank to the floor, still shaking.

"I'll heal you!" Jere rushed to put his hands on him.

"*Not here, sir, please. They wouldn't approve, and….*" Wren finally turned his face up to look at him. "*Please, take me home.*"

Jere didn't argue. He wanted to, but he fetched Wren's clothes instead and helped him to stand up and put them on, now hyper-aware of how loose they had grown. "Can you walk?" he asked, his voice unsteady.

Wren nodded. "Of course, sir. I've had worse."

Jere hadn't thought it was possible to feel worse.

He was struck with admiration as Wren walked out the door, jaw set in determination as he managed not to cry out. Jere could only imagine the pain that each jarring step must be causing, and he hated that anyone had caused him to feel that way. More than that, he hated that he had been largely to blame.

"Have a nice night," the officer bid them goodbye as if nothing had happened. She didn't care. For her, this was as insignificant as a fine for littering; no matter that blood had been drawn. Jere was more disturbed by this than he cared to think about.

They were silent as they walked, slowly, to the edge of the sleeping town. Jere kept glancing over at Wren, seeing the sweat beading up on his forehead despite the freezing temperatures. They reached the library, which had some benches outside, and Jere couldn't handle the guilt anymore.

"Sit," he ordered Wren. "I'm healing you. This is ridiculous."

"It's okay, sir—"

"It's not okay!" Jere snapped. "Nothing about this is okay. This is my fault! You either let me heal you at least a little bit or I'll, I'll carry you!"

For a second, Jere could have sworn he saw a smile flash across Wren's face.

"As you wish, sir." Wren sat lightly, facing away from Jere.

Jere put his hands carefully on his back, horrified when Wren arched away and whimpered. "Just hold on," he whispered, and he started healing.

An outdoor bench wasn't the best place to heal; neither was the middle of a winter night, but what Jere lacked in setting he made up for in guilt and determination. He didn't fix it all—he couldn't, he knew that, but he staunched most of the bleeding and numbed most of the pain. Only a short time passed before he stopped, feeling only slightly less awful.

"You're too kind, sir," Wren mumbled. From anyone else, it would have sounded sarcastic, but Wren honestly sounded grateful.

Jere said nothing. He didn't feel kind at all. He felt like he was doing damage control for damage he had caused.

Chapter 16
Showing Gratitude

They walked the rest of the way home in silence, huddled into their coats to keep warm against the cold. Well, Jere was, Wren still felt too warm all over.

The second they walked into the house, Jere glanced at him. "Clinic. Now."

Wren did as he was ordered. He was confused. Was his master still angry with him? Had he been angry at all? It was so hard to tell. The man snapped at him so much, but then he said he wasn't angry. Wren couldn't keep track. Between the confusion and the edges of pain that were creeping through the numbness, Wren wasn't sure what was real, other than the fact that his master had tried to protect him and even seemed upset that he was in pain. He couldn't remember the last time anyone had done that.

He made his way to an examination table, where he eased himself down on his stomach and tried to relax. He was unsurprised when Jere followed him in a few moments later, setting the clean clothes he had obviously retrieved on a counter. Wren he felt his master's hands brushing his skin, the pinpoint of psychic pain for the briefest of seconds as the connection was made to start the healing.

"Sorry," Jere repeated, for the hundredth time.

Why did he keep saying it? What was there for him to apologize for? Wren had been perfectly aware of the consequences of his actions when he had taken them, a master shouldn't have to bother himself with the petty hurts of a slave. Why did Jere seem to notice that he was in pain today, when he had so successfully ignored him for the past few months? Did his master really feel guilty for causing him pain?

Wren fought to hold back tears and failed. He felt his skin coming back together, and while it wasn't painful, it wasn't a pleasant feeling either, but he trusted his master to put him back together again. Jere had consistently done that, made sure he was physically taken care of. He couldn't say how long the healing took, too consumed in his own thoughts.

And then Jere was rubbing the healing cream across his skin, the motion and the smell reminiscent of the first few contacts Wren ever had with him. So much had changed since then, but so much had stayed the same as well. While Wren was less terrified, he still longed for it to end, for the pain and confusion and suffering to finally be over.

"You should have let me die, then," Wren muttered, horrified when he realized he had spoken out loud.

"What?" Jere asked, horrified.

"When you first got here, sir," Wren clarified. He had spoken the words; perhaps if he made his case well enough he could get his wish?

"Wren, why? Why would I do that?"

"All I am is an inconvenience, sir," Wren admitted. "You've been kind enough to keep me, but all I do is get in your way and cause trouble. I just, I would have been better off. Maybe you would have been, too."

"Without you?" Jere asked. "No. I wouldn't have been. You're my right-hand man, you know? At the clinic, at home, but that's not even—I like you, all right?"

Hell of a way to show it, Wren thought, feeling guilty. But how could Jere really like him? He was a slave, first of all, it wasn't like he was a person. He took up time and resources and effort, and the only interaction that Jere had with him most of the time was ignoring him or snapping at him.

"Look, I, I think you're a good person," Jere continued. "Really. And I never expected you to be so strong."

Wren nodded. To an outlander, that must have looked like a very severe whipping. When Burghe owned him, it would have been a slap on the wrist, something he would have been given for an off look or a smudge on a glass.

"And, besides, if you weren't around, who would tell me about all the stupid rules and laws in Hojer?" Jere attempted a lighter tone.

"If it wasn't for me, sir, you wouldn't have to worry about nearly as many of them," Wren pointed out. "This, tonight, it was my fault, sir. That's why I was punished."

"No. It wasn't. I ordered you to go, didn't I? Even when you told me? I had no idea—okay, that's not true. I knew damn well it was against some sort of fucking law or statute or something or other, but I didn't really think, well, I didn't think that you'd be at risk of being punished and held responsible for something that I told you to do. Something that I *ordered* you to do."

He had stopped speaking, looking at Wren sadly.

"Sir, it's the way things are done here. Perhaps I should have explained it better?"

Jere shook his head. "You've explained everything there is quite well. I'm just too damn thick to get it. And honestly... I don't want to believe it. I want to believe that things aren't the way they are. Stupid, huh?"

Wren didn't think so. He wanted to believe that sometimes, too. But years of heavy backhands had taught him that a fantasy world was not the important one to live in.

"I've promised to keep you safe, and I keep doing such a knock-up job of it, right?" Jere looked down. "I can heal you up, afterward, sometimes I feel like that's all I'm good at doing. You're feeling okay? You're a little warm."

"Yes, sir," Wren answered. "I feel good. I guess I'm a little shaken up, maybe that's why I'm warm?"

"Maybe." Jere looked guilty. "I'm sorry. I can't promise that something like this won't happen again, because I haven't had the best track record, but I can say that I'll try, all right?"

"Yes, thank you, sir." Wren responded instinctively. There was no other way to respond to a question like that.

"Then, regardless of what the law says, and who got punished, this is on me," Jere said firmly. "And, since I haven't said it, let me make it clear, I want you to take care of yourself. It's nice that you follow orders, and I know you're trained to or whatever, but first and foremost, I want you to take care of yourself."

"Yes, sir." Wren didn't know why he cared.

"Even if that means telling me no, or getting a pass when I tell you not to take the time," Jere clarified. "That's what taking care of yourself means."

Wren nodded. He would have felt like he was being talked down to, having it spelled out like that, but he did need the reminder. Jere clearly didn't want him to be getting into more trouble.

"And it means eating and sleeping and showering."

Wren's head jerked up when he heard the last part. How long had he known? His will to live had started to burn out weeks ago, and he just assumed his master hadn't cared, as long as he was still doing his job.

Jere stared at him for a few seconds, enough to make him squirm. Wren never thought he would have noticed.

"Yes, sir," Wren managed, more on instinct than anything else.

"I don't want you to just survive, Wren," Jere added, looking concerned and resolute all at the same time. "I don't like to see you suffer, no matter who's causing it. Is there something I can do differently?"

Wren was silent. Criticizing his master wasn't an option, and refusing to answer wasn't an option, either. Lying wasn't much better, but it was all he had left. "It's fine, sir."

"It's not. I treat you like you're not even there." Jere shook his head, and Wren could tell that Jere was blocking a good portion of his emotions. "I know I'm messing things up, and I realized tonight that my fuck-ups hurt you more than they hurt me. And even though it's not your responsibility, and you shouldn't have to, I need your help. I want to do better, but I need you to help me pay attention to things; things like this, things like when I say things that are hurtful. I've always dealt with free people who will call me on it, and I'll try to be better, but I need you for that. If anything was clear tonight, it's that you know a hell of a lot better than I do about *anything* here."

Jere sat there, silent for another moment, then got up and walked

132

out, leaving Wren to ponder his words and dress himself. It was so quiet in the clinic, the still of the late night sounding louder than the busy day. Finally, he stood, stretching and feeling amazed by how good he felt, how quickly the pain had been erased. His old master never healed him this well. He walked through the door into the house, where he found Jere seated at the table, a weary look on his face. Jere stretched back, twisting and contorting himself around his chair before settling into the exact same position as he had started in, looking unsatisfied.

"Just think, we get to get up and do this all again in a few hours," Jere commented. "Well, maybe not just like this."

Wren nodded. "Yes, sir." He watched his master carefully, the way he had tried to stretch, the uncomfortable way he was sitting, the hunched, alert position he held, *had* held for hours now. He had a thought, but pushed it away. But then, his master had been *so* kind to him today, and what did Wren even have to offer him in return?

"I want you to know, sir, how much it meant to me." Wren found himself speaking before he had a chance to stop himself as he usually did. "Tonight, I mean, at the police post. You tried to help, and you stayed with me. Most people wouldn't have. I know it didn't seem like a big thing to you, but it was to me. Thank you."

"It was nothing." Jere tried to be gruff, but Wren could see through it.

"It wasn't, sir," Wren insisted, trying to ignore the fear that accompanied contradicting his master. "It was kind, and it made it better, and I just wish there was something I could do in return. Something I could do in return for all the things you do for me—for saving my life, for taking care of me, for feeding me and treating me so well."

"You don't need to do anything," Jere insisted.

"But I *want* to, sir," Wren protested, realizing as he said the words that they were true. It had been too easy, even with the pain of the whipping. Jere had wiped it away and apologized for it, like he had when that woman slapped him months ago. Jere was always there like that, always giving, never demanding. Wren felt indebted to him, and debt was something he didn't want. Too much debt required too large a repayment. He thought again of how uncomfortable his master looked.

"Would you like a massage?" he blurted out. "Sir?"

Jere seemed to study him for a minute, then nodded. "I would, actually. It's been years since I've had a good massage."

Wren said nothing, but stood up and moved behind him. What had he been thinking? They were barely able to have a conversation on most days, much less touch one another. Wren was pretty sure that he should have wanted to just go back to his bed and sleep, back where it was safe, back where there was no thought of crossing any boundaries or touching or doing anything at all.

He started by placing his hands on his master's shoulders, his mind returning briefly to the way Jere's arm had felt on *his* shoulders earlier that day. So warm and strong.... He gently started to knead them, working from his neck, out to his arms, then back up to his neck, and starting down his back.

Jere, meanwhile, had stretched out nearly flat across the table, arching into Wren's hands. "My god, that is lovely. Your hands are so warm!"

"Thank you, sir."

"Thank *you*!" Jere mumbled.

Wren continued for a while longer, feeling content with the happy noises he was eliciting from his master, not to mention the tension he felt leaving his muscles. He had been told so, so many times that his hands were warm. When questioned, he always brushed it off, blaming his speed gift for the unusual heat. It made sense that someone with a speed gift would have a higher metabolism, and a higher temperature as well. No need to draw attention to himself.

"Mind if we move this somewhere a bit more comfortable?" Wren heard Jere ask through the mind connection. Wren still found the casual use of mindspeak a bit unnerving, but his master had explained, somewhat apologetically, that he had learned to mindspeak before learning to speak out loud. He tended to fall back on it whenever he was tired or distressed.

"Of course, sir," Wren answered out loud. He hoped his master was referring to the couch or something.

Jere got up and headed out of the dining room, through the living room, and, much to Wren's dismay, down the hallway to the master bedroom. Did Jere even like boys? Wren had never figured it out. Of course, that didn't really matter, not really. Any port in a storm. Wren tried to steel himself for what was coming. After all, there was only one reason to be invited into a bedroom, wasn't there?

Jere had slipped off his shirt and shoes and flopped down on the bed. Wren followed, hesitantly. Could he really do this? He was starting to tremble already, at the thought of whatever it might be that his master wanted from him. The master had left his pants on, at least—but did that just mean that he wanted Wren to undress him? And what about his own clothes? Should he leave them on? Take them off? Wait for the master to rip them off? He closed his eyes for a second, squeezing them tight against the image in his head of being stripped, held down—

"I'll apologize in advance," Jere mumbled. "I'm probably going to fall asleep."

Wren was startled out of his nightmarish thoughts. Fall asleep? Then surely he didn't mean to....

"It just felt so good, so relaxing. I haven't been sleeping well. I'm sorry if I'm keeping you up."

Encouraged by his master's sleepy tone and general kindness, Wren joined him on the bed, gingerly sitting next to him and resuming the massage where he had left off. He tried to shut out as much of the fear as he could, even attempting to use some of the blocking skills that his master had taught him to keep from projecting the fear outward.

"That is spectacular, Wren. And I'm sorry I scared you. I know, you're keeping it under wraps, but I can still — it's okay. I should have warned you. I'm just tired. You're being so good and kind, Wren. I wouldn't hurt you like that."

Wren said nothing, just kept working his hands over his master's back, trying not to think about how soft his skin was, or how strong his muscles felt, even now that they were relaxing, or how comfortable it felt to have his master's voice in his head. He had never touched him before, never imagined wanting to, and yet he found himself enjoying it. He had never felt anything other than revulsion at the thought of touching another person before. As he heard his master's breathing even out into sleep, he enjoyed it even more. He knew now, on every level, that he was safe; his master was asleep and wouldn't demand anything more of him. Despite his promises, Wren could never quite be sure about this. It was an impossible decision — to trust his master's words, or the years of experience and training that had kept him safer than the alternative.

He studied his master's face, turned so carelessly aside, one arm under his head while the other flopped out to the side. Worry free. Wren tended to sleep curled into a little ball, facing the wall, if there was one there, protecting his stomach and face, in case he should be punished for something while he was still sleeping. The habit had diminished somewhat since Jere had arrived, but it certainly still lingered. Now he sometimes stretched his legs out.

He did just that now, feeling the softness of Jere's bed, freshly made this morning, under his feet. While he continued working over Jere's back with one hand, he dared to let himself lie down, just for a minute, just to stretch. He reveled at the warmth, the safety he felt, and he shut his eyes for a moment, overwhelmed.

He awoke suddenly when he felt an arm flop over his chest. Panic threatened to overtake him as he struggled to remember where he was, and, more importantly, *why* he was there. He tried, and failed, to control the shaking as he realized he was lying in bed next to his half-naked master, and that he had fallen asleep while he was supposed to be serving him. He was tired, he was disoriented, and he could almost feel the panic coming off him in waves. Then he felt the familiar push at his mind.

"S'okay, kid. Just a dream. Go back to sleep."

Jere had the ability to mumble even when he was mindspeaking. Wren felt himself calming almost immediately. His master's half-asleep mumbling indicated that he had no idea that Wren was even in bed with him — this was, it seemed, the same panic that Wren projected still somewhat frequently when he had nightmares.

He slipped carefully from beneath his master's arm, creeping down the hallway to his own room. He wasn't about to risk a second encounter like that tonight, and what the hell would the master say when he woke up to find his slave in his bed anyway? Rather reluctantly, Wren crawled into his own bed, pulling his covers around him. Strangely, he was colder here, under the covers, than he had been lying on top of the bedspread next to his master. He tried to put it out of his mind as he willed himself to sleep.

Sleep had never come easily for him, but it had gotten less difficult in the past few months, since Jere had arrived, since his life had become so much more calm and peaceful and sane. While he often went to bed tired from long days of work, it was never the kind of exhaustion that he had grown used to while Burghe owned him, the kind that shot you down into sleep before your head even touched the pillow.

Or the floor, as was more often case with Burghe.

But since Jere had arrived, it was always a pillow. A nice, soft pillow, soft like Jere's skin had been, squishy and pliant under his hands—

Wren jerked awake, shaking the image out of his head. He hadn't really been sleeping, but certainly his *waking* mind wouldn't have filled his head with the image of his master's skin!

Although, his skin was quite soft.

Wren continued trying to push the thought out of his head. Touching and being touched only led to danger and pain. Right. He just had to keep believing that, and reminding himself of that, and not thinking about how nice it was to have Jere's arm around him at the police station, or how calming it was to lie next to him in bed, or how soft his skin was. How nice it felt under his fingers.

Half-asleep and desperate to recreate that feeling, Wren drew his fingers down the inside of his own arm, tracing a line from his wrist to his elbow, continuing up to his shoulder, where his t-shirt stopped him. His skin was soft there, too, but it didn't feel the same as Jere's, and he certainly didn't have the muscles built up that his master had.

Lying on his back, he reached for the next most easily accessible body parts, his stomach and chest. He pushed his shirt up, running both hands over his skin experimentally. It felt nice. He so rarely touched himself, except if he was hurt or showering. He had almost forgotten what his own body felt like. Burghe had forbidden it, not that he would have wanted to touch himself, then. Even if he hadn't been in constant misery, he was disgusted by his own failures. He tried not to focus on how much and how often he failed as a slave, both with Burghe and with Jere. It was so much more pleasant to focus on the way Jere's hands had felt on his skin, healing him. Would he really have carried him home?

He wondered what Jere's chest felt like, even though thoughts like that were unsettling. Other people's skin felt like fear, like waiting to make a mistake and be punished for it. But Jere didn't really feel like that. Jere felt nice.

He wondered what Jere's fingers would feel like on his skin, whether they would feel good, like his arm did around his shoulders, or not. He figured they would feel very good, and he imagined them coming up to massage his shoulders, his touch firm and gentle like it always was.

It was wrong, but he wanted to feel it. He wanted to imagine that connection to another person, even if his desire branded him as a whore. Even if getting caught meant getting punished, or worse, being touched like this for real.

Touch meant pain, but nothing with Jere meant pain. Even tonight, when Wren was hurting so much, it was Jere who kept him anchored, who finally looked at him and tried to stand up for him and *felt* something for him. By comparison, the healing was almost irrelevant. Wren knew that when his fantasy version of Jere ran his hands down his arms, it wouldn't be painful at all, it would feel nice, and maybe he would find the sensitive spots that Wren hid from everyone else in his life. When Jere finished touching his arms, maybe he would take his hands, kiss them, place Wren's hands on his skin, and Wren could feel his master at the same time.

Wren felt himself growing hard at the thought, and he smiled. It had been so, so long since he had allowed himself to indulge in a fantasy like this! He shouldn't, and he knew it, but after everything that had happened tonight, he just wanted something for himself. He relaxed, letting his legs part as his hand moved down, stroking the hair that surrounded his cock. He imagined that the hands touching him weren't his own, but someone else's, Jere's, wrapping around him and slowly teasing him, touching him.

He let a little sound of pleasure escape, something he hadn't done willingly in longer than he could remember. It was okay, though. Jere would like a sound like that. He would want him to be happy.

Once again, he thought of Jere's hands around his cock, and he started to rock himself up and down, in and out of the hand on his cock. He imagined lips on his neck, kissing him, and right as he was about to come, he placed a hand on his hip, imagining it wasn't his, imagining that it was someone else, steadying him, keeping him in the most pleasurable position possible. And it was pleasurable, in spite of everything, in spite of memories and being half-asleep, and Wren soon found himself gasping for air, his breath shallow as he continued to pump his cock, thinking of the man down the hall, wishing he were touching his soft skin. Biting back a cry, Wren stroked himself a few more times before he came, closing his eyes and letting his mind wander as he did. He tried to imagine something generic, a sunset or tranquil beach, but his mind was filled with soft skin and blond hair. He hadn't been caught. His guilty fantasy had left him worn out and confused, but he couldn't deny the good feelings. He fumbled around until he found a tissue next to the bed, rolled onto his side, and drifted into a restless sleep.

Chapter 17
Entertainment

The first of December marked the start of the Winter Holidays in Hojer. A flood of bright orange envelopes graced the mailbox, which Wren checked regularly. Jere was startled to find them dropped in front of him, as Wren sped from the door to the kitchen and back to the table again with breakfast.

Jere, still wearing nightclothes, looked at him with amazement. "How did I live without you?"

Wren smiled, taking a seat and beginning to eat his breakfast. "If the story is anything like you've told me, sir, you didn't check your mail. Or eat breakfast."

Jere grinned back at him, pleased to see that Wren had learned to see the humor in some of his self-deprecating statements. He assessed the tasks at hand, namely, breakfast and mail, and dug in, starting with the coffee, and the first envelope.

Party invitation.

Second envelope.

Party invitation.

"Wren?" he asked, tentatively. The kid had relaxed quite a bit around him, but was still somewhat awkward when Jere asked his advice.

"Yes, sir?" Wren paused, fork halfway to his mouth.

Jere decided to play it safe at first. "Are all these envelopes going to contain party invitations?"

Wren nodded. "Most likely, sir."

Jere opened a few more. Indeed, they did. "Does *everyone* in Hojer throw a party during the Winter Holidays?"

Another nod. "Yes, sir. Well, anyone who matters socially, sir."
"And do I matter? Socially?"

Jere wished Wren would have just nodded, and left it at that.
"Yes, sir. Very much."

Jere sighed, pushing the rest of the envelopes aside. "I'm not really much on parties where I don't know anyone. I don't even know what I'd do. Better to stay in and wait for the injuries to come through the clinic."

Jere saw, and felt through the mind connection, that Wren had gone very still and quiet. He waited for a second, two, maybe even three, before the feeling grew too uncomfortable. "What is it, Wren?"

"Sir, if I may?" Wren was hesitant, drawing back the tiniest bit as he tentatively asked for permission.

"Please do, Wren," Jere said, simultaneously frustrated by and resigned to Wren's usual hesitancy.

"Well, sir, you've asked me to advise you on social matters, sir." Wren's tendency to stammer and inject even more "sirs" into his sentences when nervous had finally ceased bothering Jere, who patiently waited through it. "I, uh, I would suggest that you go, sir."

Jere said nothing, just looked at him with an unhappy frown.

"I mean, of course, sir, only if you wanted to. I would never, never dream of telling you what to do, sir—"

"Go on. Tell me why I should go. It's obviously important. Although I feel like I'm being told why I should get injected with nuclear waste."

Wren seemed to calm a bit. Good. Jere had been trying to make a joke.

"Sir, the Winter Holiday parties aren't really about the holidays, they're about the social connections one can make."

Jere stared blankly.

"Networking? Sir? Building business and referrals?"

Jere raised an eyebrow. "Do I have competition I don't know about?"

"Sir," Wren raised an eyebrow back, the closest Jere had ever seen to defiance or attitude. He found it rather endearing. "It's not about competition. It's about, well, making friends. Connections.

Who would you go to if you needed help with something?"

"Well..." Jere was stumped. He had never really thought about this. He had never had things to need help with before. "I just won't need help."

"You could meet other people, sir. Equals. Others with mind gifts." Wren looked away as he said this.

Jere had never thought of it this way. He realized that he and Wren could probably not be described as friends, as he assumed that friends didn't cringe away from one another, but he at least thought that they were companions. He was lonely, sometimes, but Wren was usually willing, if not eager, to talk with him, or sit there quietly, or... whatever Jere asked. *Always* whatever Jere asked. An equal suddenly sounded appealing. An equal who could tell him no.

"I suppose I could see where this would be useful."

"Sir, going to these parties is the way things are done here."

Jere sighed. "You always get me with that one."

Wren said nothing, continuing to look carefully down at his plate. When had he stopped eating? Jere stabbed at his own food, as if it would look more appetizing stabbed to bits.

"Well, am I expected to go to all of them?" he conceded.

Wren shook his head. "No, sir. In fact, some would be surprised if you would deign to attend their parties. But you should, I mean, it would be expected of you that you pick a few."

Jere popped a piece of meat into his mouth, chewed thoughtfully for a minute, then grabbed the stack of envelopes and pushed them in front of Wren. "You pick. You know better than I ever will how many and which ones I should attend."

"Sir, I—" Wren began to protest.

"You're always asking how you can be of help, well, this!" Jere said definitively, a smirk on his face. He speared another piece of meat and used it to gesture as he spoke. His mother would have swatted him if she saw it. "Pick the parties, arrange them on my calendar, and while you're at it, make sure I have something passable to wear to a thing like this."

And that was how Jere ended up at the door of the Wysocka family home.

As Jere had said, he really wasn't much for parties. He had grown up in a small social circle, surrounded by friends, and had never needed to master the awkward art of new situations. Even when he did, professionally, he had the busy schedule of a doctor to fall back on. Nobody minded if he ran off in the middle of a conversation—presumably, he was off to do work or save a life, not hide under his desk or sit in a bathroom stall with his feet up or anything. However, he did admit that he was a little lonely. Okay, maybe more than a little lonely, at times. He could see how at least a little socializing could help him feel, well, a bit less on edge.

He was standing there, indecisive, arm raised to the door, about to knock, when the door was opened.

"Dr. Peters, how nice to see you!" Paltrek Wysocka Senior, Hojer's wealthiest investor, stood in the doorway, a slave silently holding it open. Jere assumed the man knew who he was since he was the only unfamiliar person who would be at the party.

Jere smiled back half-heartedly. "Same to you, Mr. Wysocka, and may the warmest Winter Holidays come for you and your family." Wren had, after some hemming and hawing, instructed Jere on socially acceptable responses and greetings. They were similar to those Jere had grown up with, but he still appreciated the cultural coaching.

"Come on in, let me introduce you to everyone!"

Jere allowed himself to be led around, introduced mainly as "Dr. Peters," but sometimes as "Jeremy," which never failed to produce a cringe. At least he didn't bother correcting anyone this time. He wondered again what kind of society reserved short names for slaves, anyway.

Jere barely remembered the names of the first group of people he met, much less the subsequent ones. In all honesty, he felt like he was being paraded around, his first "social outing" since moving to Hojer. He was starting to understand why he liked his usual hermit-like lifestyle so much.

Finally, it appeared that he had been introduced, to everyone but a group of young men standing around near the punch bowl. He felt like some sort of show animal.

"Now, Dr. Peters, you can meet my little PJ," Wysocka said with a grin, tapping one of the young men on the shoulder.

A rather horrified twenty-something turned around, trying to mask the horror with a congenial smile. "Honestly, Father, you haven't called me that since I was an infant!"

A fair-haired young woman walked up behind him and punched him lightly in the shoulder. "I didn't know you were an infant at breakfast this morning, little brother."

"Annika..." the young man, presumably Paltrek Junior, said, only mildly irritated. He shook his head, and turned to Jere. "Dr. Peters, welcome, I'm Paltrek Wysocka. The eighth. And this is Annika, my sister."

"The first," she said with a flirtatious smile.

"How do you do?" Jere asked, politely.

"Better, now." Annika murmured seductively.

Jere tried to resist looking around to see who else she could be making hungry wolf eyes at. He hoped it wasn't him.

"Arae!" She shrieked, suddenly, shrilly.

A tiny girl who looked no more than sixteen or seventeen came rushing to her side. Jere noticed that her outfit was interesting, to say the least. What there was of it.

"Yes, mistress?" She spoke softly, her eyes downcast.

Annika glared at her and shook her glass, which contained little else but ice cubes.

The girl, who Jere assumed was this woman's slave, reddened. "I'll bring you another one immediately, ma'am." She turned, quickly, to leave, but was caught by Annika's hand in her hair. She yelped, but went silent almost immediately as her mistress pulled her close.

"Aren't you forgetting something?" she hissed in the girl's ear, pointlessly, as everyone could hear it.

"I..." she whimpered in pain for a moment, then turned her eyes toward Jere, dropping to her knees as Annika let her go and pushed her away. "Please, sir, forgive my rudeness. How may I serve you?"

Jere stood frozen for a moment, unsure of what to do. Finally, he reached his hand out slowly to the girl. "Get up," he said softly, taking her hand and pulling her to her feet. As she did as he asked, he spoke calmly and firmly, ending any other discussions that might arise. "If you would, I'd love a gin and tonic, please."

The girl nodded, frantically. "Yes, yes, sir, thank you!" She scampered away as quickly as possible.

Annika had watched the interaction with interest, smiling rather cruelly as her slave hurried off. "I hear you've inherited a boy of your own, Dr. Peters?"

Jere nodded. He really doubted that he thought of Wren in remotely the same way as this woman thought of her slave. "Yes." A safe, noncommittal answer.

"How are you liking Hojer?" She changed the subject. "Met many people yet?"

Jere was horrified to realize she was flirting with him. "I, uh, yes. No. I mean..." Jere tried not to squirm. "I've met a lot of people, but I guess I don't know them that well?" Jere didn't like parties. At all.

"So that's why you're out for the Winter Holidays," Paltrek had returned to the conversation that his sister had more or less hijacked.

Jere nodded, relieved to be saved. "Yes. I figure, I'm moved in, I'm settled, my business is going well, now it's time to make friends and whatnot. Social life, you know."

"Yeah, it doesn't seem like you go out much!" Annika pointed out.

"Yes, you know, business, moving, medical needs for an entire town." *Social phobia, unfamiliarity with social customs, awkwardness that is physically painful.* Jere tried to guess how long he'd be here.

"It's understandable," Paltrek shrugged. "I mean, taking responsibility for the medical care of the whole town? And you're only, what, just out of med school?"

"A few years, yes." Jere saw no reason to give an exact number. As far as he was concerned, just over one counted as a few.

"Well, good for you! My father's constantly on me to start something of my own. Seems he's not content with me following blindly in his footsteps."

"You mean stumbling in his footsteps," Annika didn't seem to be entirely poking fun. She placed a rather unwelcome hand on Jere's upper arm, squeezing in an altogether too familiar way. "I'm working with a pattern analyzing company — *amazing* research on how and why different people are born with different gifts — if they're even 100% born with them!"

"Fascinating," Jere tried to sound excited. While those with pattern analyst gifts could indeed be highly successful, pattern analyzing had often been referred to as the last great pyramid scheme — something to do with some archaic business model that tended to make more money off its own employees than it did its customers.

Arae had returned with the drinks. She very carefully handed one to Annika, who did nothing more than glare at her, and then attempted to hand the other to Jere, blanching in terror as she dropped it at the last second, shattering glass across the floor.

She stood there, frozen.

"I, I'll pick it up, mistress."

"You certainly will." Annika snapped.

Arae turned to leave. "I'll be right back with a broom and — "

Annika cuffed her. "Pick it up."

Jere watched, feeling a bit nauseous, as Arae dropped gingerly to her knees. He glanced around, waiting for someone to stop it, for someone to call the woman out on her harsh treatment of the slave. Nobody seemed concerned, or alarmed, and they most certainly did not seem surprised.

"Now." Annika's voice was nothing more than a low hiss.

Arae started with the big pieces of glass, carefully picking them up with one hand and placing them into the other. When she had gotten them all, she looked up at Annika pleadingly, tears in her eyes.

"Sweep it up with your hand or you'll be licking it up!"

Jere couldn't take it. Nobody was stopping her. What if this was Wren? Would nobody speak up for him, either? "Arae," he spoke suddenly, embarrassed by the volume of his own voice. "Get up now and get a broom and dustpan. Do *not* pick that up with your bare hands."

Arae froze, trembling. She looked back and forth between Jere and her mistress.

"Annika," Paltrek elbowed her lightly. "This isn't the time or place."

For a second, Jere thought she was going to make her do it anyway.

Annika laughed, suddenly; an ugly, forced sound that went on too long as she tried to pretend that nothing had happened. "Well. You heard the man. Go get a broom and dustpan! And make it quick."

"Yes, mistress," Arae stood up, then risked a quick glance at Jere. "Thank you, sir."

"Get moving!" Annika snapped, then turned to Jere, still forcing that laugh. "You don't have to butter her up, you know! I'll let you fuck her if you want to."

Jere saw the girl cringe as she was walking away. "I, um, thank you, that won't be necessary." What did one even say to that?

"Daddy gave her to me as a gift," Annika said, sounding rather displeased. "Have you ever ordered steak in a restaurant and gotten a salad? She's like a salad. I wanted a boy. Someone who I knew would be useful at something at least. Although, she has picked up *those* skills, as much as a stupid little girl could."

"Right." It was all Jere could think of to say. Well, he also thought of calling her a dreadful troll, an ungrateful bitch, and a psychopath, but "right" was the only *appropriate* thing he could think of to say.

They continued to converse, Annika asserting her... whatever she had, at each and every given chance. The slave returned and cleaned up the broken glass, providing Jere with a fresh drink at the same time. When she handed it to him, she mouthed "thank you" one more time. Jere resisted the urge to take her away, and strategically positioned himself between the poor girl and her vapid mistress whenever possible throughout the night.

Paltrek didn't seem like too bad a guy, certainly more quiet and friendly than his sister, even if it did seem to be exclusively related to his cavalier style. In general, both Wysocka children were young adult versions of spoiled little brats — Daddy had everything, so they had everything, and the possibility of *not* having everything was incomprehensible. While Annika had developed her own gift, Paltrek Junior had followed in the footsteps — mindsteps, if you could call them that—of his father, and excelled at mathematical computations and probabilities. He had expected to take over his father's investments since he was a little boy, and saw no reason to explore the world further than his own front door.

Paltrek took it upon himself to introduce Jere to some of Hojer's other "finest" young up-and-coming members of the wealthy sect of society. Free people, all of them, although Jere noticed that a few were accompanied by their slaves as well.

"There is something you *have* to see," Paltrek told him with a smirk, pulling Jere along behind him by the arm. "Forget your city entertainment—this will be something to write home about!"

Jere was a little apprehensive as he was led down a hallway and into what appeared to be some sort of ballroom. At the center of the room, a group of people stood, laughing and cheering for something. Jere allowed himself to be pulled right into the action, where he saw two young men, both naked and covered in what appeared to be some sort of grease, wrestling each other with nervous looks on their faces.

"What is this?" Jere asked, uncomfortable at the scene. He had been to clubs where this sort of entertainment would be appropriate, but a private party?

"Slave wrestling," Paltrek said, as if it were nothing unusual. "First one pinned loses. You can place bets, the biggest winner gets the payout *and* the use of the winning slave for the night. It makes lending them out a bit more interesting, if you know what I mean!"

Jere tried not to let it show that he was horrified at the idea of lending another human being out. "What do the slaves get out of it?" he wondered.

Paltrek clapped him on the back, laughing heartily. "You've got quite the sense of humor!"

He hadn't meant it to be a joke. "I mean, I understand that they're following orders, but why would they want to win?" Jere asked, wondering if he really wanted to know. There had to be some benefit to this, right?

"Oh, the winning slave gets to fuck someone for once, and the losing slave is sort of a consolation prize to everyone who didn't win," Paltrek explained. "Wrestling must be so boring where you come from."

Jere didn't respond. He was a little confused—the winning slave got to top the free man, then? It seemed a strange prize, but he didn't really want to know any more. The looks on the faces of the spectators made Jere uncomfortable; a dozen or so men and women leered at the pair with hungry, lustful eyes. He wanted the whole scene to be over.

The slaves were evenly matched, as far as size went, but one was clearly more seasoned at wrestling. For every move his opponent made, he countered it, ducking and darting with efficiency and a resolute look. The spectators might have been smiling, but it was clear that these two slaves were seriously engaged. The grease on their skin made it hard for either of them to get a good grip with their hands, but they used the rest of their bodies to compensate, wrapping around each other and intertwining limbs. Finally, the less seasoned of the two was on the ground, and Jere breathed a sigh of relief.

"All right, he won, can we go now?" he asked, unwilling to walk away from his host.

"Keep watching, Jeremy, they're just starting!" Paltrek insisted.

"But you said, when one is pinned...?"

Paltrek laughed. "He's just *down*, man, pinned is more, you know...."

Jere didn't want to know, although the truth was threatening to invade his brain. His attention was suddenly drawn to the hard, ready cocks of the slaves, the way their sparring had taken a decidedly erotic turn.

Paltrek must have taken his silence for confusion. He leaned over, whispering in Jere's ear with a knowing smile. "One of them has to *penetrate* the other one. Fuck him. Have *sex* with him. You know what I mean?"

Jere forced himself not to shudder. "Yeah," he answered, feeling more uncomfortable than he had before. How could anyone speak so crudely of such a horrific act?

"My bet's on the weaker one," Paltrek said, oblivious to Jere's discomfort. "He's not graceful, but I hear he's desperate."

Jere said nothing. He stayed, trapped on the spot, and forced himself to watch as the two slaves fought toward their true goal — not to knock one another down, but to fuck.

He thought Paltrek was wrong about the winner, as the more seasoned wrestler had worked himself into position, holding the other slave beneath him, aiming his cock between the other man's legs. The weaker slave seemed to have given up, lying still and silent. At the last second, however, he slid between his opponent's legs, out from underneath him, and pinned the better fighter face down on the floor. He was anything but graceful as he held the other man down by his neck, trapped his legs with his own, and shoved into him a second later. Jere watched in horror as the winning slave pumped in and out of the loser's body, throwing his head back victoriously as he did so.

"If they're quick enough, sometimes they get to come before they're taken for the prize," Paltrek explained, smiling. "I called it, didn't I?"

"Yeah," Jere managed, unable to stop watching. It should have been hot, seeing this man fucking the other, seeing his hands fight to grip bruised hips and his mouth press against a slippery shoulder. He should have been able to enjoy the cry of release from the slave on top as he came. But neither of the slaves seemed to be enjoying themselves.

Before long, an older man with haughty look came to collect his prize, and the winner went with him obediently, looking relieved. The loser, however, had tears in his eyes and was begging forgiveness from his master for losing, at least until a kick silenced him. Jere continued to stare in shock as the first person came forward to claim the slave as a "consolation prize."

"Want to have a go at him?" Paltrek offered. "You didn't bet, but hey, nobody will notice one more."

Jere fought back the urge to be sick. "No."

"Suit yourself," Paltrek shrugged, walking toward the crowd.

Jere stood in shock for a moment. The gathered crowd obscured his view, but he could still hear the guttural sounds and occasional whimper of the slave, and he took both as his cue to leave. Overall, Jere tried to ignore interactions between slaves and masters as best he could, although he was relieved to see that none of the other guests were as particularly vicious to their slaves as Annika was. Still, the casual indifference with which they ignored them, cuffed them, treated them worse than most people would treat their dogs — Jere found himself sickened more than once. He couldn't even process the horrors of the wrestling, or the subsequent gang-bang.

Wren had told him that, since this was his first Holiday party of the year, and also one of the most prominent, he had to stay at least until the party died down. Of course, Wren hadn't told him this quite so explicitly. No, he wouldn't have dared. Jere hadn't been pleased, but was never one to shoot the messenger. He suffered through the party as well as possible, introducing himself, meeting people, and taking in the general scene while trying not to be too overwhelmed. He tried not to consume too many gin and tonics.

As the party finally wound down and people were starting to leave, Jere happily made his way toward his coat — and the door. He was met, rather surprisingly, with a few offers to have coffee or drinks later, including one from both the male and the female Wysockas, and many reminders to come to other holiday parties.

Paltrek grabbed his arm on his way out the door. "And what bout you, Jer'my? You gon' have a Winter Hol'day party?" He slurred his words, reeking of alcohol, and passed over those unnecessary syllables.

"Uh, well, I'd have to consult—" Jere froze. He couldn't very well mention exactly who he would consult. "—er, my schedule. Yes."

"Good!" Paltrek clapped him on the back, all together too hard. "I'll seeya 'round, buddy!"

Jere smiled and nodded, making his way home quickly. He rather hoped that Wren would still be up, although he had specifically told him that there was no need to stay up until he arrived at home.

Chapter 18
Awakening Awareness

Despite his master's insistence, Wren had stayed up waiting. He had mostly become comfortable enough to trust that the man wasn't setting him up for punishment, not like Burghe used to do. Still, he thought that his master might need something when he came home, and garnering additional favor was never a bad idea with any master. While he was reluctant to admit it, even to himself, the house did seem a little lonely without Jere around.

He heard keys jingling in the lock, and in a second, he had jumped up from the couch to open it. He still wasn't completely certain whether sitting on the couch when he was alone was acceptable or not. He'd rather not find out it wasn't.

"Wren," Jere said, a big smile spreading across his face as he saw him.

Wren tried to quell the fear that a smile like that brought with it. His other master had only been that excited to see him when he had devised a horrid new punishment or was planning to use him in some terrible, painful way in bed, and....

"Glad you're up, don't think I could sleep after all that excitement!" Jere allowed Wren to take his coat. "Say, do we have gin?"

Wren laughed inside at the use of "we." Jere tended to speak that way, as if they were housemates or something benign. So, the master just wanted company. "Sir, I'm not sure, but I do believe that Master Burghe kept a bottle of something behind the bottom drawer in his desk."

Jere's face lit up. "Wonderful! I'm not usually much of a drinker anymore, but I really could have used a few more tonight!"

Wren said nothing, just fetched the bottle, which turned out to be whiskey.

"Splendid!" Jere beckoned him toward the couch. "Will you join me?"

Wren faltered for a moment. Slaves, as a general rule, were not allowed to drink. "I, sir, uh...."

"Oh, come on," Jere insisted. "Nobody else will know. It will be our little secret."

Wren nodded. "If you wish, sir." He sped off to get glasses before Jere could respond. He grabbed a lime as well, trying to postpone going back out to the living room. He realized that his master was a bit drunk already and was terrified to imagine what would happen should he continue to drink.

Wren placed the glasses on the coffee table and poured the whiskey into them. He held out a piece of the lime to Jere. "Sir?" he prompted, drawing Jere away from his thoughts.

Jere smiled. "Yes, thank you."

"My old master, that's how he liked it," Wren said, by way of explanation.

"Whiskey with a quarter of a lime, sometimes a spoonful of sugar in the first one," Jere said with a grin. "To help it go down easier."

Wren was startled. He and Jere probably both knew Burghe better than they did one another.

"I've always preferred gin myself, but when Matthias and I went for drinks, it was always this," Jere said, tossing down the drink in one go. "Of course, he would always give me a disapproving glare for drinking this fast."

Wren said nothing, but refilled his glass. Jere swallowed it down just as quickly, and Wren filled a third with trepidation.

Jere must have caught the feeling, because he allowed the glass to sit on the table, looking curiously at Wren. "Not much for drinking, then?"

Wren answered truthfully. "I've only had sips of free people's drinks, sir." What he didn't add was that he would rather be aware of what was happening around him, in case it turned sour.

Jere grinned. "Well, have at it—if you'd like, though, only if you'd like. Honestly, I didn't mean to pressure you, Wren. I just... I didn't want to drink alone."

Wren relaxed a tiny bit. Of course, his master never had any sort of awful intentions — hell, most of the time, he just seemed like a sad, lonely little boy, too afraid to ask the kid next door to come out and play. He could have ordered Wren to do anything he wanted, but that wasn't the way he worked. Haltingly, Wren took a little sip of his drink. It was bitter and it burned, but it did leave a pleasantly warm sensation in his throat. He struggled not to cough.

Jere laughed. "I feel like I'm corrupting the youth," he teased.

Wren took another sip, trying to steel himself against it a bit better. He wasn't very successful.

"I was told I have to host a party."

Wren's third sip of whiskey nearly choked him, combined with that news. "Sir?" he managed to sputter.

"Everyone asked. It was awkward." Jere swirled his drink around, seemingly debating whether to drink it or not. He set it down. "I didn't *want* to have a party."

They had discussed this, ever so briefly, when they had discussed the parties that Jere would attend. Jere had outwardly refused.

"And now, sir?" Wren tried to maintain his composure.

"Well... it seems I don't really have an awful lot of choice."

Wren found himself struck by the irony of the situation. A free person, moaning about his lack of choice?

"Would you help me plan it?" Jere almost seemed to be begging. "I wouldn't even know where to begin!"

Wren nodded. "If you'd like, sir."

Jere smiled. "Good! We can do that tomorrow, though. Too tired tonight."

They sat there quietly, Jere finishing his third drink, and Wren getting about halfway through his.

"Wren?"

"Yes, sir?" Wren had almost been enjoying the silent company.

Jere was silent for a moment, and when he spoke, his voice was somber. "I don't really know how to say this, but, slaves are treated horribly. I'm sorry."

Wren decided that the rest of his drink was a good idea, after all. He swallowed it down. "Thank you, sir."

"Have you met the Wysockas?"

Wren nodded. Burghe had been friends with the elder Paltrek Wysocka.

"Annika, the girl?"

"Yes, sir. Although, only a few times." One only really needed to meet someone of her character a few times.

Jere was quiet for a bit. "She's a horrid person."

Wren agreed, privately, but knew better than to speak such a thing out loud. "As you will, sir."

Jere laughed. "Always the diplomat." He poured both of them another drink, before Wren even realized he wanted one. He swallowed it down, wincing slightly at the taste. "The things she did to that girl—and it wasn't just her, you know? It was everyone there. It was the way things were."

Wren wasn't entirely sure he was following the master. He nodded anyway, hoping to agree with, well, whatever it was that Jere was trying to say.

"Was he like that with you?" Jere demanded, sounding angry, but not quite. "Matthias. Was he like that?"

Wren tried to push away the fear. "Like... like what, sir?"

Jere sat back, closing his eyes. "Like they treated their slaves, like they were less than furniture, less than animals. She, Annika, she had that girl—*tried* to have that girl—pick up glass with her bare hands. Sweep it up!" He made a gesture of sweeping with his own hand. "Just like that. Like it wouldn't cut her. No. No, she *knew* it would cut her!"

Wren had felt his own back used to put out lit cigarettes enough to know exactly what kind of treatment Jere was referring to. "Master Burghe treated me as he saw fit, sir."

Jere frowned at him, eyes a little bit unfocused. "Please don't sugarcoat it."

It wasn't a request. It was an order. Wren's mounting discomfort grew. "Yes. Yes, sir, he did treat me that way."

"Bastard." Jere's tone was flat. He drew his knees up under himself, wrapped one arm around them, and held out his glass toward Wren.

Against all his instincts, Wren hesitated. "Sir, I'm not sure...."

Jere laughed, putting his head down on his knees. "You're right, I shouldn't have any more." He tossed the glass behind him, not angrily, more in a way that suggested he had forgotten how physics worked.

Fortunately, Wren was prepared, catching the glass and depositing it in the kitchen in no time. He returned to the couch to find Jere still huddled in a ball, barely sitting up. He sat down again, unsure of what else to do.

"I kind of hate it here."

"I'm sorry, sir."

"Don't be. I'm a fucking whiner, is all. I have a great job, all the money I want, I'm not eating synth food, I have heat and water and I buy clothes from fucking catalogues. I come and go as I please, and I never have to worry about anything ever again, and I'm bitching about it. And I have you. I never would have made it without you, you know? It's funny, I was terrified when I found out I had a slave. *Terrified.* Because I thought you'd judge me or something. God, was I stupid. You're the best, the best thing that could have come with this place."

Wren was struck dumb. He knew it was just drunk-speak, but still, hearing such kind words was so much nicer than just being slapped harder and raped more sloppily. "Thank you, sir."

Jere's eyes were somewhat glazed over. "It was good of you to not let me have that last drink." He nodded a few times, as if agreeing to some far-off advice. "Very good. Can we go to bed now?"

Wren's stomach lurched, threatening to betray his fear. "Yes, sir."

They stood up, and Wren understood why his master had asked if "they" could go to bed. He stumbled drunkenly down the hall, heading toward his room, and was perplexed by the door handle. Moving as quickly as possible, Wren twisted the knob and pushed it open, backing away quickly. Jere smiled, taking a few steps forward and pausing in the doorway. Wren hesitated, hoping his presence would not be required any longer.

Jere reached out an arm toward him quickly, causing Wren to

flinch back. "Thank you," he said, quite sincerely, looking him in the eyes. "And I'm sorry for everything he did to you."

Wren blinked back tears that arose, unbidden. Dammit. It was always kindness that got to him.

"You deserve so much more," Jere said softly, then, rather impulsively, pulled him close and hugged him tightly before retreating. "Good night, Wren." He pulled the door mostly closed behind him.

Wren was left standing there, shocked. He heard the bed creak a moment later, and then, silence. Shaking his head at the absurdity of the whole damn night, he wandered back to his own room, falling quickly into sleep.

Some time later, he heard his door creak open. He looked over to find his master, completely naked, moonlight from the hallway spilling in behind him.

Which was strange, because there were no windows in the hallway.

"Wren," Jere said, his voice full of longing and hunger. The light glistened off his skin, his hair, his eyes, and he smiled so kindly!

Wren wasn't afraid. He smiled back, crooking his finger, beckoning.

Jere came to him, eyes almost glowing, mouth slack with desire. He stood at the end of the bed, skin glistening in the moonlight, his cock hard and ready. He brushed his hand over it, his eyes fixated on Wren's, and he smiled. "You deserve so much better, Wren. You deserve *me*."

"Well, then, I guess I'll just have to have *you*, now won't I?" Wren purred back, turning down silk sheets to reveal himself sleeping naked under the covers. He was ready to take his master wherever he wanted to go, eager to grind together with him. He spread his legs and leaned back, stretching out and feeling his pulse begin to quicken.

With a hungry moan, the master slipped on top of him, pressing his smooth, muscled chest against Wren's, careful not to put too much weight down all at once, moving like a cat above him. He slid his body up and down across Wren's, every touch seeming to send electric sparks through their skin. Wren gasped at how good it felt, bringing his hands up to feel his way across Jere's skin, touching the muscles on his back, lifting his legs up and wrapping them around Jere's ass.

Wren whimpered longingly as Jere put one hand on his face, caressing him, and kissed him, slowly, just like that, his tongue making its way in and meeting no resistance. Wren returned the kiss, just as deep, and he clutched harder at Jere's back when he felt teeth graze his tongue ever so slightly. Meanwhile, he felt Jere's other hand on his chest, working its way down, stroking his neck and chest, down across the sensitive skin on his stomach, and creeping down lower... and lower... and lower....

As his master's hand worked its way down and between his legs, his teeth bit lightly at Wren's lower lip, pulling it carefully, making Wren moan in pleasure and thrust up at him more. He felt the hand encircling his cock and he cried out, wanting to feel it more, wanting the feeling to continue forever. He felt the hand tighten and he struggled to hold back, a battle he quickly quickly lost.

Wren woke up yelping, not in fear, as he so often did, but in shock and surprise.

A sex dream about his master? Wren had to struggle to resist rushing to take a shower, a cold, unpleasant one to wash away the excitement and pleasure and enjoyment he had just felt. The fantasy he'd had about his master after being whipped at the police post had been bad enough, but at least then he could pretend that he wasn't thinking clearly. Now he had no excuse, not unless he wanted his master to use him like this, which he didn't, it would be selfish and wrong and it would mean that he actually wanted to be touched. To be used like the slave he was. To enjoy another person.

Chapter 19
Working Together

Jere woke up to a splitting headache, with an aspirin and a glass of water next to his bed. He ignored the first, put the second in his mouth, and chased it away with the third. Then he pulled his head back under the covers to block out the horrid, horrid light, and tried not to moan.

He felt around mentally, noticing that Wren was awake. Of course Wren was awake, Wren was always awake and alert and not hungover. *"Thanks for the aspirin,"* he spoke. Mindspeak was so much less jarring to his ears.

"You're welcome, sir. Would it please you if I made breakfast, sir?"

Jere noticed that Wren seemed a bit on edge. Had something happened last night?

"Um, yeah, actually, breakfast would be spectacular. Bring some for yourself, as well."

He hadn't really meant to say "bring" some, had he? Hadn't he meant "make" some? No, no, he certainly hadn't. The thought of getting up and out of this bed made his stomach clench miserably.

Wren was silent for much longer than usual. *"Yes, sir,"* was his only reply.

A few minutes later, the smell of freshly cooked bacon and eggs and other breakfast things filled the house. Jere smiled, and managed to at least sit up before Wren came in, holding a tray with a variety of food on it.

"Good morning, sir." He was looking at the tray, as if nervous about spilling it. Jere knew damn well that he had perfect balance. His head was pounding too much to think further about Wren's nervousness.

"That smells fucking incredible!" Jere stared at the food. Suddenly, the nausea was dissipating in favor of hunger. "Are those omelets?"

Wren nodded. "Yes, sir." He stood next to the bed, holding the tray out to Jere as if he expected to stand there and hold it the entire time Jere was eating. Jere wouldn't have been surprised if that was *exactly* what the kid was thinking.

"Here, pull that chair up, sit and eat," Jere gestured toward an armchair near a window. He pulled the food tray toward himself, resting it on the bed.

Wren did as instructed, and was soon seated near the side of Jere's bed. He took up a plate and began to eat, almost timidly, watching Jere for any signs of needing something. Jere reached out to grab his own food, dropping the blankets to waist level, revealing his bare chest, as he had tossed his shirt aside at some point during the night.

He heard a choking noise, and looked up from his eggs. "Wren, are you all right?"

"Fine. Fine, sir." Wren managed to gasp, drinking some juice. "Thank you, I just, I must not have chewed enough."

Jere nodded, continuing to eat. The slave was acting even stranger today than usual. "Wren, did something happen last night?"

Wren had completely composed himself by now. He wiped at his mouth with a napkin before he spoke, always proper. "No, sir. You came home from the party, had a few drinks, and went to bed."

Jere remembered the party, remembered the drinks… remembered going on and on about how horrible Hojer was… remembered a small, warm body in his arms for a moment….

"I told you I was asked to host a party, right?" Jere did *not* want to think any more about that small warm body, or how it felt to be so close to him.

Wren nodded. "Yes, sir."

Jere would much rather have performed open-heart surgery on himself. "I suppose it's the thing to do, am I right?"

"If it pleases you, sir."

"Well, it doesn't, but I know you well enough to know that that means yes." Jere was a bit grumpy at the thought, however resigned. "So what do we do?"

"We, sir?" Wren gave him that deer in headlights look again. "I'll do whatever you require of me, sir."

"Of course," Jere sighed. "But really, Wren, I have no idea how to do this! I mean, help me out here. Tell me what needs to be done, and then I'll figure out what you can do and what I can do and how not to make this completely bomb."

So Wren explained how hosting a party would work, how Jere's party could be at the end of the season, perhaps the *last* of the season, to make an impression. He explained how there were right and wrong people to invite (and was instantly awarded the job of inviting these "right" people), and certain customs to be followed. He even ventured to explain some of the meaning and the relevance, and the importance of such parties to social status. By the time he had finished, Jere was staring at him, somewhat slack-jawed.

"Will you be there?" Jere had tried to sound casual. He was pretty sure he came off more as a child asking Mum to come to his first day of school.

Wren looked away for a second before nodding stiffly. "Yes, sir. A host's slave is always in attendance at such events to serve the guests."

Jere nodded, thinking of Arae and the rest of the Wysockas' slaves that had been running around. He tried not to shudder, pushing *that* image out of his head.

"But would you be able to keep up with all of them?"

"I would do my best, sir. But I—I would only be able to go as quickly as they ordered and dismissed me."

Jere made an active effort to avoid being rankled at the idea of someone "dismissing" Wren.

"Or, you could rent slaves from the labor services department, sir."

Jere was appalled at the idea that he could rent human beings like he could rent equipment. Of course, he was living in a country where people were *owned* like equipment, but the thought was still unsettling.

"Would that make it better for you?" he asked, a little confused when Wren started to redden.

"Yes, sir. It would serve your guests most expediently."

Jere nodded. "That settles it, then. You'll set that up?"

Wren shook his head. "I'm sorry, sir, but I can't make any sort of binding agreement like that, sir. Nor can a slave assume control of another slave."

"Right, right," Jere wanted to kick himself. "I forgot. Um, just tell me what to do and how to do it, okay?"

Wren nodded. "Yes, sir. May I get a pen and paper to write things down, sir?"

Jere nodded, and Wren cleared away breakfast and returned with a pen and paper.

"You'll need two or three slaves — would you like them for anything other than serving drinks, sir?"

"Well, I suppose it might be nice to have help with cleanup?" Jere suggested. He could tell by Wren's look that cleaning wasn't exactly what he had been talking about.

"Other… *services* for your guests, sir?" Wren emphasized.

Jere's thoughts flashed to the "wrestling" he had witnessed, and the activities that had taken place afterward, despite his best efforts to forget it. He tried not to squirm uncomfortably. He didn't succeed. "I'm not going to *rent* someone and then whore them out!"

Wren grew very still. "As you wish, sir." He busied himself writing on the pad of paper.

Jere felt the tension, the fear underlying it. "Wren."

"Yes, sir?"

"I'm not going to whore you out, either."

Jere felt most of the tension relaxing. This kid projected his feelings *so* hard for someone without a mind gift. "Is there a tactful way to make that clear to everyone?"

Wren nodded. "Don't offer them to anyone, sir. It's considered horribly impolite to ask for such a thing unless you are close friends, and you aren't that close with anyone here, not yet. By not offering, you'll seem aloof, or at worst, greedy. Nobody would fault you for being greedy, you've only recently acquired a slave. Social customs dictate that it would be acceptable to caress or touch another's slave, but not to undress or have sex with or hurt them in any way."

"I don't want anyone else touching you." The possessive growl escaped Jere's lips before he had a chance to think about it.

Wren smiled back at him, shyly, and Jere tried unsuccessfully to be less embarrassed.

"Sir, I appreciate that. Perhaps if you just, you know, do *that* if anyone tries anything...." Uncharacteristically, Wren seemed to be struggling not to laugh.

"Well." Jere said. He hadn't quite gotten his point across with just that word, had he? "Well, I like you. And you're mine. And I care about you. In a caring way. I don't want anyone getting any ideas or taking any liberties."

Wren rewarded him with a very sincere smile this time. "Sir, we can communicate through the mind connection. I trust that you wouldn't let anything get out of hand."

He trusted him? That was new. Jere smiled back. "All right, then. I do hope that this party doesn't serve to make me *less* socially acceptable."

"I'll do my best, sir." Wren was grinning at him slightly. "Now, what kinds of food would you like served?"

They continued discussing the plans for the party for a while, working out decorations, times, food, and everything else that went into such an event. The Winter Holiday parties were really set up like some sort of ball or celebration. There were a thousand little details, and Jere was certain he would never have had any idea of how to deal with them if not for Wren. He was growing to like him more and more. The tactile memory of Wren in his arms wasn't so bad, either.

Chapter 20
Unexpected Visitors

Two weeks had passed since Wren had coached Jere through his first Winter Holiday party. He eased him through three more, even encouraged him to leave one early. He was unnerved by how easily he found himself advising his master these days. He was getting an awful lot of practice at it. He had even volunteered to attend a few of the parties with him, but Jere had adamantly refused. Aside from wanting to avoid being one of "those people" who dragged their slaves around everywhere, Jere explained that he didn't trust himself to act like an appropriate "master" in public, and didn't want to place Wren's welfare on the line. Wren couldn't help but feel touched by the concern.

The party preparations were coming along well, and a part of him was starting to feel excited, like back when he was a little boy, for all the excitement that was soon to come. Of course, when he had been a little boy he hadn't had mind-numbing terror creeping in, reminding him of all the things that could go badly at the party.

Wren had come to accept, rather grudgingly, that his master probably wouldn't hurt him. It certainly wasn't out of the question, but Wren was willing to bet that Jere's moral code would forbid him from punishing Wren for anything but the most heinous of offenses. The idea boggled his mind, but he was quite comfortable with it, and he had grown equally accustomed to the luxuries his outlander master afforded him on a daily basis. Food. Furniture. Coffee. Respect.

The party, with all of its intricacies and social demands and uncertainty, made him painfully nervous. He wasn't bothered by the ten to twenty people who came by the house *daily* to have medical needs attended to; after all, Wren's role was very clearly designated there. There were rules, procedures, clear expectations. All of these things made Wren feel at least a little safer.

However, since Jere had arrived, he hadn't had a single visitor, not one person from the town or on business or anything. When he did meet with other people, Jere always went out. Jere's excuse was that he liked getting out of the house sometimes, not that he *needed* an excuse. Wren liked that nobody else was around. His master still tended to be naïve and somewhat uninformed about the way things worked as a slave-owner. Wren was perfectly thrilled with that. If things stayed the way they were, those little luxuries were much less likely to be revoked. He was further reassured by the horror on Jere's face every time he returned from a party where he had seen something "awful," which, as Wren knew, was *nothing* in the grand scheme of a slave's life.

But the thought of having other people, other *free* people in the house…. Wren was certain he had a right to be nervous. Just as certain as he was that Jere had no idea what conflicts could come up, what problems there could be, how much their peaceful life could change.

Which was why, when Jere mentioned casually over lunch that he was having visitors for dinner, Wren wanted to throw up.

"Sir?" His voice was shaking. He tried to do everything in his power to steady it. "Wh-who's coming?"

"The Wysockas — Paltrek and Annika." Jere was, as usual, oblivious. "I was hoping Annika wouldn't come, but it seems she sort of invited herself. I guess we really hit it off at the last few parties."

Wren looked down at his food. It was no longer appetizing. "Sir, I…." He didn't even know what to say. What he wanted to say was unpleasant, but he'd rather cut out his own tongue than speak such offensive words to his master. He was a slave, he reminded himself bitterly, and it was his job to serve his master *and* any guests.

Jere looked up at him, realizing something was off, and probably catching the anxiety Wren was trying desperately to hold at bay. "Oh, Wren, I'm sorry, I should have told you sooner! Paltrek caught me through the mind connection yesterday and mentioned it. I do hope, I mean, well, I don't really know how this works, having guests and all. I mean, with a housemate...."

A housemate. A fucking housemate!? You didn't have housemates serve and pamper you. You wouldn't offer your housemate up as a fucktoy to your guests. Slaves were not housemates! Housemates could leave! Housemates could say no!

"It's fine, sir. This is your house, of course you can have guests whenever you please."

Jere nodded. "Sure, but I'd also like to be a little considerate. This does affect you, too. And probably more than I even realize."

Well, that earned him points at least. "Yes, sir. I mean, it can, if you want. I mean, it always does, but how it does it—"

"How do we act when we have guests?" Jere cut him off, almost unintentionally. Wren was glad; he wasn't making much sense, anyway.

"Sir, the appropriate thing would be for me to serve you and your guests." Wren couldn't believe he was explaining this. "I'll answer the door, take jackets, make dinner, serve it to you, refill drinks, that sort of thing."

"Well, then, when will you eat?"

"Thank you for your concern, sir, but really, I'll be fine." Wren felt his face flushing with anger, and he looked down, hoping he could hide it. For as long as it had been since Jere had arrived, he was still painfully ignorant at times, and Wren wondered if the benefits of that were still outweighing the drawbacks.

"It's the socially acceptable thing to do, right?" Jere seemed incredibly displeased by this.

Wren nodded.

"Will they bring slaves?" Jere seemed appalled at the idea. "Is that a thing you do—lug slaves around with you like a purse? Is that acceptable? Do people do that for casual get-togethers?"

Wren nodded again. "Yes, sir. Miss Wysocka will probably bring her girl; she is rarely without her."

"Because she's clearly so fond of her," Jere muttered. "Okay, well then, what do I do with that? Fuck. Why didn't I ask you about this sooner!"

Wren had been wondering the same thing, but figured it was

wiser to just take things as they came. "Well, sir, there's not much for you to do. You don't have to feed her—the slave, I mean—in fact, if I'm correct, Miss Wysocka rarely lets the girl eat, just hand feeds her here and there if it amuses her. She'll stay out of the way, unless her mistress orders her to do something different."

Jere was silent for a moment. "Can I kick her out of my house if she does something awful?"

Wren assumed he was talking about Miss Wysocka, not her slave. He would like to see that! "It is your house, sir, you may do as you see fit inside of it."

"Good." Jere seemed satisfied, but only for a minute. "And what about you?"

"Me, sir?" Wren didn't even want to try to guess what exactly his master was asking.

"What do you do? I'm guessing we don't just go about our night as normal?"

Wren finally understood what he was asking. Yes, he usually served Jere, but not in any sort of formal way. Not in any sort of way that would be acceptable around company. "No, sir. I'll be serving you—like a butler, maybe?" Jere's look started to worry him. He was looking so disapproving! "Of course, I mean, sir, this is just the way that things are usually done. You can certainly do as you please."

Jere waved him off casually. "How will I know what to do? Fuck, what *not* to do?"

"Well, I've explained most of it, sir," Wren said. "And the rest, if you don't mind, sir, uh, I could guide you?" It seemed wrong, *so* wrong, but his master had asked for help.

Jere nodded. "All right. You lead, I'll follow. Mindspeak for anything more complicated."

Jere had to return to patients rather quickly, leaving Wren attempting to quell his panic and prepare for guests and the possibility of ordering his master around through mindspeak. He started by tidying up a bit, certain that things were horribly, horribly dirty, and that any and all punishment would fall on him for leaving it so. His earlier thoughts that Jere wouldn't harm him seemed stupid now, in the face of something that could actually be threatening. He had never been more thrilled to have a speed gift in his life.

It was around dinnertime when Jere looked at Wren, somewhat apologetically, and muttered, "They're almost to the door."

Wren said nothing, a bit choked up with fear, but flew to open the door the moment he heard a knock.

The Wysockas came in without so much as noticing Wren, for which he was rather grateful. He would have gotten his master and announced him formally, but Jere was there already, oblivious to the regular protocol.

"Jeremy!" Paltrek clapped him on the back like they were old friends. Wren suppressed a sigh as he readied himself to take the jacket that was about to be taken off. The young Wysocka heir was acting like he had known Jere for years, not just a few weeks, as was really the case.

"Paltrek," Jere smiled, rather reservedly. "So glad you could make it! Hi, Annika."

Wren didn't have to have any connection with his master to read his distaste for the female. But whatever sense Wren had, Annika didn't, because a moment later, she had wrapped her arms around Jere's neck in a big hug.

"Oh, hi, Jeremy," she beamed up at him. "My, it's lovely to see each other outside of big social engagements, isn't it?"

"Uh, yeah," Jere tried to wrest himself from her grip tactfully. "Shall we, um...."

"*You might offer them a drink before dinner, sir,*" Wren suggested.

Jere's face brightened. "Have a drink, before dinner?" Paltrek and Annika nodded, the latter a bit overly enthusiastic.

"Forgetting something, sis?" Paltrek mentioned as they moved toward the sitting room.

"What?" Annika was clearly irritated. "Oh." She spared a glance for Wren for the first time. "Get the door, boy."

Before Jere could protest, Wren was at the door. He opened it to find Annika's slave, cold, wet, and half-naked on the doorstep. She walked in slowly, controlled, despite the fact that her skin was nearly blue. In the same controlled manner, she went immediately to her mistress, dropped to the floor, and pressed herself to Annika's feet.

"Thank you, mistress," her voice was barely a whisper, and a shaking one at that. "I apologize for inconveniencing you."

"Keep that in mind next time you complain about the weather, slut." Annika kicked lightly at her shoulder.

As often as Wren projected emotions, it was rare for him to feel them projected back. He was suddenly consumed with rage that he knew was not his own as Jere walked purposefully toward Annika and Arae. With nothing more than a glare at Annika, Jere knelt down next to the slave and put a hand on either side of her face.

"Are you all right?" he demanded.

Arae nodded. Too quickly.

Without standing up or even turning around, Jere let out a very irritated grunt. "What is the meaning of this? She's been left out in the cold, in little more than underclothes, and she's cut up from head to toe!"

"The cuts are from earlier, the outfit is what I prefer her in, and she was being obstinate on the way over here," Annika spoke casually, as if she were explaining why she liked lemon cake more than chocolate.

Jere hadn't released his hold on the girl. "May I heal you?"

Arae began to tremble. "Please, sir," she whimpered. "You would have to ask my mistress."

Jere didn't move. "Allow me to heal her." It wasn't a question.

"Fine, do whatever with her," Annika moved away from them both. "What do you have to drink?"

Jere seemed to be pointedly ignoring her. He looked at Arae. "Will you let me in?" he asked, softly enough that her mistress wouldn't hear it over her own mindless prattling. The girl nodded, and Jere was silent as he quickly worked his way through her injuries. Wren would have guessed that there were many, ranging from visible cuts and bruises and extending to frostbite and hypothermia that must have been starting to set in.

He finished just a few minutes later. "Wren, go and get her a robe." There was no room for argument. In fact, Wren was pretty sure that he had only heard such a direct order from his master once or twice before. As such, he moved to obey very quickly.

He returned and handed it over immediately, and Jere wrapped it around the still trembling girl. "Put it on."

Wren watched his master stand up, visibly compose himself, and then stride purposefully toward the living room. He seemed to be ready to leave well enough alone, but....

"Didn't mean to bother you," Annika said, off-handed.

"You didn't bother me." Jere's tone was flat and cold, cold enough for Wren to feel uncomfortable just hearing it. "You disgusted me. Wren, a gin and tonic please, and whatever they would like."

Wren could only nod, dumbstruck. Never, in the four months since he had been with Jere, had he heard him being so harsh.

" ...and orange juice," Wren distantly heard Paltrek saying.

"Same," Annika was sort of pouty. "And don't skimp on the alcohol!"

"Yes sir, yes miss," Wren said. What had they ordered? What the hell had the man said while Wren was caught up in his self-induced terror? He wandered off toward the kitchen, trying not to panic as he made his master his drink.

"*Vodka, Wren.*" Jere's voice was suddenly in his head. "*Vodka and orange juice. Did I go too far?*"

Wren breathed in relief as he made the drinks. "*I think Miss Wysocka thinks any challenge is too far, sir.*"

"*But not socially blacklisted 'too far'?*"

"*No, sir. She's not attentive enough to care that much anyway.*"

"*Thank you, Wren. And I'm sorry I startled you. I usually have a bit more restraint.*"

"*Thank you, sir. You are very kind.*" Wren placed the drinks on a tray and walked them out, serving his master first, only partially because it was the socially appropriate thing to do. At that moment, he found himself surprisingly proud to be serving this man.

The banter, as usual, was dull. Wren was mildly attentive in hopes of saving Jere from any more social mishaps. He stood off to the side of the room, unobtrusively waiting, ready to refill drinks or fetch anything whenever necessary and as quickly as possible. It was a familiar feeling, almost comforting. When dinner was ready he disappeared to the kitchen and began to bring plates out to the table. Jere and his guests came in and were seated, and Wren refilled their drinks and stood by, in case he was needed. More mindless banter that didn't concern him.

And then, it did.

It had gotten quiet all of a sudden, the awkward lull in a conversation between people who truly don't know each other all that well. Socially graceful people might have taken a moment like this to compliment the quality of the food and drink, or inquire about a unique painting in the house.

Annika looked at Wren, standing near the doorway. "I bet you coddle him."

"Excuse me?" Jere replied, caught off-guard.

"Outlanders!" Annika shook her head. "You should whip him."

Wren felt his stomach lurch, and when his master didn't immediately respond, the feeling only intensified. Of course, he tried to remind himself that this was Jere's way of responding to awkward situations, to be calm, cool, and collected, but it was hard to keep that in mind at the moment.

"Why?" Jere said finally.

Wren wanted to run from the room. Surely, he wasn't considering this?

"He hasn't done a thing wrong," Jere pointed out, looking challengingly at Annika.

She laughed. "Honestly? That's not entirely necessary. Besides. He's haughty."

Wren's stomach continued to do flip-flops.

"Haughty?" Jere was disbelieving. "How so?"

"Look at him." Annika's eyes looked at him appraisingly. "He's all stiff and still—it's unnatural, really."

"Perhaps there's something making him uncomfortable," Jere narrowed his eyebrows.

"It's not his place to show discomfort." Annika's words were cold, detached. She may as well have been talking about the proper way to judge wine. "He's not very affectionate, either. I mean, even this stupid little slut knows who her mistress is and how to show her appreciation."

As if on cue, Arae looked up at her mistress with big, frightened eyes. Annika rewarded her with a light, almost friendly cuff on the

171

shoulder.

"I'm not particularly demonstrative," Jere said. "He follows my wishes."

Annika shrugged. "I'm just saying. It would do him some good. Show him who's boss. My father whips his slaves at least once a week, regardless of whether they've done anything wrong at all! Keeps them in line, and keeps them prepared for the whippings they get when they actually *do* something wrong. You were so kind as to help me out with *my* slave earlier, I figured I'd return the favor."

Jere's expression was drawing into a scowl. "You know, I don't actually believe in —"

"*Don't say it, you'll look ridiculous, say you don't want to discuss it!*"

" — discussing such matters over dinner." Jere had recovered quite well, coughing rather naturally as Wren pushed into his mind. "My mother always used to say that the dinner table should be reserved for fine discussions — food, art, and love!"

"Yeah, Annika, honestly, I'm sure Jeremy doesn't want to talk about such banal things as running a household!" Paltrek supported him. "Hey, tell him about that play we were going to go to."

"*I'm sorry, master,*" Wren initiated the mind connection again, despite feeling nauseous as the thought of interrupting his master again. The nausea grew as he realized that he had just addressed him as "master," but he had been calling him that all night, in honor of his guests, and perhaps he wouldn't notice, and perhaps he wouldn't be too angry, and —

"*It's all right, Wren. Actually, it's more than all right, it's — thank you. I try to stay neutral but I just got so angry at the idea that she would suggest I do something like that to you. If anyone should be whipped, it's her!*"

Wren suppressed a smile. The image of one Annika Wysocka getting whipped by his master was too perfect. She continued to yap and giggle in the most grating, flirtatious way she could manage despite its limited effectiveness.

A few minutes later, during a much more generic conversation about social events, Wren watched as his master squirmed to be away from the woman's touch. He sympathized, almost, for a minute, before recalling that Jere really could get himself out of the situation. Unlike a slave. Unlike himself.

"She's on me like a cat in heat."

Wren didn't quite laugh out loud, but did stifle it into a snort, drawing stares from both of the guests. Jere, the source of the problem, looked like he was having just as difficult a time holding it together.

"Allergies," he muttered, barely keeping a straight face. "Wren, go get some of that... that stuff. For your allergies. You know. In the kitchen."

Wren saw the opportunity presented, and bolted, barely making it through the door before exploding with laughter. She really, truly was like a cat in heat, and the mental image of her wriggling a tail in front of Jere's face was just too much.

"Sounds like one, too, sir!" Wren sent back before even thinking about it. It was just too, too fitting.

"You're awful!"

Before Wren even had a chance to get nervous, Jere had corrected himself.

"Fuck it. No. You're not awful — you're amazing! They're gonna think that your 'allergies' are catching at this rate!"

"You could use it as an excuse to come out here with me, sir." Wait. That was a bit presumptuous, wasn't it? Wren was in the process of figuring out how to backpedal, when Jere cut in again.

"Don't tempt me! I'd much rather. She grates on my fucking soul."

Wren laughed at the idea. It was true. People like her grated on everyone's soul. *"Sir, I should probably stop distracting you. Guests, and all."*

"Right, right. Guests. Come back out here when you'd like, all right? I think that's what should be done, right?"

"Yes, sir, I'll be there at once. I should be there, and, by the way, excellent cover."

Wren took a few moments to compose himself, startled by the ease which with he had just joked with his master. Of course, Jere had tried to joke before, but they had often fallen on deaf — or rather, terrified — ears. He felt that they were developing some sort of alliance, perhaps. He rather enjoyed it.

He walked back into the dining room, careful to be as unobtrusive as possible. He was startled (and, admittedly, quite disgusted), to find Annika and Jere alone, the woman practically sitting in his lap, fondling his hair. Displays of affection were nothing new to Wren, but this woman in particular? No, he was sure that Jere would be interested in a much nicer woman.

"Come *on*, Jeremy," she cooed, seemingly making her voice even higher pitched than usual. "My brother is only away for a few minutes, just *one* little kiss?"

Jere was turning his head away as far as he could without being completely offensive. "Annika, please, I really don't think this is appropriate...."

"But you're *so* sweet! And handsome," she winked at him, despite being inches away from his face, and one hand disappeared below his belt line.

Wren didn't even know how to begin to feel. He did not want this vile creature in his life, or his master's!

Jere suddenly stopped squirming and placed his hands firmly on Annika's shoulders. "I need to tell you something," he said, resolutely, as he lifted her off of his lap and placed her back on her own chair, resulting in a big, drawn-out pout. "Annika, I—you're a very attractive-*looking* woman, and I'm sure there's plenty of people out there who... Annika, I'm not interested in women."

Fortunately, Annika gasped too, because Wren's gasp was certainly audible.

"What do you mean, not interested in women?" Annika's pout looked more angry now that she was faced with the reality of not getting something she wanted.

"I, sexually...." Jere glanced nervously toward Wren. "I'm attracted to men."

"*Is this acceptable here?*"

Wren nodded back, slightly. "*Yes, sir. It's just not acceptable to Miss Wysocka.*"

"*Thanks.*"

"Annika, it's nothing personal, I just—"

"So *what* if you're gay?" Annika changed her course. "Don't you want a wife, a family, kids? A partner for your business?"

"Yes. I do," Jere said, then, before her smile became too big, "and I want it with another man."

Annika made a sound of disgust. "Well, then. Fine. Just fucking fine! I just... you don't even know what you're missing!"

"Annika, I'm sorry, I don't think I led you on or anything—"

At that moment, Paltrek returned. "Shot down?" he glanced at his sister as he returned to his seat.

"Go to hell." Annika had crossed her arms across her chest, and was pouting like the child she wasn't.

"I told you, I'd have a better chance with him!" Paltrek laughed, finishing his drink. "Not that I'm interested, well, I mean, nothing long-term. Friendly play is fine by me, but I'm not planning on settling down any time soon. Maybe ever!"

Wren was shocked, but only for a minute. This *was* the Wysocka siblings, after all. In addition to their social status, they were known for outlandish stunts like this. Despite that, Wren was still shocked that they had the gall to come over for a "social visit" that was nothing more than a pretext.

"I think I'd like to go home, now," Annika was still pouting. "Arae, get my coat."

"Oh, come now!" Paltrek tried not to laugh at her. "I told you this was a bad idea! I wanted to visit with Jeremy, and you *had* to come along to further your little plans—"

"Paltrek, I'm going home and so *help me* if you try and stop me!" Annika snapped, holding out her arms as Arae returned with her coat. "Dr. Peters, I apologize for being so forward. I enjoy your company, I'm just, I'm a little hurt right now."

Jere just nodded.

Wren showed the women to the door. The remainder of the night went much more smoothly, with Paltrek and Jere chatting about any number of things. Wren thought that Paltrek was benign enough, despite being rather privileged, and a few apologies were even uttered on Annika's behalf. Finally, the time grew later, and Jere begged off in favor of an early morning.

As the door shut and the house was quiet, Wren felt relief from himself and his master simultaneously.

"I think that went as well as possible, right?" Jere said from the doorway to the kitchen.

Wren turned and nodded. He mostly agreed, although, between Annika's suggestion that Jere beat him for no apparent reason and the revelation that his master was attracted to men, he was feeling rather on edge. He had settled comfortably into the idea that his master just wasn't attracted to males, thinking that maybe he visited a prostitute or something when he went out, although that just wasn't like Jere at all. Where was he supposed to turn for stimulation, if he hadn't had any in months? Even Wren had to admit that he had urges sometimes, desires. Dreams that woke him up feeling equally excited and unsettled. Wren's stomach clenched at the thought of his master having the same.

"Did you get something to eat?"

Jere's concern was touching, but food was the last thing Wren was interested in now. "I'm fine, sir."

Jere studied him for a moment, making him want to squirm away and hide. Wren felt like he was looking straight into his soul. He hoped that Jere wouldn't force him to eat, but he hadn't even done that when Wren had been nearly starving himself. Force didn't seem to be in Jere's vocabulary.

"All right then. I really should be heading to bed." Jere began to walk toward his room, but paused when he got to Wren. He put a hand on his shoulder in a soft, familiar way, looking down at the floor as he spoke. "I was so, so naïve when I came here, Wren. I had no idea, and the more I see of the way things are here, well, no wonder you were scared of me. I'm sorry if I made it harder. I know I'm not perfect, but at least I'm not like Annika. Or Matthias, I'd guess. I just, I want you to know, I'd never treat you like that. Even if it's acceptable and normal—it's not acceptable to me. I could never willingly hurt you."

Wren said nothing for a moment. What the hell was there to say? Without invading his mind, Jere had guessed at one of his worst fears and dismissed it, all while gently touching his shoulder. Wren could ask for nothing more.

"Thank you, sir."

Jere let him go with a slight squeeze, then walked down the hall without another word. Wren headed into his own bedroom, and was switching out the light when he felt Jere's presence in his mind.

"*Goodnight, Wren. Thank you.*"

"*You're very welcome, sir. Goodnight to you as well.*"

"*Wren?*"

"*Yes, sir?*"

"*Since you get to call me 'master' out loud when we have guests, can I persuade you to drop the 'sir' when we're speaking this way and nobody can hear us?*"

Maybe it was the tiredness, maybe it was the warm, comforted feeling that Wren always had after Jere had touched him, maybe it was just predictable, eventual dissolution of anxiety and resistance, but Wren found himself laughing at the absurdity of the whole situation. "*All right. I think that's fair.*" It was strange to *not* tack on an honorific in the sentence.

"*Thank you, Wren. It means a lot to me.*"

"*I'm glad. Sleep well.*"

Chapter 21
Getting Ready

Jere was exhausted from the social visit and everything that it had entailed, and had fallen asleep the moment his head reached the pillow. His dreams, however, were not nearly as restful, and he found himself tossing and turning, unable to get comfortable.

He heard a knock on the door.

"Sir?" Wren's voice greeted him. Wren had never dared to interrupt his sleep before. He certainly never came in without permission. Jere struggled to sit up, and by the time he managed the difficult task, Wren had opened the door and walked on in.

"Sir, are you having trouble sleeping?" Wren was advancing on him, wearing nothing but a robe. "I could help you? You've been so kind to me...."

Jere scooted up toward the headboard, suddenly regretting sleeping naked. "Wren, what...?"

Without warning, without moving, Wren was on the edge of the bed, on all fours, crawling towards him while smiling seductively. "I just want to please you, master."

Jere tried to get up, but found himself tangled in blankets. Trapped.

Wren was kissing him, and it was wrong, all wrong, as Jere tried to get away from his rather whorish ministrations.

"It's the way things are done here, *master*," Wren hissed in his ear and licked a long line down his face, across his neck, chest, and stomach, and then lower, his tongue seeming to burn a line in Jere's flesh. Jere clutched at the blankets, reminding himself that this couldn't be real.

Jere couldn't stop his body from responding to the touch, couldn't seem to restrain himself from writhing on the sheets as he felt soft, warm lips on the tip of his cock, and thought about how wrong and awful and depraved he was.

Those thoughts very quickly dissipated as he was swallowed whole, and he allowed himself to succumb to the pleasure. So what if Wren was a slave, so what if this was wrong, it felt *so* right... and *so* good.

Jere moved in response, grabbing the slave's hair, which had grown out quite nicely by now, and forced him to take him deeper, faster, thrusting down his throat, making him moan as he struggled to accommodate him. He thrust harder, harder, harder —

And woke up tangled in his sheets, which were now sticky. Jere cursed, under his breath, as he freed himself.

Jere had a quick shower and a long debate about how to hide the current state of his bedding, which Wren usually took care of washing. He settled on stripping the bed and pushing the sheets to the bottom of his laundry hamper. Wren would probably be too proper to inquire. That settled, he managed to dress himself and make his way out to the dining room. He was not eager to return to sleep. While the dream had ended quite well, the beginning had been rather disturbing. He could never take advantage of the boy that way! Well, in the dream, Wren had taken advantage of Jere — actually, he'd just rather not think about it at all.

"Good morning, sir. You're up early," Wren said by way of greeting, bringing him some coffee before he even had a chance to ask.

Jere just nodded. Nodding felt safe. The only thing on his mind was the fact that he had been incredibly turned on by one of the most disturbing dreams ever and woke up with his bed in a state it hadn't been in since he was fifteen. It was better to just nod.

"Would you like something to eat, sir?"

Jere shook his head.

"All right. Would you mind if I had something to eat, sir?" Wren was obviously uncomfortable eating when his master wasn't.

"It's fine, go ahead." *As long as it's not my cock,* Jere thought.

Wren had clearly already made himself breakfast, and now took

179

it back out from the kitchen and set it on the table. Jere wasn't really all that surprised.

"Sir?" Wren asked, as he finished his food. "I'm not sure what your plans for the day are, but I saw that there are no patients scheduled at the clinic until later today, and I know you've left most of the planning for the party to me, but, it's in a week sir, and there are really some things that should be taken care of."

Jere blinked. His reflection in his coffee blinked back at him. "Okay."

Somewhat encouraged, Wren continued. "Well, sir, I've made a list — of the things you'll need. Of course, you're welcome to change it or add or take away or — "

"I'm sure it's fine, Wren," Jere cut him off with a wave of his hand.

"Right. Right, sir," Wren nodded, seeming disoriented. "Um, so, we should go shopping, maybe. And also, we'll need to go to the rental agency."

Jere nodded. He hadn't really been looking forward to that part, but the party was coming soon, and he wasn't going to make Wren serve all those people alone. "Could we stop by the library first? There are a few things I wanted to check out."

"It's really up to you, sir."

"Right. Of course." Jere was feeling extra awkward today. "We'll go once you're finished, then."

"Yes, sir." Wren finished eating in record time, leaving Jere to throw back the last half-cup of his coffee so they could get moving.

They went into the library together, strolling up to the desk.

"Well, if it isn't my favorite doctor," Imelda grinned at them, "and Wren, how are you?"

"Fine, ma'am." Wren smiled back, shyly.

"Enjoy the latest?" she inquired.

"Very much. Thank you, ma'am."

"Don't mention it, kid. I'm just happy to have someone to discuss them with!" She glanced at Jere. "Dr. Peters here is much more amenable than that old bastard used to be — barely let you get a word out, did he?"

Wren looked away, flushing with embarrassment. "I...."

"Hey, I've got a few things I'd like your help looking up," Jere interrupted. He wasn't really sure what the appropriate way to interrupt that awkward conversation was, but he did know how to demand attention. Wren cast him a grateful look.

Imelda, temporarily interrupted, smiled back at him. "Do you have a list?" she asked.

Jere nodded, handing it over.

She perused it, nodding and pursing her lips a bit as she considered the titles.

"I have most of these. But I want you to meet someone. You can chat while I get these for you."

Had he agreed to this? It didn't really seem like he had a lot of choice. "Okay...?"

"My niece is visiting here for a few months before she leaves for University in the spring. Real bright girl, sweet, very hard working."

Jere tried to interrupt. "Imelda, I really don't think—"

"Oh, stop, I'm not setting you up on a date!" the librarian cut him off. She still had an eerie habit of knowing exactly what he was thinking. "It's clear as glass you wouldn't be interested in a *niece* of mine. Nephew, maybe, but that's neither here nor there. No, I just want you to meet her—she's been accepted to a university in Sonova, brave little thing, she's never been outside of Hojer and the neighboring boroughs, and I thought you might give her some advice on what life's like in the city."

"Oh." That didn't sound so bad. Nor did it sound like a request, so much as an order. "Certainly, I'd love to meet her."

"Good." Imelda smiled. "Kieran!"

Before Jere had a chance to say anything, a peppy-looking twenty-something bounded out from behind the library desk.

"Auntie, are you introducing me to people without telling me?" She held her hand out to Jere, who took it with surprise, and then to Wren, who looked even more surprised. Perhaps she was a *dular* like her aunt, with no gift to speak of?

"Kieran," she said, by way of introduction, her voice warm and hurried, as was her aunt's. "Nice to meet you. I've heard about you both, of course."

Jere and Wren glanced surreptitiously at one another. Jere raised an eyebrow, prompting Wren to shrug a little bit.

"So, what school are you going to?" Jere asked, somewhat feebly.

"SU," Kieran responded, rather dismissively. "But I have admissions people to tell me what that's like. What I really want to know is what *life* is like in the city?"

"It's..." Jere didn't even know where to begin. "It's different. A lot different. Are you going to be living in the dormitory, or getting a apartment?"

"Apartment. Definitely. I don't like people telling me what to do, and besides, I've heard it can get rather loud with all the people with mind gifts living in the same place."

Jere nodded. It was true, unless you had particularly good blocking skills. He realized that this meant that the girl had a mind gift, which was surprising, as he didn't get much more of a mind feel from her than he did from Imelda.

"Well, you'll be able to see a lot more of the city that way, for sure." Jere had no idea what to say to a new student. Textbooks are for reading? Don't drink until you vomit *every* night? "What are you studying?"

"Human rights and welfare," she grinned back at him. "Did you know that SU is the only place on the *continent* that offers that as a major in both undergraduate *and* master's level degrees?"

Actually, he did. "My sister was involved in that department."

"Really!?" Kieran's eyes lit up. "Can I meet her, too?"

Imelda laughed. "She's clearly *very* excited."

"She still lives in Sonova," Jere mumbled. "I could, uh...." He didn't want to introduce her to Kieran, as that would mean he would have to *talk* with Jen again, and then Jen would kill him for living in a slave state and owning a slave, and that would be bad all around.

"I'd love to meet her sometime. After I'm settled in." Kieran moved on, as if some response had been given. "So, what's it like, living without slaves?"

Jere sat there, dumb for a moment. Imelda walked off, still laughing, to collect his books. "Well, it's different."

"I'll bet!" she exclaimed. "We have a few. I just can't accept it, you know? It's wr—"

For the first time, Jere saw her hesitate, glancing toward Wren.

"It's really in need of some changes," she covered quickly. "And people with physical gifts could do so much more if they were given the chance."

"You'll like Sonova, then," Jere told her. "In your field, you'll meet a lot of people with physical gifts, who aren't slaves."

"Good! I can't wait to get out of here!" Kieran seemed excited. "So, you're here doing medicine?"

Jere nodded.

"Why didn't you stay in the city?"

Jere wondered this himself, more days than not. "The job market for new doctors there isn't exactly promising. I inherited this position."

"And him," Kieran gestured toward Wren, who looked like he wanted to hide under a table.

"Yes," Jere nodded.

"That's fucked up." Kieran shook her head.

"Kieran, watch it!" a voice called from the stacks.

"Sorry!" she yelled back, and then, more quietly, "Well, it is."

Jere nodded again. "I agree."

The girl looked puzzled. "Then why...?"

"It's complicated." Jere paused. "Actually, no, I needed help. And I like Wren. And, well, would you *sell* a person?"

"I wouldn't *own* a person to begin with!" she retorted.

"Sometimes, you don't have a choice," Jere admitted quietly. "But it works itself out anyway."

"But you stayed here?" Kieran looked disgusted. "Why didn't you sell out and leave?"

"I needed a job," Jere shrugged. "I can build experience here, build up some money. This is my only option right now."

Imelda returned with the majority of the books. "Here's most of them, the two I didn't have, I put on order. They'll be in by next week."

"Thank you, Imelda," Jere smiled, trying not to be too thrown by her younger relative's forwardness. "Say, I'm throwing a party at the end of the week—would you like to come?"

183

Imelda smiled. "Honey, I'm too old and lacking in mind gifts and *crabby* to socialize. Kieran might go, though. Dear, you don't get out that often anymore!"

Kieran glared at her. "No. I don't. Which is why I'm fleeing to the city. I'd rather not rub elbows with stuck-up socialites anyway."

Jere turned to Wren. "Did you invite only stuck-up socialites, or did you invite others, as well?"

Was that a glare? No, Wren was too proper to glare at him, but for a minute....

"Sir, I *assisted you* in inviting appropriate guests."

Maybe it was a glare, although he could see a slight smile at the corners of Wren's mouth. "Okay," Jere said. "Anyway, Kieran, it would be lovely if you could make it."

"I'll think about it," she agreed. "Maybe we could have dinner sometime?"

Jere nodded. "Sounds great. But, we really should be going now. We have some things to get for the party."

They said their goodbyes and headed out.

"She's quite lively," Jere commented, silently.

Wren nodded. *"Yes. Sir, it might not be the best idea to have her at the party."*

"Why not?"

Wren went silent for a moment. *"Well, I don't mean to be...."*

"Just say it, Wren."

"She seems to be of an abolitionist mindset, sir." Wren glanced warily out of the corner of his eye.

Jere nodded. *"I think she'd hold her tongue about it, though — I mean, not a very good strategy to just make yourself look crazy and over the top about it."*

Wren looked surprised. *"It doesn't bother you?"*

Jere laughed out loud. *"Less than you could imagine. I find it quite refreshing, actually. That's how everyone back home is. I mean, maybe not outraged by it, there's certainly plenty who don't care fuck all either way, but basically — it's the norm there. Kieran reminds me of my sister, reminds me of home. I like her."*

Wren went silent again. Jere noticed, but also noticed that he

184

was contemplative, rather than fearful or offended. He let him take the space he needed.

They arrived at the rental agency sooner than Jere expected. From the outside, it was rather nondescript, painted in a simple white and gray scheme with black lettering declaring the name. Jere went in, followed, as appropriate, by Wren. He could feel the boy's anxiety, and somewhat regretted bringing him along. However, he would certainly need help here.

They were greeted at the front desk by a young man with what seemed like a permanent scowl on his face.

"Can I help you?" He glanced up at Jere without even lifting his head.

"Yes." Jere took a moment to calm himself and tried desperately to sound less out of place. He wasn't very successful. "We, uh, I would like to rent a few slaves, to help me at a party."

"When?" The attendant asked, still not bothering to move.

"Right now?" Jere fumbled.

"When would you like to rent them for, sir?" Wren's voice prodded slightly in his mind.

"Oh, uh, I'd like to rent them today for a party on Saturday." He hoped that sounded intelligent.

The man nodded, grabbed a stack of papers, and flipped through them, looking for something that he was not disclosing. "Did you want anything special?"

"Special?"

"Speed gifts would be nice, but not completely necessary. We'll need experienced servers."

Jere nodded, thankful that Wren was there with him to handle these things. "Someone experienced serving at parties, and a speed gifted person would be lovely, if you have any."

The man nodded again. "How long do you want them for? Standard rental is twelve hours, but they can come and go sooner or later, as you wish."

"The party's at seven. If we could get them at five, to help set up, twelve hours would work."

"Standard rental, then, starting at 5 p.m."

The man handed over two sheets of paper he had been working

on. "Read over these disclaimers and agreements, I'll get the two I've got for you so you can see them and look them over."

Jere glanced through the agreements. Typical rental agreement, liabilities, terms, fees, late charges, the usual. He glanced at Wren for support and found him barely concealing a grin. Jere realized he was pretty obviously uncomfortable here, if Wren was looking at him like that.

The man returned with a man and a woman, both of whom looked to be in their mid-thirties, following with perfect poise and restraint.

"What am I supposed to do?" Jere asked Wren, trying not to sound as naïve and panicked as he felt.

"Pretend like you're sampling wine. Look at it, make a funny face, and then declare that it's good enough," Wren suggested.

Jere did just that. "They'll do just fine," he stated confidently, as if he had any idea what the hell he was looking for anyway.

"Good," the man said, waving the slaves away. "Now, we'll have them arrive at your door at the time indicated, it's up to you to tell them what to do and dress them appropriately. They'll show up clean, in outfits like they wore today. We expect them to return in the same condition. If you are so inclined to punish them, you may, but don't return them seriously injured." He paused for a moment, and laughed. "Of course, you are a doctor, so I suppose you can do whatever the hell you want with them, just patch them up before sending them home, all right?"

Jere was rather appalled, but wisely chose to keep this to himself. He agreed with whatever needed agreeing with, signed on all the lines and initialed where indicated, and was about to leave, when he felt the attendant's eyes looking past him.

He jerked a finger at Wren. "You ever think of renting that one out?"

Jere resisted the urge to snarl. "No." It was final, simple, and to the point. He glared the man down until he stopped looking at his slave.

"Your rentals will arrive Saturday at five, then," the attendant said finally, casting a final look at Wren as Jere hurried him outside.

"It's not a big deal."

Wren's voice was quiet and calm in Jere's head, but it didn't make him feel any better. In fact, he felt quite the opposite. *"Please tell me you know I could never do that to you?"*

Wren smiled slightly. *"I'm beginning to see that."*

"It's not right!" Jere was fully aware that he sounded like a whiny child, but didn't quite care at the moment. *"At least we can treat them well, right?"*

This time, Wren actually laughed out loud. *"Yes, sir, if you wish, you can do anything you'd like with them — even if that is just feeding them a good meal and refraining from beating them."*

"Well, at least there's that."

Chapter 22
Goodnight

The next few days were best described as a whirlwind. There were plans to be made, menus to create, cleaning to do—and all on top of their regular activities. It was the night before the party, and Jere and Wren had both collapsed, exhausted, onto the couch.

Wren ran though a list of things in his mind that had been done, were being done, and needed doing. He was certain he had checked all of the bases, but what was one more check? Suddenly, he tensed a bit in anticipation. "Sir?" he mumbled, still not lifting his head. "Sir, we—what should the slaves wear?"

Wren could feel Jere shrugging, despite not seeing him. "They can wear the same thing as you do."

Wren was mildly amused by the phrasing, as though the rental slaves were in a different category than himself. Then the realization hit him. "Sir? What should I wear?" At this point, he raised his head to glance nervously up at his master.

Another shrug. "Whatever you wear to these things. Just wear what you used to wear. Matthias had parties, didn't he? Wear what you wore to those."

Wren struggled to believe that his master would actually request him to wear *that*. A part of him was slowly shutting down his access to his own emotions, blocking out the pain and humiliation that was to come, while a tiny, tiny little part of him was denying it. Yes. Denial. That was all it was. He just needed to accept it and deal with it and—

"Wren?" Jere asked softly, sitting up and looking at his face. "Are you all right? You got pale all of a sudden. What's wrong? Was it something I said?"

Wren shook his head. He didn't even know how to explain, and besides, if he did, he'd just be complaining, and his master was a good man, but you could never predict how a master would react to a complaining, whining slave, so —

"Is it about the clothing, then?"

Wren flinched. He hated when Jere could guess what he was thinking. He wasn't even utilizing the mind connection. Reluctantly, he nodded.

Jere stared at him, eyes wide and innocent and expectant. "Wren?"

He looked down at the floor, before he could betray himself. This was stupid. He and the master had gotten along so well, made these plans — Wren knew better than to screw it all up now by whining about clothing. "It's fine, sir. It's no big deal."

Jere narrowed his eyes. "Fuck. Go get it, show me what it is, all right?"

Wren stood quickly, happy to at least have a direct order to follow. He hesitated before walking off. "Sir, should I put it on?" He tried, rather unsuccessfully, to keep the tremor out of his voice as he asked.

Jere shook his head. "No, just bring it. Let me see what's gotten you so damn worked up."

"Yes, sir." Wren sped to the vile, vile cellar, which neither he nor Jere had gotten around to cleaning or redecorating yet, and pulled through his old pile of "clothes." Finding what he was looking for, he repressed a shudder and brought it to his master, handing it over mutely as he looked away.

Jere stared at the tiny piece of fabric in his hands silently for a moment, turning it about and stretching it as if trying to find something else within it. "This is all you'd wear?"

Wren nodded. He didn't have any words to say.

"I have underpants that cover more than this!" Jere exclaimed.

How absurd. It was an absurd statement. And it struck Wren as hilarious. He struggled, and barely repressed a laugh, although a slight giggle slipped out.

"I mean, these could *be* underpants for *my* underpants!"

Wren was laughing openly now, not entirely sure of the reason why, a nervous, tittering laugh that threatened to take him over or turn him to tears if he tried to stop.

"My god, no wonder you were so surprised when I asked you to wear this!" Jere set the outfit aside. "I mean, you're not exactly inclined towards nudity!"

"Sir, I—"

Wren was cut off by a wave of Jere's hand. "Wren, I'm sorry, honestly, I never intended for you to wear something like this. I know you'd be horrified, and, well, I'd be uncomfortable too. You deserve the dignity of clothing, for fuck's sake."

Wren smiled back at him, touched. "Yes, sir."

"What about something more akin to a butler's uniform, or a waiter?" Jere asked, hopeful. "Is there something more tasteful available?"

Wren nodded. "Yes, sir. If you'd like, sir, I can run to the shop before the party tomorrow and purchase one for myself and one for each of the slaves you're renting."

Jere nodded, smiling back at him. "That would be great. Thank you."

They continued discussing a few more minor details for the next day. Wren was filled with relief and calm, knowing that he would be allowed to be properly clothed for the event tomorrow. The clothing he had been forced to wear in the past had given a certain impression. Not only did Jere seem appalled at the idea, which said a lot for his character, but the general appearance of formal, restrictive clothes would make the guests considerably less likely to take a "hands-on" approach to interacting with the slaves. A party that didn't involve unwanted groping would be quite welcome.

They had just finished discussing things for the night, and stood up to head to their respective beds. Jere walked by Wren, and as he did, placed a hand lightly on his arm to stop him.

"Wren, I," he fumbled a bit with the words. "Look, about earlier, I'm sorry that you were scared. I never meant for that to happen. Honestly. I just.... Please, if it ever happens again, if you ever feel like something bad like that is going to happen, please, just tell me? I can feel it through the mind connection, and I can read it on your face, but please, I'd rather you trusted me enough to ask me."

Wren nodded, feeling relief and trepidation fill him. He wished he could, but years of conditioning had taught him better than to ask stupid questions. But at least with Jere he could be honest. He didn't just have to lie and pretend to agree. "I'll try, sir."

"Then I suppose that will have to do." Jere looked sad, but still lightly gripped his arm. "Did you really think I'd make you wear something like that in public? Or, fuck, anywhere?"

Wren honestly didn't know how to answer. Now that he looked back on it, it seemed stupid. He had been panicking, thinking of just how awful it would be, how it would crush his image of his master, how he would be more vulnerable to groping and grabbing by strangers. But not once had he so much as considered the way that Jere defended him, the way he clothed him and cared for him and never, *never* so much as touched him if he didn't want it. No, looking back, it really didn't seem like something he would do.

Wren had taken too long to answer, and was met with a sad sigh.

"Well, whatever I did to make you believe that, I'm sorry." Jere let his hand drop, turning away. "I'm doing the best I can." He walked away before Wren had a chance to respond.

Wren cursed himself. The master was so kind, so considerate. So fragile. Wren realized that, as afraid as he was of being hurt by his master, the man was just as afraid, if not more, of hurting him. Before he had time to think about it and convince himself otherwise, he sped toward Jere and caught his wrist.

"I'm doing the best I can, too! Sir." He tacked the word on at the end at the last minute, wanting to cringe away from the numerous smacks he knew he deserved. Looking up from beneath his eyelashes and pushing his fear aside, he continued. "No. I didn't think you'd make me wear something like that, because I thought you were better than that, and that's why it was so hard to think that you would. But it turns out you wouldn't, because you *are* better than that, and, well, thank you." He awkwardly let go of Jere's wrist, trying to ignore the terror that he knew *should* be creeping up on him for laying hands on a free man.

Jere said nothing, but his face slowly changed from the sad

191

frown he had walked away with to a slight smile. "Thank you, Wren. It means a lot to me."

Wren nodded. "It means a lot to me, too, sir."

"Goodnight, Wren."

"Goodnight, sir."

Chapter 23
A Host

Wren slept exceptionally well. For as unusual as his little outburst before bed was, the master had seemed genuinely pleased by Wren's comment. Aside from any attempt to please or placate the man who owned him, Wren felt good seeing him smile like he did. It was strange, making someone smile for no other reason than to make them happy, no goals or gains in mind.

He finalized the preparations for the day as quickly as he could, attending to those issues while his master insisted on keeping the office open for the day. After securing a pass, he went and purchased suits that he hoped would be acceptable. They looked, he noted with a smile, like a waiter's uniform in a fancy restaurant. He came home and decorated, making sure that the holiday décor was minimal and as tasteful as possible. Jere certainly didn't seem like the type to appreciate campy, overdone garnishments. He glanced at a clock and realized that the rental slaves would be arriving at any moment.

A door opened behind him.

"Wow!" Jere exclaimed as he slipped into his home, glancing around wide-eyed as he took in the changes that had overtaken it in a few short hours. "Wren, this is really beautiful!"

Wren struggled not to blush or squirm away from the praise. "Thank you, sir."

Jere looked appraisingly at him, making Wren want to squirm away even more, although now for different reasons.

"The uniform is perfect as well. Hell, at this rate, you *and* the house will look better than me!"

Wren smiled. He had gotten quite good at pleasing his master. As reluctant as he was to take charge at times, it really did make everything go much more smoothly, and he had to admit he was better at making decisions than Jere was. "Well, sir, I found a solution to that as well—I picked up something for you to wear while I was out."

Jere was silent for a moment, studying him. It was a moment too long, because Wren felt his chest tighten with panic, fear that he had made the wrong choice, took too many liberties, acted above his station. He forced himself to stay still, and braced himself for the blows, verbal or otherwise.

"I really don't know what I'd do without you," Jere said warmly, breaking Wren's nervous paralysis. "I mean, you just think of everything. And if I know you, it's lying out on my bed as we speak?"

Wren nodded, not trusting himself to speak just yet. He was thankful that Jere never insisted he respond to every question out loud.

"Wonderful! I'll have plenty of time to shower and change after—"

Wren was pretty sure that Jere was going to say "after the rental slaves arrive," but at that very moment, they heard a knock. Wren sped off to answer the door, letting in the two slaves they had met a few days ago and ushering them to the living room.

"Hello, sir." The two spoke at nearly the same time, both bowing slightly.

They were nervous and formal. The tense, restricted way in which they moved only reinforced the image. Wren recalled a time not too long ago when he felt the same way. Deciding to take matters into his own hands, Wren guided the conversation. "Welcome. My name is Wren, and you may refer to the master as 'Master Peters' while you are here."

They looked gratefully at him and nodded.

Jere wrinkled his brow in an attempt to figure out what had just happened. He looked uncomfortable. "Hello," he managed. "What are your names?"

"Rose, Master Peters," the woman spoke first.

"Gabe, Master Peters," the man followed.

"Hi," Jere said again, glancing at Wren.

"*Sir, I apologize if I was too forward,*" Wren backpedaled a bit. The rental slaves were so formal and in their place that Wren realized how different he was. "*I knew they'd be wondering how to address you.*"

"*Don't worry about it, it's fine. But couldn't we go with doctor? Instead of master?*"

"*No.*" Wren was too busy preparing for other things to be tactful. "*They'll need to introduce guests, and addressing you properly will be necessary. Besides, it will be more familiar and comfortable to them anyway.*" That always worked on Jere.

"Right, then," Jere spoke aloud. "Welcome, and uh, I'll be leaving you in Wren's care, he can explain where things are and what you'll need to do and all that." He cast a pleading look at Wren, who nodded back reassuringly.

As Jere left, Wren motioned to the two rental slaves, beckoning them into the dining room, where he had left the suits sitting on the table. He handed one to each of them. "Go ahead and change into these. There's a spare room right there, if you prefer."

The rentals exchanged a barely perceptible look that suggested they had no preferences, but Wren really did prefer that they change out of his sight. He had grown rather prudish, spoiled as he was. They did as he asked, and he sat, meanwhile. He had forgotten just how hard it was to interact with other slaves, others like him. Was he really thinking so differently of himself?

They returned quickly, and he motioned for them both to have a seat. Obviously not wanting to disobey the person whose care they had been left in, they did as ordered.

"All right. Here's the deal," he started with a slight sigh. "The master is rather sympathetic. Toward anyone, really. He'll be kind, so don't be nervous. In fact, he would prefer it if you weren't nervous, and honestly, so would I. Here are a few ground rules. Please address him as Master Peters, as I indicated earlier. Address the rest of the guests as 'sir' or 'ma'am,' as I'm sure you've been trained."

He paused a moment as they nodded. "You'll be serving drinks, taking coats, and carrying around snack trays. I'll coordinate or answer any questions you have. You are to come to me, *not* the master, with any questions. Leave him to his guests. You will not be required to sexually service any of the guests, and, further, you are expressly forbidden to do so under any circumstances. You are to come and get me at *once* if you can't finesse your way out of a situation. Is that clear?"

They nodded again, looking surprised.

"Do remember what coats and bags and whatnot that people bring with them, so you can hand them back accordingly at the end of the night. I'm assuming you've worked together before?" Nods. "Good, then, work together tonight. I'm sure you've developed a system. After the party's over, you'll help to clean up and put the house back together before we send you back to the agency. Do you have any questions?"

The woman, Rose, looked anxiously up at him. "Sir, what should we expect as punishments?"

"He won't punish you," Wren shook his head, and had to turn away as he did, suddenly overwhelmed with gratitude. "He's—he's really very understanding. And please, call me Wren."

"Yes, Wren," they answered in unison. Not exactly what he had been aiming for, but fair enough. He supposed he must seem like he had an awful lot of power. He supposed he did. It was unusual, for a slave, but Jere seemed all right with Wren taking charge around the house—maybe he could prove himself useful with other slaves as well?

"Now, have you eaten?" Wren looked at their eyes, watching as they glanced back and forth between one another, sort of shrugging. "Never mind. I'll get you something regardless. You'll be welcome to eat after the party, as well."

Wren went to the kitchen, grabbed some plates, and deposited some of the food he had made earlier. He had thought ahead and made extra, much more than he would make for just himself and Jere. He wasn't sure if Jere would be eating before the party anyway, but he had made some, just in case. Leftovers were always appreciated. He debated with himself for a moment, and then decided to wait for his master to eat his food.

The moment he brought the plates in to Rose and Gabe, Jere strolled through the door, freshly showered and changed into the suit Wren had purchased for him. It complemented his eyes and skin tone and fit him perfectly, as Wren was quite familiar with his sizing. Jere wasn't an unattractive man by any means, but Wren hadn't realized just how nicely he could be cleaned up for a formal event.

"Wren, this is great, you really should dress me more!" Jere grinned, twirling around in a manner not unlike a fairy princess.

"Noted, sir," Wren replied, smiling a bit. He actually didn't think that Jere had purchased a single thing for himself since moving here, and he was fine with it staying that way.

Rose and Gabe stood up quickly, ignoring their food as Jere walked over. He held up his hands to calm them. "Please, don't let me interrupt!"

They glanced at Wren.

"Sit. Finish eating," he confirmed, trying not to let it show that he was shocked by his own forwardness, as though the slaves had to listen to him over Jere. Still, they nodded deferentially, and Wren felt a sense of pride.

"Eat, build up strength. I'm hoping it will be a good night tonight!" Jere commented.

Wren had been scrutinizing Jere's hair, which fell, as usual, in a shaggy pile wherever it chose. The matter was not helped by Jere's habitually running his hand through it.

"Sir?" he asked, eyebrow raised. "If you want, I could do something with your hair?"

Jere laughed. "You don't approve of my 'shake it dry' style?"

Wren tried not to laugh, mostly because he thought the rental slaves might literally die of shock if he were to do such a thing. "I just thought you might want it a bit more put together, sir?"

Jere nodded and sat at the table, obviously not noticing the tension he was causing the two rentals. "Can I at least have something to eat first?"

Wren glanced at the clock. "During, sir. You're running late as it is. Stay here."

"Okay," Jere agreed, not protesting as a plate of food was dropped in front of him.

Wren returned a moment later with a comb and some sort of

spray product that Jere had never laid eyes on before.

"See what happens when I let you do my shopping?" Jere teased, hushing quickly as he felt his hair tugged at a little more energetically than was probably necessary.

Wren worked on his master's hair quickly, taking the few moments he had to reflect on how vastly different his life had become. Just months before, he would have cringed at the idea of willingly touching his master (whom, at the moment, was wriggling away from the hands that tugged at his hair in an attempt to get it to do *something*). He would have hyperventilated at their now routine teasing. And he certainly wouldn't have appreciated the silky smoothness of the sandy blond hair between his fingers.

"I guess that's the best I can do, sir," Wren declared, whisking the comb and spray away, as well as the plates. While the rental slaves had finished their food quickly, Jere was only partway through, and he looked startled as he saw it disappear.

"I'm sure it's fine, Wren," Jere grinned at him, not daring to touch his own hair for the moment. "Have you had a chance to eat something?"

"I'll be fine, sir."

Wren tried to ignore the fact that Jere was frowning. Okay, so it hadn't been the question he had asked, but that was the point, wasn't it?

"Eat something if you get hungry?"

Wren had noticed at some point that Jere often used the mindspeak when he didn't want to give a direct order. All the same, Wren was rather touched. *"I will. Thank you."*

Jere didn't respond, but smiled slightly. He turned to address the rental slaves. "I assume Wren has filled you in on tonight's events. Just follow his lead, and you'll do fine."

Wren showed the rentals around, explaining where the liquor cabinet was, more glasses, food, bathrooms, coatroom, and even cleaning supplies, in case of any mid-activity accidents. They followed along obediently, nodding and staying quiet, as they had been trained to. It was nice to be able to tell someone else what to do, for once.

Finally, the guests began to arrive. Wren orchestrated the event perfectly, having tactfully explained the protocols and procedures to Jere the night before. He managed to greet each guest and present them for his master in a way that spoke of flawless training and social grace. Meanwhile, the rental slaves took care of things like taking and putting away coats and carrying around snack trays. Wren was thrilled to be able to manage things so smoothly, and found himself feeling none of the fear that he usually felt when faced with such imposing tasks.

It wasn't that Wren was unused to serving at such events, it was just that in the past he had primarily been involved in the so-to-speak "entertainment" end of such things. Burghe typically handed him off to guest after guest, and most of the parties were a blur of backhands and spilled drinks and drunken fumbling. Sadly, those were the good memories. There had been occasions where Wren had been forced to dance, strip, or worse for the crowd, who were encouraged to watch and jeer and touch as they so desired. Wren could see in the eyes of a few of the guests tonight that they were wondering if something similar might happen.

It didn't.

True to his word, Jere made sure that *no one* laid a hand on any of the slaves. With a mix of charm and fake naïveté, he informed the few guests that inquired about "entertainment" that there would be music and drinks and dancing. He and Wren worked beautifully as a team, checking in mentally with one another quite regularly. The few times a guest was a little too fresh, Wren alerted Jere, who directed the slave to fetch one thing or another from another room, and directed the guest to meet someone or try a new drink. Wren had conveniently neglected to invite those that he knew would be belligerent, and within the first hour or so, things had started to move very calmly. Even prior attendees of parties at the house seemed to grasp that this was a classy, upscale party, not a drunken fornicating romp.

Wren had his hands full, for the most part, directing the two rental slaves around. They were quite capable and competent, and Wren was eternally thankful that he had suggested they get some. Fortunately, the few spills during the night came from the guests, and while Wren was the one to clean them up, he was glad that he wouldn't also have to spend time calming down a panicking rental slave. They followed his lead without question.

When he wasn't busy attending the party, Wren mostly chose to hide out in the kitchen. It was quieter there, and he was in control. Still, as the night went on and the guests began to get more comfortable and request more drinks, he found himself working side-by-side with the rental slaves, directing them in the right direction to people whose glasses were empty and making sure the drinks went where they were supposed to.

"Another drink, boy."

"One minute, sir, I'll get to you once I finish over here." Wren kept his back turned to the man, focusing on the small crowd whose drink orders he was currently taking.

The man walked up next to him, close. "Whiskey on the rocks, now!"

"I will get it for you in a minute, sir." Wren said with an edge to his tone. He had been the one making sure everyone got drinks all night, and unlike this man, he wasn't on his eighth drink. He shouldn't be ordering him around. "Let me finish helping this guest."

"I *said* get it for me *now!*" the man snapped, grabbing his upper arm roughly.

He felt his face flush with rage, his fists clench at his sides. He glared up at the man, knowing full well that he should be gazing down at the ground, perhaps on his knees, at least begging forgiveness. He would rather pull his arm away and resume managing the party he had so carefully staged.

"Or would you *rather* get your *master* for me?"

Wren didn't move. He couldn't speak. He had grown so comfortable with Jere that he had almost forgotten that free people had the right to give him orders. Still, he tugged away at his arm, slightly. The grip didn't loosen.

"What's the problem, here?" Jere was suddenly at his side, his hand not-so-subtly prying the guest's fingers off of Wren's arms.

"Your boy's a little uppity," the man snapped. "You can't even get a drink around here without his approval!"

Jere smiled, placing himself between the man and Wren. "I assure you, sir, my slave is beyond capable of making sure everyone stays hydrated in a timely manner. We have a small serving staff and a large guest list — perhaps you could try something that doesn't go down so quickly? I had a vintage red wine imported, I think that would round out those whiskey drinks quite nicely."

The man started discussing wines, which Wren took as his cue to leave. He had let it go to his head, the rental slaves, the success of the party, even Jere's leniency. He had forgotten the danger he could put himself in.

"*Crisis averted,*" Jere said through the mindspeak, his voice lighter than his emotions felt. "*Is there anything I can do for you?*"

Wren relaxed. His master really did support him in this. "*No, sir, but thank you. I'm sorry.*"

"*Don't be,*" Jere protested. "*You're doing a perfect job, Wren.*"

Jere, for his part, was playing the perfect host, coming to life and smiling, greeting, and making small talk like he had been doing it for years. Wren couldn't help but listen in a few times, and was amazed by the way that his master directed the conversations away from uncomfortable subjects and on to something more agreeable. He had never really had a chance to see his master shine before.

The librarian's niece, Kieran, did show up partway through the night, and while she only stayed for a short while, it was clear that Jere was pleased to see her, and spent some time talking about his hometown. The girl was almost overwhelmingly chatty, but it was nice to see Jere warm up to someone and seem slightly more at ease. Paltrek Wysocka arrived, in style as usual, and was very quickly engaged in both talking with Jere and flirting with numerous women. His sister, as expected, was unable to make it. Nobody really missed her.

The night grew late and the booze stopped flowing so frequently, and finally, the guests began to trickle out and head to their respective homes. Matching up guests and belongings proved more difficult than anticipated, as the level of sobriety was generally low, and a good portion of the guests had forgotten that they had even brought coats along with them. Nonetheless, they were all matched except for an odd glove and hat, which Wren put aside in case anyone asked about them. He closed the door behind the last couple to leave and walked back toward the dining room, rather exhausted.

Rose and Gabe spotted him the second he walked through the doorway.

"What should we do now, Wren?" Gabe asked.

Compared with the beginning of the night, Wren found it almost comfortable to give out instructions. It was nice to see things done his way. "Start taking down decorations and picking up cups," he directed.

As he did, Jere strolled through the door, looking energetic and pleased with the way the night had gone. "Just put it all in the kitchen, please," Jere said easily, sitting at the table.

"Yes, Wren. Yes, Master Peters," they said in unison, hurrying off.

Jere winced at the term, and the tone. "Well, that works then," he muttered, then turned to Wren. "Come on, sit down a minute."

"I should really be cleaning up, sir." Wren realized he must really be exhausted—had he really just contradicted his master *and* volunteered to do more work?

"Bullshit." Jere grinned at him. "I would have had them sit down as well, but I figured you'd be easier to convince."

"Sir, I...." Wren paused a moment. He knew better than to disagree, but he had been the one taking care of all of the arrangements, and if they didn't work quickly, they would be up all night cleaning. Wren had planned the whole evening, including the time it would take to clean, and he wanted to finish the night with a clean house, according to his plans. "I need to make sure they're doing their work acceptably. And I have work to do as well."

Jere sighed, standing up. "All right, then, you lead the way."

"Sir?"

"Well, if you're going to insist on working yourself to death, then dammit, I'm going to help out and do the same!"

"Oh." Wren had expected to direct the rental slaves in the cleanup efforts, but was somewhat startled at the thought of doing the same for his master. Then again, things went so much more smoothly when he was giving Jere directions, instead of the other way around. He led them to the living room, where the rental slaves had cleared away most of the evidence of the night's party already.

"You can straighten the furniture up. Sir."

"Consider it done," Jere smirked as he joined the cleanup crew.

The work went very quickly, and if the two rental slaves were unsettled by the participation of the master, neither said anything about it, for which Wren was quite grateful. Under Wren's direction, the four worked well together, and quickly restored the house to the condition it was in just hours before.

"Anyone hungry? Care for a drink?"

Wren cringed a little at Jere's informality. It was rather endearing, but the rentals were clearly confused.

"Perhaps tea, sir?" Wren suggested gently. "*They'll be whipped half to death if they return with alcohol on their breath!*"

"*Oh.*" Jere looked a bit startled. "Tea would be lovely, Wren, a wonderful ending to the night."

Wren prepared tea and sandwiches, and was surprised to discover that he was actually ravenously hungry. Had he really forgotten to eat all night? He even picked at some of the food while he prepared it, something he rarely, if ever, did.

The four sat around the table, somewhat awkwardly. Jere seemed to be the only one unaware of the feeling. To his credit, he was pleasant in his aloofness, mostly talking with Wren about how the party had gone, if there were any suggestions or complaints from the guests, and things like that. The rental slaves both surreptitiously stocked up on as much food as they could, and Wren made every effort to keep loading their plates up, knowing fully well how delicious real food was after years of eating synthetic food product.

Finally, the time came for the rentals to return. Wren directed them to change back into their clothing and head back to the agency. He gave Jere a note to sign, granting them permission to pass and indicating that they had served well that night, and sent them on their way. The party was successful, and the new year had begun.

Chapter 24
An Unexpected Move

After they ushered the rental slaves out the door, Jere retreated to the living room, dropping down on the couch and looking back tiredly at Wren. After a brief debate with himself, Wren followed suit, sitting on the other end of the couch, reminiscent of the night after the first party Jere had attended. While it was becoming more of an everyday occurrence, Wren was too new to sitting on furniture to not feel privileged by the soft, squishy seat underneath him.

"It really did go well, didn't it?" Jere said, a satisfied look on his face.

Wren nodded. "Yes, sir."

Jere sat back and smiled. "I really couldn't have done it without you, Wren. Honestly. You're a fucking lifesaver. You were marvelous — with the guests, with the rental slaves, hell, with me!"

Wren felt himself turning red. "Thank you, sir. It wasn't a problem, really."

"You were wonderful," Jere insisted. "And I, well, I survived, didn't I? I think that calls for a toast."

Wren was about to stand up when he saw Jere shaking his head furiously back and forth. He hesitated.

"Sit down!" Jere insisted, jumping to his feet with a big smile. "I want to toast you, it's only fair I get the liquid celebration!"

Reluctantly, Wren settled back down onto the couch, allowing his master to serve him. Jere returned moments later with two shot glasses and a bottle of gin. He dropped onto the couch next to Wren, filled the glasses, and handed one over.

"To you," he said, quite seriously, then grinned, "and don't argue with it."

They clinked the shot glasses together and drank them down, even though Wren shuddered a bit at the taste. The warm feeling it left behind was most definitely worth it, and it may have contributed to his boldness in making the next toast to Jere.

The third was to the Winter Holiday parties being over, and the fourth was to the rental slaves, who, despite Jere's reluctance to get them in the first place, had certainly made things go much more smoothly. Wren, who had never had more than a few sips of alcohol at a time, was certainly feeling the first three shots, and miscalculated both the closeness of the shot glasses and the speed at which they were moving. For someone with a speed gift, this was a pretty big miscalculation.

No sooner had the glasses clinked together, Wren felt a sharp stab of pain in his left eye, and yelped before he even had a chance to think about it. Squeezing it shut against the burning, he set his glass down and tried to block out the pain.

"Are you all right?" Jere asked worriedly.

"I, I'm fine, sir," Wren mumbled, still trying to will the pain away. "I, it splashed, and it really burns!"

"Here, let me look!"

Wren shook his head. "I'm fine, sir, it's just… god, it burns!"

Jere had leaned forward a bit on the couch. "Wren, I'm serious, let me heal it. It's too easy to do damage to your eyes, and in any case, I'll make it stop hurting if you'll let me!"

Wren nodded, feeling an unwanted tear dropping from his newly gin-soaked eye, and let his hands fall to his sides as Jere leaned toward him and placed his hands on either side of his head. Moments later, he felt the familiar warmth of the mind-healing, and the dry, scratchy, fiery feeling his eye had been filled with just seconds before was gone.

Without moving his hands, Jere looked Wren in the eye with a triumphant grin. "Better?"

Wren nodded, keeping eye contact. "Yes, sir."

Warm liquor in his stomach, warm hands on his head, and then Wren felt warm lips brush his as he stared back into his master's eyes. They were and soft and gentle, moving against his own, gently parting and exploring more —

Jere jerked away as though he had been burned. "I'm sorry. I, I shouldn't have done that."

Wren thought about how he should agree, how he should stop the situation before it went any further, how he didn't want this, *couldn't* want this, but it turned out, his mouth was faster than his mind, and the words were out before he even had time to think about them. "You shouldn't have stopped."

Jere looked up hopefully, his eyes wide. "You mean it?"

Wren was pretty sure that he shouldn't mean it, but then again, the whole situation was surreal enough that he decided he should let that go. He had dreamed about this on more than one occasion. He nodded, looking his master in the eye. "Keep going."

"You're sure?" Jere asked in disbelief, a smile spreading across his face.

"Just kiss me!" Wren demanded, leaning in closer and picking up where they had left off. He had enjoyed the instant compliance the rental slaves had shown all night, and he felt the same thrill as Jere returned the kiss.

Wren was lost to the sensation. Jere's mouth was soft and undemanding, letting Wren take the lead and set the pace. While Wren wanted nothing more than to race through their hesitation, Jere was moving against him as if they had all the time in the world and there was nowhere he would rather be. It felt nice. Wren noticed a hand on the back of his head, but before he had a chance to feel uncomfortable with it, he felt the soft, careful motion of his hair being ever so gently carded through. It wasn't being pulled, he wasn't being held in place, he was just being enjoyed by someone who appreciated that part of him.

He parted his lips again, prompting Jere to do the same, feeling their tongues connect a moment later. It felt so good, so soft and right, and he could feel him breathing, he could feel the warmth of his body and hands and breath on his skin, could feel him moving ever so slightly closer on the couch. Wren wanted more, wanted to push Jere down and feel every inch of his body. Their noses touched, and he opened his eyes to look into the face of his master....

And he panicked.

If Jere had time to notice Wren stiffening underneath him, he didn't show it, and before anything else had a chance to happen, Wren had used his speed gift to dart to the other side of the room.

"This can't happen."

Jere, clearly startled, looked at him with concern. "Wren—"

"I can't do this!" Wren said, looking like a trapped animal. "I just...."

A split second later, Wren ran, full speed, into his room, pulling the door shut behind him. He climbed into his bed, burrowed under the pile of covers, and lay there shaking and crying until he finally fell asleep. He never should have asked for this. He was a slave, it wasn't his place to initiate things like this, and it certainly wasn't his place to try to stop them.

He woke up the next morning with a sick feeling in his stomach. What had he done? He was torn between what to feel more guilty for—stopping the action, or starting it in the first place. In either case, he knew better. He was tired and sore, and knew he hadn't been sleeping well, but the master hadn't come to wake him up even once. Had he not been crying out like he used to? He couldn't tell. He almost never woke up from dreams, not unless someone else woke him up.

It was New Year's Day. A holiday. Jere would only be seeing emergency patients. Wren figured that just meant that he wouldn't be needed, which gave him the perfect excuse to hide out in his room all day, like he had when Jere first arrived. He sat quietly for a moment, until he was sure he heard no signs of life from the rest of the house, and then darted to the bathroom and back. He had good plans of staying in his room all day, unless he was summoned. Resting his head on his pillow, he closed his eyes and tried to pretend that the previous night had never happened.

He was plagued by visions, memories of his time before Jere, before Matthias, even. He tried to push them away, thinking of anything else, but he couldn't. His brain alternated between old memories and the recent one, the one from last night. Both were terrible. He curled up on his side, facing the wall, and clutched a pillow to his chest as the memories swept over him.

He had been at the training facility only a week or so, but his thir-

teenth birthday and his family were all but forgotten in the misery.

He could barely keep track of what had happened, no more than any of the other kids there. Any of the other slaves. They looked at each other with haunted, fearful eyes, each one seeming to ask why they were there, why it hadn't been someone else.

One week, and they were already scheduled to start sexual training. Some cohorts started later, but this was the way the schedule had been arranged, they had been told, and it wasn't like any of them were going to argue.

Wren's memories were so fuzzy, yet so clear. He didn't want to remember them, but they were burned into his mind.

Stripping had been bad enough, that first night, when they were ordered to shed their clothing and step into the group shower, where strange trainers stood ready to hose them down. The trainers had laughed and jeered, and few of the kids had been able to keep themselves from crying. Wren watched as another boy was kicked for taking too long, and stripped his own clothes off as quickly as possible, his new gift giving him a competitive edge.

Now, here they were, lined up naked, waiting for some unknown horror. Wren pressed back against the cold tile wall, hoping he could become invisible, hoping that they would pass him over, ignore him. He had only been a slave for a short while, but it was clear that being noticed was guaranteed to bring suffering. He glanced at the beginning of the line, repulsed by the sight. Two trainers moved their way down the line, using their hands and mouths to touch and feel and caress the slaves in places they considered private, off-limits, places where many had never been touched before.

It wasn't even one of those places that put him over the edge; that he could tune out, pretend it wasn't happening. It was a hand on his chest, caressing, scratching lightly across his skin. He had been a slave long enough to know better, but it didn't matter, because he swatted the trainer's hand away and jerked backward, glaring reproachfully. He could handle force and pain, it was the intimate touch that had thrown him.

He had been so stupid, then, Wren realized. He thought about the current mess he was in, and wondered why he hadn't grown less stupid since then. The consequences....

He should have known that he couldn't get away so easily. The trainer had grabbed him, forced his touch all over him,paying special attention to the places that made Wren the most uncomfortable. Teeth nibbling behind his ears. Fingers shoved into his mouth while he was forced to suck on them. A thousand light scratches and caresses over his chest, soft enough not to hurt, hard enough to make him squirm.

As Wren felt revulsion and bile rising in his throat, he felt himself being pushed over to another trainer who held him tightly by the arms as the first trainer leered at him.

"You like that, don't you, boy?" the trainer asked, touching him again.

Wren's whole being wanted to scream "no," but he knew he couldn't. "Please, sir," he whimpered, unwilling to say anything else.

"Do you like it?" the trainer asked again, laughing cruelly and grabbing his cock. "I think you do."

Wren was horrified to realize he had grown hard under the attention. "Please, sir, please, no!"

"You'll like it if I say you like it."

While one held Wren in place, the other violated him with light touches, forcing his body to respond in ways that it never had with another person. Wren was only somewhat aware of the other slaves watching him, the horrified looks and and sounds of disgust a distant background noise.

"This one was meant for it," one of the trainers jeered. "You want to come, don't you?"

"No," Wren moaned. But he did. His body did. His mind wanted nothing more than to be dead.

"Just keep pretending," the trainer taunted, his hands expertly continuing to work Wren's cock. "You're mine, and if I say you want it, you want it."

The trainer continued until the inevitable happened and Wren came against his will, tears pouring as he did.

He hoped it would stop, but the fact that his body had finished didn't mean his torment would.

"Who does your body belong to, slave?" they asked him, over and over again, fingers and teeth and tongues on him in places he used to consider sacred. "Who do you belong to?"

Wren shuddered at the memory. It wasn't the same, his master didn't treat him like that, but he could; he had every right to. His body was no more his than this bedroom was. The bedroom, his body, his very being—they were all property of his master, and forgetting it was a dangerous offense. They didn't beat him for flinching away at the training facility, not that first time, but what they did was worse, passing him around, putting him on display. How had he forgotten that lesson? He could have stayed safe, denied his urges, kept his mouth shut. He could have let Jere do what he wanted to him, once he opened that door. But he hadn't, and he would certainly suffer for it.

The day crawled by. Wren stayed silent and isolated, reading a bit, pacing a bit, and driving himself to a near-panic thinking of the consequences that his actions would bring. Once or twice, he thought about how hungry he was, as he hadn't bothered to set foot outside of his bedroom for food. He marveled at how unused to hunger he had become. Perhaps it was better that he become accustomed to it once again. He could hear Jere moving around, doing everyday things, but he was never called, so he decided to stay hiding. Denial was so much more pleasant than reality.

It had grown dark outside, nighttime. Wren lay in bed, trying to keep his breathing steady to stave off the next panic attack. They were more and more frequent now, as he had imagined a whole string of things his master might do to punish him. He heard a knock on the door and stopped breathing, squeezing his eyes shut at the thought of what would come next. He heard a scratching sound, and looked over to see a piece of paper slipping under his door. Footsteps moved away and down the hall. He was still alone.

With caution, he sat up and made his way to the door, picking up the paper. What would it be? A receipt from his sale? An angry rebuke? With trembling hands, he unfolded it to reveal the brief message.

Wren,

There's food outside the door. Please eat. I'll be in my room all night. Don't bother joining me in the clinic until you're ready. I can cover on my own for a few days.

When you're ready to talk, let me know.

Please know—I'm not angry with you.

—Jere

Wren read the note over three times before he even processed what it meant. Numb, he set it down on the table next to his bed, opened the door, and looked at the food that sat there. A sandwich, so typical of Jere, some fruit, and a thermos with tea in it. As if Wren would let himself starve. Actually, he might. He had. He was surprised that Jere noticed this time. Shaking his head, he pulled the food into his room, sat on his bed, and ate it rather halfheartedly. At least he could do that right.

"*Please know — I'm not angry with you.*" He could just about hear his master saying that. The soft, pained eyes looking at him like he had done something wrong, instead of Wren. Like he had to try to please his slave, instead of the other way around.

Chapter 25
Companionship

Jere woke and had breakfast alone for the second day in a row. As trivial as it seemed, he was rather bothered by it. Even when he and Wren had first started living together and the kid never spoke a word to him, he was there, he was company, and Jere knew that he was at least alive. More recently, he had actually come to look forward to spending time with him, he had started to converse and smile and....

And then he had kissed him, and fucked it all up.

Jere was jerked back to reality by the unpleasant memory. Of course, the memory of the kiss was anything but unpleasant, but even enjoying that in retrospect made Jere feel guilty. He felt terrible, absolutely awful for taking advantage of the boy like he had, and the fact that Wren now felt the need to hide wasn't making it any better. Had he gone too far, or had Wren? He couldn't tell, but in any case, he was the master, he was the one who was supposed to be in control, he was the one who should have been responsible.

Jere finished up his breakfast and went through the door to the clinic. He was glad it was Monday, and the day after a holiday, because he was extra busy, and without Wren there to help, he barely had a moment to think. Only a few patients asked where his slave was, and he mentioned casually that he was working on other, more important projects for him. He was pretty sure that "hiding from me" wouldn't be an acceptable answer. He wished everyone would just stop asking questions.

Lunchtime rolled around and, with nothing to eat and nobody to eat it with, Jere sat in an empty exam room with a stack of crackers and jar of jelly and tried not to berate himself any more than necessary.

He suddenly felt a bit of a tug on the mind connection he shared with Wren.

"Sir? What would you like for dinner?"

"You to talk to me." The words spilled out before Jere had a chance to think them through, and he realized they sounded remarkably callous. *"Er, but steak would be nice in the process."* He had tried to cover up his last statement with humor. He doubted it had gone over very well.

"Yes, sir."

He felt the connection closing, and while Wren wasn't quite blocking him, he certainly sent out waves of avoidance. Jere sighed and resisted the urge to hit himself in the head for being so forward with the poor kid.

Wren made steak, as requested, and also some rather excessive side dishes and desserts. In all honesty, he was too nervous to sit still, and couldn't bear the thought of lounging around in his room all day while his master did his own work and covered for him and was probably furiously angry, despite the note, and… and he would be walking through the door at any minute.

He placed his master's food at the table, not even bothering to set his own down. He didn't deserve to sit and eat next to him and he knew it, although he had cooked himself the same food. How many times had he been ordered to do that very thing? He couldn't just ignore those orders. He had to do something right.

Wren was hiding in the kitchen when he heard his master walk in, take a few steps into the dining room, and pause. His heartbeat jumped, and he had to remind himself to keep breathing. Here it was, the moment he faced his master.

"Wren?" Jere's voice was uncertain. Wren was positive it was because he was trying to hide his anger until he saw him. "Please, join me? I really do want to talk with you."

He heard a chair pull out, then slide back in, with more weight in it. He closed his eyes for a moment, took a deep breath, and walked out into the dining room.

"There you are."

Wren didn't notice the soft tone. He didn't see the slight smile on Jere's face when he walked in the room, or the way he turned his chair toward him. He walked mutely across the room, paused next to his master's chair, and dropped to the floor, curling his knees underneath of him and dropping his head until his forehead touched the ground. He wasn't even aware that he was shaking as he knelt there.

"Wren...?"

He heard his master's voice, so full of disappointment and shame and probably anger, although Jere was so fucking *good* at controlling his anger. Not like it mattered, he'd certainly be taking it out on him in a few minutes anyway. Which he deserved. This was it. This wasn't some little thing, some misunderstanding, some petty, trivial event that could be brushed aside or dismissed. Wren had actively rejected his advances, ran off, *hid* from him even, as if Jere didn't have every right to access his body and do whatever he wanted with it.

"I'm sorry, I'm sorry, I'm so sorry, sir." That whimpering, was it him? "Please don't send me away, sir, you're so kind, I'm just, I'm just stupid, and I won't do it again, sir, please, you can have me however you want, you can use me whatever, whenever, I, I'll submit to any punishment you'd like, sir, please, god, please, just beat me or use me or whatever and get it over with, I promise I'll be better, I'll never do it again, sir, please... forgive me?"

Silence.

For what seemed like an eternity, Wren heard nothing, felt nothing but his own silent, wracking sobs. Then he heard the chair sliding out and being pushed away, and he braced himself for the first blow.

Instead, he heard his master pause in front of him, and felt his hands ever so lightly on his shoulders.

"Sit up and look at me?" The words carried an order, but they were soft and hesitant.

Wren sat up, barely, and opened his eyes. Jere knelt in front of him, his face tight. He didn't move his arms, and Wren didn't particularly want him to.

"Sir, I...." Wren had no idea what he wanted to say. "I'm sorry. Please, punish me as you see fit." That was always a good line, right?

"I don't see fit," Jere shook his head as he spoke. "Jesus, Wren, you have nothing to apologize for. I should be the one apologizing to you, except I have a bit of a hard time doing that, because you're so much better at it."

Wren thought the last part might be a joke, but it wasn't possible. Why would his master be joking when he should be about to punish him?

"Please, sir. I disobeyed you. I offended you. I—"

"Shh." Jere's hand was brushing his cheek then, ever so softly, and back through his hair. "Just stop. Please. Let me explain."

Wren leaned into his hand, certain that this would be the last kind touch he felt from the man. He trembled, his silent sobs continuing despite the gentle tone.

"Wren, I took advantage of you. You were drunk—of my doing. And, well, whether I like it or not, I'm your master, and you're my slave, and I highly doubt that you would ever have been so bold as to reject me outright, so it's my job to notice, and it's my job to be appropriate with you, and I wasn't. I'm the one at fault here. And I'm sorry."

Wren looked into his master's face, seeing nothing there but concern and regret. How could he look so upset, when this whole situation had been Wren's fault?

"Sir, it, it was appropriate," Wren whimpered, feeling like he was shooting himself in the foot as he did. He barely kept himself from sobbing as he forced words out. "I—I'm your slave, and I belong to you, and if you want to, to do anything with me, then it isn't my place to try... to try and stop you, because you own me, and I sh-should be glad that it wasn't painful and I—"

"No."

His master's voice was forceful, more than it had been in weeks, and possibly a little angry. Wren whimpered and dropped back down to the floor, curling his arms over his head to protect it.

"I'm sorry, sir. Master. I, I won't complain, even if it is painful—"

"Wren!"

Wren froze, not even breathing, as he heard his master let out an exasperated sigh.

"For the love of god, please, stop apologizing. Do you really think that little of me? And—no, don't answer that, don't say anything, just hear me out."

Wren sat silently. Don't say anything. He could do that. He could be good, please his master. Perhaps, then, he would be lenient with him? Not that he deserved leniency, but....

A strong hand rubbing gentle circles on his back pulled him back to the present.

"Wren, I haven't seen you this worked up about something since I first got here, and I like that I haven't, because I hate seeing you scared, I hate knowing that I'm the one who scares you like this. And, really, Wren, I like you. A lot, actually. You're fucking brilliant, you have such a subtle, quick sense of humor—my life here would be miserable without you in it. And I guess I just thought—oh hell, I didn't think, okay? Because, well, I was drunk too, and there you were, and you're fucking beautiful, I hope you know that, and I was, well, I was a fucking asshole—but I forgot, for a minute, who you were, and who I was, and even if that kind of thing is acceptable here, it is *not* acceptable to me. Wren, what *I* did was unacceptable, not you. And I hate thinking—*knowing*—that I'm the kind of person who would do that, but I certainly wouldn't be the kind of person who would take it out on you later, is that clear?"

Wren tried to nod, but with his head still pressed to the floor, he wasn't very successful. "Yes, sir," he managed to whisper.

"Wren." The master's voice was soft and soothing, as was his hand on Wren's back. "Sit up. And look at me. And talk to me. I'm not angry."

Somewhat reluctantly, Wren opened his eyes. He sat up slowly, his eyes moving on their own to his master's face. The hand on his back slid over his shoulder, down his arm, and rested on his hand, holding it gently, just enough to maintain the connection. He looked into his master's face, still expecting to see anger there, despite everything. He found only a soft, sad look.

"I shouldn't have run away from you."

"I wish you hadn't, but I understand why you did. I shouldn't have put you in that position."

"I ran off. And hid. And didn't even come out to work or clean or cook."

"True. You did. And look, I'm still alive!" Jere grinned a little. "And if you want to run off and hide and do nothing and have me bring you poorly constructed sandwiches for a few more days, you're completely welcome to do so. I mean, I'd rather you talked to me, hell, I'd rather you called me a stupid fucking asshole and threw things at me—not that you ever would—but Wren, please, work with me? Don't let things go back to the way they were when I first got here. I couldn't bear it."

Wren finally understood. Jere really wasn't angry with him, against all odds. He was upset—upset to disrupt their relationship. Companionship.

Wren rubbed his eyes, clearing away the tears. "I'm sorry, sir. I should have just talked to you. I know—I should know—you are better than that. You've never given me a reason to think otherwise."

Jere shook his head. "Kid, I don't think you *need* me to give you a reason to think otherwise. Someone else has already fucked that up for me. I just need to remember it."

Wren nodded. It was true, what his master had said. Years of training and time with Burghe and being raised with the social expectations of what a slave should act like had made him this upset, not anything that Jere had done or said. Jere had been following his lead, letting him set the pace, making him feel good, and that had scared Wren as much as the possibility that he would stop doing it. "Thank you, sir, for being so understanding."

Jere squeezed his hand. "It's the least I can do. And I really am sorry—that you were scared, and that I made you do something the other night that you didn't like."

"But I did like it."

Too much emotional strain and panic-induced honesty had really taken a toll on Wren's filter. There it was, his chance to agree with his master and chase off any future events like that and he had tossed it away. A part of him wished he could take back those words, hide those desires that he shouldn't be having in the first place.

"You...? But then, why? I mean...." Jere's voice trailed off, and he cocked his head in confusion.

Wren struggled to remain calm as he attempted to dig himself out of this mess. He shouldn't want this, and he shouldn't continue to encourage it. "It wasn't unpleasant, sir."

"Not exactly the best review I've gotten."

"What I mean is...." Wren had no idea where he was going with this. "Well, I, it felt good. And I liked it. And I even asked you to keep going, and you did, and I liked it, and I meant it when I asked you to keep going."

Jere nodded, his eyebrows creasing as he struggled to understand. "Okay...?"

Wren realized he *had* to continue, now that he had gotten this far in. "Sir, I just, I got scared, and I didn't know how far you would go, or if you would stop, or if I should stop you, and then I started thinking about what would happen if I did, and I knew it would be worse if I stopped you later on, or maybe you wouldn't even stop then, although I really didn't and don't think you'd do that, but I did at the time and it just seemed like the only thing I could do was leave and then I was afraid to face you again, afraid that you'd hurt me or send me away and I just—I've grown too comfortable around you!"

Jere looked at him expectantly, waiting to make sure he was finished. "Okay," he said simply.

"But you didn't get angry at me. Or hurt me. Or anything."

"Nope." Jere shook his head. "And I'm not going to. It's okay that you're more comfortable with me. I like it."

"So." Wren found himself unable to tear his eyes away from his master's face. "So that's what happened, that's why I ran away. But I did like it."

Jere was silent and still for a moment, then a wide smile spread across his face. "I'm glad. Because I liked it too. And it's really better if that goes both ways."

Wren nodded. He didn't trust himself to speak, afraid he'd say or do something too forward again.

"And if it ever comes up again—and don't feel pressured, it might not—please, try and remember, you have my *express* permission to call it off at any point." Jere raised an eyebrow in Wren's direction. "You don't need to run off, although you can if you feel better doing that, but I wish you'd just tell me, and talk to me. I won't force you, or even pressure you, and you have my word that I will never be angry at you for that."

"I would like it to come up again." Wren heard the words come out of his mouth and wondered what the hell was wrong with him! He was going to say "yes, sir" and leave it at that, all docile and agreeable and not asking for more in the future—how had he blurted that out instead? But it really had been nice, for a minute.

Jere looked at him, appraising him for a moment, then pulled Wren's hand gently toward him. "Then come here."

Wren tried to force himself to stay calm. Wren had started this in the first place, so it was only right that Jere lead now. Wren knew it was wrong to hope that Jere would continue to let him lead, knew that it wasn't his place, as a slave. He hoped that it would be enjoyable, and tried to convince himself that his heart was racing from something other than fear this time.

He was surprised to find himself pulled close into Jere's chest, his arms wrapping around him and circling his back again.

"When you're ready, I want you to come to me," Jere whispered in his ear, dropping down to press a light kiss against his neck. "I'm not going to push you, and I don't want you to do anything you don't want to. If you want to do more, you can tell me, and we'll go from there. I like knowing that you want it. Take your time to think about it, but don't feel pressured either way. I won't hold it against you, and you shouldn't have to make this decision now. I can wait."

Wren finally relaxed. As wrong as it was, he felt so much better having the choice explicitly handed to him. He vowed not to let it get out of control, not like it had last time, where he had actually dared to think that it was his right to control things. Still, things felt better this way.

Chapter 26
Something So Wonderful

Dinner that night went quietly but smoothly. Although Wren had said little more than a few words to him for the rest of the night, Jere was relieved to find that the horrible, painful tension between the two of them had dissipated. In truth, he was counting his lucky fucking stars that his beautiful, wonderful assistant hadn't shut him out for good—although he was pretty sure he might have deserved it. He hadn't really thought, well, *at all* the other night. He had just been in the exact right place, so close and so intimate, and it seemed like a good, no, a *great* idea to lean in and kiss him. Had he been asked a day, an hour, hell, a *minute* earlier, he would have said it was a crazy, stupid idea, and one he never would have tried.

But then he had done it, and it had been wonderful, and Wren had even asked him to continue.

In a way, Jere had been expecting the push back, although he hadn't expected quite the violent reaction he had gotten, and he certainly hadn't expected the way that Wren had begged his forgiveness. He understood the reason behind it on a logical level, but it didn't mean that the execution didn't still make him a little nauseous. He wanted to revive his old fling and kill him for hurting the boy so fucking much.

And yet, a few days passed, and things seemed to have gone remarkably back to normal. Jere took it as a testament to their relationship, and certainly to Wren's trust in him, that the kid no longer felt the need to tiptoe around him for days after a conflict. It was as though nothing had ever happened, although he would have sworn (and admittedly, hoped like hell) that he saw Wren sneaking glances at him here and there, a contemplative look on his face.

Of course, Wren had a speed-gift, and Jere only had his rather feeble sense of tact to hide his stolen peeks. He more or less resigned himself to simply appreciating the slave and being glad that Wren didn't hate him. That had been more than enough before, and Jere told himself that it would have to continue to be enough.

The second week of the new year started off with a rather challenging day at work for both of them. There was an unexpected number of patients, none of them in a good mood, combined with the usual irritating things happening—a vial of medicine slipping and breaking, elbows banged on tables, that sort of thing. Despite his general good temper, Jere even got a bit irritated, snapping at Wren over something little. He felt like a horrible bastard when the kid nodded and stalked out, muttering, "If that's the way you want it to be, sir." Still, a part of him was glad that Wren had gotten angry instead of dropping to the floor sobbing again. Jere was pretty sure that he would have joined him in a misery party at that point.

Of course, he apologized over dinner, but by that time, Wren had carefully masked his face to show no emotions, and dismissed it as "Fine, no big deal." A cold, dismissive Wren was rather nerve-wracking.

Jere retired to the couch after dinner, curling up in the corner he had unofficially claimed as his own and leafing through a book of modern medical marvels. The influx of new and different gifts provided a constant challenge to the medical field. There was always something interesting to find out, and, more importantly, be prepared for as a doctor.

He felt Wren's presence before he heard him speak.

"Sir?" Wren stood at the opposite end of the couch, alternating between looking at Jere and looking down at his hand, which tugged at a stray thread on the arm of the couch.

"Yeah?" Jere had no idea what Wren wanted now. Had the cold shoulder all day not gotten his point across clearly enough that he had been an asshole?

"I'm ready, sir." Wren looked away as he said it, tugging on the loose thread more aggressively as he did so.

Jere wracked his brain, trying to remember if they were supposed to go somewhere. "Ready for what?"

"Um...." Wren began to blush. "For what we talked about the other day, sir?"

Jere was confused for a few moments. Suddenly, it dawned on him, and he felt his eyes go wide. "Oh!"

Wren grinned a little. "You said, sir, when I was ready...."

"Yes. Yes I did." Jere put his book down and sat up, nodding. "I just didn't think—I've been in a terrible mood all day; I figured you wanted to be as far away from me as possible."

"Well, that's true, sir, but if you're in that terrible of a mood and the worst you do is get a little short and then apologize later, I guess I find it difficult to really worry about upsetting you," Wren admitted. "Besides, I realized that even when you were being a little mean, I was still thinking about kissing you. I mean, only if you're ready too, and if you have time and if you still want to, and...."

"Yes," Jere found himself laughing a bit. He smiled at Wren and beckoned him over with his finger. As he came closer, Jere couldn't stop himself from smiling. "I am, and I do."

Wren sat next to him, looking a little less bold than he had a minute ago. He had his hands folded neatly in his lap, and he was looking forward, not at Jere, sitting next to him.

Jere gave him a few seconds, then figured Wren probably wasn't going to move of his own accord. The alcohol had lowered his inhibitions the other night, but they were back in full force now. He reached out and put a hand on Wren's shoulder, not entirely surprised when he jumped.

"You all right?" Jere kept his voice soft, like he was talking to a scared kitten.

Wren nodded, still not looking at him. "Yes, sir."

"You know, you don't have to do this if you don't want to."

Wren finally looked at him. "But I do want to! Sir, I just...." he finally turned toward Jere. "I want you to kiss me like you did the other night."

Jere smiled. He wanted that, too. "Okay," he said encouragingly, "and you'll tell me if you want me to stop, right?"

Wren nodded, looking a little uncertain still.

Wren seemed to be trying so hard to hold back, clinging to some notion that he couldn't or shouldn't direct their interactions. Jere wished he would be as bold as he had been the other night, but it looked like it was up to him to at least start things now. Besides, Wren had made a very specific request, and Jere was eager to fulfill it.

"Lean back and relax a little — be daring, maybe put your feet up on the couch or something."

Wren shot him a sarcastic look in response to his comment, but did as Jere suggested, bringing his legs up next to him and leaning back against the couch. Jere leaned over next to him, running his hands slowly up his arms, across his shoulders, and pausing with them cupping his face. He tilted his head up to get a better look.

"Doing all right?"

Wren nodded. His breathing had sped up, but Jere sensed much more nervous excitement from him than fear.

Jere leaned in, very slowly, and pressed their lips together. He focused as much on Wren's strongly broadcast emotions as he did on the softness of Wren's lips. Of course, this soon went by the way-side, as Jere was caught up in the feeling of kissing him.

The kiss was neither long nor deep, as they weren't drunk or in any sort of hurry. Jere simply responded as carefully as he could, hoping Wren would set the pace, reminding himself to keep his roaming hands under control. Wren was still for only a few seconds before he started kissing back, parting his lips and relaxing as he leaned forward into the kiss. Wren moved on top, pushing Jere to lean back a little, and Jere felt them both becoming more comfortable.

Jere kept going, paying attention to Wren's breathing, until he noticed his breaths coming more quickly and shallowly. He pulled back slowly, keeping his hands on Wren's shoulders.

Wren opened his eyes and looked at him suspiciously. "What's wrong, sir?"

Jere squeezed his shoulder, shaking his head. "Nothing's wrong, I just wanted to breathe for a minute. Everything okay on your end?"

Wren nodded. "Yes, sir. Very okay. Keep going, please."

Jere grinned, then pulled him close again. "You just tell me if you want me to stop, okay?"

"Yes, sir," Wren whispered, his mouth less than an inch away from Jere's.

They came back together just as slowly and took their time exploring each other's mouths. Jere ran his hands across Wren's back and shoulders, and occasionally through his hair, which he noticed made him shudder quite nicely, arching into his touch. He felt a tongue slip into his mouth and welcomed it, massaging it with his own until he heard Wren gasp with pleasure. Jere felt Wren's hands rest on his legs, touching hesitantly at first, then more boldly. He smiled to see that Wren was responding, daring to make his own moves. Wren's face was twisted with pleasure, and Jere felt more confident knowing that they were both enjoying it.

He felt the change, although he couldn't quite say what had caused it. Suddenly, Wren halted his explorations, stiffened beneath him, and stopped responding to his touch. Allowing his hands to stay where they were, Jere leaned back a bit, looking at him carefully. "You okay?"

Wren opened his eyes for a second, looked at him, and squeezed them shut again. He jerked his hands back away from Jere's legs. Jere waited, not moving, unsure of what he was going to do.

"You said... you said I could stop whenever I wanted to, right, sir?" His words were barely audible.

Jere nodded, then realized he couldn't hear him. "Yeah, I did. I meant it. Do you want to stop?"

Wren nodded, opening his eyes warily. "I think I do, sir."

"Okay." Jere looked back at him, trying to appear calm. "Tell me what you want me to do."

"I want—I, I don't know, sir!" He began to tremble. "Don't make me say, I shouldn't—I just took things too far and I shouldn't have. Please, I'm sorry!"

Jere didn't move closer or further away, but gently stroked the back of his head. He wasn't exactly sure what Wren was upset about. From what he could tell, they had both been enjoying what they had been doing, and Wren had even started to get a little more assertive, right before he called it off. "Don't apologize, kid, you're doing just fine. That was lovely. Nothing bad's gonna happen, okay? Just relax."

Wren nodded, and slowly began to calm down, his trembling subsiding. His eyes stayed closed, although he did slide an inch or so closer to Jere. "I really am sorry, sir."

"I know," Jere said softly. "You don't have to be, but it's okay if you are."

They sat like that for a few minutes, until Jere noticed Wren's breathing evening out. He had rested his head against the back of the couch, trapping one of Jere's hands with it while the other one continued petting him.

"Can we stop for tonight, sir?" Wren asked, burying his face into the couch as he did.

Jere nodded, but didn't stop touching him. "Of course. Do you want to talk about it?"

Wren shook his head silently.

"Okay. Do you want to go back to your room, or for me to go back to mine?"

Another headshake, more emphasized this time.

"Okay." Jere sat like that for a while longer, until the position was obviously becoming uncomfortable for both of them. He looked at the boy curling into his hand, relaxed now, but a bit fidgety. He sat up slowly. "Here," he gently guided Wren with his hand. "Come and sit next to me, yes, there, like that. It'd be nice for us both to have feelings in our legs when we're done with this, right?"

A little laugh; that was a good sign. "Yes, sir."

"Do you mind if I read?" Jere asked.

"No, sir." Wren shifted a bit, staying close to Jere as he did.

Jere leaned away for a moment, picked up his book, and then asked, "Anything for you? A book, some tea—"

"No, sir." Wren cut him off. "I'm fine like this."

Jere settled back, one arm around Wren, who leaned into him cautiously. It was more than he ever would have expected from the person who had tensed up almost every time he was touched. He had really never expected Wren to like him, much less desire him like this. He couldn't have been more pleased with the way the situation had turned out.

He had become rather engrossed in the current case study he

was reading, and was a bit startled when he heard Wren's voice.

"I've only ever had one real kiss before, sir."

Jere didn't move. Was this really the same Wren? Talking to him? "Oh, yeah?" He tried to remain casual.

"Before I was taken. I was twelve, and a girl named Arianne Moreny kissed me behind the mail cart at school." Wren's voice had taken on a tone of far away nostalgia. "I didn't like it very much then. I didn't really like girls, or boys, either. And she had some sort of horrible lip balm that tasted like synthetic fish product. She claimed it was 'desire' flavor or something. And then, a few months later, I was taken, and I never had anyone ask if they could kiss me again."

Jere pulled him close, taking extra care to be gentle with him. "I'll always ask," he promised, "and I'll stop if you say no. And I'll certainly *never* wear fish flavored lip balm."

Wren took a moment to process what he had said, then laughed. "I think I believe you, sir."

"I certainly hope so," Jere looked down at him with a smirk. "I mean, really, if you catch me with fish flavored lip balm, you should report me to the medical authorities, because I've clearly lost my mind and I could be a serious danger to the health and safety of others."

Wren laughed, relaxing and moving a little closer to him. "I really am sorry that I get so nervous, sir."

"Don't worry about it. Six years of not having the choice to stop has to take an awful toll on you."

Wren nodded, then fell silent again for a while.

Jere returned to his book, feeling oddly comfortable with Wren tucked under his arm. A few more minutes passed.

"Sir?" Wren was looking up at him. "Kiss me? Just a little? Please?"

Jere was unable to contain his smile as he set his book down, cupped Wren's chin, and placed a very light, almost chaste kiss on his lips.

"Good?"

Wren nodded, blushing and smiling as he did. "Yes, sir. Very good."

He didn't press for more. Wren had only asked to be kissed a little, and that was it. If he wanted more, he could ask.

He didn't, although they did spend the rest of the night curled up together like that, silent, Jere reading while Wren alternated between napping and reading over his shoulder. Finally Jere realized it must have been getting late, and gently stirred Wren.

"It's late, and we both should be up and working tomorrow," he said regretfully. "But Wren, thank you for tonight. It was amazing. If it happens again, I'll be looking forward to it, and if not, well, not gonna lie, I'll be sad, but that's okay, too. Just do whatever feels comfortable for you, okay?"

Wren nodded, looking serious. "Yes, sir." He toyed with Jere's hand, which he had captured in his own. "Thank you, sir. I never thought... I like doing this with you."

Jere smiled back at him. "I do too, Wren. I like it a lot."

"Me too, sir." There was that adorable shyness again. "I'll see you tomorrow."

"Peaceful rest and pleasant dreams," Jere murmured without thinking of it. It was an old phrase, something parents whispered to their children and lovers wished to one another. He hadn't thought of it in ages.

"Same to you, sir," Wren said, hesitated a minute, then headed off to his room.

Jere followed suit, smiling at his good fortune. He had no idea what he had done to deserve something so wonderful.

Chapter 27
Trying Something Different

Wren spent three nights in a row in the same blissful, soothing pattern with Jere. Working all day, as usual, dinner prepared by him, and then sitting together and kissing and reading on the couch. They chatted sometimes, but never about very much — a funny story from their work day, something one of them had noticed in a book, plans for something the next day — but, mostly, they enjoyed the silence together.

And the kissing. And the touching.

Wren couldn't remember the last time he had enjoyed being so close to anyone. Perhaps at the training facility, but that was different, a bunch of scared, thirteen-year-old kids huddled together for warmth and protection and....

He pushed those thoughts out of his head. There was no way he was going to waste his time thinking about a training facility when he had yet to memorize every square inch of his master's body. He would much rather think about the amazing things that his tongue could do while kissing him.

He knew he was acting unusually. He thought about how he had interacted with Jere months ago, and he barely recognized the person he had been then. He was much more proper then, which kept things between himself and Jere clearer, but he liked their relationship so much more now. A collection of nagging fears still existed in the back of his mind, but every time he demanded more or called a halt to their explorations, his master's gentle acceptance pushed them further away. He finally understood sappy romance novels and love stories — whatever was bad, those soft, sweet kisses and gentle caresses could chase it away, and he could end the night curled into his lover's arm.

His master's arm.

Was there a difference?

The thought came many, many times, and Wren resolutely discarded it from his mind. It was a stupid thought, and it killed the moment, and besides, Jere didn't act like any *other* master he had ever had or heard of. Thinking of Jere as his master reminded Wren that he was a slave, and that slaves shouldn't do any of the things he was doing. He liked what he was doing too much to want to think about that.

His favorite part about the whole thing, although there were many, was simply being touched. Soft, gentle, non-demanding touches that didn't hurt him and actually made him feel good. How could he have gone so long without being touched or hugged or held by another person? Before he and Jere started this thing, he had actively recoiled from touch, most of the time. Some of Burghe's friends, the less sadistic ones, they would touch him, but it was always in the context of making use of him. They could be gentle, and maybe they would even hold him after, but he hated that more than the ones who banged his head into the floor and walked out after finishing inside of him. The thought that someone was trying to force intimacy, not just sex, had been the most repulsive.

Jere didn't force anything. True to his word, he let Wren initiate and stop pretty much everything, simply going along and encouraging him. The freedom was as terrifying as the uncertainty, but Wren was getting accustomed to it. Jere clearly preferred it that way, and while Wren was scared to be so demanding and assertive, he had to admit that he preferred it that way as well. Wren had never felt so sure of another person before. He just wondered if he could feel as sure of himself.

He found himself wanting to try something different. He thought back to the night after he had been detained and beaten at the police post, and the massage he had given Jere afterward. One of the only times, before now, that he had voluntarily laid a finger on the man he was making out with every night. How much better would it be now that they both wanted to touch each other?

The night started as usual. Dinner, some conversation, some tea afterward. As they finished, and Wren cleaned up, Jere stood to move to the living room. Wren caught him with a hand on his arm.

"Sir?"

"Hmm?" Jere smiled at him.

"I, um...." Wren struggled not to panic, to keep breathing. "I thought we might do something different tonight, sir."

The smile grew a little larger. "What did you have in mind?"

Wren bit his lower lip, blushing a little. "I, sir... remember when I gave you that massage?"

Jere nodded, still smiling.

"Well, I thought, I could...." Wren shrugged helplessly.

"Am I so lucky to be offered the pleasure again?" Jere supplied. "Or would you like me to return the favor?"

"No!" Wren was startled by how uncomfortable the idea of receiving Jere's affections had made him. Hadn't he just been thinking he was comfortable with his master? "I mean, I, I want to do it for you, sir."

Jere studied him for a moment, then nodded, smiling once again. "I would be quite honored."

Wren tensed up a bit as Jere led him to his bedroom. As he watched his master flop carelessly onto the bed, for a split second, Wren envied his carefree ease. It was a luxury he had never experienced, one he never thought he would have as a slave. Jere never seemed to overthink things, or panic, he just went along, perfectly content and relaxed, if not oblivious to everything around him.

"How do you want me?" Jere smirked.

"I think... however you're most comfortable, sir." Wren hadn't exactly thought this out beforehand.

"Hmm," Jere seemed to be thinking very hard. "Well, I really like it when I have a sweet, soft boy next to me...."

Wren looked down, trying to hide his smile as he climbed into bed next to Jere. He moved closer, smiling when Jere pulled him close and gently kissed him on the neck the second he did.

"Much better," Jere nodded approvingly. "Nice and comfortable."

Wren stayed in his arms for a few minutes more, reveling in his newfound enjoyment at being held and touched so gently. Finally, focused on what he wanted to do and eager to accomplish that goal, he pulled away a little bit.

"Shall I lose the clothes?"

Wren hesitated. Of course he wanted him to do that, but he wasn't quite sure. One less layer of clothes between them meant that other things were easier, faster, harder to stop. Would he be expected to do the same? He didn't want that. He *really* didn't want that.

A soft hand brushed his cheek, drawing him back to reality.

"Maybe I'll just lose the shirt, then, and you can tell me if you want anything else." Jere leaned in and kissed him, very softly, on the forehead. "It's up to you."

Wren breathed a sigh of relief. "Thank you, sir."

Pulling away for a moment, Jere stripped off his shirt, leaving his upper half bare. And, Wren thought, delicious.

He lay down on his stomach, resting his head on one arm and facing Wren with a smile on his face. "Like what you see?"

Wren ducked his head away, trying not to laugh. "Yes, sir."

"So do I."

Wren placed his hands on his master gently, tentatively at first, rewarded by an instant, encouraging relaxation. He worked his hands up and down across the soft skin of his master's back, marveling at the definition of the muscles he found there. The area right between his shoulder blades seemed especially enticing, and before he knew it, he had leaned down to place a kiss in that exact spot, drawing a rather surprised moan from Jere.

Wren laughed, embarrassed by his own forwardness, but certainly not put off from continuing. Inspired by the reaction he had gotten from the last one, he placed a line of kisses across his back, even flicking his tongue out a few times in the process. Jere continued to moan underneath of him, squirming a bit as Wren moved up and around his neck.

"God, that's amazing! Someone's got you trained," Jere muttered as Wren simultaneously squeezed on a knot in his shoulders and kissed around his ear.

Wren froze.

Yes, actually, someone had. Someone he preferred not to think about.

Rather mechanically, he resumed the motions with his hands, moving them over muscle groups and flesh and pressure points as he had been trained, finding the exact spots that were physically responsive and—

"Fuck. Wren, I'm sorry." Jere was pushing himself up on one arm, facing Wren, who turned away so his master wouldn't see the angry tears about to drop from his eyes.

"Hey, kid, look at me," Jere spoke softly and reached out, putting a hand on Wren's leg.

Wren jerked away, huddling at the end of the bed, wrapping his arms around his legs. This *was* what he had been trained for, after all. To be a slave. Used for sex. To make his master feel good. Was it really that obvious?

"Well, shit." Jere sighed. "Wren, I didn't mean it like that. What I meant was, you know, like, you're in a relationship or something with someone, and they teach you things. Things like that. Things like how to make someone so absolutely and completely fucking hot that they lose their mind and all common sense and say shit that is fucking stupid."

Wren said nothing, but nodded a little bit. He had heard the expression before, between free people. But it had a different connotation between free people.

As if he had read his mind, Jere continued. "I forget, sometimes. I forget that someone *has* actually trained you. Because, honestly, when your tongue and hands and mouth are on me, I don't think about that. I think about *you*."

"I *am* a slave, sir. *Master*. Your slave." Wren knew the reminder would hurt.

"Yes." The word was full of bitterness and regret. "But you're more than that to me."

Wren tried very hard to stay distant. He reminded himself that what he was doing with his master was stupid and wrong and would only lead to bad things, and that any free person who said they didn't think of their slave as what they were was probably lying. And he tried *very* hard not to think about how nice it felt to be held and kissed in return, because that was just hoping for something that couldn't be.

"Then, what am I to you, sir?" Wren found himself asking, his voice forced and controlled. He couldn't let himself seem vulnerable. He was pretty sure that he could really only tolerate a few possible answers without plunging himself into a dark, depressed void forever.

"You're the first actual friend I had here. My main — and only — source of support. My lover, sometimes. The best fucking assistant I could have hoped or asked for. My international delegate, making sure my stupid ass doesn't get into trouble."

Wren conceded a bit, turning only his head to look at Jere, who was sitting back on his heels and looking longingly at him.

"You're damn near everything to me, Wren, and now, you're sometimes willing to be more. Honestly, I get so caught up in it sometimes that I forget that the rest of the world exists, and why would I want it to?" Jere looked pleadingly at him.

Wren felt himself caving. Was he really all those things to his master? He slowly uncurled his arms from around his legs and went to Jere, burying his head in his chest, breathing in the deep, familiar smell of him as he felt his arms wrapping around him.

"I care about you, Wren," he heard Jere saying softly above his head. "I would never intentionally do anything to hurt you."

"I'm sorry I got so worked up, sir." Wren's face was still pressed into skin, so his words came out a bit muffled.

"Don't be. I was being stupid. Forgetting reality. As much as I hate it."

They sat there for a few minutes, Wren soaking in the soft caresses that Jere was tracing up and down his back, listening to his heartbeat and breathing. Finally, he turned his head to face him. "I'm going to finish the massage, sir," he said, determined not to let his past interfere with his current pleasure. "Lie back down."

Jere smiled back down at him, releasing his hold to do as Wren had asked. "I certainly wouldn't turn down a chance to feel you touching me again."

They picked up where they had left off. If Jere was surprised, he didn't say a word about it, merely arching into Wren's touch and moaning with pleasure as soft lips graced his skin in a thousand places. They continued on like that for a while, until Jere was practically melting under Wren's hands.

He had an idea. "Turn over, sir."

Wordlessly, Jere did as he was told, rolling onto his back and grinning up at Wren, who began a tentative exploration of his chest and stomach.

He worked from the top down, starting with his neck and shoulders and chest, then down his stomach, tracing the thin line of hair that went down from his navel, down to....

Well, Wren figured, that could wait for later.

He stopped at the waist of his master's pants, planting a light line of kisses where the fabric met flesh, then worked his way back up. As he did, he felt Jere's hands moving ever so slowly, coming around his shoulders and stroking his back. It was uncomfortable at first—what if he grabbed him like that and held him down, or did something worse? But after a few minutes, Wren had calmed himself down enough to realize that Jere would not do anything like that. Besides, Wren liked feeling Jere's hands on his skin.

He reached Jere's face again and leaned in for a kiss, thrilled to be met halfway. It was returned with just as much excitement. He stretched out along the length of his master's body, pressing tightly against him, and sighed in pleasure as he felt the now-familiar sensation of a tongue against his lips. He happily let it in, clutching Jere as he did.

They continued along that path for a while, both growing warm and excited and pleased, and soon, Wren became aware of something hard rubbing against him, and was almost painfully aware of the stiffness between his own legs. Without thinking about it, he moved closer to Jere, grinding against him.

"God!" Jere grunted, his face betraying his surprise. "I fucking love touching you."

Wren laughed a little, continuing to rock himself back and forth on his master's body. A little maneuvering, and the bulges in their pants were both situated against the other's legs, and Jere reciprocated, rocking and twisting in time with him.

They kept at it, the motions becoming more frantic and exciting and quick.

"Mmm, don't stop," Jere whispered in his ear, kissing it gently as he pulled Wren closer.

Wren fought the urge to be uncomfortable with the rather demanding way Jere was holding him, gripping his hips and sliding him up and down. He had been enjoying it as well, but this was bordering on too much, too demanding... but hadn't he been ordered not to stop? Was it an order?

"Wren, please, please keep going!"

Was that a whimper? Had he just made his master whimper?

Wren was sufficiently encouraged to continue on. Jere hadn't been demanding, he had been desperate, hungry, *begging* him to keep going. Wren decided he couldn't really be afraid of that. Especially not when Jere sounded so needy, so sexy.

As Wren continued grinding, he decided to be bold and reached his hand down, cupping his master through his pants, and upping the pressure. It wasn't long before he felt Jere tense up and gasp with satisfaction as he came. Panting, Jere held Wren close. Wren stilled on top of him, then rested his head on the pillow next to them and tried to turn so his own erection wouldn't get in the way.

Jere took a few moments to recover, petting Wren's hair gently, and muttering things like "so good" and "holy shit" and "fuck" with contented pleasure. Finally, he relaxed, pulling close and whispering "thank you" as he did.

When he pulled him close, he must have noticed something.

"Wren, didn't you...?"

Wren shook his head. "No, sir, I...." He was a little afraid to say it, but after what they had just done, should he really be embarrassed? "I didn't know whether I was allowed, sir."

"Ahh," Jere nodded. "Of course you were. Are. I want you to— if you want to, of course. I'd never stop you from it."

A little late now, Wren thought bitterly. It wasn't that he wasn't still excited—no, he certainly was—it just wasn't at that mind-blowing-I'm-going-to-explode moment any longer. But, he supposed, that wasn't really his master's fault.

"Let me make it up to you?" Jere smiled, so sure of himself. "Besides, then I get to touch you more!"

Wren grinned back at him. This was something that they would both enjoy. He loved when his master touched him. "Okay, sir."

Jere leaned over him, capturing his mouth in a kiss. "Can I go down on you?" he asked, barely leaving space for words to pass between their lips.

"I..." Wren stalled. Had his master really just asked that? Was he really volunteering to do that? Wren used to hate having to do it, but then, he had hated everything he had been made to do. Could he ask his master to do it? Then again, he didn't think Jere would offer if he didn't want to.

Jere had moved to his ear, ignoring the fact that Wren hadn't responded, and drew his tongue in a delicate line around his earlobe. "I want to. I want to take you in my mouth, feel you growing harder and harder, swallowing you deep...."

Wren was hoping he could avoid listening to the sensual promises, but his cock had other ideas, poking rather unpleasantly into his pants. He moaned a little as Jere strategically rubbed his leg against it.

Jere's lips were moving down, across his neck, to the collar of his shirt. "I can go for hours, you know. Letting you thrust into my mouth. Maybe even humming a little as I reach your balls with my tongue."

Christ, could he do that? Wren couldn't help rocking against him, raking his hands across his back, feeling his soft, warm skin. "I, I don't know, sir, I mean, I don't know if I'm ready...."

Jere kissed him, long, deep, and passionate. "That's okay, too. We can just keep doing this for as long and hard as you'd like."

Wren smiled at his cheesy pun. "I want to, sir, but I...." *I don't want to take my clothes off. I don't want to like it too much.* Wren was irritated with himself for the thoughts. It didn't even make sense. But, still, the thought of being naked, vulnerable, wanting something so bad that he might get carried away, might hurt someone, like he had been hurt.... He felt himself growing nervous just thinking about it.

"Talk to me, kid."

Jere's voice was in his head as he kissed him again. This was certainly more intimate than he had expected. But in a way, it felt better. Easier to say things this way than to have to say them out loud.

"*I – it's stupid, but I don't know if I want to take off my clothes.*" He didn't mention the other part, the part where he thought he might like it, even if Jere didn't.

"*Would it be easier if I took mine off too? Evened it out a bit?*"

"No!" Wren yelped out loud, forgetting to use the mind connection and breaking the kiss. "*I mean –* "

"It's okay," Jere whispered in his ear. "It's okay to tell me what you want—and what you don't."

Wren nodded, glad that his master understood.

"I'd go through your pants if I could, but I think that would just be awful messy and entirely unpleasant for both of us," Jere said, raising an eyebrow. "So what would you say to me slipping a hand down there?"

Wren's breath caught, but he felt pretty certain that it was much more from excitement than fear. This was safer, easier to start and stop. "That... that sounds good, sir."

Jere grinned, moving himself completely above Wren, who looked up at him with wide eyes for a moment before shaking his head a bit.

He struggled to remind himself that nothing bad would happen, that Jere was good and kind and sweet to him, but too many men had been positioned above him like this before they hurt him, badly. He couldn't move, couldn't get away, and he didn't know what he might do if he was trapped like that. He certainly couldn't throw the bulk of another person off quickly enough if he started to hurt him, or take him too roughly, or –

Jere rolled off of him and onto his back. "You on top," he announced, pulling Wren above him. "Better?"

Wren kissed him and nodded. "*Much* better, sir."

The change in positions didn't hinder Jere any, he seemed perfectly comfortable reaching up, sliding his hands across Wren's body, and soon slipping one beneath the waistband of Wren's pants, touching him softly.

Wren felt like his head would explode from the contact. It had been so, so long since anyone had touched him like this, and certainly longer since anyone had done it so kindly. The last time had probably been at the training facility, when—

His thoughts of the training facility were cut short by incoherent moans and grunts and words of ecstasy, which he realized were coming from his own lips. Looking satisfied, Jere continued doing whatever he was doing, and Wren all but cried from the unfamiliar pleasure.

Finally, Wren wasn't sure he could hold back anymore, and didn't really see why he should. He thrust harder and harder against Jere's hand, moaning as he did, and felt Jere's grip tighten around him. He gasped as he came, thrilled to realize that Jere's hand never left him, his other hand never stopped clutching at his back, and his lips never stopped kissing him. He shuddered in pleasure, letting his weight drop to lie on top of his master once again.

At some point they managed to separate, get up, and don clean pants. Wren wondered briefly if Jere had put on the pajama pants for his benefit, since he had often seen his master wearing only boxer shorts to bed. If he had, he didn't mention it. Clean again, they came back together, falling asleep in each other's arms.

Chapter 28
Sharing History

Jere woke up later than usual the next morning, still wrapped around a warm body. It was Sunday, which meant it was a short day of work, which meant sleeping in. Jere stretched and smiled at the thought.

He pressed his lips to Wren's neck, kissing him softly. God, but he felt wonderful! And it was so nice to sleep next to another person again—for a minute last night, he felt Wren get up, as if to leave, but he had beckoned him back, kissing him again until they fell asleep together. Shameless, but it worked. Jere meant what he said the night before—Wren really was damn near everything to him. Jere was perfectly fine with this.

"You awake, sir?" Wren mumbled sleepily next to him.

Jere nibbled on his neck a bit more in response, getting some moans. Wren was obviously tired, and he didn't want to impose, but he couldn't resist touching him and kissing him some more. Not only that, but Wren was starting to respond, arching and stretching his neck to offer up the most sensitive spots.

A few minutes passed. Jere was perfectly content lying here doing this all day, but Wren was stirring a little.

"Would you like breakfast, sir?"

Jere kept nibbling on his neck, his ears, whatever he could reach. *"Can't I just have you?"*

"Mmm," Wren replied, squirming a bit and twisting around to face him. "I'm kind of hungry."

"I was actually thinking I could make breakfast for you," Jere whispered in his ear, reluctant to take his mouth too far away.

"Since you always make it for me. I thought you might be a bit tired after last night."

Wren laughed a little. "It's not a problem, sir."

"I can actually cook a fairly decent breakfast," Jere insisted. "It's one of the only things I *can* cook—eggs, that is. And toast. And I know we have some fresh fruit, you just brought it home the other day. Do you know how long it's been since I've had *fresh* mangoes? Or, at least, since I could afford them. Come on, let me make breakfast."

"If you really want to, sir." Wren looked a little uncertain.

"I do." Jere quieted any further protests with a kiss, then hopped out of bed. "Wait here, I'll bring it back!"

He hurried out of the room and into the kitchen. He just wanted to do something nice for the kid, and who in their right mind would turn down breakfast in bed? Even if his cooking skills were a little lacking.

About twenty minutes later, Jere returned, balancing two plates and tea on a tray. Wren, to his credit, had clearly gone to the bathroom and washed up a bit, and was waiting patiently in bed. He smiled when he saw Jere returning.

"It's nothing fancy, but, you know," Jere said, by way of explanation, as he set the food down.

They got settled in, and began to eat.

"This is actually quite good, sir," Wren commented, trying the eggs.

"It's nothing special," Jere grinned. "Strangely enough, well, Matthias actually taught me how to cook eggs. He got me out of bed one day, took me to the kitchen, and said 'Boy, you need to be able to cook *something* for yourself!' and showed me how to cook eggs. Of course, looking back, it was a rather effective way of ensuring I would cook for him in the future."

Wren paused, looking at Jere carefully. He said nothing, but continued to eat a moment later, looking distressed and closed off.

Jere studied him. He had gotten better at guessing what the boy was thinking, but he still wasn't sure whether to ask him what was upsetting him now.

"Sir?"

Jere's musings were interrupted. "Mmm?" he replied, mouth still full of food.

"I, uh, I was just wondering...." Wren looked a bit guarded. "You and — and my old master. How did you know each other?"

Jere smiled. "Huh. I guess I've never talked much about that, have I? Well, the fucked up thing is — looking back, I don't think we really did."

At Wren's confused look, he continued. "Oh, I don't mean we didn't know each other — we did — quite well, in, er, a few ways. And I think he knew more about me than I did about him. We were... lovers? No. That's not the right word. We fucked. We were friends, sort of? We definitely fucked. And he introduced me to the right people, in the right places. A good connection. Like this deal, here, Hojer. He could always be counted on for things like that."

Wren said nothing, but kept looking at him, solemn, expecting.

"He was a visiting professor, when we met. And I was a student. *His* student, to be exact. He made the first move; that was for sure. He always did. But I was always happy to go along." Jere laughed. "I suppose he liked them young. Me. A bit naïve, even. We'd talk about medicine and fuck and sometimes he'd take me around and introduce me — he used to tell people I was his protégé. I think everyone knew I was a little more, but it was okay. In the circles we ran in, that was accepted, if not expected. And I liked it, you know, an older man, more experienced...."

Wren's eyebrow had lifted ever-so-subtly, as if to say, "Are you fucking kidding?"

Jere shrugged. "Well, I liked it, anyway. He taught me a lot. About all sorts of shit, actually. He wasn't my first, wasn't even my first relationship, but he was my first in a lot of other things. And then, one day, just like that, he told me he was moving back home. I didn't even know where 'home' was for him at the time, just that it was some rural outland. I certainly didn't know it was a slave state. And, well, shit, it must have been about that time that he bought you."

Wren shuddered a bit. "Did you... did you like the things that he did, sir?"

Jere contemplated the question for a moment. "In bed, I'm sure you mean?"

A wary nod.

"Most of them, yes," Jere admitted. "Actually, it was one of the most exciting times in my life."

"Oh."

Jere watched as Wren began to tremble a bit. He sighed. "Wren, you gotta understand—he was good to me. He made it enjoyable. All but a few things, and even those—well, those things, we didn't do again. And it was always my choice." He reached out and ran a hand through Wren's hair. "And it will always be *your* choice. With me."

Wren looked up at him, not saying a word.

"Look, I enjoyed a lot of the things he did. I'm sure I would still enjoy them. But that doesn't mean I need to do them to feel good. And I know—I *know* that he was into some fucked up things. But I wouldn't expect someone else to be."

"But you know I've done them before, sir," Wren said, his head turned down.

"And I'll bet that you didn't enjoy them," Jere pointed out. "Which is why I wouldn't expect you to do them."

"But... but, would you want me to, sir?"

Jere pulled him close, kissing him on the head. "Only if you want to. Besides, there're an awful lot of things for us to try before we try the fucked up things."

He felt Wren relax into him.

"Listen, kid, I haven't pushed you into anything so far, and I promise that's not gonna change. Nothing's gonna happen until you're ready. And when you are, it will be *good*." Jere grinned at him, quite sure of his skills. "I'm sure you know this better than I do, but while Matthias wasn't exactly easy to please, he was an excellent teacher."

"Perhaps he had different methods, sir," Wren supplied hesitantly.

Jere nodded. "I would imagine. Mine were certainly more pleasant. He would never have dared to treat me like he treated you. But, at the end of the day, I can still give a hell of a massage. And some of the best head in the Sonova metro area, as I've heard a few times!"

Wren made a happy noise, probably thinking of last night. "I wish I had learned that way, sir."

"I do, too," Jere ran his hand through his hair. "Last night, the way you touched me... it was exactly the way that he would touch me. It was almost eerie—like seeing a ghost. Or feeling one, rather. He must have given massages exactly like he trained you to give them."

"He never...." Wren looked away. "He never really wanted to be on the giving end of a massage, sir. There was only one thing he was interested in giving. Aside from beatings."

"He never much liked bottoming," Jere agreed. "Although he did it on occasion."

Wren's eyes went wide with disbelief. Jere choked back a laugh.

"I like either. Top, bottom, whatever. Tie me up, make me beg— I like it all. Matthias was different with me, I'm sure. He would try most anything once, if I asked nicely enough. Honestly, I'm glad I didn't know about him then what I know about him now. I would have been disgusted, not to mention scared to death!"

"He used to...." Wren shook his head. "He used to do horrible things to me, sir. I'm glad he was kinder with you."

The words were polite, too polite, thick with cold formality like most of Wren's communications had been in the first few months Jere spent in Hojer. Familiarity and a sneak peek at the mind connection confirmed Jere's suspicion that the artificially polite tone barely concealed the anger beneath the surface. Jere looked into his eyes as he spoke. "It must be hard, knowing he could have treated you better, like he did me."

Wren didn't answer for a moment. When he did, his voice remained cold and forced. "I saw it every day. At the clinic. He was kind and patient and gentle with his clients, just like he probably was with you, sir."

"I want to give you that experience. Enjoying new things. Learning without fear. Knowing what it's like to be treated kindly."

Wren smiled slightly, looking doubtful. "I guess, if anyone can, it would be you."

Jere ran his hands lightly over Wren's arms, pleased when he shuddered and smiled more fully at him. "Aside from Matthias, have you ever enjoyed it?"

Wren shook his head. "Of course not," he answered, bitter. "Even if I could have, if I hadn't been too busy being scared and in pain, I probably wouldn't have been allowed to. That's how it was, the rule, at the training facility. We couldn't, you know, without permission. Not that I ever wanted to. It's hard now, sometimes, to remember that I'm supposed to, that it's *supposed* to feel good. I think I can, though, with you."

"Thank you," Jere kissed him, wishing he could go back and erase all the horrors that Wren had lived through. "I want you to know what it feels like to feel good. They shouldn't have stolen that from you — the training facility, and especially Matthias. He was capable — "

"It doesn't matter. I don't want to think about that."

Wren's tone said he was finished with it, but in the brief second he glanced up, Jere was startled to see pure, unadulterated hatred in his eyes. It was gone in the time it took him to blink.

"I'd rather think about you," Wren smiled suggestively, leaning into Jere's arms and cutting any further serious conversations short.

Their conversation was interrupted by a knock at the door.

Before Jere had time to react, Wren was up, dressed, and at the door. Sighing, Jere followed suit, albeit at a much slower pace.

"It's ridiculous, I can get him myself!" a female voice echoed in from the entranceway.

"Miss, it's not really proper — "

"Please, I don't *care* about proper!"

Jere stepped out into the hallway, shirt still in his hand, to see what the commotion was. Much to his chagrin, he saw a very agitated Wren trying desperately to place himself in the way of a rather unstoppable young woman in a Sonova University sweatshirt.

"Kieran?"

She smiled brightly at him, as though nothing were happening. "Hi!"

Grunting with irritation, Wren stepped aside, throwing his hands up. "*I tried!*"

"*Thank you, Wren,*" Jere answered, then took a moment to slip his shirt on. "Kieran, I—what are you doing here?"

"I have a proposition for you," she smiled hopefully as she said it. "I'm leaving tonight for Sonova, but I wanted to talk with you first."

"Can we sit? Or something?" Jere had no idea what the girl was on about, but her energy was overwhelming.

"Of course!"

They moved to the dining room, Wren looking awkward and uncertain. "Can I get you anything to drink, miss?"

"I'd like something, but you don't have to serve me," Kieran shook her head, turning to Jere before anyone else could cut in. "Listen, Jere—it's Jere, right, that you go by? I've heard rumors, and honestly, the whole name thing is just outrageous—anyway—I need your advice. I'm being courted by an active abolitionist group and I need help figuring out whether to accept or not."

Jere sat silently. Wren was looking at him with his eyebrows raised in disbelief, wordlessly asking what to do. Jere looked at him desperately. "*For the love of god, don't leave me alone with her! There's water on the stove, bring some tea back for all of us and join us, please?*"

Wren nodded, disappearing into the kitchen.

"Well?" Kieran prodded.

Jere sighed. "Why on earth would you want my advice? I'm a medical doctor, and a slaveowner at that. Why would you possibly want *my* advice?"

Wren had returned, poured tea for the three of them, and sat next to Jere, highly uncomfortable.

"Because you're sympathetic to the cause," Kieran said casually, as if there was no debate. "And you're an outlander. You're not like most of the people here. And your sister is involved in the movement, too!"

Jere squirmed uncomfortably. She was right, but the way she had stated it so certainly, was it that obvious? "I'm not my sister," he muttered, eager to have *some* response to that last set of undeniable truths.

"I'm an empath," Kieran stated. "I see the way you feel about slavery, the way you feel about Wren—which, by the way, is a lot more than a master feels for his slave, and maybe even more than friends feel for each other—and I could tell that you liked me and weren't put off by my... different interests."

That made a lot of sense. "You know, it's considered polite to warn people if you're planning to use an invasive gift like that."

"It's for the cause." She shrugged, waving her hand dismissively.

"How long have you been interested in this?" Jere asked.

"Well, I never really thought it was right, I mean, my family has a lot of *dulars*, and even some slaves." Kieran shuddered. "I came into my gift rather late, and I was *terrified* that I might have a physical gift!" She glanced at Wren. "Sorry, but, you know how it is. Growing up in a family with mind gifts, the absolute terror you feel at not having one."

Wren nodded. From what he had told Jere, he knew all too well.

"Anyway, I finally got my gift, and it was empathy, and you can't really, well, I guess you can if you're a fucking sadist, but most people can't really handle so much pain and suffering as an empath, it affects you too strongly. And that's all slavery is about, pain and suffering." Kieran paused, drinking tea for a moment before finishing her story. "It started with the slaves my family kept, and I started to see that even when they acted happy, they weren't, and I started doing a little research, and the more I learned, the worse it got.

"I had a hard time making friends, because my skills were too out of control. I was homeschooled for a while, but that didn't make it better. I didn't go to college, because I couldn't handle the spoiled little brats here—did you know, they take their slaves *with them* to class? It's disgusting. I couldn't be around that. I couldn't learn in that environment anyway. It was my auntie who suggested I go to a school in the city—my father was *furious*, but I was really just wasting away at home. Drinking too much—it was bad. So I applied, and I'm in, and I know this is what I want to do!"

Jere sighed. He had the urge to slip a sedative into the girl's drink. This had been a really, really calm day. It had been lovely. And now…. "And so you think I can help, how?"

Kieran was silent for a moment, looking at the table. "I needed *someone.* And I needed someone I would have a good enough excuse to speak to."

Jere waited. There was more to this.

"I'm not...." Kieran hesitated for a moment, and Jere could tell that she was actively feeling him out with her gift. "I'm not the only one around here with these interests. There are others, but we're obviously not very vocal about it. It's not the way things are done. But they're not necessarily people I would be socially expected to talk to; questions would be raised if I started sending them letters, and *especially* if I were to send them a telegraph or a speed message."

"Right." Jere looked at her encouragingly.

"But you would work." Kieran admitted. "You're from Sonova, you're friendly with my aunt, and you're the kind of guy that a girl like me might have a crush on. It would make sense that I would seek you out as a mentor or something."

Jere was a little stunned by the cunning behind this plan. "Um, okay...."

"I don't *actually* have a crush on you, Jere." She wrinkled her nose at the idea. "No offense, but you're a little too... " she waved her hands, looking for the right word, "...gay for my tastes. Besides, I wouldn't want to intrude on whatever you and Wren have going on."

Jere's jaw dropped, and Wren froze up, looking like he was about to bolt out of the room.

Kieran held her hands up. "Oh, no, I didn't mean it that way! It's not that obvious! It's just, Wren, you're very comfortable with Jere, and Jere, you care about him *so* much, much more than would be expected, and, well, you were both somewhat undressed at noon on a Sunday, so what the hell else were you doing?"

Jere felt himself blushing, and felt Wren's absolute horror and mortification through their connection.

"For the record, most slaveowners feel that using their slaves sexually is normal and a right, and wouldn't be embarrassed about it," Kieran said with a grin, proving her point.

"I'll need to ask you to refrain from using your gift on me or Wren," Jere scowled at her. "Or I'll get my hands on you and make you regret it. Healers don't just have to heal, you know."

"All right, all right!" Kieran pulled her empathic senses back immediately. "You don't have to threaten, you could have just asked!"

"I already warned you that it was rude!" Jere retorted. Truthfully, he was a little frustrated at himself that he hadn't noticed her gift sooner.

"It's justified, for the cause!" Kieran protested. "That's why they're recruiting me — a spy with an empath gift can get in and identify potential supporters and problems!"

"So they want to use you?"

"Not like that! I mean, they use everyone's gifts. If they recruited a healer to help after protests, would that be using them?"

"Quite possibly," Jere muttered.

"Whatever it takes. That's their motto." Kieran smiled.

Jere shook his head. "Of course it is. It wouldn't have anything to do with safety or reservation or making sure you don't get arrested."

"Irrelevant." She shook her head back at him.

Jere sighed. There was no arguing with someone who was *this* set on a cause. He had heard his sister rant about them often enough. His response was usually the same. One thing caught his interest. "You said there are other people here, in Hojer, who're supportive of the cause?"

Kieran laughed a little at his disbelief. "How much do you really know about Hojer and the boroughs?"

Not a damn thing, really. He had been bored by the general history of Hojer, and appalled by the extensive list of laws that restricted and punished, but never protected slaves. He had forced himself to read through those after Wren had been held and beaten at the police station. "Well, I know it's in a slave state, and there are a lot of in-depth slave codes, and people get sick or injured and need my services."

"I'm betting that's about the extent of it!" Kieran grinned. "Listen, Hojer was one of the first towns to promote slave codes, or so it's rumored. After The Fall, and then the rise of the gifts, Hojer was still a pretty rural place, so it wasn't nearly as affected, but there were a lot more people with mind gifts than physical gifts. You know, these things do have *some* geographical relevance."

Jere nodded. It was true. Despite an inability to determine why, mind gifts and physical gifts tended to converge in geographical areas.

"But those with physical gifts were seen as being able to take power too easily. After The Fall, military law ruled, and it just so happened that the majority of the leaders had mind gifts. Uprisings started, and uprisings by those with physical gifts are more noticeable. I mean, really, someone throwing you a few hundred feet with a strength gift, or someone manipulating your feelings with a mind gift, which is more noticeable? So the laws were put in place first to restrict use of physical gifts. Then the resource crisis started, well, got worse, anyway; it had been a problem for years. For so many years, people had relied on technology or machinery for so many things, but technology was suddenly useless and materials and fuel for resources dried up, and we needed something to replace them. That's where slaves came in.

"See, you won't find this in a history book, because it's awful, and that's why it's hidden. Or maybe—do they teach it in Sonova? First, slavery was used judicially—to punish criminals who had used physical gifts 'inappropriately.' But, soon, the value was too great, and the slave codes were passed, back then under a different name, putting the same restrictions that we have on current slaves on all people with physical gifts. But this was just a trick—with those sorts of restrictions, of *course* people with physical gifts failed to stay out of trouble, and soon laws were passed declaring them all slaves, for the betterment of the state, and the people."

"Okay...." Jere had heard this version of history at some point in his childhood, but hadn't really paid much attention. He wasn't paying too much attention now. He didn't want to be a part of this. He had enough on his plate, and already didn't fit in here at all; this would be just another strike against him.

"So, years pass, and this is just the way it is. There are no more people with physical gifts who can remember being free, and no more people with mind gifts who can remember not being part of the slave owning class. Textbooks change, laws change, and it's like this is the way it *always* was. And it's beneficial for them. The free people. They can get free labor and other things for *no* reason, other than because they have slaves! For a few years, there was a breeding program started amongst slaveowners, but it became too problematic, because too many of the slaves were giving birth to children with mind gifts, which fucks everything up.

"Because, you see, even people with physical gifts are more likely to have kids with mind gifts here. Nobody knows why, but there it is. But in the last few years, it's started to change—a lot more kids are being found with physical gifts, and a *lot* more *dulars* are being born—like my auntie. And that's why there are dissenters. You can be a supporter of slavery, even ambivalent, but an awful lot of parents change their minds when it's their little boy or girl being taken from them. Or their grandchild. That's why pattern analysis is so popular in slave states—we are trying *so* hard to figure out how to change this—do we blame genetics? Do we blame parenting? Do we blame location? If the family moves down the street, will their child avoid the curse of a physical gift?"

Kieran grinned proudly at the shocked looks she had inspired. "Or, do we try to destroy the slavery system as we know it?"

"Remind me again why you think I'd want to destroy *anything* with you?" Jere asked, still trying to process the information she had dumped on him.

"Well, you don't think it's right, do you?" Kieran asked, the question bordering on rhetorical.

"No, but...." Jere frowned. "Listen. Here's the thing about me. It's cruel and callous and will probably make you sad, but it's true. I don't care. I think it's wrong. I don't think people should be slaves. But *I*, personally, don't want to get involved."

"That's different than not caring!" Kieran cut in.

"But it means the same thing," Jere continued. "I don't want to go to a rally or protests or overthrow the government. I'm a doctor. I want to make people who are sick or injured not be sick or injured anymore. I want to have a comfortable house where I have hot water and good food and don't have to worry about getting evicted. I want to have friends and family and I want to keep them safe and I'll fight for them, but I really don't have the time, energy, or desire to fight for random strangers. I'm sorry, Kieran, but I have no desire to be anybody's white knight."

He thought he'd crush her with his little speech. He thought she'd storm off, get upset, and write him off. He kind of hoped she would. He was wrong.

She smiled back at him. "Jere, we—I don't want you to be a white knight! I don't even want you to be a white knight's page. And certainly I would never ask you to go to a protest! We're trying to work *within* the system. And you're *in* the system. You're neutral. You're like a doorway. All we need from you is for you to be there. I'll do all the rest."

Jere had noticed her alternating use of "I" and "we." "Did they ask you to recruit me?" he asked tiredly.

"They emphasized the importance of establishing a safe contact point for while I'm away," she answered evasively. "I liked you anyway."

"Kieran...." Jere started to shake his head.

"Just think about it, okay?" she begged. "You don't have to decide right now. But it would be nice, too, if I could write you about other things? Like I said, I don't really have many friends. I'm a little scared."

Jere conceded. He understood how hard it was to uproot and move away from your life and home and friends. "Of course. Feel free—starting college in a new town can be a little intimidating. Maybe we can talk more about it when you're back to visit?"

She nodded, the small victory won.

"And Kieran—look, I won't tell you what to do, but be careful, all right? These groups can be dangerous. Make sure to keep yourself safe."

Kieran nodded. "I will. I can't do anything from inside a prison cell, right?"

"Yeah. Or dead," Jere shook his head. He was glad he had never been such an idealist. He didn't have that sort of drive or commitment.

"Thanks," she smiled back at him. "I should probably be going. I still have packing to do, because I refused to let my father order the slaves to do it. Do you know he thinks I have obsessive compulsive disorder because I insist on doing everything myself?"

"That… " *probably isn't the only thing he thinks you have.* " … does not surprise me."

"And, Wren, sorry I barged in," Kieran apologized. "It was rude, but I was excited. Maybe we can talk some other time? I'd like to get to know you better."

"As you wish, miss," Wren said.

The words were submissive and appropriate, but Jere could see the disdain and irritation he felt behind them. He tried not to laugh.

Kieran wrinkled her nose at the term, but said nothing. She looked to Jere. "You will write back, yes?"

Jere nodded. "As soon as I get a letter from you with the return address."

"Okay." She smiled as she walked to the door.

"By the way, Kieran?" Jere asked, halting her in her steps. "I never told you my sister was anti-slavery."

Her eyes went wide as she realized she had been caught. "I, um… I might have had someone research her. When you said she was in the Human Rights and Welfare program at SU."

"Difficult, as she goes by my mother's maiden name," Jere commented wryly. "Please don't do that again."

Kieran nodded. "I won't. I promise."

"And if you see her, don't mention me," Jere said finally.

"Are the two of you not close?"

"We're… we used to be close. She doesn't know I'm here. And I really can't deal with her right now, she'd come in and raise hell, and I don't need that."

Kieran nodded. "I get it. You keep my secrets, I'll keep yours?"

Jere nodded, not entirely sure whether he really wanted to agree to this or not. "Goodbye, Kieran."

"Bye, Jere! Bye, Wren!" She bounded out the door.

Jere said nothing as he walked back to the dining room and dropped back into the chair he had been sitting in. Wren came up behind him and placed his hands on his shoulders, prompting Jere to place a kiss on one before looking up at him. "I think I just agreed to help her…."

Wren smiled at him. "In some ways, sir, you did."

Jere sighed. "Well. Shit." He stood up, facing Wren. "I liked what we were doing before much better."

Wren grinned shyly. "Me too, sir, but you have a patient scheduled in just a moment, and it really would be responsible to get changed and ready."

Jere rolled his eyes. Grinning a bit, he reached one hand out toward Wren. "Come here."

Wren did as he was asked, and Jere pulled him close. He could feel his heart racing, but he smiled encouragingly and gripped his hand softly, making sure not to hold him in place. He leaned forward and kissed Wren, lightly at first, then more passionately, hungrily, bringing his free hand up to cup the back of Wren's head and pull him close. Wren seemed stiff and still for a moment, but quickly relaxed, melting into Jere's arms and almost purring with pleasure as they continued. He felt Wren starting to grind his body against his own and he reluctantly pulled away, looking into his eyes for a moment before muttering "I hate being responsible."

Chapter 29
Let Me

They made it through the short workday without further interruption. Wren was quite relieved, as Kieran's presence made him nervous. Having a friend who was involved in the anti-slavery movement was one thing, but for his master to get involved in the "cause" himself was dangerous. And Wren was very clear that danger for his master meant danger for him as well.

Despite his disdain for the girl's energy, he found himself liking her. Admittedly, the disdain he felt had mostly been irritation, as his rather pleasant morning had been interrupted. Kieran promised excitement, danger, and an optimism that had been beaten out of him within months of being taken as a slave. Besides, it was nice to see Jere relax around someone, no matter how eccentric the girl was.

He and Jere had a quick dinner, neither one of them up to waiting for anything complicated to cook. When they finished, they retired to the couch, mere seconds passing before they started kissing one another.

Wordlessly, they arranged themselves into a familiar pattern, Jere reclining back against the arm of the couch on the side that had become "his," while Wren climbed on top of him, slipping between his master's legs. Their lips stayed together, as if glued that way, while their hands roamed and explored, feeling above, below, and between layers of clothing.

For the most part, it was Wren's hands that were the most likely to explore. Jere was exceptionally careful to avoid going too far, a consideration that Wren didn't even know how to express his thanks for. Certainly, Wren could tell that Jere enjoyed touching him, but he often contained himself to running fingers through his hair, stroking his back, or lightly gripping his upper arms. Wren echoed his thanks in the best way he knew how — by being bolder with his own ministrations.

He toyed with the buttons on Jere's shirt, finally deciding to undo them as their tongues intertwined. He moved slowly, sensually, but was soon overcome with the desire to feel skin, to get the damned shirt *out* of the way. Holding his gift very tightly in check, he continued to kiss his master at a normal pace while his hands rapidly undid the remaining buttons on the shirt and pulled it open. He felt Jere grin beneath him.

"That's a hell of a useful skill."

Wren was pleasantly embarrassed, blushing a bit as he felt evidence that Jere was certainly enjoying his skill. He ducked his head down, trying to hide the blush, and taking advantage of the new expanse of skin to explore.

He moved his lips in a soft, slow line from Jere's throat down to his chest, marveling at the soft, smooth skin, covered with a ghosting of hair, filled underneath with lean, taut muscles.

Muscles that rippled and shuddered as Wren dragged his tongue across them, drawing a soft, pleased sound. He felt Jere's hands across his back, gentle, but still full of desire. He drew in a sharp breath, inhaling the clean, earthy smell he had come to associate with his master. Wren closed his eyes and tried to picture what they'd look like, just for a minute, before the abstract thought brought him too close to the reality — that he'd look like a slave serving his master.

Jere shifted beneath him, not-so-subtly pressing his leg into Wren's erection, and drawing him immediately back to the present. Throwing off all cares of what he might or might not look like, he wriggled around on Jere's leg, working his own leg into a mirrored position, and soon felt his back arching with pleasure at the contact. He leaned down and continued to kiss at his master's neck, humming gently and feeling quite pleased when the soft sounds made the other man shudder.

Holding himself up slightly with one hand, he slipped the other between their bodies and increased the pressure for his master, causing him to yelp with pleasant surprise. He quickly recovered, thrusting in time against Wren's hand. He was panting after a few minutes of this, and Wren felt the arms around him slide down. He felt Jere's hands brushing his own. Jere hesitated at the waistband of his own pants.

Wren quickly understood. "Do you want me to—"

"Only if you want," Jere cut him off, quickly. "I just, I need... I have no problem finishing myself, but I won't lie, I'd fucking love to feel you touch me."

Wren's nervousness was washed away with desire for the man so passionate beneath him. "I want to, sir."

"I've died and gone to fucking heaven," Jere muttered, quickly undoing his pants and sliding them down, with some help from Wren. Wren slid his hand around him, and Jere sighed. "Oh my fucking god!"

Wren grinned. Jere was so expressive during sex. He liked seeing him this way, liked seeing him so relaxed and turned on. He tightened his grip and began pumping in time with Jere's thrusts, sitting up a bit to look at his face.

Jere's head was thrown back, a smile on his lips, which were slightly parted. He had no worries, no demands, he just succumbed to the pleasure. Wren was struck with a pang of jealousy at that carelessness, but it was overridden by the low moans of pleasure he was inspiring. Tapping into his speed gift again, he alternately tightened and loosened the grip of each of his fingers as he continued working Jere's cock. It was one of the few tricks, learned long ago at the training facility, that he enjoyed using on himself.

Jere let out a stream of unintelligible curses, and reached up to pull Wren toward him, his hand catching the back of his head and tangling into his hair. "Get over here," he breathed.

Wren was as turned on as Jere was, and what they were doing felt good, but he hated that hand on his head, and the order in Jere's tone stirred up memories he'd rather escape. He tensed, his mind protesting at how wrong it was, but his body had other ideas. On some level, he did want it, and he felt as betrayed by himself as he did by Jere. He felt old anger building inside of him, warring with excitement, and he did the only thing that had ever worked to soothe that rage, hiding away from his true feelings. Wren squeezed his eyes shut and tried to focus on the pleasure he had been thinking about a minute ago, on being on top of Jere, on using a speed gift....

Strong hands gripped his arms very, very lightly. "I'm sorry, Wren, so so sorry, fuck, don't stop, please, I need... keep going, won't hurt you. Just forgot. Fucking, lose my mind."

Wren rarely felt Jere through the mind connection, but he could tell that his master had stopped blocking as much, and he could feel the regret, overpowered a hundred times by lust and passion and desire. It cut through the numbness he tried to cling to.

"It's all right, sir," Wren heard himself saying. And it almost was. He almost felt reassured that he could make Jere lose *this* much control, and that this would be as far as things went. "I believe you were wanting to kiss me?"

"Mmm," Jere agreed, wrapping his arms around him again, less demanding this time.

Their mouths crashed together with near-bruising velocity, and they continued to kiss as Wren's hand continued to move, up and down, squeezing and not, doing things that drove Jere completely wild. Finally, Wren felt his master's hands clench fistfuls of his shirt, and he kissed him deeply, knowing he was almost there. Seconds later, Jere came, thrusting hard one final time as he clutched Wren to him. It was almost uncomfortable, but for the satisfied, grateful murmurs of "thank you," in his ear, and the now-gentle arms around his back. Wren slid his sticky hand out from beneath them, careful to avoid touching the couch with it.

Jere squirmed a bit, reached down next to them, and pulled up the shirt that had been discarded earlier, bringing it to Wren's hand for him to wipe off the mess. Jere kept kissing him for a minute before pulling back and whispering "I suppose I should clean myself up a bit."

"I could —" Wren started to suggest something.

"You just sit back," Jere ordered lightly, a playful grin on his face. "Please."

Wren did as he was asked, smiling as he accepted the game they were playing, whatever it was. Jere stood, taking the opportunity to run a hand across Wren's chest as he did, and hurriedly cleaned himself off with the shirt. Wren itched to fetch him a towel or something more proper, but Jere didn't seem to mind. He finished, and tossed the shirt carelessly on the coffee table.

"Now, where were we?" he grinned, coming back, still entirely nude, to sit by Wren. "Ahh, yes." He leaned over and kissed him, making Wren gasp with the pleasure. He had half expected his master to be finished after he had, well, finished.

Jere seemed to have no such intentions. He kissed Wren carefully, eagerly, exciting him with his mouth and tongue and hands, then suddenly slid down to the floor, dropping to his knees.

Wren looked at him with confusion.

Grinning, Jere placed a hand on either of Wren's thighs, moving them apart with no resistance. He leaned in a bit, then looked up eagerly at Wren.

"Let me?" he asked, eyes big and wide and hopeful.

Wren was speechless. How the hell was he supposed to respond? He couldn't deny his master—not that he really wanted to. If he was honest, he had to admit that a part of him *did* really want to deny him, but there was the other part as well, the part that wanted to force himself down his master's throat just to see what it felt like.

Jere sat there silently, looking up at Wren with a hopeful grin plastered across his face.

Wren found himself struck by the absurdity of the situation. Here he was, the supposed slave, fully clothed and reclining on a couch while his master was naked on his knees in front of him. Waiting to be granted permission. Offering to…. Wren's mind flashed back to last night, the description that Jere had given of his talents. He started to think that this might not be such a bad thing after all.

A hand reached up, trailing lightly across his chest, and down, all the way down until it lingered at the top of his pants.

"Are you gonna make me beg?" Jere asked, an eyebrow raised. "Because you know I will."

"Um…." Wren wanted to let him. He really wanted to feel Jere, to feel his mouth, but it would leave him so exposed and vulnerable. A certain part of him also wanted to say "yes" and hear Jere beg, and Wren wasn't sure what to do with that thought.

"*You have my word, I'll stop whenever you tell me to,*" Jere's voice was clear and sincere in his head. "I know you want it," he spoke aloud, much more teasing than his voice had been in the mind connection.

"I do." Wren heard his own voice answering before he could think about it, making him a traitor to himself. He did want it.

Jere slid up, his teeth catching on the button of Wren's pants. Without moving his body, he tilted his head to look up at him. "Please?"

Wren felt a thrill of excitement at the pleading tone, and found himself nodding. "Okay. Yes. Let's try."

Jere laughed, low and sultry, as he softly undid the fastening. "I'll make you glad that we did."

Wren felt his pants being undone, much more carefully than any other person had ever undone them before. The sensation was still too-familiar and uncomfortable, but Jere's mouth was there, suddenly, pressing a line of kisses across his stomach, distracting him, reminding him that he was supposed to be feeling *good*. He had to admit, he did.

He felt hands moving around to reach behind him, and realized that his master would want him to lift up, to allow him access to slide the pants off of his body. To take the last barrier between them away, exposing him, naked....

"Just a little," Jere coaxed, talking more to Wren's cock than to Wren.

Fitting, as his cock was the part of him that was so fucking interested in this.

Wren lifted himself a little, bracing for the rough pull, the feeling of being stripped and violated — and was startled when Jere eased his pants down only a few inches, taking his time and stopping to caress his lower back in the process.

Without moving his head away from its target, Jere slid his arms back to the front, slowly dipping inside of Wren's pants to free his cock the rest of the way. Yelping with pleasant surprise, Wren thrust into his hand.

"Let's not spoil the main event, shall we?" Jere smirked at him, keeping his hand still on purpose. He waited a moment until Wren's eyes focused again and looked down at him. "Are you comfortable?"

Wren nodded, not trusting himself not to yelp again.

Jere grinned back at him, holding eye contact while he leaned down and barely touched the edge of his lips to the head of Wren's cock. "Good," he said softly, warm air making Wren moan. "And you'll tell me if anything changes?"

Wren's eyes closed with pleasure. Had he nodded? He thought he had nodded. But Jere seemed to be waiting. Best to make sure. "Yes. Yes sir, please...."

A small chuckle sent shudders of ecstasy through Wren's body.

"You don't have to ask me twice." Jere leaned in, encompassing every inch of Wren in his mouth.

Wren was caught between shock and pleasure and nervousness and more pleasure. Certainly, he had felt another person's mouth on him before, but never like this, never so eager. He felt himself flushing as he forgot about taking clothes off, forgot about being proper, and seemed unable to stop himself from thrusting up into his master's mouth.

Jere accommodated him easily, wrapping his hand around the base of his cock and filling the gap that his mouth left when he pulled back, only to return and go deeper. Wren felt the tips of his fingers sliding around, caressing his balls as he continued to work his mouth over him. He tried his best to stay still, but it was nearly impossible with such sweet torment.

Before he realized what he was doing, Wren had reached a hand out and clutched it in his master's hair, desperate for touch, connection... and to pull him closer. As Jere moved up, and then slid back down, Wren jerked him closer by his hair, forcing him further down the length of him. For the first time in his life, Wren understood why all the men who had forced their dicks down his throat insisted on tugging on his head like this—it felt so good! Even so, he loosened his grip a little bit, but was encouraged to continue on by a half-grin from Jere, who somehow managed to still have facial expressions in this position. It was strange, but Jere seemed to be enjoying it.

"Sorry," he muttered, feeling a bit guilty for treating his master so roughly.

"*Don't bother,*" Jere replied through the mind connection, "*I like it.*"

Wren doubted he hid his shock very well. If it wasn't for the mind connection, he might not have believed it, but Jere felt just as pleased and excited now as he had when he came earlier. Wren could admit, grudgingly, that it was exciting to be on the giving end of such rough treatment, but to enjoy receiving it? He struggled to understand it. Then again, Jere viewed everything so differently than he did, and he had no reason to lie. He certainly had no reason to hate it, not like Wren did.

Wren's mind flashed back to his own memories of sucking cocks, the way he would barely take them into his mouth, the sour expression that no amount of smacks could clear from his face, the way he worked to make sure as little of his own body touched that of the man doing it to him. Based on that description, Jere looked like he couldn't be performing the same act. He wasn't just sucking Wren's cock, he was savoring it, teasing it with his tongue and lips and teeth like he just couldn't get enough of it. His hands were making contact elsewhere, stroking Wren's shaft, playing with his balls, grazing lightly and carefully up and down his thighs. When he glanced up, his face was that of pure contentment, and Wren knew that Jere's experiences were so monumentally different than his own that he just needed to stop comparing them and take Jere at his word. Jere's eyes flashed up at Wren again, and Wren was pretty sure he might lose control.

It wasn't long before he did. The constant pressure, rhythm, sucking... the feeling of soft hair between his fingers, the way his master's hands caressed his legs, his stomach, his balls, every part of him was consumed with fire, burning so hot....

"Please, sir," he whimpered, having no idea what he was even begging for.

"*Whenever you're ready.*" Jere's voice was clear in his head, as real as the tongue flickering up to his balls as he was pulled in deep again.

Moaning, Wren continued to thrust against him, pushing, ignoring the small voice in his head that said things like "be careful" and "what the hell are you doing?" He felt the pressure building, and it was too much, and not enough, and at the exact right moment, he felt Jere tighten his grip with his hand and increase the pressure in his mouth, and Wren gave one final thrust before collapsing back against the couch, making noises he didn't even know could come from him. His eyes closed of their own volition and he sunk as deep under the lovely sensation as possible.

Jere's mouth stayed on him, gently working his quickly fading cock, feeling much more like a massage than the frantic sucking that had been going on moments before. Wren's mind briefly flitted around the unbelievable idea that his master had not only sucked him off, but swallowed as well, but it was too much, too soon, and he pushed the thought away. He barely managed to lift his hips as his pants were pulled back up where they belonged. He felt the older man climbing up to sit next to him on the couch.

A soft hand brushed the hair out of his face.

"Was that good?" Jere asked softly, his voice still playful.

Wren kept his eyes closed, leaning into his master's hand. "Mmhmm."

Soft lips brushed against his earlobe. "Did I tire you out?"

"Mmm," Wren nodded. Words were too hard.

"Come to bed with me?"

Wren said nothing, but allowed himself to be led to bed by his master. He collapsed into the bed, still completely sated and satisfied, and felt the familiar, warm body press next to him, wrapping an arm around his waist. After what Jere had just done for him, he couldn't bring himself to feel uncomfortable, even though Jere's arm could potentially trap him. It just felt nice.

As Wren felt sleep descending, he felt a light kiss being pressed to the back of his neck, sending pleasant thrills down his spine.

"Thank you," Jere whispered, and they fell asleep.

Chapter 30
Things to Think About

Morning was a hurried affair, as both Jere and Wren were tired from having been up so late the night before. Wren tried to behave, for the most part, but Jere couldn't seem to resist stealing a quick kiss and grope right before they walked through the door to the clinic. He was absolutely thrilled when Wren returned his affections. He wondered how he had ever seen Wren as anything less than perfect. The fact that he had been irritated and bothered by Wren, just because he was a slave, seemed horrible now that they were so much closer. More than just sex, Jere was starting to see the personality that Wren hid so well behind the slave persona he had built.

The day went well, though busy. A client who had had an unfortunate accident with a saw taxed most of Jere's mind-healing abilities, leaving him with the highly unpleasant and rather tedious job of applying stitches. The patient was chemically and mentally sedated, allowing Jere to talk while he carefully sewed up the long, gaping wound.

"You've checked in the rest of the patients out in the waiting area, right? And given that woman directions to the pharmacy?"

"Yes, sir."

"Great, thank you," Jere continued to deftly stitch. "I'd be lost without you, Wren. Of course, I'd also be a bit more awake without you," he teased.

Wren blushed, but kept his grip steady. "It's my pleasure, sir."

"Indeed." Jere looked up from his task to smirk playfully at Wren, who laughed a little and shook his head. "Can I ask you something?"

"Yes, sir," Wren said, nodding.

Jere paused a moment, trying to think of how to phrase this. He knew he had to tread carefully. "Wren, listen—no, don't say anything just yet, just think about it, okay? I just want you to think about what I'm about to say."

Wren nodded, looking a bit wary, but also curious.

Jere smiled encouragingly. "Remember a while back—back when I first came here? We were talking about how you'd address me, and I said we could talk about it again later? Well, I think we should, sometime. I mean, I mean, you don't *have* to, but I'd like to, and I'd really...." He made himself stop rambling and collect his thoughts. "Look, when I asked you about it when we first met, it was a knee-jerk reaction, a way that I felt I could rebel against owning a slave. It had nothing to do with *you* then, but now it has everything to do with you, and with how I feel about you. What I'm trying to say is, I'd really love to hear you say my name. All the time, really, well, I guess, when we're alone, customs and all, but really, especially when we're... doing stuff. Sexy stuff."

Jere forced himself to stop speaking. Wren had grown visibly tense, but didn't seem to be terrified or panicking like he had the first time Jere had broached the subject, months ago. Jere watched Wren's hesitant nod and felt himself growing nervous in response.

"I—" Jere wasn't really sure what he was planning on saying next, and years of exposure to literature and a college education did nothing to improve his speaking ability. "I just... I wish you didn't need to be so formal around me. Just think about it sometime? Please?"

The room was silent for a moment, except for the faint sound of stitching going through skin. Wren nodded.

"You're more than just some boy to me, you know?" Jere muttered, wishing he could stay quiet and stop pushing the issue. At the same time, he was glad that he was saying this. It wasn't just about the name, or being sexy, it was about how he felt for Wren. He couldn't remember the last time he cared about someone this much. "I hope you know that."

Wren smiled, looking down at the patient. "I do."

Jere noticed the lack of honorific at the end of the statement, and, knowing Wren, was nearly positive that it had been intentional. The slavery thing made everything so complicated. When he first moved to Hojer, he wanted the "sir" or "master" dropped because it was uncomfortable and morally wrong; now he wanted it gone because he felt so intimate with Wren, and not just sexually — to continue to be so formal felt distant and wrong. He finished stitching the man up, brushing his hand against Wren's intentionally.

The day didn't slow down until it was nearly closing time. Exhausted, Jere and Wren slipped through the door into the house, where Wren had found time to prepare dinner earlier.

Jere paused, catching Wren's hand. "If I go shower and change, will dinner keep?"

"Of course, sir," Wren smiled up at him, allowing himself to be pulled closer. "I suppose I could shower, too."

"Want to join me?" Jere teased.

"Um..." Wren started, hesitating before finishing.

Jere cursed inwardly. One would think he tried to rape the kid every chance he got! But he forced himself to smile, leaning in to brush his lips against Wren's. "It's all right. I'll meet you back out here, okay?"

The big, almost innocent smile was reward enough.

"Yes, sir," Wren darted forward to kiss him again, then sped off to the hall shower.

At a normal, human speed, Jere went to his own bathroom off of the master suite. He tried to shower quickly, hoping to ignore his body's demands for attention and sensation. The way his cock was practically *begging* to be touched. The way it would only be a minute, in between soaping himself up and washing his hair... no. He had much more important business to attend to, and every minute spent wanking alone in the shower meant one less minute that he could be with Wren. The hand wrapped around his cock would be Wren's, and he would touch him in that perfect way he had. If he could just wait, he could be feeling that mouth on him, feel Wren in his mouth.... He leaned back against the wall of the shower, picturing himself between Wren's legs, taking him deep into his throat, and his own grip on his cock tightened one last time.

Well, at least it was good that he was young, and therefore had plenty more left where that came from.

Jere returned to the dining room not long after he finished and found Wren waiting patiently for him. If he had any idea what Jere had been busy doing, he gave no indication. Jere counted this as a blessing.

Wren brought out fish and couscous and vegetables, all steaming hot and edible. Jere couldn't wait to get his mouth around them, taste them on his tongue.... He was thinking more about the person *serving* the food than the food itself. He tried some, smiling at the perfection with which it was cooked.

"Amazing," he muttered, smiling at Wren.

"Thank you...." Wren let the sentence trail off. "Sir, can we talk tonight?"

Jere pulled himself back from the fantasy he was indulging in, forcing himself to be serious despite his massive lack of desire to do so. Thinking about the way Wren's skin tasted was great, but the chance to talk honestly with him was worth infinitely more. "Of course, any time you like."

Wren nodded, looking down at his plate. He was still eating, which was a good sign.

Jere studied him for a while, trying to guess at what was making him so cryptic. He figured that part of it was the request he had made earlier — for Wren to call him by his name, at least sometimes. He didn't regret asking him to think about it. He felt confident that he wasn't forcing anything, and besides, he really *did* want to hear it. Not only that, but Jere realized that they should talk about some things, anyway. The physical connection was great, but he cared about much more than that with Wren. He wasn't completely sure what he felt for him, but he knew it was more than friends, more than coworkers, and certainly more than a master should feel for a slave, according to anyone around here.

None of this made him any less nervous. Would he call it off? Now? When they had come this far? Jere's feelings for the dark-haired young man sitting next to him had grown considerably, despite his best efforts to stop them. He would be more than a little sad to have them go back to being just friends. Although, a few months ago, even friends had seemed an unreachable ideal.

He picked at his food. "Is everything all right?" he blurted out finally, unable to contain himself.

Wren nodded. "Yes, sir. It's just.... I just need some time to think before I talk with you, and I'm a little tired. After dinner?"

Jere nodded, trying to look encouraging. He had been the one to bring this up, after all, so he figured he deserved the suspense. Wren deserved the time to collect his thoughts.

They talked about work and food while they finished eating. Not only was there dinner, there was also dessert, and Jere began to suspect that Wren was trying to avoid the conversation he had postponed. Finally, when they had each finished a cup of coffee and a piece of tiramisu and Wren offered him a drink, Jere decided to put an end to it.

"I'm tired," he said softly, a pleading look on his face. "Let's go to bed."

Wren looked down at the floor, cleared the table in seconds, then returned to look at the floor some more.

Jere walked slowly toward him, placed his hands on his fore-arms, and leaned in close, lingering a moment before brushing their lips together.

"*Anything you do or don't say, it's fine. Nothing changes unless you want it to.*"

He felt Wren nod against him, and thought for a moment that he felt him sob, but, no, he wasn't... was he?

"Okay," Wren said quietly, twisting out of Jere's arms so he could go first, leaving Jere to stare at his back, wondering.

Wren didn't turn the light on when he entered the room, and Jere followed his lead. They slipped into bed, Wren facing toward the window, and Jere pressed against his back. He had an arm around him, gently pulling him close. They lay there for a minute, neither one saying or doing anything.

"What does it mean to you?" Wren's voice cut through the dark, the silence.

"The name?" Jere felt Wren nod. "I'd like to hear it. I think it's sexy, and more than that, I just, I hear you say 'sir,' and it makes me think 'master,' and I don't like thinking of you that way."

"As your slave?"

"As *any* slave." Jere tried to keep his frustration in check in spite of the rage he felt toward the institution of slavery in general.

"I am." Wren's voice was quiet, resigned.

"Technically," Jere challenged. "It might not matter to anyone else, but I don't think of you that way. I never have. I certainly don't now, not now that I've gotten to know you."

Wren was silent. Jere dared to test out the mind connection, Wren often let emotions leak over, but now Jere was only privy to the slightest hint of apprehension. But Wren had agreed to talk, even asked to do it tonight. Jere rested his head against the boy's neck and waited. The minutes ticked by like hours, and Jere found himself focusing on Wren's breathing, timing his own to match.

Finally, the silence was broken.

"My old master, he—he'd let his guests use me."

Jere was silent, guessing there was more to the story. He didn't move a muscle, even as he felt the body in his arms tense.

"There were some that liked to pretend—that liked *me* to pretend that I liked it. Even though I never did. One asked me to call his name out—I begged him not to, *begged* that he let me say something else, and, after he had beaten me half to death, I did as he asked. Screamed it, good and loud, for anyone to hear. He seemed pleased, but once he left... my master, he came in. He cut my tongue out."

Jere felt his stomach churn in disgust. He blocked his end of the mind connection, shielding Wren from his emotions. The last thing Wren needed was to think that Jere was disgusted with him, when it was so far from that.

"I don't know if it was for refusing to do as I was told, or for finally giving in and addressing a free person improperly. Probably both. I never asked. I couldn't.... He healed it up, later, after making me beg, after making me...." Wren was trembling now, his voice shaky. "Making me suck him off. I was still bleeding and it hurt, god it hurt. He said I wasn't doing it right without a tongue. I don't even... I don't even know if he would have healed it otherwise, you know? If it wasn't for that?"

"Wren, I wouldn't—"

"I know you wouldn't. I'm not finished!" Wren snapped, quite uncharacteristically, although he was shaking as he said it.

Jere felt him curling into a ball next to him, pushing his arm away. He pulled his arm back, heeding Wren's wishes, but trailed it lightly across his back. He was relieved when Wren didn't flinch away.

"This wasn't out of the fucking ordinary!" Wren drew a sobbing breath before continuing. "I've told you that my father gave me my first beating—I literally couldn't *count* the ones I had after that. I spent two fucking years in a training facility. All I had done was kiss a girl at school and wank to dirty magazines, and all of a sudden, there I was, doing everything they asked. I was beaten, raped, starved. And then I was sold and it got worse. It fucking got worse.

"I tried. I tried really hard to be good for him. But I just couldn't, it seemed like whatever I did, whatever I tried wasn't good enough. It's so fucked up—I *wanted* to please him. I thought that maybe he'd like me, maybe, if he just had me long enough, and... but he never did. He'd push me, see how far I could go, how much I could take until I lost consciousness, how much I could scream before I lost my voice and couldn't scream anymore. He liked that, you see, because he liked me quiet. He'd throw me down in that cellar—I was terrified, at first, because it was dark, and sometimes he'd tie me up, and I was always just so afraid of what would be down there.

"He liked to 'experiment.' That's what he called it. He'd 'experiment' with fire, knives—sometimes even new medications. He'd 'experiment' in bed. He let anyone and everyone use me however they pleased. He was always changing things up. Making up new rules. Playing new games with me. He'd tell me one thing, hell, tell me a *lot* of things, and then take it all back later. He would create these elaborate mind games to make me feel safe, cared for even, and then he'd snatch it all back and beat me for being too stupid to figure it out."

Jere stayed silent, feeling quite strongly that Wren wasn't finished. As he waited, Wren turned to face him, the moonlight behind him creating an almost ghostly appearance. His face was streaked with tears, but his eyes glowed with rage. Jere pulled back, startled by the dark hatred he saw.

"Everything that was done to me was fine. Because I'm a slave!

Nobody can be held accountable, except me for making mistakes. There are no laws. He could have maimed me, killed me, done whatever he wanted, and nobody would have cared or stopped him. *You* could do the same thing, and nobody would stop you. Or you could sell me, and the next person could do it too."

Wren covered his face with his hands, rocking back and forth as he wept silently. The silence, more than anything, was unnerving.

"No matter how *you* see me, or what we do here, I am a slave. I will always be a slave. And no matter what fancy names you put on it or how nice you are to me or whether I call you master or sir or something else or nothing at all, I will *always* be aware of that. And we will never be equals. How *dare* you ask that of me?"

For a moment, Jere found himself feeling afraid of Wren. Usually so calm and controlled, he lay there fuming, glaring, and clenching his fists. He was telling a story about terrible abuse, but he didn't look scared. He looked explosive and dangerous.

The moment passed quickly. Jere could feel Wren blocking his emotions, extinguishing the feelings, rearranging his facial expression to a neutral one again. Jere sat silently, waiting to see if there was more to the terrible story, more that this kid, his *slave*, felt he needed to tell him. He was met with silence.

"I'm sorry," he finally whispered, feeling trite and ineffective.

"For what?" Wren muttered. "You've been nothing but kind to me, and all I seem to do is try and fuck it up. This is too hard. I fucked everything up before, and I'm still fucking it up."

Jere reached out in the darkness, gently covering Wren's hands with his own. When they weren't pulled away, he held them both lightly, the hot, sweaty palms a reminder of how agitated Wren had become. "I'm sorry that you went through such hell, and I'm sorry that it hurts you so deeply. But you're not fucking anything up, and this isn't a game, and even if I can't promise you that everything will be perfect and happy all the time, I can promise you that I will be next to you, whenever you need me or want me, and you're not gonna change that. Not because what I say goes, but because I care about you. And I like you. And... and I guess we don't have to be equals. But I don't want you to think of me like you thought of Burghe, or that training facility, because that was something else.

Something wrong."

Wren said nothing, but sniffled a bit and gripped Jere's hands tightly.

"I've seen you," Jere said, trying to look into the kid's eyes despite the darkness. "I've seen you let down your guard a bit, relax, enjoy yourself. Hell, enjoy me, even. And the point is, that's the side of you I lo-like." He rushed to continue, covering the almost-confession he had just made. "Wren, what I'm trying to say is, it's not about denying reality. As much as I'd like to, as much as I'd like to pretend that you're just my housemate, or my assistant, or my boyfriend, well, I know it's not the case. Regardless of whether either one of us likes it, I own you, and I'll do my best to do that honorably, but dammit, when we're alone, I want the way we interact to be different, to be less fucked up by what's socially acceptable. I want to see you let your guard down, not to trick you into punishing you, but so I can get to know you—all of you—better."

Jere forced himself to stop talking. He felt Wren drumming his fingers across the palms of his hands, simultaneously calming and arousing. He wanted nothing more than to sweep him away, out of a state so backward that it turned people like Wren into slaves.

Wren let out a little laugh. "Did you call me your boyfriend?"

Jere found himself struggling not to laugh out loud. "I guess I did," he said, barely repressing a snicker. It was absurd! They were talking about horrible abuse and slavery and what stuck out was that he had called Wren his boyfriend?

"I kind of like that," Wren said, a bit shyly, still laughing.

"Well, if you only *kind of* like it, we could certainly stop!" Even the darkness of the room couldn't hide the grin on Jere's face as he teased.

"I don't want to stop!" Wren protested playfully, then grew serious. "I really do like it. I like being with you. Talking to you. I know I probably don't seem like it sometimes, but I'm happier now than I've been in years. I never thought... I never thought I'd enjoy another person's company so much. You say you want to know all of me, but nobody knows all of me. When my family found out I had a physical gift, they disowned me. Burghe knew more about me than anyone, at the end, but then, well, he's dead now. It's dangerous to let people get close."

"That's all in the past," Jere insisted. "I promise, you won't be in any danger. I love being around you, Wren, I couldn't imagine anything that could change that."

"I can tell," Wren smiled. His eyes were sad in comparison. "I never expected that. I never thought I'd find someone to care about me that I cared about as well. It not something you do as a slave. You survive. At any cost, you survive, and if you're alive at the end of the day, that's all you deserve. Being happy is something that free people do."

"You'll look back on this in a few months and laugh if you think you're happy now," Jere said, a bit of his usual, playful cockiness coming out. "It only gets better from here—at least, if I have anything to do with it!"

Wren smiled, big and sweet and at ease, and pulled himself closer to Jere, who wrapped his arms around him instantly. They stayed like this for a few minutes, and Jere forced himself to be quiet again. Wren seemed to need some time to think, and he was willing to give it to him—after all, it had been quite a bit of information they had just dumped on one another.

"I'm willing to try, sir."

Jere let the comment stand as it was, ignoring the end.

"I've spent six years addressing free people in a certain way," Wren explained. "I was rarely even around other slaves once I left the training facility. It's a hard habit to break, and I won't lie, it does make me nervous, even though I know it shouldn't. But I do feel myself being more comfortable around you, letting it slide, and I like the way it feels when I speak casually with you through the mind connection. The best I can do is… I'll think about it, and I'll try."

Jere kissed him on the forehead. "That's good enough for me, kid."

Wren arched into him, pressing their bodies together. "It helps, you know, to know how you feel about it—to know that you understand. That we're not just lying to ourselves, or each other. Not about this."

"I'll do my best never to lie to you," Jere promised, feeling his body respond to the closeness, the ever-present heat.

"I know," Wren said softly, letting out a breathy sigh as Jere's hands stroked across his body. He managed to keep his tone serious. "And thank you for listening to me. I'm sure that some of what I told you was shocking, to say the least. I'm sorry if it disturbed you. I'm probably not the person you wanted to be with."

"Of course you are," Jere protested.

"You don't know…" Wren started. "You just don't know everything that happened. Everything I've done. Everything I'm capable of, how much damage—"

"Hush!" Jere captured his mouth and kissed him, deep and passionate. "I want to hear about your past. It is disturbing, but it happened to you, and it affects both of us, and nothing you can tell me will ever make me pull away from you."

"Nothing?" Wren asked, looking doubtful.

Jere shook his head, imagining the sorts of abuse that must have been piled on to make Wren so unsure of himself. "If anything, it reinforces how strong you are, how brave."

"I don't feel very brave," Wren mumbled.

"I know," Jere whispered, kissing him again, moving down to his neck, and holding him close the whole time. "But you are. I don't think I could have handled it. You've told me so little, and I think it would have been more than I could have dealt with—at least, and stayed sane."

Wren laughed, bitterly. "I wonder if I did, some days."

"You're one of the sanest people I've met here," Jere said, trailing his hand along his back. "Mmm, and one of the sexiest."

They fell asleep soon after. In contrast to the previous night of hot, insistent passion, tonight they simply reveled in one another's touch. It wasn't about sex, or getting off, rather, they took comfort in the closeness that each had to offer. Jere could sense that Wren was still rather unsettled from the conversation, and he wouldn't dream of pushing him past those boundaries. The information that he had shared tonight had been so personal, so painful—there was no way he would ever forget any of it, nor would he take it lightly.

He kissed him, over and over again, wishing he could convey with his mouth what his words didn't seem able to convince his lover of; that he was strong and beautiful and brave and valued. He tried to worship the body that held such an amazing person inside of it, and he tried to make him feel good, as if he could undo all the awful touches with more good ones. He soaked in Wren's touch, focusing in on it, trying to use each and every one to push out the reality of the rest of the world, the state that made him a master and Wren a slave. They held each other close, blocking out the world that placed demands, restrictions, and unwanted limitations on both of them.

Chapter 31
Playing with New Toys

A few weeks passed. As promised, Wren did try to be more casual with Jere, rarely addressing him as "sir" unless they were in the clinic, preferring instead to avoid addressing him directly at all. Jere still longed to hear his name coming from those beautiful lips, but was satisfied to hear "hey" instead of "sir" all the time. He attempted to get Wren to open up again, as he had that night, but was unsuccessful. Wren didn't want to talk about it, and both were much happier kissing or cuddling, or, much to Jere's delight, getting one another off. Wren wasn't always up for it, but on those occasions that he was, Jere had grown familiar enough with him in his mouth that he knew *exactly* how to make him feel wonderful. Even his aversion to nudity had faded somewhat, and Jere was pleased to be able to sleep next to him wearing only boxers.

Nonetheless, Jere saw the nervousness that flitted at the edges of Wren's emotions when they were together. He felt the fear that forced them both to pull back when things were heating up, and he woke up to muffled cries and pleas more nights than he cared to. He hated the fact that the kid was still so afraid of him at times, and wished that something other than time and promises would help him to see that Jere really wasn't a threat. Finally, he had an idea.

The clinic was having a rather quiet day, and Jere found the time to sneak out to buy something. He insisted that Wren stay behind, in order to check in any patients that might stop by unannounced. He tried his best not to smirk when Wren asked what he was buying, and he replied simply, "Supplies."

They finished the workday, and Jere remained closed-mouth

about his plans, drawing a few curious looks from Wren. After a leisurely dinner, Jere got up, a mischievous grin on his face. "I have a surprise for you."

Wren raised an eyebrow, not saying anything.

Jere caught his hands and walked him toward the bedroom slowly. "I know, you don't really like surprises, but I promise this one will be fun."

"Okay...." Wren allowed himself to be led to the end of the hall.

Jere stopped outside of the bedroom door, which was suspiciously closed. "Give me five minutes, then come in," he instructed, his eyes eager.

Wren smiled a bit. "Okay."

Kissing him quickly on the lips, Jere disappeared into the bedroom, setting up the "surprise" he had bought earlier. It didn't take him nearly as long as he thought it would, although his excitement might have helped him to move a bit faster. He couldn't contain his eagerness. "Okay, five minutes was too long, come in now!"

The door opened and Jere watched as Wren stepped through, his eyes going immediately to the bed where Jere lay on his back, entirely naked, arms and legs restrained to the bed with tasteful padded leather cuffs. After attaching his legs to the bedposts at the foot of the bed and snapping cuffs around both of his hands, Jere had fastened the cuffs to a chain attached to the headboard, a small lock completing the task. He could move a few inches to the left or right, but for the most part, he was completely at Wren's mercy. Wren said nothing, but his jaw dropped a bit.

Jere smiled at him, beckoning him over with one restrained hand. "Come here."

Wren did as he asked, wordlessly.

"I know it's hard for you sometimes — you don't know when I'll stop, and sometimes you think that I won't stop at all, or not soon enough, or sometimes, I think you're just not sure of what I'll do at all," Jere explained. "And so, like this, Wren, you're entirely in control. Do whatever you like, or don't do something if you don't like it, but you can be certain that nothing else is going to happen. Explore me, use me, do whatever you want — I just want to see you enjoy yourself."

Wren said nothing, staring with a blank expression. Jere found himself growing a bit nervous. He had made the right decision, hadn't he? He hoped he had. In any case, he was securely locked into the cuffs, so Wren would at least have to participate enough to let him out.

"You went out today to buy this for me?" Wren said softly, his hand coming up to brush lightly against the restraints.

"I did. I thought it would be helpful," Jere nodded. "Also, I really enjoy being tied up."

"You do?" Wren's voice was doubtful.

"Mmhmm," Jere wriggled around a bit, straining the restraints. "I like feeling something holding me back, making me wait for whoever I'm with to put their hands on me, to run their tongue across my body, to do whatever the hell they want to with me. Knowing that all I can do is squirm and struggle and hope that they'll do what I want them to. Every movement is a surprise, and the waiting makes it *that* much more delicious."

Wren seemed puzzled by this explanation. "But what if... what if you don't like what's happening?"

Jere smiled. "First off, I can't recall anything that you've done to me in bed that I haven't liked."

Wren blushed a bit.

"But mostly, if I don't like it, I'll ask you to stop, or to do something different," Jere said more seriously. "And I'm sure you will. Wren, I trust you completely. I know you wouldn't hurt me."

Wren was quiet, an uncomfortable look on his face. "I guess."

"What?" Jere asked. He couldn't quite put a finger on it, but Wren seemed to be pulling away, blocking the mind connection more than usual. He decided to keep the mood light, teasing. "Do you have some sort of evil plan I'm not aware of?"

"Of course not," Wren shook his head, looking nervous. "Why would you think that?"

"I'm joking," Jere smiled. "I know you well enough to know that you could never do something like that."

"Right," Wren agreed, looking away. Jere was surprised that the teasing had made him so uncertain.

When Wren looked up again, the uncertainty was hidden by a carefully blank face, although Jere could still feel it through the mind connection. He decided not to push it further, putting it out of his head as Wren looked him over for a minute. Jere felt somewhat scrutinized, but it only increased his desire.

"I hope you're not entirely opposed to the idea," Jere said, only half-kidding. "Because I at least need you to unlock these things if you are."

"No, I, I see the appeal." Wren shook his head, erasing the small smile that had threatened to creep onto his face as he considered the situation. "It's intriguing. You're *sure* you enjoy this?"

Jere nodded. He was perfectly comfortable and excited by the idea. He thought he had mentioned it to Wren before, but certainly hadn't gone into details. There were plenty of stories he could have told, but somehow, he felt it was best to let them develop their own stories.

"Okay." Wren looked at him, as though he were considering something vitally important. "Is there anything that you want, or don't want?"

"Well, I would certainly like to feel you touching me," Jere felt his lust growing at the thought, and was relieved that Wren seemed to be less thrown by the idea. "But, other than that, I'm leaving it up to you."

Wren smiled. "Well, I suppose I can try and see what it's like." He approached Jere carefully, and knelt next to him on the bed. "Now, where to start?"

Jere was quiet, assuming it was a rhetorical question. He relaxed against the pillows he had strategically placed near the headboard to prop himself up, hands curling around the restraints. It was a feeling he was quite comfortable with, and quite a fan of as well. He missed these games.

Wren decided to start at his legs, running his hands up them softly, almost chastely. He continued on over his hips, up his sides, and across his chest, where his hands lingered and explored with more confidence. As he did, he kept flickering his gaze from Jere's body, to his face, then back again, carefully observing the reactions he was causing.

Jere was shuddering from the anticipation, not to mention the tentative way in which he was being touched. He could still sense some fear, but Wren was so often afraid. Jere wondered if it was really him that Wren was afraid of, or if it was something else entirely.

After a few moments, Wren continued his trail upward, up his arms, straddling him as he stretched his own arms up to clasp Jere's hands. He leaned forward and brushed his lips across Jere's lightly, dipping down to his neck a moment later, leaving him wanting more.

Jere enjoyed feeling the weight of his lover pressing gently against his abdomen. Wren wasn't exactly sitting on him — no, he was too well-versed in sexual ways to do that — but the slight, confining pressure and heat made him catch his breath, not to mention the hardness he could feel pressing into his stomach.

A hardness that increased as Wren moved back up to his mouth, kissing him boldly, grinding on top of him as he devoured him with his tongue. Jere tried to thrust up against him but found himself unable to move. A needy moan escaped his lips.

Wren, despite his concentration, couldn't hold back a slight laugh, and seemed to take that as an opportunity to trail himself down Jere's body again, making contact pretty much everywhere. The fabric of his clothes was both soft and rough, and the feeling contrasted with soft hands and an even softer tongue. Wren tantalized him, dragging his tongue experimentally across every inch of Jere's neck, chest, and stomach. Jere yelped with pleasant surprise as he felt teeth, very light teeth, grazing across his nipple. Wren looked up at him, a curious expression on his face.

"Uh huh," Jere felt himself breathing heavily, wanting to feel those teeth everywhere, those hands everywhere….

Between the delicate pulls with teeth, Wren had started to flick his tongue across his skin as well.

"Jesus!" Jere gasped, wanting to kick himself when Wren pulled back and froze.

"Did I hurt you?" Wren sounded alarmed.

"No, god no, don't stop, please!" Jere mumbled incoherently, pulling at the restraints, wanting nothing more than to pull Wren back to what he was doing. He couldn't leave him like this! It wasn't fair! He forced himself to sober up a bit, opening his eyes and smiling. "Really, honestly, I'll tell you to stop if I want you to. But right now, god, keep touching me!"

Wren looked relieved, and he kept his eyes on Jere's face as he leaned down and alternated between licking and biting at his skin again. Jere couldn't tear his own eyes from Wren's intense gaze. Suddenly he stopped again, causing Jere to make a sad little groan.

"What—"

Wren pressed a finger to his lips, soft, but insistent. "Shh." The smile on his face was playful. "I made you squirm. It's kind of fun."

For as hesitant as Wren had been, he was catching onto the game quickly.

Jere obliged him happily, squirming as desperately as he could. It wasn't an act.

Wren slid back, allowing his still-clothed ass to brush against Jere's cock, making him squirm and thrust against it. Wren looked satisfied, getting the reaction he had hoped for. Seconds later, Jere cried out as he felt lips and tongue and teeth along his inner thighs, so close, but not quite there. He trembled with the need to move, to thrust against him, to make some connection, but a part of him knew better. He wasn't calling *any* of the shots tonight it seemed.

"You like that," Wren observed, his voice quiet. Jere could barely nod in response.

When Jere was least expecting it, he felt a hand grip him and squeeze, pumping two or three times in rapid succession.

"God shit god, Wren, yes, please!"

He was pretty sure that he wasn't making sense, but he didn't care. Wren jerked his cock a few more times, eliciting the same response, and then settled into a lighter touch, almost tentative again. Jere closed his eyes and threw his head back, unintelligible moans still coming from his mouth. Suddenly, the hand disappeared, and he felt lips on the head of his cock. He whined, pleaded, and then found himself whimpering as he felt nothing more and heard the bed creak a little.

He opened his eyes to see Wren standing next to the bed.

"Wren?"

He was greeted with a look of amazement.

"I've never gotten completely naked for you, have I?" Wren's voice was teasing and sultry.

Jere shook his head, eyes widening. There had been healing, and that terrible night at the police post, but that was different. That didn't count. That didn't turn him on.

"Would you like me to?" Wren's hands tugged at the edge of his shirt, not pulling it off yet, but soon.

"God, yes!" Jere was almost able to ignore the longing between his legs to watch this show.

Indeed, it was a show. Wren removed each item of clothing slowly, intentionally, fully aware that Jere's eyes were on his every move. Not to mention on every inch of his body. It was too soon and too long before he was naked, and he stood there, uncertainty evident on his face.

Jere let out a long sigh. "You're fucking beautiful," he said, glancing up and down the young body in front of him, but settling on the eyes. "Do you know that? Do you know how much I want you?"

Wren blushed and ducked his head, somehow making him more adorable.

"I can't wait to feel your skin, feel your body pressed to mine, knowing I can't touch you, *wishing* I was touching you," Jere groaned, tugging at the restraints to prove his point. "Don't make me wait anymore to have you next to me!"

Wren smiled, climbing back into bed.

A tiny part of Jere was sad that he wouldn't get to touch Wren right now, that it wasn't him who was dragging his tongue across Wren's body, but to see the kid so fucking comfortable and free to explore, it was worth it. And the wanting was its own delightful torment.

Jere found himself pinned under the full naked length of Wren's body, squirming beneath him, exploring his skin with the parts of his body that still had a little bit of movement available. He whimpered again when he felt Wren returning to kiss his neck, letting his head drop to the side to give him better access. Suddenly, an idea crossed his hormone-flooded mind, and he whispered in Wren's ear. "Can I make a suggestion?"

Wren smiled, kissed him deeply, then returned to his neck, nodding.

"Let me suck you," Jere found himself proposing. "Keep me tied up, and let me take you in my mouth. Please?"

"Hmm," Wren returned, kissing him once again, using a hand to reach down and stroke Jere once, twice.... "Are you sure I won't hurt you?" he asked finally.

"No," Jere said, shaking his head. Truthfully, he didn't care if Wren hurt him, he just wanted him. "I mean. Yes. I'm sure. You won't. Really, I trust you. And I really, *really* want you!"

"It's strange. This is so—I never thought I'd do something like this." Wren smiled lustily at him and slid his legs up, straddling him again.

Wren arranged himself over Jere's head carefully, though not without a bit of challenge, ending up with his knees spread wide, trapping Jere's arms. The tip of his cock waited just inches from Jere's mouth, stiff and ready and enticing.

"Are you comfortable?" Wren asked, quite considerately.

Jere nodded, bringing him a bit closer to his goal. He figured "comfortable" was relative.

"If you're not, then, uh...."

"I'll tap the headboard," Jere supplied, eager to reach his goal. He demonstrated, rapping his knuckles back against the wood. "Or, you know, mind connection."

"Oh!" Wren smiled, looking relieved. He slowly inched himself down to Jere's open, waiting mouth.

Jere took him in one movement, tugging against the restraints and straining his neck to pull him in deeper. He moaned around the cock, the vibrations making Wren shudder above him. He wanted to feel him thrust, wanted to feel him lose control and let him swallow him deep, but for some reason, he wasn't.

"*Don't hold back,*" he pleaded through the mind connection. "*I can take it, go deeper. I want it Wren, I want you so bad!*"

Without another word, Wren leaned forward, pinned Jere's wrists to the headboard, and began thrusting down his throat.

"Like this, sir?" His voice was a deep whisper.

All Jere could do out loud was to whimper through his nose. *"God yes, Wren, yes, keep going!"* It didn't matter that his own cock was untouched at the moment, it was as hard and ready as if it were being sucked as well.

While he had worked Wren's cock carefully, artfully in the past, at the moment he was simply struggling to take it all. The position provided Wren with quite a good angle, and the more Jere responded, the more excited he got, the harder and deeper Wren thrust into his mouth. Jere worked hard not to gag, as it had been so damn long since he had given head quite like this. He felt Wren tense up, and smiled a bit around him, certain he was about to come.

He pulled back, instead.

Jere couldn't find words, out loud or through the mindspeak. He whined instead as Wren slid down his body, and Jere felt their mouths pressed together. Wren's tongue moved softly over the lips that his cock had just bruised.

"I want to come with you," he whispered, and continued to slither down Jere's body, making him writhe.

Jere looked down to find Wren kneeling between his legs, reaching out with both hands for Jere's cock, which Jere thrust up to meet his touch. Wren toyed with it for a few moments, exciting him, but certainly not bringing him anywhere near orgasm. Wren was silent, watching Jere's response to the different touches. After a few minutes he stopped, daring to stroke himself for the first time that Jere had ever seen. They both moaned in pleasure, though for different reasons.

Wren leaned over, letting his head rest on Jere's pubic bone, cruelly taunting him as he ignored his cock.

"Here's the deal." He glanced up at Jere. "If you stay still, you get to feel my lips around you. If you move too much, I'll stop."

Was that a question? "Okay," Jere agreed, regardless.

"And I don't...." Wren faltered for a minute. "I don't want you to...."

Jere understood immediately. "I won't come until you tell me to," he promised, "and I'll tell you if I'm getting too close."

"Good." Wren looked satisfied, and leaned over to brush his

lips up and down Jere's shaft.

The amount of control it took for Jere to hold himself still was stupendous. He squeezed his eyes shut, too amazed by the sight of his lover between his legs to look. He tuned in to the mind connection, mostly detecting excitement and curiosity. He grasped at the tiny sliver of fear that he felt around the edges of Wren's arousal. The last thing Jere wanted to do was to add another negative experience of this sort to Wren's life.

Wren moved from brushing his lips across him to dragging his tongue around, from balls all the way to the head, slow and careful. Finally, he circled the tip of it a few times and pulled Jere into his mouth the tiniest bit.

Jere whimpered pitifully, begging for Wren to take him deeper. He clutched the restraints as hard as he could, forcing the lower half of his body to stay still.

After a few moments of teasing like this, Wren did as he was being begged to, accommodating the entire length into his mouth, cupping it with one hand to hold it steady. Jere sighed as he finally felt relief, and pressed down into the mattress to avoid thrusting up as he wanted to. A few minutes later, a hand began stroking his balls again and unexpectedly brushed along his ass. He jumped with a startled yelp, and felt a rather punishing pressure on his cock before Wren pulled back.

"I'm sorry, I'm sorry, please keep going, I won't move again!" he begged, feeling terrible that he had moved when he said he wouldn't, but also wanting that hot, sweet mouth back on him. "Shit, you caught me off guard!"

Wren laughed, his mouth still over the head of Jere's cock. The vibration caused him to flatten himself back against the mattress, yelling out all the obscenities he had ever heard. Without a word, Wren continued, bobbing his head up and down as Jere arched his back, flexed his calves, and clawed at the restraints, all in a desperate attempt to hold still. Finally, when he wasn't sure he could handle it anymore, he heard himself saying, "Please... about to come...."

Wren slowed down, sliding back off his cock, much to Jere's dismay. A moment later, he stretched out on top of him again, and Jere felt his cock caught in Wren's hand, along with a partner.

"Fuck," he muttered, daring to wriggle and thrust again. The combination of pre-come, saliva, and sweat provided just enough lubrication to keep the friction from being painful. Still, Wren was rough. He gripped both their cocks in one hand, while using the other to grab the back of Jere's head. Pulling him close, he kissed him as intensely as he worked their cocks. Barely a few minutes had passed before they were both grunting, thrusting, and riding the barrier between pain and pleasure as they ground into one another.

Wren pulled back ever so slightly and looked Jere in the eye. There was a glint in his eyes, the likes of which Jere had never seen from him before. It was sexual and demanding and dark. "Come for me, Jere."

Hearing his name escape those lips pushed him over the edge. Within seconds, both were coming, yelling and kissing and biting and thrusting until neither one of them was sure who was doing what. Time seemed to stop for a moment, and when it started up again, Jere found himself pressed tightly against the mattress under Wren's body, his face buried in his neck, a sticky pool forming between them.

"*That was fucking spectacular.*" Jere wasn't sure if real, out-loud words were possible at the moment.

"Mmm," Wren replied, nuzzling closer to him.

"You are... you're amazing." Jere tried words, with some success. "Thank you, so much. God, Wren...."

"Mmm," Wren still wasn't capable of much more.

Jere started to fidget, noticing that the restraints had become uncomfortable at some point.

Wren noticed, sitting up reluctantly. "Where are the keys?"

"Second drawer," Jere indicated the bedside dresser with his head.

Wren retrieved them without completely moving himself off of Jere's body, and unfastened the arm restraints, leaving his legs tied for the moment. He pulled Jere's arms to him, one, and then the other, gently rubbing the sore muscles and wrists, encouraging him to stretch. Jere almost felt like purring under the attention.

Wren sat up, pausing for a moment as he looked at the leg restraints.

"You can leave me tied if you'd be more comfortable," Jere said quietly. It was like reality was crashing back. "Or, if you want to leave, I could —"

"No." Wren undid the restraints. "I'm okay, it's just, it's strange, you know?"

Jere nodded. He did know, sort of. He knew how much of a challenge it was for Wren to be naked, to be vulnerable, to be around anyone else in such a sexual way.

Wren rubbed his legs and ankles, as he had his wrists, then flopped down next to him on his back. "I didn't hurt you, did I?"

Jere laughed. "If you did, I liked it too much to complain." He wouldn't lie to him outright, but he didn't want to give him the idea that anything wrong had happened. So often, Wren seemed so afraid of being hurt, hiding behind perfection and obedience. Still, the way he enjoyed being rough and controlling made Jere wonder if there wasn't something more to Wren under the surface.

"You really do like it rough, don't you?" Wren asked, looking puzzled.

"Yes." Jere saw no reason to lie.

"It turns you on." Wren's statement was more of a question.

"Yes."

"It doesn't, I mean, you're not worried? I could really hurt you."

Jere shook his head. "It never crossed my mind. I wouldn't have done it if it had."

"And you like to be tied up?" Wren asked, looking skeptical.

Jere had answered that already, but figured Wren had been too surprised to really think much about it. "I love it," he answered honestly. "It turns me on, just thinking about it."

Wren said nothing, but he was studying Jere's face again. "What do you like about it?"

"I like to let someone else control it," Jere said, shrugging. It was hard to put into words. "I like the surprise, the things I would never think to ask someone to do, and I like knowing that the person I'm with is going to be in control of if and how I feel things, and trusting that they'll make it feel good for me. I like pain, too, a little.

Just the way it feels."

"You like pain?" Wren asked, looking uncertain. "Like, really like it?"

Jere smiled. Logically, it sounded strange, but logic had nothing to do with the way his body responded. "Not a lot of pain, and not every kind of pain for that matter, but certain things I like. Things like feeling your teeth on my skin, or being grabbed roughly. Having my hair pulled. A good slap, depending on the circumstances."

Wren still looked puzzled. "So it's not just that you put up with it, you actually *like* it?"

"I was the one who begged you to do it," Jere reminded him lightly. "I guess it might sound weird, I mean, I've never really enjoyed being on the giving end of pain, I just take people at their word when they say they enjoy it. Besides, did I look like I was unhappy tonight?"

Wren shook his head. "Definitely not," he agreed. He looked like he had more to say, but he was silent instead.

Jere figured that maybe he just needed some time to think about it. "Did you enjoy yourself?"

Wren blushed, looking away. "Yeah," he mumbled. "I didn't think I would. I mean, why would I enjoy something like that?"

"Because it turns me on, and there's nothing wrong with doing something that turns both of us on." Jere turned his head, kissing Wren on the shoulder. "Thank you for trying it with me. I'll leave it up to you whether you want to use them again. I'm completely in favor, but I'm completely in favor of anything you want to do with me."

Wren let out a contented sigh next to him.

"I'm gonna go get a towel for us to clean up, all right?"

Wren nodded, eyes closed blissfully.

Jere stood up, stretched a bit, and retrieved a towel from his bathroom, wetting one end of it with water. He returned to find Wren exactly as he had left him, stretched out naked on his back.

He sat on the edge of the bed. "May I?" he asked, when Wren opened his eyes.

For a second, he thought Wren was going to reject him. He had never let him touch him this way before, why would this be any different?

But he just nodded, relaxing back into the bed.

With careful reverence, Jere went over every inch of his body with the towel, following it with his hands. His touch was barely sexual, and certainly not very arousing. They were both tired from their activities earlier, and neither was interested in attempting a second round, but Jere took the rare opportunity to explore Wren's body, feeling him respond to certain areas, and vowing desperately to remember which ones those were for future reference. They were silent, except for quiet sounds of pleasure. There was nothing more to say.

Finally, when Jere was finished washing and exploring, he looked down at his slave, who looked up at him from half-lidded eyes. "Clothes?" he offered, somewhat regretfully. He didn't want to be rude. Not after such a lovely gift.

Wren nodded. "Pants. Just pants. You wear whatever you want. Or don't. Just don't want to panic in the morning."

Jere smiled at him, retrieving a pair of pajama pants and helping him slip them on. He joined Wren in bed, pulling him into his arms, which was becoming their regular sleeping position. Sleep descended quickly.

Chapter 32
An Unexpected Visit

The restraints, as it turned out, were a wonderful, wonderful idea. True to his word, Jere really did seem to like them, and while Wren had been quite reluctant to do such an unthinkable thing at first, well, who was he to deny his master that much pleasure? Jere did seem to enjoy it, and Wren thrilled with the excitement of knowing just how much he could make the man enjoy his touch. Wren felt powerful for once, and it was almost intoxicating. It was terrifying as well.

The security of knowing that things could never go too far was amazing. It wasn't that he didn't trust Jere, it was just hard to trust anyone who could hurt him. Seeing his master tied down and *enjoying it* reminded him how different things were — in the past, restraints had meant punishment, pain, force. But with Jere they were fun, and Wren discovered that he enjoyed teasing him, something he would never have thought of doing otherwise. It was strange, just like it had been strange the first time Jere had given him head, but Jere proved repeatedly that he liked different things than Wren. Once again, Wren let his observations and Jere's passionate responses convince him that Jere truly was enjoying himself.

Still, Wren struggled to trust that he wasn't hurting Jere. As scared as he was of someone taking advantage of him, it was worse still to imagine himself losing control, making a mistake, hurting someone who so willingly turned himself over to Wren's control. He made sure to check in, with words and mindspeak and touch, to make sure that Jere was still enjoying it, that his rough play didn't go too far, that everything was as comfortable as possible. It was a challenge, being so responsible for another person. In the same way that nobody had ever cared for him so closely, he had never had the chance to care for another person. It brought them to a level of closeness he had never witnessed before, certainly not in his own experience, but not even in relationships between free people. The society they lived in valued culture, tradition, respect — it left little room for trivial things like affection and attachment. People here took care of one another out of duty or to garner favor for the future, not simply because they enjoyed seeing the other person happy.

At Wren's tentative suggestion, they used the restraints almost exclusively for a few days, until Jere's wrists started showing slight bruises, despite the padding. He said he didn't mind, and Wren decided to believe him, although he did insist they cut back.

Besides, feeling Jere's hands roam across his body was something that Wren didn't want to stop. They both felt free to touch and kiss and explore each other, and Wren started to relax enough to enjoy feeling Jere touch him without reservation. Whether it was soft, gentle caresses, warm strokes of his tongue, or, occasionally, hungry grabs of desire, Jere made him feel hot and cherished and utterly out of his mind in a way that no one had ever done before.

Wren was just starting to lose his mind in the best of ways when he felt Jere stop.

"Someone's coming."

"Mmm, not yet," Wren writhed above him, seeking more contact.

Jere put a hand on his hip, stilling him. "No, not like that," he said, eyebrows furrowing. "Someone's coming to the clinic."

Severe medical emergencies were few and far between, but when they happened, they arrived at the clinic at any hour of the day. It was the downside of being the sole medical practitioner in town. In the eight months that Jere had been living in Hojer, only three people had shown up with emergencies outside of normal business hours. Tonight looked to be number four.

"What can I do to help?" Wren asked, sliding off of Jere to allow him to get out of bed. His excitement faded quickly in the face of necessity.

"Find us clothes."

In a matter of seconds, they were both successfully dressed, and Jere ushered them both in the direction of the clinic. He paused suddenly as they passed through the living room, causing Wren to stumble into him.

Wren was about to apologize, but was startled by his master's change of course. Jere muttered something he couldn't hear and moved to the front door. Wren followed him, confused. He knew Jere could sense people through the mind connection, but why would someone be at their front door at this time of night?

Jere opened the door to reveal Paltrek Wysocka, looking irritated and nervous. An unusual look for the flighty aristocrat.

"Paltrek, what's wrong?" Jere asked, looking confused.

"Jeremy, I'm sorry to bother you, but I need your help. As a doctor." With this, he stepped aside a bit to reveal a male slave carrying what Wren was pretty sure used to be Arae.

Jere paled. "What happened to her?" he demanded, ushering them inside.

"My sister happened to her," Paltrek said wryly. "Took after the poor girl earlier tonight and damn near killed her. She's breathing funny now, and she won't wake up. Annika couldn't care fuck all if she never did, but I'm just… this is wrong."

"Bring her inside. Quickly!" Jere snapped to action.

"Yes, sir." The slave carrying her hurried to follow the order.

"Wren, go set up an exam room and get her into it. Get me some of the Crucial Care and some bandages."

"Yes, master," Wren said as he sped off. He was surprised that the Wysocka boy had brought in a slave at all, let alone as an emergency. While the statewide healthcare arrangement took care of the citizens of Hojer, slaves were considered property, not citizens. Payments for their care were made out of pocket. More often than not, slaves were taken to veterinarians, whose skills weren't as good a match, but who charged far less for their services.

The room was set up, and Wren heard the others entering. The male slave was cradling Arae in his arms, heedless of the blood that was dripping onto him. Wren couldn't even tell where the blood was coming from, or how such a small person could lose so much and still be alive.

"Dane, put her down on the table," Paltrek said quietly.

"Yes, master," the slave said, doing as he was ordered. He returned to Paltrek's side. "Master, will she be all right?"

"Don't pester me," Paltrek said, without much conviction. "I'm not the fucking doctor."

"I'm sorry, master," the man mumbled, head down toward the floor.

Wren felt nervous for him. Asking questions out of turn and irritating one's master could be a dangerous offense. He was overcome with a sudden desire to kiss his own master for his kindness.

"I'll do what I can," Jere was saying, looking more at the male slave than at Paltrek. "What was done to her? It'll give me an idea of where to start."

"I don't even know what she did, really, except belong to Annika," Paltrek shrugged. "But I came home tonight and she was after her with a cane—not even the normal kind that you'd use for discipline, an actual walking cane. Big and thick and—"

"What else?" Jere interrupted, looking ill. "Clearly, more has happened than a simple beating."

"I don't even know, Christ, I wasn't home!" Paltrek shook his head, then looked to Dane, who was looking pleadingly at him. "You know more than I do, probably, tell him what you know."

"Yes, master," Dane looked relieved as he turned to Jere. "Sir, Arae was being punished for the past few days—Miss Annika was beating her on most days and hadn't allowed her to eat or drink—"

"At all?" Jere asked in disbelief.

Dane looked nervous. "Well, sir, she might have found something."

"Dane sneaks her things when he's not supposed to," Paltrek explained, rolling his eyes when his slave flinched away. "It's not like I'm stupid. The girl would have been dead years ago if Annika had it her way."

Jere shuddered at the callous disregard. "Okay, so what changed today?"

"She failed to please her tonight, sir, she threw up while she was supposed to be servicing her. The mistress, she, she made her eat it, but she couldn't, and Arae tried to run away from her and hide, and Mistress Annika really lost control and started beating her with whatever she could find. The cane. A fireplace poker. Her fists — "

"Did she burn her, too?"

Dane nodded, tearing up as he did. "Yes, sir. Sh- she burned her, and, and when she screamed she put it in her... in her mouth...."

"Dane, get a hold of yourself," Paltrek muttered, looking entirely uncomfortable.

"I, I'm sorry, master," the slave replied, obviously trying to keep his voice steady.

Wren was disturbed by the scene. He had no idea what the connection between the Wysockas' two slaves was, but it was obvious that Dane was in nearly as much pain as the girl lying on the examination table. She was naked, prominently displaying the various abuses that had been visited upon her body. Wren was horrified by the severity and thoroughness of the multiple beatings she must have suffered through. The only part of her body that wasn't bleeding or burned or both was her face, aside from a split lip. Dark bruises competed with pale skin, and Wren had never seen so many bones visible through another person's skin. At least she wasn't conscious.

Jere reached out and put a hand on Dane's shoulder, subtly pulling him away from his master. "Hey, it's okay," he said softly, looking more at Paltrek as he said it. "You're doing just fine. Now, tell me, is there anything else that I should know, anything else that happened?"

Dane nodded. "Sir, she, she cut her up. All over. But on the inside, too. With a knife. Like... like she was... fucking her with it."

"God dammit!" Paltrek's tone caused both Dane and Wren to jump. He didn't notice. "She's fucking disturbed. Jeremy, I'm sorry you had to see this."

"It's all right," Jere said. "Why don't you have a seat while I get started? Wren, go and get some drinks — bring some for yourself and Dane, too, please."

"Yes, master."

"And take Dane with you," Jere tacked on at the end. "*Keep him out of here for a little while, okay? He's too upset; I'm worried what will happen. Try to calm him down or something.*"

Wren nodded, pausing in the doorway to wait for Dane, who followed after a quick nod from his master. Wren led them into the house and to the kitchen, where he leaned back against the sink. "What does your master like to drink?" he asked, rather stiffly. He wished this task hadn't been pushed on him. He hated dealing with emotionally overloaded people.

"Um, vodka," Dane said, distracted. "Vodka and orange juice."

Wren nodded, remembering from the first time the Wysocka boy had visited. "And you? Will your master allow you anything?"

Dane shrugged. "He doesn't really care too much. He'll allow it, since Master Peters requested it."

Wren was glad to hear it. He guessed that the female Wysocka wouldn't let someone piss on her slave if she were on fire. He wondered about the repercussions for the healing that was undoubtedly going on in the next room.

"Hey, my master... he's very good at what he does." Wren tried to be comforting. "I mean, I was nearly dead when he acquired me, and you can't tell now. I'm sure she'll be fine."

"She'll just hurt her again." Dane looked no less distressed. "I should get back...."

"I'm keeping you out of the way," Wren told him. The favor to his master was work enough, he didn't need to pretend it was a secret on top of it. "Help me make drinks. I'm sure you know how your master likes them?"

Dane nodded, silent. If he had any feelings about being kept away, he wasn't showing them yet. Wren couldn't blame him. Showing feelings left you vulnerable, and if you were vulnerable, you could be hurt. He directed the other slave to the liquor cabinet, pulled out supplies, and left him to mix the drink. Meanwhile, he put some water on the stove, heating it for tea and wishing he was back in bed. He turned to find Dane crouched on the floor, leaning back against a wall.

"You can sit in a chair." Wren hadn't meant to sound so harsh, but it was late and he was irritable.

"I'd rather not be beaten later, thanks."

Wren sighed. It was true. "Do you belong to just him, or his sister as well?" Shared slaves were uncommon, but not unheard of in families.

"Just my master," Dane said quietly. "He's a fair man, but there are rules that I am expected to follow."

Wren nodded. This slave didn't really seem too afraid of his master. After all, he wasn't the one lying half-dead on the exam table in the next room.

"I think I've met you before?" Dane asked. "You look familiar."

"You probably saw me with my last master, Dr. Burghe. He was friends with Mr. Wysocka, senior."

Dane nodded. "That explains it. You look different now. Better."

Wren turned to the stove for a moment, under pretense of checking on the tea, but really to hide the redness on his face. Was it that obvious? "My master is very good to me."

The water was boiling, and Wren carefully poured it into two teapots, adding identical teabags to each. "Carry the cups, please."

"He lets you drink tea?" Dane asked, surprised. In general, slaves were only allowed water. Along with the synthetic food product, it ensured that their diet remained bland and unexciting.

"Yes." Wren artfully arranged the two teapots, cream, and sugar in his own hands. "Don't mention that it's the same, though, I doubt your master will be so agreeable with the idea."

Dane said nothing, but followed Wren back into the examination room where Jere was already deeply out of touch with reality, set on healing the girl. Wren set the beverages on an exam table, trying to dismiss the absolute absurdity of the situation. Dane handed Paltrek his drink, and Wren turned to fulfill his duties, holding out a teacup to the man before offering anyone else any. "Tea, sir?"

Paltrek shook his head. "My boy got me just what I need right now," he muttered taking a long drink.

Wren picked up a new cup and the second teapot. "May I offer your slave something to drink, sir?" He cursed at how formal he sounded.

Paltrek shrugged. "Whatever. Have at it, Dane."

Wren filled a cup and passed it over, then poured himself one. He left Jere's in the pot for now, until he was ready for it, but added a bit of sugar to his own, out of habit. "Cream or sugar?"

Dane, who had knelt on the floor at his master's feet, looked up, questioning. Paltrek shook his head, resigned. "When in Rome, eh?" He laughed a bit at his own joke. "Knock yourself out, kid, we'd both be killed at home for this!"

Dane let a little smile spread across his face he glanced at Wren. "Both, please?" he pressed his head against his master's leg, and was rewarded with a slight ruffle of his hair.

Wren smiled back as he held the cup out to his fellow slave. A few months ago, he would have been bitterly envious of the kindness with which Dane was being treated — a far sight from what he was used to now, but so much more considerate and gentle than the way Burghe had treated him, how Arae was treated. At that thought, he pulled up an examination stool and sat next to his master. It was bolder than he usually would have attempted in the company of others, but this was a medical clinic, and any and all decisions were explainable as medically necessary. He smiled a bit, realizing that he trusted Jere to have his back.

"*Is everything okay, sir?*" he asked, pressing lightly at the mind connection.

"*Give me a minute.*" Jere dismissed him, following quickly with, "*Sorry, just a little involved. I'll update everyone in a minute, okay?*"

Wren touched his arm lightly, waiting.

"Dane, what the hell did she do that got Annika *this* pissed off?" Paltrek had nearly finished his drink, and still looked rather unhappy.

"Please, master, all I know is that she angered one of Miss Annika's suitors a few days ago, and then, little things, and then, tonight, she took her to bed and—"

"All right, Dane, it's all right, relax!" Paltrek said irritably, although Wren noticed that his hand was still gentle as it stroked his slave's hair. "Relax. You don't have to know. This is just... it's more than usual. Even for Annika."

"Yes, master. Thank you."

Paltrek sighed, looking around and then at his watch, as if he had somewhere to be. He tipped his drink up. "Dane, go get me another drink," he ordered. "I think we're gonna be here a while."

Muttering, "Yes, master," as he went, Dane did as he was ordered, leaving Wren uncomfortably alone with Paltrek, as Jere was otherwise occupied.

"So, uh, what do you do around here?" Paltrek asked, looking as uncomfortable as Wren felt.

Was he really trying to make small talk? "I assist Dr. Peters with his medical work, sir. I do as he asks, and manage patients as they come and go. I also have duties around the house, cooking, cleaning, whatever is required of me."

Paltrek nodded. "Jeremy's a good guy."

Was that some sort of trick question? He trod carefully. "My master has been very kind to me, sir."

"Bet he'd never get you in *that* state."

The usual, diplomatic, "as he sees fit" answer seemed out of place. Wren answered truthfully. "No, sir, I don't believe he would."

Wren felt his master's presence returning before he heard him swivel about in his chair. Dane returned at the exact same moment, and Wren was mostly glad to be saved from having to make awkward conversation with a free man for any longer.

"She'll be fine," Jere announced solemnly. "But it will take a little while. She has a host of pretty serious injuries—a few broken bones, one rib that's puncturing her lung. It's surprising she can breathe at all. There are quite a few internal injuries as well. Sepsis, blood loss, dehydration, malnutrition. Dammit, she's damn near dead!"

"It wasn't me who did it to her!" Paltrek protested weakly. "I'm just trying to help."

Jere paused for a moment, collecting himself. He touched Wren lightly on the arm. "Go pull up a painkiller and an antibiotic shot, please." He turned to Paltrek. "I know it's late. If you'd like to rest, you're welcome to one of the guest rooms in the hall—Wren can show you the way."

Wren returned with the supplies Jere had requested and shot him a questioning look. Offering to let a slave take a guest to a bedroom could mean more than just sleep, and he was pretty sure Jere wouldn't do that....

Jere's eyes widened as he understood. "Of course, if you'd like company, Dane can accompany you. I'll be needing Wren's full attention immediately."

Paltrek laughed. "Don't worry, I'm not gonna lay hands on

your prize possession. I'm tired anyway, and this really kills any mood I might have had. Show me the way, and Dane, stay here and make yourself useful."

Wren escorted him to the first guest room, checking perfunctorily to make sure there was nothing else he required before he left. He sped back to the examination room to find Jere downing a few cups of tea and washing his hands. Accustomed to the more frantic pace that usually occurred during the workday, Wren felt rather relaxed as he settled onto his stool, waiting for Jere to need him. This, finally, was familiar.

"Please, Master Peters, how may I help?" Dane asked, voice filled with concern, enough to make him speak out of turn.

"Just stay out of the way," Jere answered. He was always so brusque when he was at work.

Wren pulled another high stool over to the opposite side of the table from himself and Jere. "Dane, come sit here, hold her hand. If she wakes up, it will be nice for someone familiar to be around."

Dane looked at him gratefully. Not only could he pretend that he was doing something to help Arae, but he was being allowed to follow his master's orders to do something useful. Wren knew how important this was, even if Jere seemed to have forgotten it for the moment.

"*Honestly!*" he exclaimed, silently, and Jere turned to look at him, a bit surprised.

"*I'm working! I don't have time for formality and shit!*"

Wren returned to his seat, daring to reach a hand under the table to lightly stroke his master's leg. "*I took care of it. And I'm sure she'll be fine. Just tell me what you need.*"

He felt Jere's mood soften at once.

"*Sorry. I'm being an asshole.*"

Wren didn't respond. It was true, but in addition to it being horribly inappropriate to agree with such a thing about one's master, he knew Jere hadn't really meant it. At the same time, he respected him too much to lie to him.

"*Make it up to you later?*" Jere flashed a bit of a grin at him, and Wren couldn't help but smile back as he nodded at him.

Chapter 33
Different Lifestyles

The healing, as Jere had indicated, took quite a while. A solid four hours of repair were needed to stabilize the girl, and once he was finished, Jere debated sedating her further so she would continue to sleep. Dane had fallen asleep long ago, sinking down into the office chair that Wren had rolled into the room in place of a stool, while still holding Arae's hand.

Jere pulled back, exhausted. He turned to Wren, who was waiting with something for him to drink. He wanted nothing more than to drag Wren back to bed and fall asleep with him there.

"Should I go wake their master?" Wren indicated the sleeping slaves next to him.

"I suppose." Jere stood up and stretched, uncomfortable from remaining in the same position for so long. "Make some coffee too, would you? I'm about to fall over."

Wren nodded, placing a kiss on his lips before speeding out the door.

Some barely perceptible noise must have been made, because Arae stirred a bit, opening her eyes and looking confused for about half a second before sitting up in complete terror.

"Where am I?" she asked, to no one in particular.

Dane woke up immediately, sitting up and taking her hand again. "Arae, it's okay, you —"

"What happened?" She attempted to get off the table, but found herself gently restrained.

"Hey, it's okay, calm down," Jere said as he eased her back. Too much exertion could cause serious damage this soon after such an intense healing.

"M... Master Peters?"

Jere nodded. "Yes, hey, relax, it's all right. You were a little sick, so Paltrek and Dane brought you in here? Just lie back, let me get you something to drink."

"Where's my mistress?" Arae's voice was more panicked than before. "Please, sir, I need to find my mistress. If she comes for me, and I'm not there — "

"It's all right. I'm sure Paltrek will tell her — "

"No! Please, I have to go back, I have to — "

Jere and Dane both struggled to hold the tiny girl down on the table.

"Arae, it's okay, you're safe here, master will — "

"No! You don't understand! Please, Dane, let me go! She'll kill me, she'll — "

Paltrek walked in, eyes red from sleep, and obviously a bit disoriented. "Arae! Knock it off immediately and lie down on that goddamn table until I tell you otherwise!"

Arae drew in a shaky breath, looking at her mistress's brother nervously, and did as he ordered.

"Jesus." Paltrek muttered, then glanced at Arae again. "You were damn near dead when we found you last night, and Dr. Peters healed you up. You still need to rest. And you will obey *every* order that he gives you, is that clear?"

Arae nodded, finally relaxing. "Yes, sir. I'm sorry, I — "

"Don't apologize! Just be quiet." Paltrek shook his head and looked to Jere. "Sorry, I should have warned you — she doesn't respond well to kind and gentle."

Jere shook his head, a bit unsettled. "That's fine. If I may, I'd like to give her something to drink that will help speed the healing, as well as a mild sedative to help her rest. A few more hours to observe her would be necessary — "

"I'm not going home without her," Paltrek said, somewhat resigned. "She was right, Annika's likely to be furious when she finds out about this. Actually, my plan is to wait until around breakfast time so I can speak with our father first. He'll be furious — with Annika. Never did like to see her break her toys."

Jere felt his lip curl back in disgust at the sentiment, but the man in front of him had at least brought the poor girl in for treatment. As it was, Paltrek wasn't really a bad guy. Of course, before anything else, he'd need to get the girl taken care of.

"Wren?" he called. He couldn't resist smiling when his "assistant" strolled through the door. The smile grew when he saw a tall glass full of green liquid in one hand, a coffee mug in another.

"I've added a sedative, master," Wren handed the beverages to him.

Jere took them, letting his hand brush over Wren's a moment longer than was proper. He didn't care. It was now five in the morning, and he hadn't slept since yesterday. His night and his time with Wren had been interrupted, and he was exhausted and cranky. The fact that Paltrek and Dane were undoubtedly watching made no difference. "Thank you, Wren."

Wren pulled back a bit, ever proper, and turned quickly to Paltrek, bowing a little in apology. "I apologize sir, how may I serve you?"

"Coffee's fine," Paltrek said, dismissively.

Wren caught Jere's eye. "If I may suggest, master, it is nearly time for breakfast. Would you and Mr. Wysocka like me to make something for you?" At Jere's somewhat confused look, he added wordlessly, "*After they leave, you can have a nap before your first patient.*"

Jere smiled, understanding. "That would be most appreciated. Please, just fix the usual?"

"Right away, master!" Wren scampered off, leaving Jere to try to move things along.

He started by giving the drink to Arae. "Drink this," he ordered, unable to bring himself to summon up the vicious tone he had heard Paltrek use with her. Obediently, she did as she was asked, choking a bit on the taste and thick texture, but managing to get it down. She relaxed quickly, falling asleep in minutes.

"Right then, let's move to the dining room, see what food there is!" Jere tried to sound energetic.

Paltrek stood. "Come on, Dane, let's go."

Dane hesitated. "Um, master, I could stay here with Arae—"

"You could do as you're damn well told!" Paltrek said, quite irritably. He glared at Dane until he hurried over to stand next to him, hands clasped behind his back. Paltrek reached out an arm toward him as he did, and Jere cringed away, certain he was about to witness an uncomfortable moment of discipline that he would rather not be present for.

Instead, Paltrek put his arm around Dane's shoulder and guided him out toward the dining room. "She'll be all right, Dane, trust me. Just let her sleep it off. Come with me and let her rest."

"Yes, master." Dane walked silently with them to the dining room, where Wren had laid out coffee, orange juice, bagels, and fruit already, along with two place settings.

Jere realized, rather uncomfortably, that the two place settings were for himself and Paltrek. But then, the other two?

"*Just go with it,*" Wren advised him, his voice firm. "*Just follow my lead, and Mr. Wysocka's.*"

"*Yes, master,*" Jere teased, feeling a little loopy, not to mention tired of hearing the honorific thrown around all night.

Wren held a straight face while he finished setting the table, announced that more food would be on the way, and turned back toward the kitchen. When he passed Jere, he grinned, brushing into him lightly.

Jere and Paltrek seated themselves at the table, and Dane rested on his knees at his master's feet, leaning his head against Paltrek's leg. They began to pick at the food that was sitting on the table already, and Jere was careful to notice the way that Paltrek handed food down to Dane occasionally, mindlessly, as though this was an everyday occurrence. It probably was.

"Write up a bill and I'll take it home with me. Make sure it's in Annika's name," Paltrek broke the silence. "Father will see it and be absolutely outraged with her."

"Honestly, if it's that big a deal, I don't have to—"

"No, it is a big deal. She won't stop unless someone calls her on it." Paltrek took a long drink of his coffee and continued. "I can't get her to lighten up. And if I just tell Father, he'll see it as petty squabbling—he didn't have a chance to see what Annika did to her. But an itemized receipt from you would mean a lot. He'd have to acknowledge what Annika actually did."

Jere nodded, considering the logic. It was rather different from how things worked in his own family, but little about the rich, frivolous Wysocka family was familiar.

"The other thing is, well, Annika is making a goddamn spectacle of herself," Paltrek confided. "Has been for a while, but it's been worse since you turned her down. Not that you shouldn't have, but she didn't take it well. She never takes rejection well. But the way she's been treating that girl—Jeremy, you might not know this, being from the city and all, but only trash would treat their slaves that way in public. What you do behind closed doors is your own damn business, but doing it in public or so severely that it has to be addressed outside of the home is just tacky and wrong. I mean, what if it hadn't been the middle of the night? We couldn't have just walked her on over looking like that! We're Wysockas, not some sort of goddamn barbarians!"

Jere didn't say anything. He couldn't. The most upsetting thing about the situation was the social repercussions?

"Jeremy." Paltrek was looking at him with a raised eyebrow. "Come on. Don't look at me like I'm shallow. I'm rather disgusted by my sister's behavior, too. I know you are—hell, you told her as much the last time she was here! And it was a disgusting show. But even at home, hell, somehow I ended up being the softie in the family. I can't stand to just arbitrarily punish the slaves, you know? I can't take life so fucking seriously."

Wren had returned with the remainder of the food—eggs, potatoes, sausage—and placed them on the table before kneeling at Jere's feet, shaking his head quickly to stop any protests. Jere wanted to protest, badly, but knew better. He tried to content himself with running a hand through Wren's hair instead.

Paltrek smiled as he looked at them. "Like that," he said, vaguely. At Jere's look, he continued, "I bet you don't so much as raise your voice to that boy, do you? And he's perfectly well behaved. Perfectly. That's something special you've got, right there."

Jere blushed, and felt Wren turn his head into his leg to avoid doing the same. "I am... very fond of him."

Paltrek laughed, open and honest. "Not a damn thing wrong

with that! At least, I don't think so. My family, however…. Well, the people here, *especially* the people here who have owned slaves for years and years, they tend to have a different attitude toward it. Take my father, for example. What Annika told you about him a while back, that he beats new slaves just because, and keeps up weekly beatings? It's true. He does. And I'll admit, I gave Dane a hell of a beating when my father first gave him to me."

Jere nodded, unsure of what to say.

"I regret it to this day." Paltrek looked down at his slave, sadly. Dane rubbed his cheek against his leg, almost reassuringly. "I didn't know what I was doing; here I was, just some stupid kid. I thought my daddy's way was the only way, you know? And he comes up to me, after I had just laid his back open, and begs me to tell him what he did wrong, so he wouldn't do it again, and to punish him for not knowing in the first place. I'll tell you, man, I was *sick*. This wasn't some crazy, rebellious slave who needed to be put in his place — this was a scared little boy! But I wasn't much more than that myself, really."

Jere shook his head, shoveling some food into his mouth to save him from having to speak.

"Our father got the twins for us when I turned twenty-one," Paltrek explained. "Annika, as usual, was pissed, because she was older, and she still got Arae at the same time as I got Dane."

"Twins?" Jere asked, confused.

Paltrek grinned. "They don't look it, do they? Arae and Dane — they're twins. That's why he's so concerned about her. Not too many slaves get to stay with their family, but the novelty of twins who are slaves, well, it's unusual. Quite a talking point."

Jere was stunned. He had thought friends, maybe even lovers, given Dane's strange devotion, but…. "They don't even look the same age!"

"Twenty-two, both of them," Paltrek replied. "They were slightly used when we got them, but already trained. Father didn't want us having green slaves. No, they were both small and young when we got them, but the difference, well, I feed Dane. It's sad to see, but Arae hasn't grown a damn inch since Annika got her hands on her. Dane's shot up quite nicely, filled out, keeps himself in shape.

I like that."

"That's...." Jere let his voice trail off. Wrong? Terrible? Worthy of horrified looks and anger? "Wow."

"Yeah." Paltrek shook his head. "Annika took after our father, but took it a step too far. I mean, he'll beat his slave, and the household slaves, for that matter, but it's always calm, controlled. With Annika, it's like she just lets all her rage out on that girl, for whatever reason. Not that Dane and I didn't have our days, huh?"

"As you say, master," Dane replied tentatively from the floor.

"Hell, I was young, headstrong. He was too, really. I took my youthful frustrations out on him more times that I care to recall. It was usually stupid shit, really, but isn't it always? Not getting ready quickly enough, taking a tone with me — I suppose, things you could expect from any slave." Paltrek reached down to pass Dane a choice bit of food, almost indulgently, suggesting there were no hard feelings. "Now, it's few and far between, isn't that right, boy?"

"I try my best to please you, master."

Jere watched the scene with fascination. The combination of criticism and comfort, humiliation and blatant disregard — it was like a mix of someone talking to an infant, a criminal, and a pet dog. He knew where to categorize people like Annika, but what to do with a slaveowner like Paltrek? Dane was clearly uncomfortable with the conversation.

"Lately, our conflicts seem to be over Arae and Annika," Paltrek said, shaking his head. "You know, I can hardly blame him, it is his sister after all, but I won't tolerate disrespect. And even when I disagree with my sister, she's still a free woman, and I won't tolerate disrespect toward her either. Or lying. I've only had to whip Dane, what, twice, in the last year or so? It's been a damn long time, hasn't it?"

"Yes, master," Dane closed his eyes, and Jere guessed it wasn't for a good reason. "Thank you for being so kind, master."

Paltrek ruffled his hair a bit, oblivious to the embarrassment he was causing. "Eh, he's a good kid," he said affectionately.

"Then why — "

"*Sir, no!*" Wren interrupted in his head.

" — would you whip him at all?" Jere continued, undeterred. He didn't care if he offended Paltrek or not, he had to know. Had to at least *try* to understand how one person could do this to another. Wren looked up at him nervously, and Jere couldn't tell if he was nervous *for* him or *because of* him.

Surprisingly, Paltrek laughed. "Jeremy, it's different views, different lifestyles. You city folk are all delicate and forward-thinking, and I suppose that might be the way it is there. But out here... hell, I'm no stranger to the whip myself!"

Jere tried, rather unsuccessfully, to stop his jaw from dropping.

"First time, when I was twelve, 'just in case' I might have developed a physical gift. Daddy didn't want me soiling the family reputation by being weak and crying. I did cry, anyway, because I was twelve, but it happened." Paltrek shrugged, as if this were normal. "Before that—and after, but after that, it varied—it was the cane. Annika, too; just because she's a girl didn't mean she avoided it. Around here, that's what it means to be part of an important family—you need to carry yourself properly at all times. It doesn't matter if you're six years old, and you want to run around and play, you do it when it's damn well time to do so, or you're up to that many strokes of the cane, then sitting on a hard chair for the rest of the day. Believe me, by the time I was a bit older, and the number of lashes was up to fifteen or sixteen, I started thinking before I did stupid shit."

Jere reminded himself to close his mouth, before he looked like a fish. "I... I'm sorry that happened to you. My mother never a laid a hand on me when I was a child!"

"It's the way it is out here," Paltrek said, casually. "There are rules, and they are meant to be followed. I'm not gonna whip a slave for something trivial, but a major infraction, yes, that does deserve whipping. They know it."

"I'm sorry, I don't even know what to say." Jere couldn't comprehend the magnitude of a society built on that much violence. *"Was it like that for you?"* he asked.

"We'll talk later," Wren promised.

"You might not notice it, because he's a bit smitten with you," Paltrek said congenially, nodding his head toward Wren. "Or, because you're a bit smitten with him, too. Or hell, maybe the late Dr. Burghe had him appropriately cowed. But usually, they try you, push your buttons, test your limits. And you've gotta be firm, make sure they know their place. Not destroy them, like my sister, but, get them like Dane. A little goes a long way."

"I'm pretty sure Wren is perfectly aware of his place," Jere said quietly. "*And it's not on the goddamn floor!*" he added to Wren, aware that he sounded sullen.

"Hey, I didn't say you were doing anything wrong!" Paltrek held his hands up. "Hell, what you've got there is a good thing. Wish I liked boys more, I'd probably take up with Dane the same way. And Arae… Christ, when I can wrestle her from my sister, she's so terrified I feel bad trying to do anything with her. I've done it a few times, on principle, but hell, I'm not a bad person. Then Annika started asking for Dane in trade, and I had only been doing it to get Arae out of her clutches, so that had to stop. Say, you wouldn't have a use for Dane for a bit while I'm out of town on business, would you?"

"I, uh, I don't—"

"*Agree. He wants you to get him out of the house!*" Wren cut in.

"—uh, remember, uh, what his gift is," Jere finished lamely. "What I'd use him for."

"Organizational skills," Paltrek replied, oblivious. "He can look at a room and put things in the best places to maximize space so you have a ton more. It's really amazing, actually. Part of the reason my father bought him for me, an underhanded dig at my, er, messiness."

Jere nodded. "Of course. I can have him help clean up the cellar. Been meaning to do it, and, well, just haven't had the ambition."

"Great, great!" Paltrek smiled. "I don't like leaving him with my family. Honestly, I come home and it takes days to get him to calm down—sometimes nearly as many to get him healed. I don't understand it, but they are constantly finding fault with the kid. Not that I like to believe a slave over my own family, but I think they provoke him. And since I'll be gone for so long, I'd have to officially pass him over to their ownership, no way to protect him."

Jere looked confused. "How long will you be gone for?"

"Oh, just under a week, but you know, well, no, you probably don't, but that new senator a while back passed that ordinance that there officially needs to be someone in charge of a slave if the master is away for more than 48 hours. Which, usually, means I hand him over to my father, which has its own complications, but he has no issues with what Annika does. Damn disrespectful, if you ask me. No, I'd rather keep him with me when I can, but I'm sure you'd be kind to him. Especially after I pull this stunt with Annika. She'll get me back however she can, I just know it."

"Of course, any time," Jere smiled, trying to process what he'd just agreed to. "Why can't you just take him along with you?"

"Fucking business in a non-slave-state," Paltrek said, obviously displeased.

"You couldn't just leave him at a hotel while you were out?" Jere inquired. Surely that was easier than this arrangement? It wasn't as if money would be a problem.

"Outlanders," Paltrek shook his head. "You can't take a slave into a non-slave-state. Can't even cross the state line, except in a licensed freight train transport."

"Oh...." Jere was startled. From what Paltrek was saying, he and Wren couldn't travel, at least outside of slave states.

"Of course, the freight trains are for slave trading business only, and they aren't even allowed to stop for repairs in non-slave-states," Paltrek continued. "They break down, they send out another train to tow them. Too risky, losing slaves like that."

"And what about people with physical gifts who would visit here?" Jere asked, still amazed that this society could function.

"Doesn't happen!" Paltrek laughed. "If they go to buy a ticket here, and I couldn't imagine why they would, they'll be told that it's a slave state. Nobody in their right mind would just travel right down to somewhere that they'd be enslaved!"

"I never heard that when I bought my ticket here!" Jere couldn't contain his shock.

"Didn't you notice it was a blue ticket?" Paltrek asked, surprised.

Jere hadn't noticed anything about the damn ticket. "What the hell does that mean?"

"Blue tickets are slave states for people with physical gifts. Red tickets are non-slave-states. Green tickets are slave states for criminals. There's a myth that there are orange tickets for slaves states for people with mind gifts, but that's ridiculous," Paltrek dismissed the idea that people like him could ever be slaves. "That's why they ask for your gift along with your name and date of birth when you sign up on the security register. The employees will inform those who *need* to know about it when they go to buy a ticket. Even if they get on the train, they won't be let off, although at that point, they'd probably need a police escort back. Pesky differences in laws, really."

"Yeah," Jere agreed. He wasn't thinking about that, so much as he was trying to reconcile the strange reality that he would never get to go home again. There was no way in hell he would abandon Wren here with anyone else, and he was stuck otherwise. He pushed the thought aside, the reality of it a little too much to handle. "When are you going?"

"A little over a week," Paltrek answered. "I'll be gone the whole business week—Monday through Friday."

"That's fine, then," Jere nodded. What was he agreeing to? This was insane.

They finished breakfast at a rather leisurely pace, Paltrek filling up most of the conversation explaining his work and the deal he hoped to make while out of town. Jere, at Wren's urging, even brought himself to hand feed his slave little bits of breakfast, and was pleasantly surprised to feel his fingers being licked and sucked passionately. Perhaps there were benefits to this arrangement....

Wren cleared the table off once they were finished, and Paltrek stood as well, bidding Dane to fetch his sister. The lack of sleep had gotten to all of them, and Paltrek seemed quite eager to head home.

"I'll be in touch about the trip, then," he said, heading out the door.

Jere bid him farewell and dropped down on the couch, exhausted. He heard Wren tidying up a bit, and looked up to see him standing in the hallway, a peculiar look on his face.

"Come here."

Wren walked over, pausing in front of Jere for a moment. Jere reached out and wrapped his arms around his waist, holding him silently for a moment with his chest pressed into his stomach. He and Wren had been enjoying their little fantasy world of sex and happiness, but the rest of the world was out there, waiting, full of reality and misery.

He felt Wren's hand softly running through his hair, comforting him for a change.

"Are you okay, sir?"

Jere shook his head, still silent.

Wren stood there, petting him, not saying a word. After a few minutes passed, he reached around and gently detached Jere's arms from his body. "Let's go to bed. Things will make more sense once you've had some sleep."

Jere didn't respond, but allowed himself to be guided to bed. He knew that there would be very little sleep, but more than anything, he wanted to take comfort in Wren's closeness, to pretend that the rest of the world didn't exist for a little while longer. They lay in bed, curled around one another. Neither bothered to take off their clothes, which they would need for work in just over an hour anyway. Jere fell asleep, trusting that Wren would take care of waking him.

Chapter 34
Pillow Talk

The day dragged by, almost blending into the next. With no need for discussion, they decided that dinner and bed were to be top priorities, both worn out from the previous night. At least this time they managed to change out of their work clothes before crawling into bed and falling asleep in each other's arms.

Which was where Jere woke up, feeling Wren's eyes on his face.

"You're awake early," he mumbled, noticing that it was still dark outside.

Wren smiled back at him. "We fell asleep right after dinner last night. Couldn't have been much later than seven."

"Mm, that's right," Jere moved closer. "I was tired."

"We both were, sir," Wren agreed, returning the affection.

"God, did I actually agree to slave-sit?"

Wren tried unsuccessfully to stifle a laugh. "Yes, yes you did."

"Fuck. I have no idea what I'm doing," Jere laughed. He wondered how he had managed to end up taking care of his friend's slave by accident. "What do I even do with him?"

"Whatever you want to," Wren gave him a smile. "You'll be effectively standing in for his master, so whatever you do or don't want to do is fine. Short of permanently damaging him, I mean."

"Like I would," Jere grinned back. "Did Matthias ever lend you out like that? While he was out of town?" The thought of leaving Wren with anyone else made him shudder a bit.

Wren nodded. "A few times, sir, when he was gone for business. He didn't leave very often, though."

"How was it?"

"They were...." Wren looked away a bit. "They were kinder, kinder than my old master had been."

"Ha." Jere shook his head with disgust at the memory of the man he had once taken up with. "Probably wasn't hard to be kinder."

Wren said nothing to him, just nodded and relaxed into his arms a bit more.

"Wren... you know I would never do that to you, right?" Jere asked, after a moment.

Wren was silent for a few seconds. "I know you have family and friends back in the city...."

"Yeah, but..." Jere tried, but he couldn't imagine abandoning Wren with anyone he had met here. "Can't I just leave you here?"

"It's not really like that here. I mean, a night or so is fine, but it is forbidden to leave a slave alone for any length of time. It was always sort of frowned upon, but with the recent law change, it's a serious offense now."

Jere resisted the urge to curse. "But shouldn't I, I mean, if I own you and all, shouldn't I get to say what happens to you?"

Wren shrugged, avoiding Jere's eyes. "There are a lot of laws like that. They restrict both the slaves and the masters."

"So I don't get to go back and visit my family, my friends?" Jere asked, disbelieving. It was too much. "I don't get to catch a speed train into the city if my mum gets sick, or if a friend has a wedding? I've been thinking about it since Paltrek mentioned it the other day, and I just don't want it to be true!"

"You are allowed to travel, sir," Wren mumbled.

"Not really," Jere retorted, wishing things were different. He thought about it more, about how he could get around it, or escape it, and he came up with nothing. He thought about Hojer and how much he hated it, how much he wanted to leave, and he was struck with an unpleasant fact. "I don't get to move back home. Ever."

Wren stared at him, a guilty expression on his face as he waited for him to continue.

"I mean, I never had any real plans. Okay, any plans at all. But I think that staying here until I got old and died was certainly *not* the plan, you know? I wanted to be able to move back to the city one day, take a bunch of years of experience and expertise back with me and have a job there all secured and stuff...." Jere tried to put his unfinished plans into words. "I mean, it's sort of amazing here, I don't have to worry about working under somebody at a hospital or anything, I get paid extraordinarily well, I have this house—I don't even know, I mean, I guess I was thinking I'd sell it or something. Like I said, I hadn't really thought about it—but this isn't where I want to end up. I miss the Indian takeout place that was by my shitty apartment. I miss the flurry of speed messengers on lunch hours. I miss the noise of a hundred people walking by on a Saturday night to go try out a new club. I don't want to give that up! I want to go back!"

"You could." Wren's voice was quiet and tense.

"Not really," Jere frowned. "I'm stuck here. Is there a way to get *you* out?"

Wren looked down as he spoke. "No. There's not."

"Wren, I hadn't had time to think of visiting for months, and even now that I do—I thought that taking you might have been difficult, but I figured I could just leave you here, you know, to take care of things on your own!" Jere tried to put his feelings together, to get them across to Wren, who was looking more closed-off and detached with every passing moment. "I didn't realize what a goddamned burden it could be to have the 'privilege' of owning a slave!"

"I'm sorry," Wren mumbled.

"I looked into it, and there was nothing I could find," Jere continued, trying to process his own mess of thoughts. "Getting you out of Hojer. I mean, unless there's some sort of alternative. From what I've seen, it doesn't matter, money, influence, anything, it's unavoidable. You're stuck here, and so am I. There's no way for you to get out of here."

"There's not," Wren confirmed, his voice still quiet. "But you could still go."

"Not without leaving you." Jere frowned. He hated it, hated the whole system.

"You said it yourself, in a few years, you'd be able to move back permanently, have a job, have some money. That sounds like exactly what you would want."

"It *is* exactly what I want, but that doesn't mean I can do it," Jere said. If Wren wasn't here, it was exactly what he would have done, exactly how the next few years of his life would be working out, and he would be planning just how long he had to stay here in Hojer before being able to return home.

"Once you establish yourself, I'd be the only thing keeping you here," Wren said, giving voice to Jere's thoughts. "It's because of me that you're stuck here. It's not fair to you."

"You're right," Jere agreed. It wasn't fair to him or to Wren. Nothing here was fair. He looked over, startled when he realized that Wren had pulled away a little, looking upset.

"You shouldn't let me get in the way of living your life. You might get tired of me, or want to move on, or you might realize that I'm just not what you expected."

Jere considered it briefly, for argument's sake, but he felt nothing but horror at the idea of abandoning Wren. "Even if we're not doing whatever we're doing now, I still couldn't do that to you. I'd be sick every night worrying about you."

Wren said nothing at first, but the look on his face told Jere he didn't believe it. Finally, he asked, "Why would you stay here if we weren't together? It has to be hard enough as it is, being with me, having me mess up your life?"

"You did not mess up my life," Jere said firmly, pulling Wren close. Where had he gotten this idea? "This *state* messed up my life. You were just the one thing in it that made it worth it, and I wouldn't ever leave you here. Not forever, not even for a weekend. That's been true since the first few weeks I was here."

"Thank you," Wren tightened his grip around Jere's waist for a moment. "I doubt you have any idea how much that means to me."

That's because I doubt you have any idea how much you mean to me, Jere thought, then spoke aloud, "The other night, when Paltrek was talking about what it was like growing up here? You said we'd talk later. Was it really like that for you?"

Wren nodded. "Yes and no. I mean, our family wasn't as much

in the social spotlight as the Wysockas are, so things were a bit more lax. Certainly, there were significant demands placed on behavior, even from children, but I think our parents only punished us physically a handful of times. The cane, though, yes, that was the torture implement of choice. We hated it."

"We?" Jere inquired, making an almost conscious decision to avoid processing the sheer barbarity of this state.

"My brother and I," Wren answered. "He was two years younger than me, certainly the one of us that was most likely to get in trouble."

"I didn't realize you had a brother," Jere mused.

"Dalen," Wren supplied. "I kept an eye out for him, at the training facility, even though I knew it was unlikely he'd be brought to the same one. All I hope is that he wasn't cursed with a physical gift like I was."

Jere was quiet for a moment, processing the horror he would have felt not knowing where his sister would have grown up, whether she would have been free or a slave. She was older than him, though, she would have been the one having to worry about those things. Not that it mattered anyway, there weren't slaves in Sonova.

"Do you ever want to see them again?" Jere inquired.

Wren shrugged. "Dalen, maybe. Yes. He'd be seventeen, now. Almost finished with high school... or... or a slave. I would certainly like to know how he's doing. Probably not see him though."

Jere said nothing, but looked at him curiously.

"I told you," Wren hesitated for a moment. "I told you when you first got here how my father rejected me once it was revealed that I had a speed gift, right?"

Jere nodded.

"Well, he was the most vocal about it, but everyone else had to disown me as well. It's the way things are done. My mother, Dalen, extended family—I'm sure that once I was taken, the family pictures were edited out, my room was turned into a study or office or something—when someone is taken as a slave, it's like they don't exist. They aren't talked about again. Ever."

Jere shuddered at the thought.

"Dalen would have become the heir, legally and socially. He would have been regarded as an only child. He would have been even more spoiled than he was already," Wren tried to manage a smile, but was largely unsuccessful.

"I just—I have a hard time believing my mum would have done that," Jere said, looking sorrowful.

Wren shrugged. "It's the way it is here. It's a weakness to have a physical gift. You're taken as a slave, so at least you're not around to remind your family of their genetic failures, but there's still shame to it."

"But that's your family!" Jere didn't want to understand the sheer awfulness of this culture, but he couldn't help trying.

"It's not like anybody here really gets close to their children, Jere," Wren pointed out. "We were taught discipline. Taught to obey and agree and go along with social customs. Once the gift shows, then it's safe. Most families have elaborate parties when their children show their mind gifts, because then they are finally part of the family. Until then, it's a gamble, a calculated risk."

Jere shuddered. His childhood stood in huge contrast, full of hugs and affection and security from his friends and family alike. He didn't know what to say.

"So you, your mum, and your sister?" Wren asked. "Was that the whole family?"

Jere nodded, relieved to have the distraction from thoughts of family in Hojer. "Yep. We had a father, when we were very young, but he wasn't really involved. Jen has more memories of him than I do. He and my mum had an agreement—no promises, no commitments, the kids were hers. Sometimes he'd send a card or something, but I think the last time I saw him I was ten or eleven. My mum had always wanted children, and hey, he was cheaper than a fertility clinic!"

Wren laughed.

"That's how she described it to us, at least," Jere grinned. Thinking about his childhood was so much more preferable than thinking about Wren's. "We never held it against either of them. Although, personally, I think if my mum wanted children, she could probably have just split her own genes off and forced them to grow. She's rather a force of nature."

"Must have been nice," Wren said. "My mother obeyed every little thing my father told her, I guess in hopes that she didn't fall out of favor with him."

"What, did she owe him something?" Jere asked, confused by the relationship that Wren was describing. "Why would she marry someone just to spend the marriage worrying about things like that?"

"It's not like they were in love or anything," Wren dismissed the idea. "That's not really how things work around here. They were married, they wanted children together. It was functional. My father was from a much better off family, so my mother was glad to be with him. I remember good times with her when I was young, when we were alone. But when they told me about my gift and I begged her to help me, she just told me I wasn't her son and walked away. I never saw her again. I never want to."

Jere had no words for this. He pulled Wren close, kissing him on the top of the head. "She has no idea what she's missing." He felt Wren sigh against his chest, not moving.

"She knows exactly what I am," Wren said quietly.

Jere stayed silent. He couldn't really contradict Wren, but he didn't agree, either.

"Do they have mind gifts?" Wren asked, after a moment. "Your family?"

Jere nodded.

"They could always come and visit," Wren pointed out. "No law keeping them away."

Jere smiled. "My mum has been on me to visit since I moved here — well, since she terrorized my old landlady into giving her the address." He looked a little sheepish. "And Jen... I hope Jen doesn't know, although I'd expect she does, and that's why I haven't heard from her. She really will kill me if she visits — Kieran wasn't lying, Jen is pretty actively involved in anti-slavery movements."

"Hmm, maybe have your mum visit first, then," Wren teased. "I mean, I'm guessing she'd be pretty upset if she came all this way to find you dead already."

"Good point," Jere laughed with him. "It would be about the

right time too, she does have a holiday coming up soon."

"It would be good for you," Wren said, a bit more seriously. "I mean, not to assume, but you seem lonely sometimes. I love spending time with you, but it's probably not enough to just be with me."

Distracted, Jere nodded. "Yeah. I miss home."

Wren looked down, turning away a bit. "And if you want me to, you know, be out of the way, or hide, or whatever...." His words were tense and stilted. "You'd probably want to show her around, introduce her to other people here, who aren't—"

Jere put a gentle hand on his chin, tilting his head upwards. "Never. I've told my mum about you—and not just that you're my slave, or an amazing assistant, or that you're keeping me well-fed and clothed. You go on like there's something terrible about you, but the more I get to know about you, the more amazed I am by you. Of course I want her to meet you! Why wouldn't I?"

Wren shrugged, glancing away again. Jere felt the hesitation, the fear, and he couldn't understand it. Didn't Wren see how much he meant? "Wren, I've told her that we're dating or whatever."

Wren looked up at him, still doubtful. "What did you tell her?"

"I told her that we're together. That you're more than a slave, or an assistant, or a lover. That you're my boyfriend." The word was still so new, it caught coming out of his mouth. "You're such an important part of my life, how could I *not* tell her about you?"

"What did she say?"

"About you being a slave? Nothing. Which isn't a good sign," Jere frowned, knowing *exactly* what his mum's reaction would be. "I'm sure she's waiting to give me hell in person. But about the more important part about who you are and what you are to me—she's happy that I'm happy with someone."

Wren smiled.

"Oh, although I do believe she told me she'd beat me herself if she ever found out I mistreated you."

"I like her already," Wren smirked.

Jere made a face and started tickling him, hoping that the various sensitive parts on his body could be exploited in non-sexual ways. His hopes were right, and they soon found themselves rolling and giggling like little boys, each one trying to defend himself and go after the other at the same time. Finally, when they had both become effectively tangled up in the sheets, not to mention each other's limbs, they stopped, breathing a bit more heavily. Wren raised the stakes, leaning close to place a kiss on Jere's lips and wriggling his legs into just the right spots to turn them both on.

Jere still didn't really understand what Wren was so worried about, why he thought that Jere wouldn't want to introduce him to his family. Wren always seemed so uncomfortable talking about those sorts of things, like family or history caused him actual pain. Jere couldn't help but want to know more, but seeing how uncomfortable it made Wren, he let it go, focusing on kissing and touching instead. Talking could wait for another time.

Chapter 35
Exchanging Letters

Mum,

I'm glad to hear that things are going well. Congratulations on the promotion, I'm sure you deserve it! What's the next promotion, "full-time retirement?"

I can picture your face at that last comment, not to mention the grief you're going to give me next time you see me. You know I can't resist a perfect opportunity to tease!

Things are going very well here. I still don't necessarily like it, but I'm getting used to it, I suppose. And, yes, I am even social on occasion. Definitely not as much as I was in college, but there aren't as many people here that I really connect with. Actually, there are very few people that I fit in with at all, and even then it's sort of limited. But I really don't work all the time, so please stop worrying. I talk with Paltrek occasionally, and sometimes he even manages to drag me out of the house for a few drinks or a party or something. He's a pretty decent guy, now that I've gotten to know him a little better, at least for what I know of people living here. We mostly just agree to disagree on things.

I did meet someone I really like, this girl, Kieran. She can be a bit much at times, but she's one of the only people I've met here who's opposed to slavery, which is such a relief. It's hell for her, she says she's never really had anyone who understands where she's coming from before. She's sort of adopted me as an older brother, especially because she's started up at SU. I get my city fix by talking with her when she comes home on break. She's trying to set me up to meet with some more people that she thinks I'll get along with better. I'm doubtful, because this is Hojer, but she seems pretty confident.

People here are so different Mum, everything is just so different and weird and hard. I can't help but wonder sometimes what kind of person I might have turned out to be if I had been raised in a place like this — would I have been able to be so callous and cruel as everyone else here is, or would I be miserable and outcast like Kieran? I'm so glad that you didn't raise us in a slave state. It does things to people, it makes them mean. And I don't even think they see it at all. I try not to think about it too much, but it's always there.

Wren is doing well, we were talking about you the other night and he thinks you sound very nice. It's hard to believe that this is the same kid I met when I first moved here; so much has changed. He's become so much more comfortable, with me and with everything else, and he's really starting to come out of his shell. I'm getting to see all these sides of him that he's kept hidden away for so long. He's so sweet and wonderful, and I know it sounds sappy, but he's really perfect. It scares me sometimes how much I care about him. And you're right, as much as I don't want to admit it, I would be devastated if I lost him, but I don't think I will. Even if this whole thing goes south, if we break up or whatever might happen, I think we'll still be friends. I know I would still want him in my life as more than an assistant. He's become such a huge part of my life, and I care about him so much.

And no, I'm not ready to say, as you put it, "the four-letter 'L' word" yet. Even if that might be true, I just don't know if I'm there yet. It's been a long time since I've been in a serious relationship, and I feel like Wren and I are moving really fast. He's a great guy, and I don't want to rush things.

He is looking forward to meeting you, though, which reminds me, when is your break? I know you said you had a holiday coming up, would you want to come out here and visit? I discovered the other day that I probably won't be traveling much for a while. We can talk about it more when you come to visit, but let's just say you'll be able to come and visit me well before I'll be able to come and visit you. Slave state stuff. It's better discussed in person.

I'm very busy with work, which I guess is another reason why it would be easier for you to visit. It takes a lot of time and energy to provide healing for an entire town, even a small one like Hojer. I never imagined I'd have an opportunity like this, even though I hate some of the aspects of living here. It's not quite an even trade, but it's okay, all things considered. I love my work, and I love healing people, even if I don't particularly like the people I'm healing. It was so painful not being able to do it back home, not to mention being completely out of money, and all of a sudden I'm here and I have the clinic and I have my own assistant. The fringe benefits that come with my assistant now aren't too bad either. I guess it's the best of a bad situation.

As I'm sure I've mentioned before, the house is just fantastic. I look at it sometimes and I can't believe that I actually own it. I never thought I'd own a house! Not to mention one this huge and beautiful and clean, no thanks to me. Again, I have no idea what I'd do without Wren. There are plenty of rooms, so there will be a spare for you to stay in. I don't understand why there are so *many* rooms, since Matthias lived here alone, except for Wren, but I guess it's what you do when you have a lot of money and a lot of space. Sure beats my place in the city!

The speed train drops off not far from here, so I can come and meet you. Aside from the general unreliability of the speed trains, it's not terribly inconvenient to get here from the city, you should have no problem. Let me know when you'd be able to come, I'd love to have you! I miss seeing you and can't wait to show you the place.

Love,
Jere

Hi Kieran,

I got your last letter. Glad to hear you're getting settled in. The pamphlets and brochures you sent were very informative, but I probably shouldn't put them out in my office. I think you suggested being neutral? I hope you understand, but they aren't very neutral. But if anyone is looking, I do have them stashed away in a drawer under a box of gloves. I'll make sure to hand them out to anyone who seems like they might be interested.

Sorry to hear your apartment is so awful. Water problems are pretty common in the city. I'd recommend a place to you, but all the places I've lived have been dismal as hell. You'd do better looking on your own. Stay away from the Cooke neighborhood.

I appreciate your offer to join some of the activist groups around here, but I'm going to have to pass, at least for now. I really don't want to be too visibly involved, and I don't have that much spare time, either. People might notice, and I'm guessing they won't be pleased. Like I said, I'll do what I can to help, but I don't want to cause disruption here, it wouldn't be worth it. I've got my job and Wren to think about.

Hope your studies are going well and that you're finding time to have some fun. I know firsthand that SU has some great parties, so stop making fliers or whatever you do for a night and go enjoy yourself! And keep fighting the good fight, I know it means a lot to you, and I'm sure that if anyone can make some changes, it will be you.

-J

Dear Jere,

University is wonderful! I love it in Sonova, and can't believe you ever left! I bet you just can't wait to come back one day, right? Although, now that you have a certain "special someone" keeping you there, maybe not, hmm? I went into the city with some new friends I met from the one of the groups I'm in and it was absolutely awesome! I tried this new-age fusion food place and was blown away, and then we stayed up all night at this soup café place talking about the cause and how we were going to change things and everyone's like, *shocked* that I'm from Hojer. Christ. It's like having a tail, you know, it makes me *so* weird! But, they say it can help the cause, and that's awesome, so, yeah, I'm happy to contribute! I guess I understand about not wanting to be too visible — one of my mentors was explaining to me the other day the value of transparency versus blending in versus — something. Being a ninja, more or less. Anyway, I'm going to send a list later this week of some people who I think you'd get along with. I don't want them associated with my contact info, though, so I'm sending it from a different name and address with the title: Wedding Invitation on the top. But of course, there is no wedding! But yeah, some are business owners and some do and don't own, you know, and so, it might just be a good place for you to start meeting people! Got to head off to class now, more later!

Kieran

PS — Tell Wren I said hi!

Dearest Jere,

I was wondering when you were going to ask me to visit. I miss you, you know, and it's been over a year since I've seen you, thanks to the disappearing act you pulled last year. Between you and your sister, I can't tell who is worse about writing me. I hope you have children one day and they are exactly as challenging as the two of you!

I'm glad you could tear yourself away from your pretty, wonderful, opening-up boy to talk to your ancient, decrepit mother. After all, the ripe old age of 53 is just about time for a nursing home, don't you think? I mean, my grandmother just retired last year, but if my sweet son would like to put me away, what's this old lady to do but grin and bear it? After all, you are a doctor.

I suppose I should save some of the teasing for when I come to see you in person. I'm so excited to come; I can't wait to see my baby boy's house! From what you've described, it sounds grand, lots of space and land. It must have been quite the change from living in the city. It's excellent that the fire insurance paid out to cover everything that had been damaged in the house. That man must have had a very good policy. You had quite the luck meeting him like you did, so nice for a professor to take on a student like that.

I'm glad to hear that Wren is doing well and starting to adjust a little better. It's good that he's looking forward to meeting me; I'm certainly interested to meet him. After all, I've heard enough about him! He's really someone special to you, isn't he? I don't recall ever hearing you describe a boy like that before, not even that one you dated for a few months in high school. I'm glad he's not still running away from you and scared all the time, that must have been horrible for both of you. The things that poor boy must have gone through, it just makes me angry that anyone could treat another person so poorly! I'm sure you're treating him well, though. I didn't raise you to treat people like that.

I don't really know what to make of this slavery thing. In principle, it's horrible, but I know that you're there and that's the way it is in the state; it sounds like everyone there has slaves. I suppose that's something we can discuss once I arrive. You're right when you say that it's more of an "in person" topic, I'd hate for anything to be misconstrued in a letter. I won't be expected to have a slave, will I? If I recall, that's something that only people who live there tend to do. In any case, I would simply refuse. It's an evil practice, even if you treat them nicely.

I do have a holiday coming up soon, and I would love to see you as well, darling. I miss you very much, and I've only seen one of your places since you left university, and that one was nothing to write home about. I'm so proud that you actually live in a place that you want to show me, it's like you're growing up overnight.

I hope you don't mind, but I went ahead and booked a ticket on the speed train for a little over a month from now, on the 18th. I wasn't sure if that was one of the trains that fills up early, so I figured I'd be better booking my ticket well in advance. Is there anything you'd like me to bring from home? I did toss out all your old clothes and school papers like you had asked me to, but are there any books or anything else that you would like? You have quite a collection of things still in your old room, and I would be more than happy to bring them along with me. I certainly should have room for an extra bag or two, I don't bring too much along when I travel.

If there's any reason you wouldn't want me to visit then, let me know and I'll cancel the ticket or rebook it for a better day. I know how the messages can get delayed through the messengers and the post system, especially when you're sending mail between states, and especially so far out into those rural states. I figured there was no sense waiting to see if it was a good date, your last letter made it sound like you didn't really have a specific time frame in mind. I'm really looking forward to seeing you, and tell Wren I can't wait to meet him!

I love you!

Mum

Chapter 36
Lightening Up

Things had lightened up between them considerably, and Jere was nothing but pleased. Between the introduction of the restraints and Jere's encouragement, Wren was finally seeming to let go a little bit more, relaxing more naturally, daring to call him by his name, and the way that their bodies fit together made Jere hot just thinking about it.

Their sex life continued to be absolutely astounding. It was almost strange to think that they had done little more than kiss and cuddle and give each other head, when it seemed like so much more! Jere wondered, intermittently, if and when they were going to move on to other things, but every time they started, he quickly found himself too distracted to think about anything else. Further, he wasn't even sure how to broach the topic—Wren certainly seemed comfortable enough with what they were doing, but every once in a while, that nervous, haunted look came into his eyes again. Would there be a point past which they simply could not go? Not that it really mattered too much. What they were doing was amazing, wonderful—cause for lovely dirty thoughts and washing extra, extra well in the shower....

A knock on the door interrupted Jere's alone time.

"Unless you're planning to finish what you've started in there on your own, I really suggest you come out here." Wren's voice cut across the pounding water in the shower, taunting him.

Somewhat reluctantly, Jere removed his hand from his dick and finished showering quickly. He had tried to convince Wren to join him under the running water, but he was still somewhat skittish about the idea of showering together. Jere didn't push. The fact that Wren even tolerated their explorations while both of them were naked had been a big enough move. Jere could wait.

He stepped out of the shower, grinning as he saw Wren leaning in the doorway to the bathroom, arms crossed over his chest. For once, he was wearing nothing more than a pair of lounge pants, which clung quite nicely to his hips. Jere stepped over, reaching for his towel, which he had left on the sink again, causing him to drip water everywhere.

In a flash, Wren had snatched it up and darted out into the bedroom, a smirk on his face as his speed gift put him far out of Jere's reach.

"Hey!" Jere protested only slightly, laughing as he stood at the edge of the tile in the bathroom, debating whether to get the carpet wet or not.

"Hey, yourself, you know who'll end up cleaning up that mess you just made," Wren laughed, dangling the towel in front of him. "Oh, if only you had simply *asked* me to give you this!"

Shaking himself dry and feeling ridiculously similar to a wet dog, Jere headed into the bedroom, knowing he had no chance of chasing Wren and actually catching him if he decided to use his speed gift, but going for the challenge anyway.

To his credit, Wren played fair for the most part. They darted around the room like children, taunting and teasing, until Jere finally managed to outmaneuver him, feinting left, then right, then left again, and finally pouncing on him and pinning him to the bed, water still dripping from his hair.

"I win!" he declared, grabbing for the towel, which Wren was still stubbornly trying to hold out of his reach.

"Or maybe not!" Wren giggled as he tossed it behind him, off the bed. "Now what, you can't hold me down *and* get the towel, can you?"

Jere laughed. He had been outmaneuvered in return! "Now we've gotten the whole bedroom wet," he pointed out.

"Pretty sure there was only one person involved in that!" Wren smirked, laughing as Jere released his grip on him and started tickling him instead.

Wren began to tickle and wrestle back, and they rolled around on the bed a few times before ending up in the same position, Jere pinning Wren beneath him with a little more force than before. He heard him draw a sharp breath, his eyes widening.

"Don't!" Wren began to struggle, pushing Jere off of him quickly.

Jere backed off immediately, startled by the slight burn he felt where Wren grabbed him. He didn't think he had fought back, but Wren had grabbed him so unexpectedly, he must have. He moved to lie beside him, running his hand down his arm. "You okay? That was a little rough."

"I'm fine. You just caught me off-guard."

Jere could see on his face that that probably wasn't all he had done, and Wren's reaction confirmed that. He knew better than to mention it, Wren would just keep denying it and become more withdrawn. Instead, he motioned for Wren to come closer. When he did, he kissed him softly and passionately, running his hands across his arms and back until he felt him relax again. "*Sorry,*" he said, silently, their mouths still locked together, "*I'll make it up to you.*"

He broke off the kiss, pausing for a second to look at his lover's face, smiling back at him, trusting and calm again, now that the moment of panic was over. It was so different from before; where Wren wouldn't have dared to say even a word against him, now he was pushing back, reacting like anyone would if they were startled. Maybe Wren was more sensitive than most, but Jere felt relieved that he was more comfortable. His lower inhibitions made him even more desirable. Unable to resist, he kissed him once more, then trailed down his neck, kissing, touching, biting here and there, ever so gently. He took his cues from Wren's body, increasing the pressure slightly, being rewarded with little moans and whimpers. He made his way lower, his teeth brushing against the waistband of the pants that dropped so low on his body. At the same time, he worked his hands behind and beneath Wren, cupping his ass and almost massaging it.

"May I?" he asked, looking up at Wren, taking in the upper half of his body with his eyes while feeling the lower half with his hands.

"Mmhmm," Wren squirmed underneath him, wriggling seductively. He obligingly lifted his hips as Jere slid the pants off to reveal his perfect body.

"God, you're sexy," Jere muttered, running his hands up and down his legs, slowly. Wren relaxed into his touch, stretching out his legs and allowing Jere to work his muscles a bit as he did. Jere massaged his calves, then up his thighs, and was rewarded by soft purrs of pleasure.

"Turn over," he said, his hands still gently resting on Wren's legs.

He felt Wren stiffen, and a wave of fear shot over him through the mind connection.

"Why?" Wren's tone was accusatory and nervous.

Jere kept his hands where they were, but didn't move them. He hadn't forgotten Wren's fierce reaction earlier, and he didn't want to make any sudden movements. "Because you seem to like the way I'm touching you, and I thought you might want me to do the same to your back," he said softly. "I would certainly enjoy it. And I'll stop if you want me to."

"I don't want you to stop." Wren sounded uncertain of this. "That's all you want, then? Just to touch me?"

Jere wanted quite a lot of things, but he wasn't going to bring that up now. "Yes," he said softly, rubbing circles into Wren's heated flesh. "Well, and maybe to drag my tongue across your skin. And kiss you. And drag my teeth very lightly...."

Wren drew in a breath, this time of longing. He grinned as he looked into Jere's eyes, then rolled onto his stomach, clutching a pillow and turning his head to the side to look at Jere. "Sorry," he muttered.

Jere slid up next to him, intensely aware of their body positions. He knew better than to even consider moving on top of him at the moment. He kissed him. "You don't need to apologize," he said softly, before his hands and lips moved on to the back of his neck.

As he had in the front, he worked his way across Wren's neck, back, and shoulders, alternately massaging and kissing and touching him until Wren was squirming, taking the utmost care with him. He slid down eventually, stopping between his legs, and paused with his hands on his ass.

Gently stroking his skin, he asked, "Is this okay?"

"Mmhmm," Wren replied.

Jere massaged gently, even dared to bring his lips to the soft skin a few times, then drew his hand toward the cleft of Wren's ass and paused again. "How about this?"

Wren was silent for a moment, although he didn't move away. "What are you going to do?"

"I just want to touch you," Jere reassured him. "Just my hands. Well… and maybe my mouth."

"I don't want… I don't really like…." Wren struggled to speak. *"It hurts to have something inside of me."*

"I won't," Jere promised, leaning down to place a kiss in the dip of his lower back, sending shivers through both of their bodies. "Has this never felt good?"

"A lot of things have never felt good." Wren was still struggling to speak out loud.

"Well then, I guess that gives me a lot of things to change for you, huh?" Jere teased, softly caressing him once again.

He worked the flesh with both hands, mirror images of one another, and slowly eased his thumbs further down, pressing between the round, smooth mounds of flesh, never demanding, but still firmly applying pressure. He felt Wren relax into it after a few minutes, his breathing calmer, but still coming quickly. Jere leaned over, dragging his tongue in the path behind his thumbs, over and over again, quickly circling in on his hole.

Wren let out a whimper, squirming beneath him. "Shit…."

"That feel good?" Jere couldn't help grinning, but did manage not to laugh.

"Mm… mmhmm," Wren muttered, spreading his legs a bit more.

Jere kissed his skin again, then decided to test his luck. "Can I use my tongue—"

"You can do anything you want with your tongue!" Wren replied, squirming underneath him.

Jere laughed out loud at this, and used his hands to spread Wren's cheeks apart while his tongue continued to circle the hole, probing and pressing at it, getting it wet, and finally, slipping in the tiniest bit.

Wren moaned, low and deep, arching his back.

Jere kept up the motion, kept gripping his skin, kept dipping his tongue in and out, flicking it, plunging it in.

"Jere..." Wren moaned.

He kept at it for a few more minutes until Wren was thrusting into the mattress, seeking release. "Turn over again," he suggested.

Wren did exactly that, and Jere was rewarded with his very happy face and very hard cock, which he wasted no time taking deep into his mouth.

"Fucking Jesus!" Wren gasped, lying back.

"I think there's porn by that name," Jere commented, pulling back for a second. Wren thrust up at him and grunted desperately in response.

Jere obediently dropped his head back down, resuming the task he enjoyed so much. With one hand caressing the base of Wren's shaft, the other roamed about his body, under his legs, cupping his ass. He had an idea.

"*I won't go any further than I did earlier, I promise,*" he told him, taking his free hand and pressing it against his ass, fingers carefully finding their way to his entrance.

Wren said nothing, but did continue to thrust against him after a moment.

While his head bobbed up and down, Jere carefully increased the pressure against Wren's hole, his fingers in a loose fist, with no intention of going anywhere. The combination of the pressure and the blowjob had Wren coming in seconds, yelping and grabbing on to Jere's hair as he did. Jere responded to the pain by taking him deeper, relishing the sensation. He continued until he felt Wren soften in his mouth, then slid back carefully, eying him, before crawling up next to him.

"That was a dirty trick," Wren muttered, pressing closer to him even as he said it.

Jere was pretty sure he was talking about the tongue and fingers on his ass earlier. "You didn't seem to mind," he pointed out.

"I fucking loved it," Wren confessed, smiling despite hiding his head in Jere's arm.

"I love you," Jere said, startled that the words had just escaped his mouth.

Wren was silent for a moment. "Jere—"

Jere kissed him, silencing him. "Don't say anything. Don't feel like you have to say anything. I wouldn't want to pressure you into that."

Wren nodded. They lay there in silence for a few moments, until Jere felt a hand grazing his still-hard cock.

"Can I put my mouth to better use, then?" Wren asked suggestively.

Eager to feel that soft mouth on his cock, and somewhat wanting to change the subject, Jere nodded. "Mmm, please?" He rolled onto his back, spreading his legs shamelessly and biting down on his lower lip. "Please, Wren?"

In seconds, the sexy young man was between his legs, gently sucking, expertly working over the head, down the shaft. At some point, as usual, Jere lost words for what was even happening, and simply clutched the sheets as he tried to stay still. It was part of the game, part of the agreement. No squirming, no thrusting. It was nearly impossible to perfect.

Finally, Jere barely managed the words, "Please... come?" between incoherent vowel sounds. He heard Wren laugh, almost cruelly, before drawing his head back slowly, his tongue trailing from the base all the way to the head and eliciting a series of whimpers from Jere as he struggled to hold back.

Finally, he felt Wren's hand close around him, and heard him announce, "Okay, you can come now."

He thrust one time, Wren's hand clenching around him, the other resting on his hip, not quite holding him down, and he came.

They lay there for a while, utterly spent, in each other's arms. Jere loved these moments, soft and calm and one of the few times Wren seemed tired and relaxed enough to be this intimate with him for a longer amount of time. Smiling at the thought, he nuzzled against his neck a bit, kissing him softly.

Wren made a happy little sound of contentment, craning his neck to allow better access. "I love the things we do together."

"Me too," Jere agreed. "Although, between the water and everything else, we've quite destroyed this room!"

"Well, then, it's a good thing there are more, now isn't it?" Wren retorted, quite bold. Jere loved it when he was bold like this.

"Should we sleep in yours tonight, then? Or one of the others?"

"Mine's far away," Wren said, overly dramatic and pouty. "I mean, it's *all* the way at the other end of the house."

Jere laughed. "I suppose we've already gotten our exercise for the day, then?"

Wren nodded.

"You know, I've been meaning to ask you — do you want to stay in that bedroom? I mean, it is in a rather odd place, all the way over there, and far from — " Jere had been about to say "me," but thought better of it, " — the bathroom and stuff."

"It is, but I mean," Wren hesitated. "Would you want me in here all the time?"

Jere shook his head. "No, I mean, one of the other rooms down this way. Of course, I want you in here whenever you'd like to be, but I want you to have your space, too. You know — in case, well, whatever. Sometimes, it's just nice to have your own space, and I wouldn't want you to think otherwise."

"Oh." Wren sounded surprised, but pleasantly so. "I think I'd quite prefer the one across the hall, then. The colors are nice, and it's right across the hall from the bathroom and stuff. And a certain someone."

Jere felt himself blushing. He wasn't nearly as transparent as he had hoped. "Shall we go try it out, then?"

"Yes, but let's keep the sheets clean on this one for tonight, hmm?"

Chapter 37
What to Do with Slaves

Mind-blowing orgasms made time pass quickly, and the week of "slave-sitting," as Jere kept referring to it, was upon them quickly. Paltrek was supposed to bring Dane over some time after dinner, and they were looking forward to closing up a little bit early so they could have some time alone before they arrived. Wren had finished organizing papers and charts for tomorrow, and he walked in to see Jere stirring at something on a prep table.

"Here, try this." Jere was smiling as he held out a small cup with an unidentified liquid in it.

Wren took a step back, the fear and the memories all but paralyzing him. No. He wanted to say no, but he couldn't, he wasn't allowed to, couldn't disobey.

"Come on, it can't be any worse than my cooking," Jere said, moving closer, smile still on his face. "Tell me what you think."

Jere was there, but he wasn't, and Wren took another step back, trying to move away, clutching the table behind him for support so he wouldn't slip, wouldn't fall.

It didn't matter anyway. Even if he turned, even if he ran, even if he managed to get out of the room, there was nothing he could do. It would just make the punishment worse, maybe get him chained up for days again, like last time, and it was so cold this time of year.

"Give me your arm, boy. If I have to fight you, I'll break it!"

His arm was barely healed from the last time the threat had been carried out. Wren felt the last of his resolve slipping as he mutely held his arm out to his master, hoping that this would be the one that killed him, the one that stopped his heart or his breathing or his brain or anything for just long enough to let him die and end everything. He welcomed the pain, if only it had a hope of relief at the end.

But all that came was the pain. First the needle, stabbing sharp and deep into his skin, finding a vein, twisting. Why did it always feel like master was twisting it when he did this? None of his patients ever seemed to be in this much agony when their dear Dr. Burghe gave them injections, was it just him?

Then the burning, the stabbing pain that shot up through his arm and down into his stomach, and he was down on the floor, sobbing in misery as his guts seemed to twist inside of him. He was on fire, oh god, what was happening?

The mind-pain came next, as he felt his master invading his mind, searching out the pain and the effects of the medication, running the tests and comparing it to the last batch. The last batch had at least rendered Wren unconscious for a few hours; it looked as though he wouldn't be that lucky this time. His master's hands were on his head, holding him there, hurting him, and all he wanted to do was to get away, to escape, to do anything but be subject to this anymore. He was calling his name, but Master Burghe so rarely used his name, always just calling him "boy," or "trash," or something equally horrible.

He wanted to push the hands away, but he couldn't, fighting back only brought more pain, he just had to let it take him over. He heard his name being called again and all he wanted to do was to give up. He had to keep fighting, had to keep himself away from Master Burghe. But something felt different.

"Wren!" Jere's hands were on his head, holding him close, rocking him slightly. "Wren, for fuck's sake, tell me what's wrong!"

Not Burghe. Not an experiment. Not real. He was crying, though, and that was real, and Jere's hands were on him, and they were real, too, and real hands could hurt him.

He pulled away, the effort almost exhausting. Jere moved closer, following him, and Wren started to panic. He still knew better than to fight back, but he couldn't shake the memory.

"Please," he begged, unable to say anything more as he moved further away from his current master, the one who he more often thought of as his lover. He wanted to lash out, to fight, to do everything he hadn't been able to before. He needed the space to keep himself safe, but distance kept Jere safe, too. Safe from him.

He had backed himself into a corner, but Jere kept coming, the confused look on his face somehow threatening. Wren cowered and recoiled as a hand touched his shoulder, and he all but threw himself to the floor to wrench himself free. He felt the heat rising through his body, the fear threatening to consume him.

"Get away from me," Wren mumbled, terrified to even utter such words. The terror paid off when he felt Jere retreat.

"Wren, it's okay," Jere said softly, looking bewildered. "Whatever I did, I'm sorry. Tell me, and we can fix it."

"No, you can't!" Wren snapped. "You can't fix what's wrong with me. Just stay away!"

It wasn't Jere, it was never Jere who hurt him. But Wren still wanted distance, because as many times as Jere had proven he wouldn't hurt him, he didn't trust himself not to lash out at Jere right now.

"Just stay back. Don't touch me," Wren muttered, his voice shaky.

"It's all right," Jere said. The reassuring tone just didn't work like it usually did.

"No it isn't." Wren sagged against the wall. "It's not all right and it isn't fair to you and you deserve better and I should just...."

Jere waited for a moment before asking, "What?"

Die, Wren had been thinking, but he wouldn't say that out loud. "Just give me something. Sedative. Pain killer. Poison. Just give me something to make this go away!"

"I'm sorry you're in pain," Jere said, letting the room go silent before he spoke again. "I might be of more help if I understood what just happened, though."

Wren didn't really think that anything could help, but he did owe Jere some sort of explanation. If it hurt to give the explanation, then maybe that was punishment enough. "It just... it just came out of nowhere, I, he used to... experiments."

"He experimented on you?" Jere asked. "Medical experiments, like, medications? Surgeries?"

Wren nodded. Both were true, although it was only the first that he had been thinking of today. He still didn't trust himself to speak.

He didn't want to talk about it. He didn't want to do anything but curl into a ball and hide.

"Flashback?" Jere asked, finally.

Wren nodded. He appreciated that Jere was there for him, but he couldn't talk about it. He had spent so long trying to ignore memories like this, all he wanted was to have it go away and pretend that it never happened.

Jere was silent, not saying a word as Wren calmed down. Wren was glad. Talking was hard, putting anything into words at all was hard, and as much as he wanted to be left alone, he knew he would still be panicking if Jere wasn't there.

"You should just go back to whatever you were doing," he muttered. "It's embarrassing. You don't need to sit here and watch me break down again."

"There's nowhere else I'd rather be." Jere's voice matched his face, and Wren couldn't help but believe him. "I'll stay unless you really need me to leave."

After that, Jere stayed quiet, letting Wren take what he needed, or didn't. He didn't push, and Wren had no idea how to even begin to express his gratitude for that. Finally, he felt his own trembling subside, the terrible memories fading into the background again. He glanced up at the cup that Jere had held out to him earlier, forgotten on a table. "You, you wouldn't?" It was all he could manage.

"No," Jere said firmly, finally meeting Wren's eyes. "You had no way of knowing, but no, I wouldn't *ever* do anything like that. I picked up a flavor additive for the Crucial Care — supposed to be banana, for kids — and I think it's pretty decent. Wren, I would *never* give you anything that could hurt you!"

Wren closed his eyes. Eye contact was too much. He reached out a hand, relieved when Jere took it. He really wasn't going anywhere. "He always healed it," he mumbled. "After. When he saw what it did."

"Wren, I'm sorry," Jere whispered. "I'm sorry I reminded you of him, even for a minute."

"I know," Wren mumbled. Reality was starting to filter back in, taking over the memories and making him feel foolish. "I just need a minute alone." He stood up, a bit wobbly on his feet, pulling away from the man he was developing such deep feelings for. He stalked off toward the bathroom and shut the door behind himself.

Glancing in the mirror, he was unsurprised to see his skin pale and eyes wet. He splashed some water on his face and stared at his reflection as it dripped down in little rivers, mixing with the tears that were starting to dry up already. For years, this had been his only reprieve, crying alone and trying to hide the tears. He hated it, always, but it had kept him safe. Safer, at least, than showing he was afraid. But it felt different with Jere. In some ways, it scared him more to hope that Jere could really care about him than it would to just hide from him.

When he finally felt calm enough, he walked out, finding Jere standing exactly where he had left him. He walked over and pressed himself close to his chest, feeling Jere's arms come up around him. It felt comforting, secure. Is this what it was like to feel safe? He wanted nothing more than to hold on to the feeling, to keep it forever, to prove to Jere and to himself that he could do it.

Impulsively, he reached past Jere and grabbed the cup of liquid.

"You don't have to!" Jere protested, moving to grab it from him.

"I want to," Wren insisted. He didn't. The last thing he wanted to do was put the liquid in his mouth, but he had to prove to Jere that he trusted him, and he had to prove to himself that he could do this. He looked at the cup, so little, so insignificant, and he swallowed it down. He trusted Jere, at least this much.

He had to fight to keep from throwing up, which had nothing to do with the taste. The taste wasn't even that bad. Jere watched him the whole time, not moving, a confused look on his face.

After a moment had passed and Wren convinced his body that it wasn't about to be poisoned, he turned his head toward Jere and forced a smile onto his face to match an artificially light tone. "It's still pretty awful, sir, but the flavor does hide some of it!"

"You didn't have to try it," Jere whispered, brushing his lips lightly across Wren's.

"I know," Wren replied, breathing in the familiar smell of him. "That's why I did."

They stayed close through dinner, unwilling to break the physical contact that was so reassuring. In lieu of going to bed immediately after dinner, they waited at the table in the dining room, dawdling over dessert and coffee.

"What do I do with someone else's slave?" Jere asked.

Wren was pretty sure this was the fifth time he'd heard that very question. Jere was looking for reassurance more than any sort of real answer. "You'll do fine. Make a good impression, show off your masterly abilities...."

"Ha," Jere raised an eyebrow at him. "Even if I *had* what anyone around here would qualify as 'masterly abilities,' I certainly wouldn't want to show them off!"

Wren smiled back at him. It was so strange to see his master so put off by the thing; anyone who had grown up in a slave state would have seen this as completely common "Just relax. If you want, I can handle him for the most part, give him tasks or whatnot. And if you want or don't want him to do something, just tell him. I'm certain he'll obey you."

"I don't want people fucking obeying me," Jere muttered.

"And that's one of my favorite things about you," Wren smiled at him.

A knock sounded at the door, and Wren answered it quickly, nodding deferentially to Paltrek as he strode in. Dane was silent on his heels and carried a small bag. Wren closed the door behind them and followed them into the dining room where Jere had risen to greet them. He couldn't help but notice the familiar smell of sex on the two of them.

"Sorry I'm a bit late, got a little 'caught up,' if you know what I mean," Paltrek said, a wolfish grin on his face.

Wren thought he might be sick at the display.

"Um, not a problem," Jere said smoothly, although his nose wrinkled a bit, the way it did when he was healing someone with intestinal problems.

"Well, I'll be gone just over a week, god-willing and speed train running," Paltrek motioned for Dane to stand beside him. "Dane is yours to do with as you wish, just return him in good condition — not that I'd worry about anything else from you, Doc."

Jere laughed uncomfortably while Dane stared down at the ground. Wren found himself feeling extremely glad that he wasn't either one of them.

"He gives you any trouble, you're entirely free to discipline him as you see fit," Paltrek continued, oblivious. "Dane, if I hear you've given Jeremy *any* trouble while I'm gone, I'm gonna come home and whip you bloody, is that clear?"

"Yes, master." Dane was still frozen to the spot, eyes glued to the floor.

Paltrek reached over and ruffled his hair affectionately, then looked back at Jere. "Listen, I know this whole thing is unusual, I guess, for an outlander, but I just didn't feel right leaving him with my family. Annika's likely to kill *me* in my sleep, I wouldn't leave Dane there. Just treat him as you do your own, you know what I mean?"

Wren was surprised. In his own way, Paltrek was asking Jere to be *kind* to his slave.

Jere nodded. "Of course. He'll be perfectly fine here. I'm sure there will be no trouble."

Paltrek nodded. "All right, then. I better be going before the damn train leaves. Dane, remember what I said. Jeremy, thanks a lot! I'll see you soon." Wren opened the door for him, and he left, taking his exuberant energy with him.

The three of them stood there, uncomfortable. Wren sent a pointed glare Jere's way to encourage him to move things along.

"Right. Well...." Jere looked completely out of his element. "Uh, Dane, let me show you to your room, then."

"Yes, Master Peters." Dane followed along obediently.

Wren wondered how exactly Jere planned to handle the whole situation. The master really was unused to slave matters, and his interactions with Wren in that way had been few and far between, even when Jere first arrived, before they started kissing and exchanging whispers of sweet nothings in each other's ears every night. With little else to do, Wren followed them. Knowing Jere, he was probably going to treat the quiet, nervous slave as a hotel guest or something.

"So, you can use this room while you're here, feel free to make yourself comfortable. Are you hungry?" Jere tried a smile.

Wren resisted the urge to slap a hand to his forehead. A slave wouldn't respond to a question like that. It was like asking to be called ungrateful—not to mention exposing a weakness that could be exploited.

"*Be more direct with him, he won't answer a question like that,*" he advised.

Jere glanced at him, a little confused, but did rephrase the question. "Have you eaten yet tonight?"

Dane shook his head. "No, sir. My master had better things to do with my time."

"Right...."

"I'll get you something," Wren supplied, eager to help both Jere and Dane avoid further awkward communication. "Come into the kitchen with me."

Dane followed obediently. Wren glanced at Jere and quickly shook his head. He didn't need to come along and complicate matters.

Once they reached the kitchen, Wren assembled a sandwich, allowing them to speak without the intensity that eye contact would have demanded.

"We're rather casual, here," he tried to explain. "My master will ask you questions if he really wants to know the answers, and he actually does want to know—it would be best for you to just answer upfront. Not that he'll get mad or anything—really, he never gets mad."

Dane nodded. "You seem comfortable around him."

It was true. Wren was more comfortable around Jere than he had been around anyone since he could remember. It was a good feeling. Secure. "I enjoy a rather privileged life."

Dane said nothing as Wren handed him the sandwich. He probably hadn't been allowed to eat real food for a whole meal since becoming a slave, but Wren couldn't quite bring himself to mention it.

"Will he want to use me sexually?" Dane asked. His eyes were carefully blank, hiding anything he may or may not have felt about the act.

Wren shook his head. "He wouldn't dream of it," he informed him, feeling quite relieved when he realized it was true. He decided he most definitely wasn't feeling jealous. That would be stupid. Slaves weren't jealous of their masters. But boyfriends....

"That will be nice," Dane actually managed a half-smile. "Do you know what he will be doing with me, then?"

"Um, probably just having you help around the house," Wren shrugged. Neither he nor Jere were actually sure what to do with the extra help. "He did mention a project cleaning and organizing the cellar under the kitchen." It was best to stick with the story that Jere had mentioned to Dane's master.

"Oh," Dane nodded, devouring the majority of the sandwich in one bite.

Wondering how long it had been since the other slave had been fed, Wren pointed to the small table in the kitchen. "Sit," he muttered. "I'll get you something more, and something to drink." His lack of comfort around slaves—around *other* slaves—was disconcerting. He knew he had let his guard down far too much for his own good.

"You help in the clinic?" Dane asked, pausing to take a break from his food and rediscover basic social manners.

"Yeah, that and clean up a bit around the house, cook—whatever needs to be done, I suppose."

"Must be nice, only having the one mento to serve," Dane grinned at him.

Wren was startled for a minute. Mento was an old slur against people with mind gifts, back from the days when the gifts first started to emerge, a twisted combination of mental and psycho. He had never thought of Jere that way. "I, uh, yeah."

Dane studied him for a minute. "Sorry. Didn't mean to offend."

"I just, he's been very good to me." *And I'm oddly protective of him, because I've started to think of him as "boyfriend" instead of "master."*

"So you've mentioned." Dane shook his head. "You don't socialize much, do you?"

Wren shrugged. It was true. When Burghe had owned him, he

wasn't allowed to socialize, and with Jere... well, he'd rather stay in and be comfortable with Jere than go out and socialize uncomfortably with other people's slaves. Single slaves in a household rarely had the opportunity to socialize, if they were fortunate enough not to be passed around like toys to the master's friends. "It doesn't come up often."

"It's fine. You seem like more of the quiet type anyway," Dane smiled, polishing off the remainder of the food. "The Wysockas have me and Arae, and the master's father's slave, and three more household slaves on top of that. The six of us, we get to keep each other company most times."

Wren had no idea what that would even be like. He cleared the dishes away quickly. "Come on, I'll show you the rest of the house."

They didn't say much else as Wren showed Dane the bathroom, entrance to the medical clinic, and gestured vaguely toward the cellar, trying not to shudder as he did so. Jere made himself scarce, which Wren was both saddened and relieved by. As much as he could have used some moral support, he was pretty sure that Jere would have made the situation twice as awkward as it already was.

He finished the rather short tour back at the guest room that Jere had shown Dane to earlier. "That's it. If you want, there are some books in the living room, I think a deck of cards is around there as well. Feel free to help yourself to anything in the kitchen if you're hungry later."

"The master won't have anything for me?" Dane asked, skeptical.

Wren shook his head. "No, he, uh, he asked me to make sure you got settled in and such. Free him up for other things." That sounded better than the truth, which was that Wren had suggested Jere leave the other slave to him.

"All right," Dane shrugged. "Good night, then."

"Good night."

Wren took off down the hallway as if he could outrun the awkwardness. He found Jere in the bedroom, half-dressed and reading some sort of obscure medical journal he had been waiting for. Slipping off his shoes, Wren crawled into bed next to him, silent, so as not to disturb him.

"Hi," Jere smiled, putting an arm out and pulling him close. "Dane all settled in?"

Wren nodded, wriggling closer.

"Did you explain to him that I'm not some sort of evil rape monster?" Jere grinned, setting the journal aside.

"Oh, did you overhear that part?" Wren smirked back at him.

Jere laughed. "Part of it, yes. I wasn't trying to overhear, I just went in to find something to read, and, well, voices carry."

"It's fine," Wren smiled. "I do hope you don't mind me taking over like I did?" It happened so frequently, Wren did it without thinking. Aside from healing in the clinic, Jere deferred to him, followed his lead without question. It was strange, but it fit, and Wren had to admit that they were both more comfortable that way. But always, after the fact, the old doubts surfaced, and Wren wondered whether he had pushed too far.

"Of course not! Saved me the trouble." Jere was so nonchalant about it, as if it had never occurred to him to *want* to take responsibility.

It was nice, knowing Jere trusted him so much, and it made him feel safe. Wren wanted to sit and revel in his good fortune, but he did have a question, one that made him feel anything but safe. "Um, are you... did you want me to help him? In the cellar?" He struggled to keep his voice neutral, as if he didn't care either way.

"I take it the thought upsets you?"

Dammit. He really was getting terrible at lying. "I'm sure I'd be of more use elsewhere, sir." He should have just kept going with his plans, having Dane do it, acting like he was just trying to be "helpful" like when he was showing Dane around, like he had been at the holiday party with the rental slaves. He battled between staying safe and in control and being a good slave and deferring to his master.

Jere studied him silently for a moment, just long enough to make him uncomfortable. Suddenly, he leaned over and kissed him briefly, although Wren really would have enjoyed more.

"I wasn't going to ask you, and I certainly won't if it upsets

344

you," Jere promised, looking into his eyes. "From what I've heard, it certainly isn't a place full of good memories for you."

Wren shook his head, grateful that his master seemed to get what he was feeling without needing to be told.

"It's simple, then," Jere smiled. "Dane can do it. I'll help with whatever you need me to, so you won't even have to go down there. You should tell us what to do; this really is your area of expertise. I'd just as soon board it up and never look back."

Wren tried not to be shocked, and wasn't so successful. "At breakfast, you'll explain to Dane that he needs to clean and organize and throw things away, let you know what's broken, make space for storage. I'll leave to get things started in the clinic. You'll get him set up in the cellar, and then you can come back up and join me in the adequate lighting, ventilation, and lack of crawly things for the rest of the day."

"Sounds good," Jere nodded.

Wren thought back to the single time that Jere had been in the cellar. "If I recall correctly, you weren't exactly a fan of the cellar either."

Jere kissed him again before answering. "I'm not, but I'm a very big fan of you, and I'm at least hoping Dane can make it useable. You were right when you mentioned food shortages, did I tell you I had to special order the last case of coffee we got? It cost a fortune! I bet we're the only household in the state — the Wysockas, obviously, excluded — with real coffee."

"Mmm, you didn't tell me, but I do appreciate your consideration for our shared caffeine addiction," Wren kissed him back, wishing he could send his gratitude through a kiss.

"Caffeine isn't the only thing I find myself wanting more of...."

Chapter 38
As You Command

Breakfast the next day was only slightly awkward. Wren started the day by fetching Dane from his room, where he was unsurprisingly awake and dressed. Wren had him help out in the kitchen, not because he really needed help, but because he figured he could give Dane some warnings to ease him through the meal.

"We eat together," he said, flipping eggs with practiced ease. "At the table. I know, it's unusual, and quite informal, but that's the way he likes it, and he's asked me to tell you the same."

"Okay." Dane continued to butter toast.

Once they were seated at the table, Dane doing his best not to look uncomfortable, and Jere looking more or less oblivious to the situation, Wren decided to provoke at least some conversation.

"Master, I believe you wanted me to remind you to let Dane know what he would be doing today?" Wren smiled as he spoke. Subtly pressuring Jere was becoming one of his best skills.

Jere wrinkled his nose for a moment. "*Master?*" he protested through the mind connection, but said, out loud, "Of course, yes."

"*Jere, we really should keep up some appearances,*" Wren reminded him. Regardless of Jere's hatred of the title, it was right and proper to use it.

"*It's just Dane! Fuck it. I don't like it!*" Jere had stuffed a forkful of eggs into his mouth to buy him time. As he finished chewing, he glanced at Dane. "I'll be having you clean and organize a cellar. Pretty dirty work, but it needs to be done. I can't spare Wren much, things are pretty busy in the clinic, so I'll get you set up and show you what needs to be done and leave you to it, all right?"

"Yes, Master Peters."

"I, uh," Jere looked uncomfortable, but it didn't stop Wren from shooting him a warning glance anyway. Wren knew exactly what he was about to do, and was highly disapproving.

Jere ignored it.

"Look, Dane, things are a bit different here than they are back home, all right? You're a guest in my home, and I'm not about to change the way that I live, nor do I expect Wren to act differently either. I'm gonna ask you something that might be a bit uncomfortable, but I'm asking it anyway."

Wren contemplated strangling him.

"Wren and I have an agreement. It works for us." Jere shook his head at Wren, effectively silencing him. "I don't talk down to him, or make him eat off the floor, or insist upon him calling me by some stupid fancy title, and I won't insist that you do either. Here's the thing — I know it's unusual, and socially unacceptable, so what I need you to do is, well, just don't mention it. Of course, if Paltrek is pressuring you, don't get into trouble, but I know him well enough that I doubt he sent you here to spy on me, and I assume that you're able to keep a secret when you need to. You're going to be here a week, and I just — this is my home, and damned if I put on an act in my own home!"

Dane looked a bit confused, but nodded slowly. "Yes, Master Peters."

"So. You can call me whatever you'd like, but I'd really prefer Dr. Peters, or sir is fine, if you must, because I think Paltrek would literally kill you if you called me Jere. Don't think twice if you hear Wren calling me something else, because it's my house and I said he can!"

"Yes, sir," Dane mumbled, still confused.

Wren said nothing aloud, but looked down at the table and shook his head. *"Honestly? Honestly, you felt this was necessary?"*

"Yes. Besides, I know some of the Wysocka family's dirty little secrets, don't I?"

For once, Wren couldn't help but relent. Jere had a point — he was the master of the house, and groveling and playacting for a slave was a bit taxing. Still, it created a feeling of discomfort that

347

was almost as unpleasant as, if not more than, the original situation. Jere's rather devious plan of blackmail startled him as well—he never expected his master to be capable of plotting something so carefully.

They finished eating in silence, and rather quickly.

With a grin, Jere stood, glancing at Wren and Dane. "Wren, if you would, please go and get things set up in the clinic? Dane, come with me, I'll show you where the cleaning supplies are and what I'd like you to do."

Wren headed through the clinic door without another word. The whole situation made him uncomfortable, but the worst part was Jere's dismissal of his advice. The more he thought about it, the more it irritated him, because they had talked about it, and Jere was supposed to follow his lead! He stormed into the clinic, going through his daily activities with extra speed just to get them done. The first patient had already arrived, and he managed to check him in without seeming excessively irritated, or so he hoped. This done, he walked back and plopped onto a stool, intent on waiting for his master to join him.

Jere strolled in with a smile on his face that was only slightly diminished by Wren's glare. He walked over to where Wren remained sitting, placed his hands on his shoulders, and kissed him quite passionately. Despite his promise to himself to stay angry, Wren felt himself melting under the hot touch and contagious happiness.

"I'm sorry," Jere whispered in his ear, while he nibbled on it. "I know I said I'd follow your lead, but dammit, this is ridiculous. I'm too fucking happy with you to pretend I'm not, and if I have to be a master in this goddamn slave-state, then I get to make some choices too, don't I?"

Wren couldn't help but laugh. "Of course, yes, of course you do, I just, I think I get worried, you know? About you."

He was silenced with another kiss.

"I worry, too, but honestly, Wren, I refuse to keep living like this. I have to be able to let my guard down at least a little. If I don't, I will lose my fucking mind!"

Wren glanced into his lover's eyes, unable to stop himself from laughing harder as he saw the overly dramatic "crazy face" that Jere was making at him. "I suppose you're right," he relented. "Besides, if Dane spreads any rumors, you can just say he's lying, and you'll be believed over him."

Jere's face showed his distaste. "My, that's...."

"True." Wren interjected.

"Well, I was aiming for cynical, but I suppose you're right. Let's just hope it doesn't come to that, okay?"

"Of course." Wren knew he was being a bit cynical about the whole situation, but he was also being honest. It was true, a free person would be believed above a slave at any time. He saw nothing wrong with putting this bit of information to use.

The work day went by as usual, with a quick lunch break where Jere reassured Dane that he was doing fine with the cellar project. By dinnertime, things had calmed down considerably, and Wren was pleasantly surprised to find himself comfortably settling into his normal routine with Jere, despite the addition of an extra person to the room. For the most part, Dane kept to himself, taking things as they came along. More than likely, this was considerably calmer and quieter than any day at the Wysocka estate.

Dane asked to be excused immediately after dinner, claiming he was tired. Wren couldn't blame him, it had been a very strange day. Being lent out was difficult enough as it was. Despite the fact that Burghe's friends had been considerably kinder than Burghe when he had been lent out, he still recalled the stress and uncertainty that accompanied any of those trips. The old feeling of helpless rage flared up for a moment before he recalled that Jere had promised never to do the same to him.

After clearing away the dishes, Wren walked out to find Jere sitting at the table, a blank expression on his face. He walked up to him boldly, straddling one of his legs, and taking his hands in his own.

"We should go to bed early, too," he proposed, a suggestive grin on his face.

Jere's face brightened considerably and he sprung to his feet, following Wren into the bedroom. They were on each other in seconds, mouth meeting mouth, body meeting body as they collapsed onto the bed together.

"Mmm, I think I like going to bed early," Jere laughed as Wren pinned him to the bed. "Something's got you in a bit of a mood!"

"What can I say?" Wren pretended to be innocent, all the while biting down on Jere's neck. "I couldn't think of anything better to do!"

"Nice to know," Jere paused for a minute, catching his breath, "that I'm your backup plan."

Wren moved up again, kissing him on the mouth. "You know you're more than that."

Jere nodded, moaning as Wren made his way down his neck. "You're my first plan, Wren. Always."

Wren felt a rush as he heard the words, feeling the truthfulness behind them through the mind connection. More and more, Jere had been letting the shields on his side of the connection drop, letting his feelings spill over more clearly, opening his world up to Wren. "You meant it?" he asked, softly, kissing his neck, conveniently avoiding his eyes. "What you said the other night?"

"Of course."

Just like that. So typical of Jere.

"It's been true for a while. Just too damned thick to say it, I guess," Jere pulled him close for a second before holding him back a little, almost at arm's length. "I wouldn't say it if it wasn't true. I do love you."

Love. What the hell did that even mean? Regardless, Wren couldn't stop the big, wide smile that spread across his face. But still, he didn't know what to say, how to respond. "I think this will be better if you're not wearing clothes."

Jere said nothing about the change of topic, but obediently stripped, tossing his clothes aside carelessly and dropping back onto the bed. "Better?" he teased, leaning back comfortably, catlike.

Wren nodded, fighting the shyness that always tried to take him over in these moments. "Much," he added, then began to work his way up and down and over his master's body. It wasn't an unfamiliar task any longer, but sometimes Wren still preferred to be clothed. Jere, as far as he could tell, was just as comfortable nude as he was in a three piece suit, if not more. Trust took Wren a long way, but old habits still died hard.

Jere moaned, stopping himself suddenly. "Can he hear us?" he mumbled, twisting and squirming under Wren's touch. "Dane. Can he hear us down the hall? That would be—"

"Shh," Wren silenced him with a kiss. "Thick walls. Very thick. Trust me." He thought for a second about the times he had been in here, screaming, nobody else having any idea—no, he wouldn't think about that. He bit down on Jere's neck, drawing a gasp. "Just trust me."

He worked Jere over with his tongue, hands, and teeth. Light grazing teeth on his skin was certain to drive him mad, an experience Wren enjoyed every single time. He settled in to give him head, a skill he was perfecting by the day, given the noises of pleasure he could elicit now. And Jere, as always, was the perfect gentleman, lying still and undemanding, struggling only to stop himself from thrusting. The torment was wonderful.

Wren brought him *just* to that edge, where he knew Jere would soon be begging him, through mumbled words or mindspeak, for release. It had become a thing for them—Wren couldn't handle the feeling of the stuff in his mouth, and Jere was fine waiting. While Wren would usually back off immediately and finish him off with his hands, sometimes he liked to tease, torture, or move on to something else entirely. Jere seemed to enjoy any combination of these things, and they both loved the variation.

"Wren," Jere's voice was strained, lustful.

"Mmm?" Wren stayed focused on his task, the vibration of the word causing Jere to shudder.

"God, you feel so good!"

Wren snickered a bit, never interrupting his motion.

"I want you."

Wren figured it was just a passionate statement. He went with it. "*I think you have me!*"

"I want you inside me."

Wren froze, startled, then pulled back a bit. "You... you do?" Surely, he didn't mean... like that?

"Mmhmm," Jere squirmed underneath of him, thrusting, his hands running softly across Wren's arms. "I want to feel you inside of me!"

Wren was completely at a loss for words. People wanted that? They wanted someone to do that? As distasteful as it was, he tried to recall his own experiences. Pain, stretching, ripping, burning, begging—no, there was never anything he would *want* in there. He understood it must have felt good for the men doing it to him, but why on earth...?

"I... shit, um, only if you want to, I mean." Jere had shifted a bit, tilting himself so that Wren could see his face.

Fuck. He had been silent too long. "I... if you want it...." Wren fumbled. "I just don't know why?"

Jere laughed. Hurt, Wren looked away, sitting back on his heels and starting to move back from his master. Jere caught his hand, gently, sitting up a bit as he did.

"Wait, Wren, I'm sorry," he said sincerely. "I forget, sometimes, that you have no idea how good it can be. How nice it is to have someone inside of you like that. So close. So...." His voice trailed off as a big, horny smile covered his face. "I promise you, there are few things I want more right now than to feel you fucking me."

Despite his disbelief, something about Jere's attitude stirred the lust that lived inside of Wren—mostly the lust in his cock. He felt his pulse quickening at the idea, but he was still not convinced. "But... but won't it hurt you?"

Jere smiled, sitting up and pulling Wren into his arms. "I'm sure it will, a little, at first. It's been a fucking while. But I don't mind, and I know you'll be careful, and it's not bad pain anyway."

Wren said nothing. From what he remembered, it was only "bad" pain, or, if you were lucky, "slightly less bad" pain.

Jere kissed softly at his neck. "It's like curry, you know? Like really, deliciously spicy curry. It's almost painful, and sometimes, it actually is painful, but it's so fucking good and you know it would be lacking something if it wasn't that tiny bit painful, because it wakes up your whole body, and you just want to take more and more and more of it...."

Wren heard himself gasping slightly at the words. Could he really want this? And what kind of monster would he be if he really *did* hurt his master?

"You just want it inside of you, filling you, taking you places you never thought you'd be...."

"We're not still talking about curry, are we?"

Jere grinned and shook his head, trailing his hand down the inside of Wren's leg, then back up.

With all his willpower, Wren resisted the urge to thrust into his hand, even through his clothes. He was quickly losing this battle. "I just don't want to hurt you," he muttered.

"You won't," Jere's hands were at his waistband, not undoing it, but toying with the fastening. "I trust you, and I trust that you'd stop if I asked you to."

Wren nodded. Maybe that was the part he had been missing? Nobody had ever stopped for him before. Not when he asked, begged, pleaded.

"I want you so bad," Jere whispered in his ear, his hands still deviously working Wren's pants and groin area.

Wren drew a breath and nodded again. "Okay," he said, his voice a little shaky.

A big smile spread on Jere's face and he literally *bounced* back a few inches. "How do you want me, love?"

Wren grinned back, but honestly, he was at a loss. He had no idea how how he wanted him, or even what his options were, really. He had never done this! Well, not from this side, anyway. He realized that Jere was still sitting there, looking like an excited puppy ready to catch a ball. "Um—"

Jere kept looking at him, just as excitedly, as he tried not to squirm uncomfortably.

"Jere, I've never...."

A look of realization flashed across Jere's face as he stammered. "Oh," he said, eyes wide, then returned to grinning. "Well, then, this will be fun!"

Wren found himself feeling torn—from anyone else's mouth those words would have meant the exact opposite.

Jere was shimmying across the bed as Wren had his internal debate, and returned seconds later with a bottle of lube that he must have had stashed in the dresser next to the bed, although Wren had never laid eyes on it. It was about half empty.

"You pick," Jere instructed, his eyes sparkling. "Do I get myself ready, or do you want to do it?"

Wren knew how to do this. He had been ordered to do it to himself enough times, and sometimes to other boys, at the training facility. While he had always detested the task, he knew it made it hurt a little bit less at least, and even when he had been with Burghe he would sometimes sneak and do it, particularly if he knew his master would be coming home drunk and wanting him immediately. It was humiliating, always, for him to do it to himself, but then, others usually hurt him more....

Jere had come up in front of him, face-to-face, and leaned in close, pulling for eye contact. "Are you okay with this?"

Wren hesitated. "Yes?" It wasn't that he was *un*-okay with it!

Jere leaned forward and kissed him deeply, passionately, but just for a moment. "I'm okay with it." Another kiss. "*Very* okay with it." And another. "With you feeling me. Touching me." Another. This time with teeth, oh-so-gently. "Fucking me and making me feel wonderful." Another, this time, nibbling on his lower lip. "Slipping inside of me, feeling me squeeze around you, all hot and tight...."

Wren found himself clutching on to Jere, wanting more, wanting the contact, wanting to feel his skin. He allowed his hands to roam over Jere's body even more freely than usual, hesitating only briefly when his hands seemed to move on their own, down below the curve of his ass, gently grazing his hole.

"Please," Jere whispered, arching his back and positioning himself closer. "Please take me, Wren."

Between the lust and the heat and the excitement and the begging, Wren felt himself cave, and when Jere moved away and positioned himself on all fours, Wren found himself moving on instincts he never knew he had.

In seconds, the lube was carefully dripped onto his finger, which was just as carefully worked around Jere's ass. He reasoned that one finger couldn't hurt too badly, it fit, and, well, he had quite enjoyed Jere touching him there the other night. It couldn't be all bad.

Meanwhile, Jere was rocking himself slowly, back and forth. "Yes, god, yes, more!"

Wren eased a second finger in, applying a bit more lube, and was rewarded with a slight squeeze and a moan from Jere.

"God, Wren...." Jere said nothing for a moment, and Wren concentrated on the task at hand. He was surprised by how much enjoyment he got from Jere's pleasure.

"Fuck me now? Or should I suck you first?" Jere managed, pounding back against Wren's fingers as he did.

"I, um." Wren had actually been thinking about taking more time.

"I'm ready," Jere promised with a glance over his shoulder. "I'm *so* fucking ready. I just want you to fuck me already!"

"I'm ready too," Wren said, quiet excitement building. He was actually... he actually wanted this.

Jere handed him the lube, which had rolled up closer to the front of the bed. "Just go slow at first, okay?" he smiled. "I want to feel every inch of you!"

Wren slicked up his cock, and rubbed a bit more of the lube against Jere's entrance for good measure. More was always better, right? As he did, Jere wriggled back against him, laughing playfully.

"Think you can catch a moving target?" he teased.

"Don't make me tie you down!" Wren heard the words come out of his mouth before he had a chance to think.

Jere gasped. "God, don't make me come before you fuck me!" he muttered. "Also, I'm taking you up on that!"

Wren grinned, gripped his cock, and... and....

"Please?" Jere dragged it out, wriggling, although much more slowly.

Biting his lip in concentration, furiously glad that Jere couldn't see him, Wren slowly guided the tip of his cock to its destination, pausing at the resistance he felt there.

"I want you inside me now!" Jere said, his voice almost a whimper.

Wren pushed, ever so slightly harder, wishing he would slide in as easily as his fingers had. How could he—

Jere met him with a backward thrust, and he felt the strange and wonderful sensation of his cock being squeezed inside of a tight, warm space.

"Fuck!" he managed, steadying himself with his hands on Jere's hips. He started to push deeper, until he heard a sharp intake of breath, and he froze.

"Are you okay? Am I hurting you? Do you want me to—"

"I'm fine, really, and don't you *dare* pull out!" Jere said through what sounded like slightly clenched teeth. He took a deep breath and let it out. "It's been a *hell* of a while, though. Just go slow. Fuck, you feel good!"

Wren could hear the smile coming back onto his lover's face, and did as he was asked, inching in and out slowly, smoothly, and feeling Jere relax and stretch to accommodate him. As for what Wren was feeling, never before had he felt such smooth, soft pressure, squeezing him, pressing every inch of him. He burned with need as he started to move, feeling the heat building between them.

"Harder," Jere demanded, thrusting back. "Fuck me harder!"

Wren didn't respond, but leaned forward, putting himself at a slightly easier angle, and braced his arms on either side of Jere, daring to drive himself in not only harder, but deeper. He thrust in deep, slid out, and started again.

"Jesus, fuck," Jere muttered. "Stay right there, fuck, yes, keep going, fuck, right there!"

Wren wasn't quite sure whether to stay or go, but it didn't matter much, as Jere worked himself up and down. He felt a hand on his, and he allowed it to be pulled, wrapped around, and placed on a very, very hard cock.

"Are... are you? Is this good?" Jere finally managed, dropping his hands back to the bed and slowing his thrusting only the tiniest bit.

"Mmm," Wren replied, wordless. This was what it felt like, fucking someone. He suddenly understood the attraction. All the men who had done it to him over the years—this was what they got out of it while he suffered. But Jere didn't seem to be suffering, in fact, he seemed quite happy. Could he be hurting Jere without knowing it? "Is it good for you?" he asked, solving the dilemma.

"Oh my god yes!" Jere exclaimed. "You've got me so fucking hot."

Wren felt ecstasy ripple through him. He pushed himself into Jere again and again, speeding up, needing more. Jere was right when he said it was hot—Wren felt like the temperature in the entire room had gone up. He closed his eyes and tried to regain some semblance of calm, taking deep breaths to steady himself.

"You... you get to feel me come around you," Jere managed, between thrusts. "Feel me tighten and squeeze...."

As Jere spoke, Wren moved his hand the same way, tightening on Jere's cock, starting at the base, and working up, and down, up again, his thumb encircling the head lightly, and all the while thrusting in and out of him. Neither one could say who was thrusting more or harder, and neither one cared. He kept going, relaxing and letting his guard down, and let himself get lost in the heat between them. His hand, his cock, every inch of his body seemed to be burning with excitement, stoked by their motions.

Suddenly, he felt it, the tightness, the way Jere's entire body tensed up, and he knew that he was coming. Jere's frantic pleas for more devolved into little more than whimpers, and Wren slowed down a bit, uncertain.

"Keep fucking me, baby," Jere breathed, shuddering. "Keep fucking me until you come, too."

Wren moaned in relief and joy, slowly starting up again, but building quickly to his original pace. For the most part, Jere was still, panting quietly while Wren pushed inside him, excitement building to a fever pitch.

"Jere," he whispered, about to come. He clutched at Jere's sides and drove in deeply.

"God, yes, Wren, fuck, fuck," Jere's words fizzled out as Wren gave one final thrust.

The world didn't explode and there weren't choruses of angels, but Wren did experience one of the most intense and amazing orgasms of his life, sheathed inside of the man he had once called "master," his arms wrapped around that same man, whom he mostly thought of as "boyfriend." An internal debate raged inside of him, whether to keep his eyes open and keep looking at Jere, or succumb to closing them. In the end, the stimulation was too intense, and he let them close, dropping his head down and almost stretching over Jere's back.

With shuddering breaths, they collapsed, mindless of the mess in the bed for a minute, reluctant to separate.

"That was... Jesus. Jere." Wren finally slid out, missing the warmth instantly, and pulling Jere closer, turning him so they were facing.

Jere leaned in and placed a gentle kiss on his lips. "All you ever hoped and dreamed?"

Wren had stopped dreaming long ago, and hope for anything more than a quick death was something that had only recently started to cross his mind. His old hopes were limited to minimizing pain, being safe, maybe escaping punishment. But real hopes and dreams? Those were things free people had. Even now, when things were going so well, all Wren hoped was that they stayed exactly the same, that nothing ruined it, that Jere never found out anything that would make him reconsider. It was that desire to keep things the same that prompted a little white lie. "More." Wren buried his face in Jere's neck. "I had no idea. Thank you."

"Thank *you!*" Jere countered. "Jesus. I haven't been fucked like that since before I left Sonova!"

Wren felt himself blushing. He couldn't be sure, but... "You really liked it, didn't you?"

Jere laughed. "Of course I did! One of my favorite things in the world. Hell, I'd do it every night!"

"Mmm." Wren, half-asleep, enjoyed that thought.

Jere laughed. "But we're—grab that shirt I had on earlier. Just off the bed."

"Too far," Wren decided, and stripped off his own shirt, which he had somehow managed to keep on. "Here. Take it."

"As you command, my love," Jere smirked, mostly succeeding in cleaning them up. They rolled to the cleaner side of the bed, pressed together naked in each other's arms, and fell asleep, utterly exhausted from the night.

Chapter 39
Handling Accidents

The remainder of the week that Dane stayed with them passed quickly, and he made considerable progress with the cellar. For one reason or another, he had started with the sub-cellar, where Wren had been kept. Jere found himself quite pleasantly surprised when he went down to find that the small room no longer looked like a torture chamber, but was simply an empty room. Wren said nothing when Jere curtly ordered the chain and collar to be disposed of, but the way he grasped Jere's hand under the table had certainly been thanks enough.

On the last day of his visit, Dane asked rather nervously what he should focus on, as the entire downstairs would certainly not be cleaned out, despite his efforts. Jere realized, with a shudder of disgust, that he was covertly asking whether he would be punished. He assured him that finishing up the shelves would be fine. Dane still looked nervous.

It was probably this very nervousness that caused Dane to drop something. Jere and Wren were enjoying a quick break between patients when they heard the sound of something falling and smashing to the ground, followed by an almost palpable silence. Wren's eyes widened as he looked to Jere, who frowned and walked toward the entrance to the cellar.

Dane met him at the top of the stairs, dropping to his knees when he saw him and hiding his face.

"Master Peters, please, punish me as you see fit for being careless in your home." He was trembling, but his voice was steady and calm.

"Dane, what happened?" Jere asked, too horrified with the situation to even address the man's request. Punish him? It was the last thing on his mind.

"I was cleaning off a shelf, sir, and something fell," Dane recounted, almost robot like. "I was careless and didn't move quickly enough to catch it. I apologize, sir, and I'll present myself for any punishment you deem necessary."

Jere was pretty sure that no punishment was necessary, and was almost sickened at the thought. He stood there, frozen for a moment, until he felt Wren come up behind him.

His musings interrupted, he shook his head. "Dane, please, get up. It's no big deal."

Dane stood immediately, head still tilted down toward the floor, clutching his hand as blood dripped down it and onto the floor.

"Jesus Christ, Dane, you're bleeding all over the place!"

Dane dropped to the floor again, lower this time. "Please, Dr. Peters, I'll clean it up after my punishment, sir."

Jere dropped down next to him.

"Give me your hand!" he ordered, frustrated.

Hesitating for the slightest fraction of a second, Dane held a trembling, bleeding hand out and looked up at Jere fearfully.

"*He thinks you're going to hurt him more, Jere,*" Wren supplied. "*Most would.*"

It was all Jere could do not to scream in frustration. He held Dane's hand gently in his own and took a deep breath, trying to calm himself enough to communicate rationally. "Dane," he said softly, waiting until he had the slave's attention. "I'm not angry with you. You're not going to be punished. I just want to heal you. That's all. This looks like a nasty cut, and I don't want you to be in pain, okay?"

Dane nodded slowly. "Yes, sir."

Jere nodded, keeping eye contact with him for a moment. He looked down at the messy, bloody hand, and was shocked to see that the cut had gone straight through the skin and nearly to the bone on the palm.

"My god, what did you cut yourself on?" he wondered out loud.

"I, I'm not sure what it was, sir," Dane replied, still trembling. "I think it was a picture frame or something—glass. It fell and I tried to catch it, but it broke and I kept trying to catch it, but I couldn't hold on. Please—"

"You couldn't hold on because you cut through tendons!" Jere tried, unsuccessfully, to keep the shock out of his voice. "Hell, it was probably broken before you ever even got to it! It was a goddamn mess down there."

Dane said nothing, but kept looking at the ground, breathing shallowly.

"It's okay, Dane, just relax, let me heal it," Jere spoke calmly, soothing him with his best doctor voice.

Dane nodded, and Jere carefully began his work, reconnecting the tendons and blood vessels and skin cells. It was delicate work, as hands always were, but with an injury so fresh it wasn't nearly as difficult as some of his work had been.

"*Bring me some healing cream and bandages, would you, love?*" Jere spoke to Wren mentally, as he often did while they were working. Wren returned before he knew it, and had brought along a bucket of water and soap as well.

"*I'll clean it up,*" Wren offered, "*if you can stop Dane from trying to do it instead.*"

As if on cue, Dane moved to protest. "Please, I can take care of that—"

"You'll do nothing of the sort!" Jere said firmly. "And stay still."

Dane was instantly subdued, and Wren began cleaning at the top of the stairs.

A few more minutes passed, and Jere slowly pulled back from the healing connection.

"Move your fingers for me, one at a time," he ordered, his hand lightly stretched out against Dane's palm. They moved smoothly, fluidly, and naturally. Jere nodded. "Good," he said, and reached for the bandages.

"I, I'm probably fine, sir," Dane said, looking nervous again.

"Your skin is still fragile, and you'll want to keep it wrapped so it can finish healing on the inside," Jere explained, carefully applying cream and bandages, following up with a thicker, more supportive wrap. "Just take it easy for a few days."

"Please, Dr. Peters, my master is coming back today!" Dane's voice had risen to the tone of terror.

"Dane...." Jere hadn't even considered this. Hadn't considered the possibility that Paltrek wouldn't be amenable to this plan. He let Dane's hand go and stood up. "I'll take care of your master, Dane. Don't worry about it."

Dane nodded, looking reluctant, and Jere wished he had something more reassuring to tell him. Paltrek would probably be a bit put out by his orders, but it was good medical advice. He had seemed at least passingly fond of his slave, and Jere couldn't fathom being upset at someone for something so trivial. Besides, Jere figured that if Paltrek insisted on pushing friendship on him, he could push back with a little human compassion.

Wren came back up the stairs, carrying a now-bloody bucket of water, as well as a box with shards of broken glass in it. He caught Jere's eye and smiled, making him feel at least a little bit better.

"Master Peters," Dane stood slowly, looking just as nervous as ever. "Thank you, sir, for healing my hand. Are you going to punish me now?"

"No, Dane. I'm not. I want you to go have something to drink, change clothes so you're wearing something that isn't covered in blood, and then you are to spend the remainder of the day resting. It was an accident, and I have no plans of punishing you for it, now or ever."

Dane was quiet for a moment, nodding while looking down at the floor. "Thank you, sir." He walked toward the kitchen, presumably to follow Jere's orders.

Shaking his head, Jere made his way back to the clinic, where he was relieved to find that his two o'clock appointment was running a bit late. He felt arms circle around his waist.

"That was kind of you," Wren said, pressing into him for a moment.

"It was nothing," Jere tried to brush it off. "I'm a doctor. It's what I do."

"Yes, and you're also standing in for his master. Letting that go was kind."

"I'm not going to get mad at him for breaking something that wasn't even mine," Jere protested, somewhat weakly, as he spun around to face Wren.

Wren smiled back at him, rather smugly. "You wouldn't have gotten mad at him even if it was yours," he pointed out. "You handled him very well."

Jere made a sort of muttering noise. Personally, he thought he had been a little brusque with Dane, but it had seemed necessary at the time. He nearly shuddered to think that a person would actually beat someone else for something so petty, especially when he was already injured.

The day passed smoothly after that, although Jere did have to remind Dane that he was not to continue working after dinner. Not long after, there was a knock on the door, and Wren opened it to let Paltrek in.

"Shit, it is good to be back!" he exclaimed, strolling through to the dining room.

"Paltrek," Jere waved hello as he approached.

Dane stood, walked toward him, and knelt beside him, a smile on his face. "Master," he glanced up at him.

Paltrek smiled at him, almost affectionately, placing a hand on his head as Dane wrapped his arms around his legs. "Miss me, boy?"

Blushing, Dane nodded. "Yes, master."

Paltrek laughed, motioning for him to stand up. "I'll tell you what, a whole week without anyone taking care of me was quite the inconvenience. Fucking non-slave states!" He glanced at Jere. "Eh, no offense, of course."

Jere grinned back. "None taken." He could say the same about Hojer. He often *did* say the same about Hojer.

"Dane, go get me something to drink, something a bit harder than water," Paltrek ordered, taking the seat at the table that Dane had previously occupied.

"Yes, master," Dane jumped to do as ordered, but was stopped by a strong hand on his upper arm.

"What the hell happened?" Paltrek was eying up the bandage.

"A picture frame broke and I was cut, master," Dane replied calmly, although his body had tensed visibly. "Master Peters healed me."

"Goddammit, Dane!" Paltrek didn't loosen the grip on his arm. "I leave you here for one goddamn week and you're breaking shit? What the hell got into you?"

Dane dropped to the floor again. "I'm sorry, master. Please—"

"Go get me my goddamn drink, I'll deal with you when we get home," Paltrek frowned irritably at him. "*Just* what I want to do."

Jere was silent for a moment, planning his attack. Dane returned with the drink, dropping to kneel next to his master again, looking strangely calm. After the display of nerves that Jere had witnessed through most of the week, the fact that he looked so calm in the face of impending punishment unsettled him.

"Paltrek, really, it was an accident," he said calmly. "Nothing to worry about."

"He knows better," Paltrek said coolly, sipping at his drink. "Knowing you, you were too busy healing him to punish him properly."

Jere dug his nails into his palm under the table. "There's no need to punish him. It was an accident, and the thing wasn't even mine. It was probably broken already. Honestly, it was a terrible mess down there, most of the things ended up being thrown out anyway."

Paltrek considered this for a moment. "That true, Dane?"

Only now did Dane start to tremble again. "I, I'm not quite sure, master. Many of the things down there were broken. If Master Peters says it was broken already, then I would be in no place to correct him."

Paltrek glanced back and forth between Dane's wide eyes and Jere's hopeful smile. "Dane's far too polite and well-trained to openly correct a free man, but he's also smart enough not to lie to me, even if it meant he wouldn't get beaten tonight. I'll go lightly on him."

Jere felt his eyes narrowing in response. He wanted to scream. He wanted to punch the man sitting across from him. He wanted to move back home.

"Thank you, master," Dane was leaning against Paltrek's legs, honestly looking grateful.

Jere felt revulsion rising.

"Paltrek..." he said, with a pointed glare.

"Jeremy, I know you do things differently, but the boy has to learn, and nothing gets through to him like a good whipping," Paltrek pointed out.

"It's not worth it, Jere, let it go." Wren advised in his head.

Jere shook his head, almost imperceptibly, than focused back on Paltrek. "Look. Correct me if I'm wrong, but you said that taking Dane for a week was a favor to you, right?"

"Well, of course —"

"And where I come from, at least, you repay people who have done favors for you."

Paltrek looked back at him, confused for a moment. "Well, yeah...."

"Well, I'm asking a favor of you in return, then," Jere said, a too-big, fake smile consuming his face. "I mean, really, what's a favor between friends, right? Friends help each other out, last I checked. It's only fair."

"Well, sure, but I don't see what that has to do with anything," Paltrek was looking at Jere like he was making no sense.

"My favor: let it go." Jere laid his cards out. "Dane has done a spectacular job helping here this week and I enjoyed having him. Simple as that. What I want from you is to leave him alone. See, if you punish him for what happened here, I will feel like it's my fault. No, nothing will make me think otherwise. I'll feel bad and guilty and, really, you will be the only one to blame. *You* will be the cause of those feelings."

Paltrek said nothing, but scowled a bit.

"I know it's nothing off your back to *not* punish him — hell, you just said yourself that he was polite and well-trained, and I've seen nothing but," Jere smiled as Paltrek was trapped with his own words. "But if you did do it, I'd take it as personal offense — both against my abilities as a slaveowner, as well as a betrayal of my kindness and friendship. Perhaps I'm unfamiliar with the ways in slave states, but in Sonova at least, we make every effort to meet the requests of our friends and guests."

The room was silent. Jere thought for a moment that he had pushed his luck too far, that his tentative "friend" was going to tell him to go to hell. Worse, he worried that his words would have no effect on the way Dane was treated. He was still pretty sure that it had been worth the gamble.

Suddenly, Paltrek broke out laughing. "Well, I'll be damned, Jeremy, I've never heard a better argument. Hell, if you didn't have a healing gift, I'd say you'd make an excellent salesman! Might have to pull you into the business now and again anyway—you know, I'm feeling guilty just *thinking* about doing anything now. Shit. I haven't felt that ripped up since my grandmother was alive!"

Jere smiled, pretty certain he would get his way. "It was an accident. If he had done something wrong, I wouldn't be so opposed to your punishing him. And if there had been any actual wrongdoing, I would have dealt with it."

Wren was silent, but a slight smile had crossed his face, and Jere could feel the laughter that he was holding back through the mind connection. "*I didn't say how I'd deal with it!*"

"You know what, you're right!" Paltrek agreed, his mood seeming to lift. "Hell, I'd rather not go home and be miserable anyway. How about you, Dane, you agree?"

Dane's head was still down, but he was smiling. "As it pleases you, master."

"Well, I think it does!" Paltrek tossed back the rest of his drink, and Dane was instantly getting him another one. "Besides, home is miserable enough as it is."

"Oh?" Jere raised an eyebrow. The lap of luxury was unpleasant?

Paltrek rolled his eyes. "Ever since I pulled that stunt with Arae, Annika has made it her personal mission to make my life hell. Our father is angry at her for being a spectacle, so they're not talking, and he's angry at *me* for starting shit—even though he was glad for the intervention—so he's glaring at me all the damn time. Arae is even more on edge than usual, even though Annika has lightened up on her, somewhat. Shit, I think Dane and I are the only civil beings left in that house!"

As if on cue, Dane returned with his drink, and Paltrek ruffled his hair affectionately. Dane leaned into the touch, and Jere found himself startled by how much more content he looked when his master was around.

"Well, if you ever want to go out, or visit, or, whatever..." Jere mumbled. He felt out of place, but he had just called Paltrek out by citing their friendship, and friends did things like invite each other over. "You and Dane are welcome."

"Thanks," Paltrek replied.

The rest of the night went smoothly, and Jere was pleased to find Paltrek in good spirits, especially after a few drinks. They talked for a few hours, and Jere finally sent them home with instructions for continued medical care. He elicited a promise that Dane would not be punished, threatening Paltrek that he would not be doing any more favors for him again if he was.

Once the door shut and they were left alone, Jere looked at Wren, rather tired. "Bed?" he suggested, taking his hands and leading him in that direction. "I'd really enjoy it if you'd fuck me until I forget today."

Wren smiled back at him, following obediently. "I think that could be arranged."

Not much time passed before they were naked, entwined, fucking, gasping, then they collapsed next to each other.

There were a few minutes of silence in the dark.

"Jere?"

He heard Wren's voice, despite being half asleep. "Mmm?"

"That was good of you. What you did for Dane." Wren's arms wrapped tighter around him.

"It was the least I could do," Jere mumbled, placing his hands on top of Wren's. "Glad it worked."

Another moment of silence.

"Jere?"

"Mmm?"

"Do you ever, I mean, do you want to...?" Wren fumbled for words for a bit, burying his head in Jere's shoulder as he did. "You let me fuck you all the time, do you ever want to do it to me?"

Jere turned so he was facing his slave, his lover. He couldn't see his eyes, but he could make out the outline of his face, and he put a gentle hand on his chin to tip it upward. "I've *wanted* to do it for a long time, love. But I wouldn't ask that of you. It's not my place. If you want to do it, I'd love to, but I'll wait until you ask. I can promise that it will feel good, but I know it's hard for you to believe, and that's okay. And if you never want to, that's okay, too. Just being with you is good enough for me."

Wren said nothing, and Jere couldn't think of anything else to say or do. He leaned over and kissed him, caressing his head as he did. They fell asleep like that, wrapped up in each other's arms, mouths close, bodies close.

Chapter 40
A Visit from Mum

The next few weeks passed quickly. Jere and Wren took care of business in the clinic and prepared for Jere's mum to visit. Things between the two of them had gone remarkably smoothly, and the interactions they had while Dane was around somehow set Wren at ease. He didn't think about it much, what with work and a fantastic sex life keeping him busy, but something about the way Jere handled Dane—and his master!—reassured Wren in a way that no words or actions toward him could have done. He had always assumed that Jere gave him special treatment because he cared about him, and because they were dating, if that was the right word to call it in this situation. Beyond that, Jere was a genuinely nice guy. More than nice, he was strong, sharp, and loyal to his beliefs.

The part that had really gotten Wren was watching his master stand up to Paltrek. It was Jere, of course, so it was soft, subtle, and gentle, but Jere had made his point exceedingly clear—he was not going to allow Dane to be hurt. The cool, calm manner he had, the way of convincing, it was remarkable how Jere's unassuming friendliness could be turned into a cutting weapon, when needed.

Wren wondered if he had gotten that trait from his mother. Jere had warned him to "go along" with her, whatever she demanded, whatever that meant. All Jere had been able to explain was that his mother was a "force of nature" and "wouldn't take no for an answer." Of course, he had also said she was lovely and quite fond of Wren already, so he wasn't really sure what to make of her. Wren was certain that anyone who had raised a son like Jere had to be someone special.

Regardless, Wren was anticipating her arrival with a mix of curiosity and apprehension. Jere had taken a half-day off from work to meet her at the speed train station, despite her adamant insistence that she could find the place on her own. While buttoning his coat, Jere remarked that his favorite thing about the slowness of letters was that it was one of the only things that could stop his mother from arguing. Jere was so passive and easy-going; would his mother be assertive, threatening, even? Wren dusted away some invisible dirt as he waited, calming himself with the familiarity.

Wren might have lacked the mind gift necessary to sense people at the door, but the sound of laughter reached his ears before the footsteps did. Out of habit and propriety, he rushed to open the door, pulling it open even as Jere's hand reached for it.

"Hey," Jere smiled at him, his face wide with the remnants of whatever he had been laughing about.

"Hello, sir," Wren spoke softly, hoping to downplay the fact that he wasn't comfortable addressing Jere informally in front of company, as well as to hide the nervousness that tried to clamp his vocal chords together.

A petite blonde woman stepped inside a second after Jere. Despite the tall son she had produced, she was a good head shorter than Wren. Like her son, she had soft, grey eyes, and an open face that curled easily into a smile. Faint wrinkles graced the edges of her mouth and eyes, providing a dignified tribute to her age.

"You must be Wren," she said, that familiar smile brightening on her face.

"Y-yes, ma'am?" Wren froze, unsure of how to answer, and his statement came out as a question.

"Don't 'ma'am' me," she raised an eyebrow at him, the smile still there. "And none of that 'Mrs. Peters' crap either—I firmly intend to go by my name until I'm interred in my burial space or a nursing home. You can call me Janet, and that isn't a request."

Wren was startled, to say the least. "Uh, okay," he managed. Of all people, it would be terrible to offend his boyfriend's mother.

"*I warned you!*" Jere's voice cut into his thoughts, teasing. "*Didn't I tell you she was a handful?*"

"Jere! Stop talking about me through the mindspeak!" Janet

swatted at his arm. "Don't look surprised, you have the same damn look on your face as you did when you'd talk with your little friends when you were in high school! Make yourself useful and put our coats away, since you *insisted* on dragging yourself outside in the rain to come and get me."

"All right, all right!" Jere threw up his hands in mock surrender, grinning as he did so. "Mum, Wren, Wren, my mum. Make yourself at home."

Janet proceeded to do exactly that, strolling through the front hallway and into the living room. Uncertain of what to do, Wren followed a few feet behind in case she needed anything. Jere and his mother seemed exceedingly at ease, which only made his own anxiety worse. His training had never covered this sort of a situation, and he wasn't sure whether to treat this woman as his boyfriend's mother or his master's mother. He couldn't even use his own family as reference; interactions between the two sides of his family were always conducted in a tense, business-like manner, much like how the marriage between his parents had been conducted. There was no room for joking or teasing.

He felt Jere behind him, and a sly arm wrapped around his waist.

"*She really is nice,*" Jere reminded him. "*Just a bit much all at once. And she forgets, well, you didn't grow up with her. She and my sister are both rather animated.*"

"You want me to show you around, Mum?" Jere suggested. "The house is amazing—huge, too!"

"Certainly, yes, I've been dying to see it!"

Wren was glad for Jere's arm around his waist as they gave Jere's mum—*Janet*—the tour. It saved him from having to guess where he was supposed to be, or what he was supposed to be doing, for that matter. She made a few comments here and there, polite things about the structure of the house, or the décor, which, Wren realized, hadn't exactly been changed at all since Jere had moved in. She seemed to be appraising Wren as much as she was appraising the house, although she didn't comment on him. Wren was glad, but felt himself growing tense whenever she looked in his direction.

They made their way through the clinic, which made Janet's face beam with pride as she saw how far her son had come. Wren thought, only for a second, what it would be like for his own parents to visit. Had things been different, they could have been proud of him, too—a life, a home, a job, someone who loved him. But that was ridiculous. He was a slave, and that's all *his* parents would ever remember about their firstborn son.

"Well, Wren, I want to applaud you!" Janet's voice cut through his thoughts. "It looks quite nice and tidy in here—certainly something I won't attribute to my son!"

"Mum!" Jere protested weakly.

"I, thank you," Wren blushed, caught off-guard by the praise. "I do my best."

"Give Jere a chance, and he ends up living like some sort of takeout-caveman," she smirked, even as Jere's face grew redder. "I'm glad to see he has someone to take care of him."

Wren nodded. Praise was uncomfortable, but the criticism of Jere made his skin crawl, even if it was meant to be playful. It simply wasn't done, and while he was used to Jere's oblivion to social protocols, seeing it from another person still shook him.

"Hey, Mum, I bet you're hungry," Jere struggled to change the subject. "Come on, we can sit down and Wren can find us something to eat."

Janet followed her son to the dining room with a skeptical look on her face. "Adjusted so quickly to having a slave?"

"*Mother!* Christ!" Jere protested, blushing furiously as he said it.

Wren grabbed the opportunity to escape for a few minutes. "Uh, it's really all right, uh, it will give you and my—and Jere a chance to talk. I'm a bit more skilled in the kitchen anyway."

"Well, it wouldn't be hard," Janet remarked, a pointed glance at Jere. "You know, when I tracked your old landlady down, she said there was a *mountain* of takeout boxes in your living room?"

"Well, I didn't really have a kitchen," Jere protested. "Wren, darling, if you would, please?" "*And get me a drink, too. I don't care if it's four in the afternoon.*"

"Of course," Wren smiled. "Janet, anything in particular you'd like to eat? Or drink?"

She shook her head. "Whatever you boys are having is fine by me."

Wren took off to the kitchen to prepare food and drinks. Janet was friendly, and Jere seemed thrilled to have her here, but she was unsettling. Her disregard of social customs seemed so intense as to be purposeful, and Wren couldn't shake the feeling that she was watching him, sizing him up. Was this something that all mothers did, or was it something about him?

He wasn't trying to overhear, but he heard them talking anyway. It didn't help the unsettled feeling.

"So you just... go about, I mean, with a slave, like—"

"Mum, he's not just a slave! He's my assistant, and my friend, and we're, you know...."

"Jerry, honey, you might not notice it, but he *is* doing all the work around here. If he's not your slave, then he's your 1950s housewife!"

"Christ's sakes, Mum! If I didn't have Wren I'd, well, shit, I'd probably hire someone to get it done, anyway. You know, get a cleaning service or something. I'm the only doctor in the area, and my time and energy are a little more valuable! But you don't hire a cleaning service here, you buy a slave!"

"*Jeremy!* No one in our family has ever owned another human being!"

Wren winced at the tone, even though it wasn't directed at him. He understood why Jere didn't like his full name.

"Yeah, well, I didn't have much of a choice! I inherited this place, and I fucking inherited him, and what else was I supposed to do, sell him off? I wouldn't do that to him. And I can't set him free. So I'm stuck just doing the best I can with him. Hell, I'm stuck *here*. In Hojer."

"Jere, you can always leave—but you said things were going okay here!"

"They are going okay, but I don't like it, and I can't leave. Not without leaving Wren, and I'm not leaving without him. I'm stuck here. I'm not exactly happy about that!"

Wren tried to focus on making drinks, tried not to be hurt by the words he shouldn't even be overhearing in the first place. He shouldn't care. He was a slave. Jere owned him. He was kind to him. He shouldn't care that Jere was a nice person who was stuck with him, and that was the only reason why he was kind to him. He shouldn't be feeling angry at the world for making him a slave and at Jere for teasing him with lies of compassion.

"Listen, Mum, the thing is—I don't necessarily like it here. That's a lie, I hate it here. I think the slave laws are horrible, and a good portion of the people here are equally horrible. But I have my job, and I *like* my job, and more importantly, I have Wren. I know you have your doubts, but what we have is real. I love him. I could lose my job tomorrow and I'd sell this place in a heartbeat and look for a shitty, entry-level job in *another* slave state, just so I could be with him. Even if we were... if we weren't doing anything dating-like, I'd still stay with him. Because if I were to leave, I'd spend every day thinking about whether he's okay or not."

Fuck. The tears had been easier to hold back when he thought Jere was being hurtful. This, this devotion, he didn't deserve it. What would Jere say when he got to know him better, when the newness wore off and he had become really fed up with living in Hojer?

"Jere, honey, isn't there any way you could just bring him back with you? I mean, I know you like your work here, but I'm sure there would be something you could find back home?"

"Mum, Sonova isn't going to be home for me again. I've researched it, looked at laws, even had my lawyer look into it for me. There is no way to get a slave into a free state legally, and smuggling success rates are below fifty percent. I love him too much to risk that, and I won't go without him. Even if it does mean 'owning another human being,' as you seem so intent on pointing out."

It was quiet in the dining room for a minute. It was Janet who finally spoke. "Honey, I never meant it like that. I shouldn't be angry that you have a slave when I know so little about your situation. Just... love makes it too easy to hurt someone. To take advantage, or to be taken advantage of. I can see that Wren is special to you."

Wren realized he was taking an awfully long time for someone with a speed gift. Carefully, he wiped at his eyes, grabbed the plates, and brought them out to the table, as if nothing had happened.

"Looks delicious!" Janet exclaimed, a little too excitedly. Wren hoped she didn't realize that he had overheard their conversation, but she seemed very perceptive.

"Thanks, hon," Jere smiled up at him.

Wren smiled back, dropping into the chair next to him and taking his hand under the table. He wasn't sure whether Jere knew he had overheard the conversation, but all he wanted was to feel something grounding. That, and to be alone with him again.

"So, Wren, what is it that you'd be doing if you weren't working with Jere?" Janet asked brightly.

Wren looked away, uncomfortable being the focus of attention. "I, well, I never really thought about that."

"No hopes and dreams and inner ambitions?" she asked, still smiling. Still missing the point.

"I, uh, here, we don't really..." Wren fumbled. "People don't really make plans until they uh, until their gift...."

"Oh, well, even aside from the gifts you have, surely there must have been something you've always wanted to do?"

Wren bit his lip for a moment. "If you have a physical gift, you don't get to make plans. There's no point. It's not encouraged to think about that until you find out."

Janet's face dropped, then reddened. "Oh, I, Wren, I didn't realize...." She, like her son, hid behind her glass for a moment. "I forget how different things are here."

Wren shrugged, wishing the conversation would just shift away from him and back to Jere, back where things were safer and he could blend into the background and observe. "It's okay. I've had plenty of time to come to terms with it."

Janet nodded. "It's a pity, someone with such special gifts like you have."

Wren felt tension rising. He forced his expression to remain neutral, even smiled a bit. "Well, a speed gift certainly is useful."

"Yes, but that wasn't—" Janet stopped abruptly. "Jere mentioned that you had a speed gift."

"Yes," Wren answered, unsure of what else to say. He wished desperately for the conversation to move away from him. "Speed gifts are pretty common here. I'm glad it can be useful."

"Do people spend a lot of time developing their gifts here?"

Janet asked. "You know, exploring them, learning how to use them, things like that?"

Wren hated many things about himself, but especially that part of him that made him so different. "Free people do. They have classes every day in high school on various parts of using their gifts. Slaves are taught the basics of their specific gifts, but mainly are taught how to control them and use them as well as possible to serve their masters."

"So, not that much, then," Janet mused. "Must be a shame, then, if someone has a special gift, or something that could take a little coaxing out?"

"I wouldn't know. I have a speed gift. It's pretty common." Wren was trying desperately to avoid being rude, but he wished she would stop asking so many questions about gifts. He couldn't figure out why she was so interested.

"Wren is special for much more than his speed gift," Jere cut in, trying too hard to smile and pretend that the room hadn't grown uncomfortable. "Even though nobody here would notice it!"

"All anyone here sees when they look at me is a slave with a physical gift," Wren said quietly. "I guess that's only somewhat true."

Janet wrinkled her brow at Wren, just for a minute, before steering the conversation away. "Jere wanted to be something different every week when he was a little boy," she smiled at her son. "His gift showed early, though, in little bursts. I remember he was maybe seven, eight years old when he brought in a little bird he had found outside, half eaten by the neighbor's cat. He didn't understand how, but he had fixed it, just a little. He turned out to be much more skilled with humans, though!"

"If I recall, the bird never did learn to fly," Jere mused.

"You showed such surprisingly strong skills," Janet smiled. "Better than most I had seen, most I've seen since."

"What do you do, ma—er, Janet?" Wren stumbled.

"Oh, Jere didn't tell you? I work at a gift identifying agency. I'm a talent scout!"

Wren struggled to keep his eyes from widening, to keep from responding at all. A talent scout? As someone with a gift for identifying other's gifts, she would be highly sought-after in a slave state, to identify kids like him, to condemn them to slavery. He tightened down the hold he already had on his emotions and on the mind connection, praying that Jere didn't notice it too much, or at least ask too many questions. No wonder she had been so interested in Wren's gift, and all the other questions. This was her job.

His stomach churned and he thought for a moment that he might be sick, but he had had years of practice ignoring those urges and keeping his face blank. Janet might look like a loving, friendly mother, but here in Hojer she would have the power to determine someone's fate just by peeking at their gift. She would know what it was, how powerful it was, and if there were any abnormalities to it. And she would know —

"I've seen so many interesting gifts," she said with a grin, "and it was so exciting to see my own kids come into theirs!"

"I, I'm sure," Wren managed. She would know too much about him. Things he had never told anyone else, things that could ruin everything he had worked so hard to find with Jere.

"She was always predicting what my friends would turn out with," Jere rolled his eyes. "Drove their parents nuts — although, she was always right."

Janet shrugged. "It's rather fun. Besides, affluent families pay good money to hedge bets on which skill their child will have. Of course, those are usually the kids that decide to ignore their gifts in favor of art or academia or something. That's why we didn't put too much pressure on you and Jen."

"Ahh, reverse psychology," Jere teased. "Honestly, I think I just enjoyed having something I didn't much have to practice for!"

Wren let the conversation fade into the background, relieved that the topic had switched away from him. Janet, as a caring mother *and* someone who could sense gifts, had the potential to know far more about him than he ever wanted revealed. Surely she hadn't really meant anything by saying he had "special gifts." She was probably just being nice. Friendly, or something, like Jere had suggested. Jere always accepted the simplest conclusions, why could Janet not do the same?

They finished out the evening without further conflict, mostly Jere catching up with his mum, explaining how the clinic worked, and even getting into a little bit of the history and workings of Hojer. Janet was actually more appalled by most of it than Jere had been, despite his keeping most of the grittier aspects quiet. Wren found himself liking her, and would probably have gotten along better with her under different circumstances. Still, she made him uncomfortable, her eyes and questions too probing.

Wren couldn't help but avoid being left alone with her; when Jere went to the bathroom, Wren excused himself to get more drinks, or snacks, or even to use the other bathroom. If Janet noticed how long he was taking, despite his speed gift, she was tactful enough not to mention anything. Having Jere there helped him to feel more calm, and seeing the interplay between them made a few pieces of the puzzle fit together as well. With his own parents, before he was a slave, at least, they had been kind enough, but there had always existed a certain level of formality, if it could be described that way. Detachment was probably a better word. Ultimately, Wren knew his place, as did his brother, and their parents. Knowing one's place was vital to the functioning of society, and had been instilled, not to mention beaten, into them from an early age.

Watching Jere and Janet was different. Certainly, his lover respected his mum, even went so far as to take trouble to make sure she was comfortable and happy, but it wasn't the same. Wren would have done it out of obligation, out of fear, out of propriety. Jere and his mum seemed to share so much, to be so connected. The way that they joked with one another, the way she hugged him when they parted ways for the night. They were so close, despite the time they had spent apart. He felt like he had missed out on some part of that in his life.

He was still thinking of this when he and Jere went to bed, after no small amount of teasing about them sleeping together. As they slipped beneath the sheets together, he felt Jere's arms wrap around him.

"What did you think of her?" he asked, grinning.

"She's nice," Wren said, completely honest. "You're right, she is a bit much, but in a good way."

"She's been excited to meet you," Jere confessed, blushing. "I may have told her all about you."

"You're a lot like her," Wren said, not quite putting words into how he felt, but coming close. "It's nice, just seeing where you came from."

"I wish I could take you home with me," Jere said, pulling him close. "It's so different there. I think you'd like it. I mean, even aside from the obvious."

Wren smiled. Going to Sonova would mean he wouldn't be a slave. It was almost impossible to imagine, something he would never even have considered before. Now that he was with Jere, he could at least explore the fantasy. "You really looked into it?"

"Taking you out of here?" Jere asked, surprised. "Of course I did! I looked at freeing you when I first got here, and that was out, and then when I found out that I wouldn't be able to take you if I went on a visit, I looked into taking you with me for good!"

"Wouldn't I stick out, though, I mean, even if I wouldn't be a slave there, I am here. Wouldn't it be obvious?"

Jere shook his head. "Not really. Everyone here is all into every-one's business and set in their ways; back in the city, it's more open, more anonymous. There're too many people to know who or what everyone is, so nobody really cares. And there's not this ridiculous division between gifts— like my mum said, plenty of people ig-nore their gifts and go for something they care about more, instead. Taking you there, you could do whatever you wanted; your gift wouldn't hold you back."

Wren was touched. He hadn't even considered it. Of course, anyone growing up here would know it wasn't possible. "Thank you," he said softly. The lengths that Jere went to for him never failed to amaze him. He appreciated it, even though he felt that Jere's affections might be better spent on someone else. If only things were different, he would love to be as perfect to Jere as Jere was to him.

"It's nothing," Jere assured him, kissing him. "You know, my mum isn't the only one who's offended at the very idea of slavery!"

"I do hope I don't put your mum off too much...."

"Love, it's Hojer that puts Mum off, not you!" Jere protested. "She just, well, you know how odd it was for me when I moved here? Now, imagine I was twenty-some years older and a bit more assertive."

Wren giggled a bit at the thought. "I suppose it is a shock."

"People here with skills like my mum has...." Jere looked uncomfortable. "They're the ones who identify slaves, aren't they?"

"Yes. It's not a very common skill, so they're paid quite well. Some of them don't like to be present when the child is taken, but some do. They like to see the results. Of their work." The man who identified him did. He had sneered down at Wren in satisfaction, like an exterminator who had caught a rat.

"Is that why you were so uncomfortable when she was talking about it, then?"

Wren was horrified to realize that he hadn't been blocking that well. "I, uh, yeah," Wren muttered, not wanting to meet Jere's eyes. "Yeah, it, it's weird to think about it. People with that gift here are sort of like the boogeyman or something. You hope to never see them around."

Jere hugged him. "I'm sorry. Is that why you were kind of avoiding her? I haven't seen you so fidgety since I first moved here."

"I guess," Wren mumbled, feeling like he would never be able to swallow the lump in his throat. "Jere, I'm not used to being around other people. And she's not like a slave, or like a free person here, and so I don't really know how to act around her. It's just better when you're around. I hope I'm not being rude."

"Of course not, love, I've told her that people out here are a little standoffish, and that you might take a while to warm up. She won't blame you for this terrible place."

Wren hugged him back, pushing the rest of his feelings aside. They didn't matter now. The past didn't matter now. Everything was perfect. He wouldn't let his buried feelings ruin that. "It's okay. It worked out. I have you now."

Jere ran his hands up and down his back, dipping suggestively lower. "How about if you have me right now?"

Wren grinned, equally happy for the distraction and the activity to come. He pinned his master to the bed in one super-fast motion, setting the pace for the night. Once again, the thick walls proved themselves to be valuable.

Chapter 41
Revealing Conversations

Janet had been in town a few days, and the visit had mostly gone smoothly. Wren was thrilled to see Jere so happy, and to learn more about him, both from the stories Jere and Janet recalled and from the way they interacted. He thought he knew a lot about his master, but the different sides of him that were able to come out around his mum were enough for Wren to feel almost at ease with the two of them.

Really, it was only uncomfortable when they were alone, because Jere provided a convenient and willing barrier. He had accepted Wren's excuse that Janet unsettled him due to her gift, and due to the fact that people with that gift were used to identify slaves. Even aside from that, Jere knew he was uncomfortable around new people, and he let this discomfort seep through the mind connection as often as he needed to keep Jere by his side. As expected, Jere did his best to make sure that Wren was as comfortable as possible.

The only time when Wren *might* have been caught alone with Janet was during the work day, when he sometimes caught up on cleaning or started dinner, but he made sure to do neither of these things, sticking to meals that could be prepared quickly when he and Jere were both finished working, or slow-cooked dishes that he could start during lunch and ignore until dinner. Jere commented on it, but Wren said that he just didn't want to disturb Janet. The fact that Jere hadn't pushed the issue had helped considerably, and Wren was hopeful that he could keep himself and Janet from spending time without Jere for the rest of her visit.

On top of that, Wren made sure to give Jere and his mum "alone time," where he didn't intrude. Mostly, he picked up extra work around the clinic, insisting that Jere take advantage of the visit. Jere appreciated it, Janet appreciated it, and Wren successfully avoided spending too much time in discomfort. He felt almost guilty, because he was coming to truly like Janet, but she set off all the self-preservation alarms he had ever established for himself. As aloof and oblivious as Jere could be, his mum was anything but. She had tried to catch him alone for a few days now, but between having a speed gift and having years of experience evading an abusive master, he had outsmarted her every time.

Wren was brainstorming dinner ideas, and debating whether to use the "tired and going to bed early" excuse or the "spend some private time with your mum" excuse for after dinner when Janet announced that she was in the mood for steak.

"I don't think we have any," Wren said apologetically. "We used up the rest of it just the other day."

"That's all right," Janet smiled back at him, then glanced at her son. "Jere, honey, go and get some."

"Mum, they might not even have any, you know, it's not like in the city where everything is stocked all the time," Jere reminded her. "The last few times Wren has gone, they haven't had any beef at all. I guess it was a tough year, and there was a strike by the nature growers."

"Well, then, get something else," Janet persisted. "Something fresh. I'm sure you can find something."

"All right." Jere looked a little confused, but went to do as she asked.

"I can go," Wren stood, intent on keeping himself comfortably away from Janet. "It'll only be a minute, just get me a pass—"

"Don't be ridiculous!" Janet was looking at both of them, eyebrow raised. She looked quite determined. "Jere can go and pick up things for dinner, and you and I can chat a bit."

"I'm sure you're hungry, I'll be much faster, speed gift and all," Wren pointed out.

"You made such a nice, big lunch," Janet countered, one step ahead. She had requested the big lunch. "Jere, you go ahead. You don't get out enough anyway. It seems like Wren and I never get a chance to talk alone—when was I supposed to tell stories about when you were a little boy?"

"Mum!" Jere looked at her with pleading eyes. "Is it your mission to embarrass me?"

Wren had a sneaking suspicion that Janet had a far less innocent mission, one that involved terrifying conversations and getting him alone for some reason when Jere couldn't intervene. Jere didn't get it; he was acting like the worst thing in the world would be an embarrassing story. Jere couldn't possibly understand that Wren was worried about Janet doing something to upset their peaceful lives. He tightened down on the fear that was threatening to leak through the mind connection, because as nervous as he was, he didn't want to give Jere the idea that he was afraid of his mother. Then Jere might ask *why* he was afraid of his mother, and that was a conversation he wanted to have even less.

"Get to it, the sooner you leave, the sooner you'll get back," Janet said with a smug smile.

Jere sighed. "Be nice," he said, eyes on his mother.

"Always," she grinned back at him as he left.

Wren made his way back to the table, sitting down uncomfortably. He wished Jere was still there. He wished he had dinner to make, or something to turn off in the clinic, or some sort of illness that would force him to lock himself away in the bedroom.

"Wren, honey, I don't bite, you know!" Janet smiled at him. "I just wanted a chance to talk with you. I trust my son, and I know he's a good man, but things like this can go to a person's head."

"Things like what?" Wren could barely form words. What was she talking about? Who was she talking about even? He was too terrified to figure out even the most basic parts of the conversation.

"Slavery. Does he hurt you?"

Wren let out a breath he hadn't realized he had been holding. She wanted to make sure he was okay. Of course she did. Because that's exactly what Jere's mum would do. "No. He never has, and I doubt he ever would."

Janet nodded, seeming relieved. "This isn't just a show for my benefit, right? He's not just taking note of everything and planning something for you later?"

Wren shook his head, thankful that they were talking about safe topics that he knew how to deal with. "Not a bit. He's nothing but kind to me, has been since the first day he arrived here."

"Good." Janet seemed satisfied. "And he's not forcing you, I mean, in bed...."

"No, no!" Wren protested, caught between wanting to defend his lover and wanting to never, ever talk with Janet about sex. "He's... he's good to me. Patient, kind. He would never take advantage of me."

Janet smiled. "It might seem strange of me to ask, but every horrible man who has hurt someone is someone's son. Perhaps their mothers should have asked the same questions."

"You raised a very good son," Wren smiled, again wishing Jere were there with them, but for a different reason. Talking with Janet was okay when they were talking about Jere; that was a comfortable topic, one that wouldn't lead into dangerous areas. Still, he wished Jere could hear this conversation, too. "Most would have been more affected by the culture here, taken in by the power. Jere resists it every step of the way, with me and with others. You've definitely got many reasons to be proud of him."

"Good!" Janet said, looking much more relieved for a moment. Her gaze turned serious and demanding again. "And you?"

"Me?" Wren resisted tacking "ma'am" onto the end, but only barely. This was what he didn't want to talk about, what terrified him and made him do his best to avoid being alone with the woman. What could she want to know about him, and how much could he tell her without putting himself at risk?

"Yes. What are your intentions for my son?"

Wren was silent for a moment. It wasn't the worst question, given all the things Janet could have asked. It was still potentially dangerous. He went with what he hoped was the safe answer. "I'm his slave."

Janet winced at the truth, but didn't back down. "Is that the only reason you're doing this? Just another way to keep safe? Convince him that he loves you so you don't have to worry as much about what he could do to you?"

"What! No! No, it's nothing like that!" Wren was surprised to find himself defensive at the accusation. Realistically, it wasn't the worst thing a slave could do to keep safe, and when he and Jere first got together, he had considered it. "I mean, I know I wouldn't need that. Not with Jere. I could make his life miserable, ignore him, probably flat out disobey him, and I still—I could trust that he wouldn't hurt me. He's too good a master, too good a man for that."

"That sounds like my boy, all right," Janet nodded. "But why then? Why do you do it?"

"Because I care about him," Wren skirted around that other word. "I want to be with him. I like to see him happy, and make him feel good, and I trust him like I haven't ever trusted anyone before, and just being away from him for a few hours seems like forever. I tried really hard not to, to just be his slave, but it didn't work. We both tried to ignore it, but it didn't work for either of us. And I'm happy with him."

"I'm glad to hear how much you care about him, Wren," Janet said with a smile. "Jere's my baby. I'd really hate to have to come back here and hurt you."

Wren felt his eyes widen. She was smiling, but her eyes and her tone were completely serious. "Yes, ma'am..." he managed, wondering where the hell Jere was.

Janet laughed. "Oh, don't worry, I told Jere the same thing plenty of times already. It's bad enough that my son owns a human being, but if he hurts you *and* breaks your heart, he'll have you *and* me to answer to!"

Wren shook his head. "That's... scary."

Janet laughed again, almost as though she was embarrassed by her protectiveness. "I'm all talk," she said lightly. "But seriously— don't hurt my son. And if he hurts you, let me know. He may be a grown man, but he's still my little boy. I worry about him being hurt, but I worry more about him losing himself here. People can change so drastically. Burnout, if you will."

"I'm sure it would never come to that," Wren replied, his throat tight.

"I hope you don't mind, but Jere's told me about some of what that man did to you," Janet said. "To think that my son was involved with someone like that! I didn't raise him that way. It might be cruel, but I'm glad to know that he's dead. It seems quite fitting that he died the way he did."

Wren would rather not think about exactly how fitting it was. He would rather not think of it at all. "It was a tragic accident, but it brought Jere here."

"Yes, and it brought him to you," Janet smiled. "You're not like everyone else, Wren. I'm glad that Jere is with you."

Wren tried not to squirm. There was nothing special about him. You didn't want to be "special" as a slave. He tried to think of something to say, but ended up sitting there in silence.

They heard a noise, and Jere strolled in with a bag. "I'm back. Miss me?"

"You have no idea."

Jere was greatly enjoying having his mum in town. He had successfully pushed his homesickness away for the most part, but having someone else around from Sonova made him feel so much more at home, so much more comfortable. He loved never having to watch what he said or did, or wonder what he and Wren must look like.

Wren. The thought brought a smile to his face, even as he was writing up the co-pay bill for one of his patients.

"Have a nice day," he said, receiving a rather strange look from the man, who probably wondered if the local doctor always had such a dreamy look on his face while working.

Wren and his mum had gotten on quite well, as he had predicted, and Wren had even warmed up to her quickly, even if he was a little skittish to be left alone with her. He was surprised that Wren was still so guarded and nervous around her, but Wren had been right when he pointed out how infrequently he was around people other than Jere. Since it seemed to make his lover more comfortable, Jere did his best to be around, and he was pleased to notice that Wren was much less nervous that way. His mum had a way with people, even if she was a little forceful. It was something Jere had never quite mastered. His mum had been able to draw both of them into conversation without a problem and had even convinced them to play a few card games together. She insisted on teaching Wren some common games played in Sonova.

It was the last night she was going to be in town, however, and Jere wanted to do something special. Useless for ideas of his own, he asked Wren, who suggested he take her out for dinner.

"But, would you want to come out?" he asked, uncomfortable with the idea.

Wren smiled at him. "Babe, you know I couldn't—not like you *or* your mum would want."

Jere was quiet for a moment. His hatred of the state grew.

"I'd be kneeling at your feet, eating out of your hand," Wren explained with a shrug. "Neither of us would like it, and your mum would probably destroy the place before she left for insisting upon it."

"Well then, maybe I should do something else," Jere backtracked. He hated excluding Wren from things.

Wren kissed him, destroying any resistance he even thought of having. "Look, you should take her out anyway. She's barely seen the town—"

"She hates the town," Jere reminded him. "On principle, she hates the town."

"There are nicer parts to Hojer," Wren grinned. "Honestly, I won't mind. Go out with her. Have a little bonding time or whatever. I promise, I'll be here when you get back."

Jere kissed him again, felt Wren pinning him to the wall, and was glad that the clinic was empty for the moment. "*Smart ass.*"

After the workday was over and he and Wren had showered and changed, he found his mum and told her the plan. Initially, she was nearly as resistant as her son had been, but Wren gave her the same story as he had given Jere, and she finally agreed.

It was a short walk into town. They went to Hojer's nicest restaurant, which Wren had suggested. Jere didn't want to think of the circumstances under which his lover had been brought there before, but he did appreciate the recommendation.

Like the gentleman he pretended to be when he was with his mum, he led her in by the arm, following their host to two seats. Janet took a few minutes to look around, taking in, Jere was sure, much more than the subdued lighting and the aroma of other people's food. Her eyes lingered on a kneeling slave for a few seconds, and her nose wrinkled.

"When in Rome, huh?" she sighed, looking at Jere.

"Yeah...." He knew how she felt.

A slave who introduced herself as "Rain" came and took their orders, smiling brightly and moving quickly. Jere doubted his mum realized yet that she wasn't an actual employee.

"Jere, I am so proud of you," Janet told him, beaming at him over a glass of wine.

"Eh, I fell into the job," he tried to deflect the praise. He had never been too comfortable with compliments.

"Well, yes, I'm proud of that, too, but Jere, putting up with the society here! My god, I don't think I could have managed it for a week! I'm sure this is just because I'm some stubborn old lady who can't leave Sonova, but honey, this is such a huge change! I don't even think I realized the half of it until I came to visit."

"It can be a bit overwhelming."

"I'll say. Makes me uncomfortable just to think about it."

Jere said nothing, just smiled back at her. No, his mum would never be comfortable in a place like this. She wasn't an activist like her daughter, but she certainly wouldn't partake in such activities. He felt guilty for his own part in it, however small.

"And what you and Wren have...?" She gave him that all-knowing mum-smile. "Something special, there. Really. The two of you have come so far, and I doubt I have the slightest idea of what you must have gone through to get here!"

Jere nodded again, blushing this time. "You're right. I could never have done this without him. He's been... he's been everything to me."

"I just don't understand how they could make someone like him a slave!"

"Mum, it's just the way it is here, I told you, people with physical gifts are slaves, people with mental gifts aren't. It's nothing personal."

The slave-waitress arrived with their food, and they paused their conversation for a moment as it was placed on the table and she went away.

"Jere, it's not that, I mean, of course he's a sweet boy and all, but his gift is very special! It's a pity that something like that is being squandered!"

Jere raised an eyebrow. "Mum, what are you on about? He has a speed gift. Hell, hundreds of people with speed gifts run about Sonova every day delivering messages!"

Janet looked up from her food, studying Jere for a minute before saying anything else. "Surely you've noticed that he's a bit more expressive than most people with physical gifts? As far as what he's feeling?"

Jere thought back to before they had initiated the mind connection, so long ago. Back when he was having nightmares every night. "Sure, yeah, but some people are like that."

"Well, have you noticed that he's a bit warmer than most?" she continued.

Jere was a bit confused. "God, Mum, when have you cuddled up with my boyfriend? This is starting to get a bit weird."

"My god, you don't actually know, do you?" Janet's eyes widened. "Hell, I wonder if he even knows?"

"Mum?" Jere's confusion was building. He didn't like the way this was sounding.

"Jere, Wren certainly has a speed gift, that's obvious, but he has a semi-latent mind gift as well," she told him hesitantly.

Jere froze. "But that's —"

"Ten, fifteen years ago, people would have said it was impossible," Janet said gently. "But I'm sure you've read of cases where it has happened."

Jere shook his head, in disbelief. "No, I, I have. But I mean, it's what, one in a million?"

"Actually, I think the recent statistics are closer to one in 500,000," Janet shrugged. "So, two in a million."

"Two in a million," Jere repeated numbly, cutting into his food. "And he's a fucking slave."

"See why I was so surprised, honey?" Janet asked, a sympathetic look on her face. "I just thought you knew."

"But he never told me," Jere said. He felt slightly betrayed.

"Well, I doubt he knows," Janet smiled. "The poor boy looked as confused as you did when I mentioned that he had a special gift. I'm sure in this society nobody encourages kids to explore their gifts, especially not slaves!"

"No, probably not," Jere agreed. "But they have people—people with *your* ability—they're the ones who identify kids, who...." Did he really want to clarify to his mum what people like her would do in a state like this?

"I know, we're the ones who mark prepubescent children for a life of slavery," Janet nodded, merely shrugging at Jere's shocked look. "Don't think I haven't had a slew of offers. Probably five or six a year, from different slave states. They get our names from job listings, from word of mouth, who knows, but plenty of my colleagues get the same offers. Terrible business, that. Part of the reason your Wren didn't get identified properly."

Jere blinked. "Come again?"

"Look at it this way—unless someone with a gift-identifying gift is born and raised in a slave-state, they have to hunt down people from other states," Janet explained. "And any self-respecting person in a non-slave-state would be horrified to come here—oh, don't give me that look, your case is a bit different! But the outlanders who come here are the ones who aren't quite cutting it at home—primarily, those with weaker skill-identification abilities. Someone with a weak skill or poor training or both wouldn't notice a latent gift, especially when another one is more apparent. To put it quite frankly, I'm quite good at what I do, so I noticed it."

"But...?" Jere sputtered. "The people who made him a slave didn't notice it? Nobody else in his whole life noticed it?"

"Jere, I know you, and I've seen your reviews, and I can see your skills. I know you aren't just a good healer, you are an extraordinary one, and yes, *some* of that is due to the fact that you have an extremely strong gift. Your father has one as well. So do I. Your sister wastes hers extremely well, but that's beside the point—it runs in families. I know, they've never been able to prove it, in part because they can't quite figure out how to quantify it, but trust me, I do this day in and day out, and I see very powerful kiddos come from very powerful parents."

Jere didn't even know what to do with this information, any of it. Although, it was true, he and his mother were amazingly good at their jobs. "Have you met someone with multiple gifts before?"

Janet nodded. "Just once." At Jere's surprised look, she laughed. "Well, I've been working a long time! She was a little girl, who could stretch like crazy—an elastic gift, and who also had a hearing gift. Lovely kid, the elastic gift was far more prominent, though."

"Those are both physical gifts," Jere mused.

"Yes, and we both have forks," Janet rolled her eyes. "Honestly, Jere, the distinction between physical and mental is so fine and inconsequential, outside of here, anyway."

"You're right, you're right," Jere shook the idea away. "So, what is his other gift, then?"

"Oh, right, totally slipped my mind! He's a firesetter."

Jere suddenly felt cold and he tried unsuccessfully to swallow his food.

"Jere, are you all right?"

"Mum, if that was a joke, it wasn't funny!" Jere protested, but when his mum's face didn't change, he continued. "I told you why I came here—the last doctor was killed in a fire and Wren nearly lost his life!"

"Of course you told me, and you said it was accidental," Janet shrugged. "I don't see what the big deal is. You could kill someone with your healing gift, but I wouldn't think you were to blame if your neighbor turned up dead. Accidents do happen, even unfortunate ones."

Jere tried to calm the racing thoughts in his head. "So you don't think, I mean, he couldn't have…."

"Of course he could have, but do you really think he would? Starting a fire of that sort intentionally would take considerable energy, but more importantly, well, could you see Wren harming someone? He's perfectly sane and kind, far too timid, if you ask me! Besides, most people with a firesetting gift can put it out, too, but only if they know how to use it. It could have been an accident, untrained gifts can show up uncontrollably, but usually they show up gradually at first," Janet said. "Sounds like he had no idea at all, and probably still doesn't! Poor thing, could have saved himself a lot of suffering—well, maybe not, from what you've told me about the old doctor."

"Yeah...." Jere was silent. The fire investigators would never even have considered a psychic-started fire. There was a healer and a slave in the house. Or so they thought.

"Jere?"

He shook his head. "Yeah. Sorry, I just... wow. I'm a little shocked."

"Oh, I hope I didn't make things awkward," Janet frowned. "I didn't realize it would, but, I guess I should have. But Jere, it's so uncommon! It's exciting, I mean, I'd be excited to find out something like that. Although, I suppose, in his situation...."

"It's all right, Mum," Jere pushed the thoughts—*all* the thoughts—out of his head and forced a smile.

"You'll tell him, though, right?" she questioned. "After all, something that powerful—I'm sure he'd like to know. And, used properly, it could come in quite useful one day!"

"Sure, Mum, definitely. I'm sure he'll be thrilled."

They continued dinner on a much lighter note, but Jere had a hard time focusing on the conversation. A firesetting gift? No, surely he wouldn't have.... He was sure that whatever had happened in the house had been an accident, perhaps a random burst of his gift. Hell, kids that didn't know how to control their gifts had accidents like that all the time. Although, he had never thought to ask what had occurred that night.

They came back to the house in good spirits, and Jere firmly decided to pretend that nothing had happened. Everything was perfect, why bring up the past and interrupt? They had a few drinks at the restaurant and came home to have more with Wren. They passed the rest of the night talking and playing games, enjoying the rest of the time they had to spend together. Janet left the next morning, nursing a bit of a hangover, as were Wren and Jere. At the train station, she grabbed them both up in a hug, placing a motherly kiss on both their surprised and embarrassed foreheads, and shot a glare of death at the single other passenger who dared to give them a dirty look.

Chapter 42
Do You?

It was nearly June and summer had almost taken hold, freeing Ho-jer from the cold clutches of winter. Things were going well; at the clinic, at home, everywhere. Wren could barely recall the last night he had spent alone, and looked forward to going to bed with his lover every night. During the day, they worked seamlessly togeth-er, at night, they fit seamlessly together.

Since Janet left, Wren had noticed Jere watching him occasion-ally, squinting slightly, as though he were trying to see something there. Wren couldn't help but be uncomfortably reminded of the way that Janet had looked at him, and he wondered what had changed. Had Janet said something? But he had been so careful. So perfect when he was around her.

He asked casually how dinner had gone, and for the first time he could remember, Jere had been almost evasive, looking away as he answered vaguely.

"Well, did she say anything about me?" Wren pressed, digging for information so he would know what he was dealing with, what kinds of things Janet might have mentioned. He hoped he came off simply as an anxious boyfriend.

"She liked you," Jere answered, still evasive. "She said it was a pity that you're a slave, but you know that. Is there something, anything that you were worried about her saying?"

Wren tried not to stiffen at the question. "Of course not."

"You know, if you have anything you wanted to tell me..." Jere shrugged. "You can tell me anything. There's no part of you that I don't love."

Wren was silent. Those kinds of statements were only true until they were disproved, and he was certain that he had things in his past that would absolutely disprove them. If Jere really knew something, why didn't he just come out and say it? "I'd tell you if there was something important."

Jere nodded, and he gave Wren another one of those strange looks, like he hadn't gotten the answer he wanted.

The looks made him nervous, and so did Jere's questions. Odd things, about what it was like when he found out what his gift was, and how did he know, and what else would he have liked to have. Where had these questions even come from? Nobody from a slave state would even think about such questions, and Wren was confused as to why Jere felt it was so important to ask him about it now.

He finally asked Jere about it one night.

"Why are you so interested in gifts all of a sudden?"

Jere shrugged. "My mum and I talked a lot about gifts while she was here. When I was growing up, too, I mean, it is her job and all. Some people have the most fascinating gifts. Don't you ever think about it, the possibilities, what other gift you could have?"

Wren most certainly did not think about those things. He did his best to think as little about gifts as possible. "I guess," he lied. "But it's different, living here."

"I'm sure," Jere relented. "I just wonder what it would be like. To be able to fly. To move things with your mind. To control the weather, or animals, or to make energy or fire. I think it would be amazing."

Wren felt his pulse start to race. The room was suddenly too small and uncomfortably warm, or maybe that was just him. "I just wish I didn't have a physical gift *and* live in a slave state," he mumbled.

"I think you're perfect the way you are," Jere said.

Wren took that as his cue to kiss him, ending the uncomfortable conversation. He noticed Jere watching him over the next few days, when he thought Wren wasn't looking. Once or twice, he had even asked his master about it, but each time, Jere just smiled, shook his head, called him beautiful. He never got a clear answer.

He never really wanted one. He just wanted things to go back to the way that they were. As nice as it had been to meet Janet, he couldn't help feeling that something had shifted between him and Jere since she came, and he could only imagine what she might have told Jere about him. Not knowing was almost worse than facing the consequences of whatever terrible truth it might have been.

They were curled up on the couch together one evening when Jere looked up from his book suddenly. "What do you remember about the fire?"

Wren carefully ignored the cold pit of dread in his stomach at the thought. "Not a whole lot. It was painful and... and a long time ago. What made you think of that?"

Jere was silent for a moment. "The little boy who was in at the clinic today — who burned his hand on the stove. It made me think of you, of how badly burned you were."

Wren thought there was something else there, something more.... "You put me back together again," he forced a smile.

Jere brushed a hand across his leg, so familiar, so comfortable. "What even started it?" he persisted.

"Didn't the accident report say it was some sort of electrical fault? I never really knew. I just remember the fire. And then you." Wren hoped he could bring the conversation back to the present. The present was so much easier to deal with than the past.

Jere smiled at him. "You're probably right. It also commended you for trying to save Matthias."

Wren nodded. It did say that.

"Why would you have saved him?" Jere wondered aloud. "He was nothing but a bastard to you."

Wren was silent for a moment. He forced himself to stay still. To stop trembling before he couldn't stop. "I was his slave. It was my duty. And the next person could have been much worse."

Jere, so perceptive now that they knew each other so well, noticed his fear, noticed his trembling. He certainly couldn't have known what it was from, but he set his book aside and pulled Wren close anyway. "I'm sorry, love," he whispered, kissing his neck. "I didn't mean to bring up bad memories. I understand — it must have been terrible."

Wren closed his eyes, hiding himself. "It's okay," he replied, allowing himself to melt into the familiar body.

Jere didn't press anymore, and Wren was glad to let it go. Too many skeletons hid in that closet, skeletons they'd both be better off ignoring.

But as he lay there in his lover's arms, cold compared to his warmth, he thought about Jere saying "I understand," and he wondered, *do you?*

It was a few days later when they heard a knock at the door. Wren opened it to find a grinning young woman in an SU sweatshirt on his doorstep.

"Hi, Wren!" Kieran stepped through the doorway, catching him in a hug as she did.

He struggled not to pull away from her. "Miss Kieran."

"Ew, Wren, don't!" she protested.

He sighed. The girl had no sense of what was appropriate. "Kieran, then," he acknowledged, damning himself as he smiled a bit in response to her wide grin.

"Jere!" she strolled through the house without waiting for further invitation. "Jere, I have a wonderful idea for you!"

"Shouldn't you be at school?" Jere asked, although he didn't seem overly surprised to see her.

"Spring-Summer break," she said, flouncing down on a chair. "Quarter system, you know. We have this week off, and even though I'm super busy with planning, I have this thing that I wanted to talk to you about, and my family really wanted me to come home, even though I would rather have stayed at University and kept up with my work, well, they said I could use a break too!"

"Glad you're enjoying yourself." Jere's voice sounded slow and overly controlled by comparison.

Wren tried to stop himself from laughing, but was mostly unsuccessful. He took a chair next to Jere, figuring that all social customs were to be damned with Kieran around. He turned to smile at Jere as he felt a hand on his leg.

"So anyway, what we were thinking, is that people really need a place to take their slaves, you know, for medical care, right?" Kieran continued on without waiting for a response. "And so, even though they can take them to a veterinary, well, that's not always the best, because, you know, they're not cut out for it or whatever, and plus the nearest vet isn't even that close to Hojer, but you're, like, right here!"

"Right," Jere tried to make sure he was following her. "Animal healers aren't quite as good a match for humans as human healers are. And vice versa."

"Right. So, what has happened in other states, and what some people have suggested, is that slaves could go and see a regular doctor, see, and then that would be healthier, and it would, more importantly, put the society in mind that slaves are humans, too!"

Wren cringed at the thought that this kid and her "cause" put theoretical social change and paradigm shift above actual, everyday suffering. As the property of a doctor, he had never been taken to a vet's office, but the stories he had heard from those who had made his stomach churn. He thought back to the story Jere's mum had told about the little bird Jere had tried to heal as a boy, the little bird who never flew. He knew of some slaves like that, who never quite recovered.

"See, people take slaves to a vet mainly because it's cheaper," Kieran continued, oblivious to everyone around her. "Like, *way* cheaper, because of the healthcare subsidy, and the different training, and—"

"Yes," Jere interrupted. "We know."

"Well, the thing is, you wouldn't have to do it *any* more cheaply to make it worthwhile," Kieran's eyes glowed as she proposed her plan. "In fact, you could go a little more expensive, because, after all, you're right here! Closer. Less time wasted. And, what's more, people will instantly start seeing that their slaves are healing faster, better—and getting back to work sooner. It's a win-win situation."

Jere nodded. Wren knew he wasn't opposed to the idea, he had actually seen a few slaves as emergency cases, or taken care of those who had been brought along with their masters. Payment tended to be questionable, but Wren knew, as he suspected Kieran did, that Jere would have gladly healed each and every slave in the town for free if need be.

"So, how would I go about promoting this?" he asked. "I mean, it's not as though people would want this advertised."

"Word of mouth," Kieran grinned. "That list of people I sent you a while back — who, by the way, have not heard from you *at all!* They would be the starting group."

Jere didn't comment on his lack of socialization. "I thought they were against slavery?"

"Well, so are you, but you seem to have a slave."

Jere winced at the comment, and Wren gave his hand a squeeze. It was rather adorable how uncomfortable his master was with owning him, after all this time.

"There are plenty of people who've come into slaves through different circumstances," Kieran pointed out. "Gifts they couldn't return, inheritance, pity, whatever. It's a way of life here."

Jere nodded, casting a glance at Wren.

"So, they'll start, they'll consider you their primary doctor not only for themselves, but also for their slaves," Kieran continued. "And then, at social gatherings, at parties, across the fence to the garden — whatever, they'll pass the word on. That you're offering affordable services for slaves, and that their slaves are better and healthier as a result."

"But how would I justify the cost?" Jere asked. "Sure, I can go higher than a vet would, but without the healthcare subsidy, the cost of medical care is astronomical! They couldn't afford to pay that for slaves, and people would be up in arms if I was giving low cost services for no reason."

"Just tell them you aren't using painkillers or something, people have no idea what the costs are for anyway," Kieran shrugged, with a wave of her hand.

"I would *not* consider that!" Jere protested.

"It's called 'lying,' Jere," she pointed out.

Wren laughed. "She's right. People barely understand what their co-pay covers, not to mention what's being used. Tell them you'll only use half of your healing gift, they'll buy it."

Jere considered it. "All right, but what good would this do me?" He held up a hand at Kieran's outraged face. "No, not like that, but I mean, why would I say I wanted to do this? I'm a fucking doctor, not an activist, and the people in Hojer like it that way. What's my excuse?"

"Oh, right! It's extra revenue. It's convenience to your customers. It's a way of giving back to the community," Kieran seemed to be reciting top business models' mottos. "Hell, you could even get away with saying it's professional pride, I mean, you're a doctor, you're supposed to be all snooty and stuck on yourself, right?"

"I think that was a compliment," Jere shook his head, laughing a bit. "I'm up for this."

"Great!" Kieran seemed about to burst with joy. She dug into her back pocket, pulling out a sheet of paper, which she slid across the table to Jere. "This is an outline of how best to go about this. See, pamphlets on slave health, setting up separate exam rooms so free people aren't at risk of sitting where a dirty slave sat, you know, people *will* ask about that, fee structures and explanations, a separate check-in system to make sure that slaves are never prioritized over free people—"

"Wait, this is sounding—"

"She's right, Jere," Wren was surprised to find himself agreeing with the girl. "If you want to do this, you have to do it right, and for Hojer, that means shit like this."

Jere still looked uncomfortable. "This has worked in other places?"

Kieran nodded. "Yep. Really helps to improve the quality of life."

Jere glanced over at Wren. "Would you, I mean, I'd need your help—not just in setting this up, but in keeping it going...."

A part of Wren felt like saying no. Felt like saying he didn't want to get involved in this mess, didn't want to worry about how other slaves felt, didn't want to feel the terror at seeing others like him abused. It was easier to just pretend. But, now that Jere was more comfortable with life in Hojer, what *was* his purpose? How could he prove his usefulness to the man who owned him? If Jere ever decided to break off their relationship, where would that leave him now that his master knew his way around and seemed capable of managing on his own? Encouraging a business move that would more or less *force* Jere to have an extra set of hands cemented his place in the house.

"Of course, I'd be glad to help," he heard himself saying. He damned himself with agreement, but he secured his place at Jere's side.

Kieran and Jere ironed out the rest of the plans, and Wren found himself wondering how much of it was Kieran's "cause," and how much of it was simply her desire to get Jere involved in the social circle. Strangely, for as antisocial as his master could be at times, Jere had connected with two rather persuasive social hubs in town — Kieran, connecting him to the anti-slavery types, and Paltrek, connecting him to the "right" people, and defending his methods and lifestyle with the fierce protectiveness that only young men seemed to feel for one another. Wren had grown more and more used to Paltrek's presence in their life, and took comfort in knowing that little suspicion would ever fall on Jere with that sort of association to fall back on. The Wysocka family, for as strange and petty as they could be in private, were public figureheads, and neither the head of the family or the two ruthless children would hesitate to financially destroy anyone who got between them and their inner circle.

And Kieran? Well, she was enough of a loose cannon that nobody took her seriously. That she was going to University in Jere's hometown was enough for most of the town to accept, and most assumed that he was just pitying her. Jere's friendly, open nature made most underestimate him, which worked in his favor.

After Kieran joined them for dinner, she finally made her way out in a flurry of manic energy, pausing only to wrap her arms around Jere.

"Thank you! You'll be helping the cause so much! I just hope you don't have to stretch yourself too thin!"

Jere smiled back at her. "It's okay. I like to help, and besides, I have the energy."

Kieran smiled back, eyebrow raised. "Do you?"

That night, Wren found himself in the shower with Jere. It was still a relatively new thing for both of them, showering together, but since the first time Wren had slipped in next to him, it felt right, safe, okay to be there. It was stupid really, the hesitation he had held on to for so long. And now, feeling his lover's lips wrapping around his cock while the water streamed down over both of them, Wren wondered why they hadn't been doing this for months. He hated that he was still afraid of so many things. Stupid fear had held him back. What else was it holding him back from? Everything Jere did with him felt wonderful.

Jere was on his knees, he arms wrapped around Wren's legs to keep his balance on the slippery floor. He didn't kneel in the graceful, perfectly trained way that a slave would, but with reckless passion, desire, and need that simply poured from his body. Wren fisted his hair, jerking him closer when he wanted to, forcing his cock into his mouth and down his throat with punishing roughness that had Jere whimpering under him. The fingers that caressed his ass only added to the ecstasy for Wren, as he trusted his lover completely in that regard. Jere had never gone any further than Wren wanted.

Reflecting on Jere's valiant self-control, Wren felt himself coming, exploding into Jere's mouth, and jerked Jere's head down one last time, holding him tightly as he felt his mouth working, his throat struggling to swallow. Wren fought with himself, wanting to hold him there forever. He remembered the last time he had held him there too long, and Jere had struggled to breathe, leaving Wren feeling terribly guilty. He moaned with continued longing as he pulled Jere away from him a bit, trying to remind himself that this much control came with quite a bit of responsibility as well.

The water washed away anything excess, and Jere gently continued to suck him as he grew soft, before standing, sliding his body up the whole way, and kissing him on the mouth.

"God, Jere," Wren moaned. "I can't wait to get you into bed and do the same to you!"

Neither one of them liked Wren on his knees. They had tried it, twice, actually, and Wren couldn't get comfortable, which meant Jere couldn't relax, which meant they ended up in bed together. Neither minded.

"I could think of some other things you could do to me, too," Jere wriggled his ass suggestively as he turned off the shower and grabbed towels for both of them.

Wren reached out and swatted playfully at the moving target. "Shameless," he muttered, allowing himself to be dried off.

"But you love it," Jere grinned at him, sure of himself. He let the towel drop to the floor and sprinted to the bed, jumping on it and flopping down on his back, his cock already erect and waiting.

Wren pounced after him, biting and kissing and touching everything *but* his cock, until he felt him start to squirm and heard him whine. "Oh, am I neglecting something?" he teased, purposely speaking close enough so his breath warmed up the cock he was so pointedly ignoring.

"Wren..." Jere pleaded, his eyes hungry. "You promised!"

Wren laughed a little at his desperation. He raised his finger to his own mouth, sucking it slowly, grinning back at Jere, whose eyes were glued to him. Removing the saliva coated finger from his mouth, he trailed it down the tip of Jere's cock, swirled it around his balls, and pressed it against his ass, rewarded by a series of yelps and jerks as Jere tried not to move too much.

"Jesus, Wren," Jere panted. "Feeling a bit evil tonight?"

"Mmm," Wren smiled in return, grabbing Jere's cock in one hand while working his finger into his ass with the other, roughly, quickly. He squeezed hard on his cock, not letting up until he heard whimpers that went from pleasure to pain. He knew Jere liked to play on that line, and Wren was starting to enjoy it as well. It felt good, and it was wonderful to see his master enjoy himself; having such unquestioned control helped him to relax more than anything he had ever imagined.

"Reach over and get me the lube," he ordered, releasing his grip on Jere's cock ever so slightly, but twisting his finger around in his ass.

Jere's eyes widened a bit. "But, I...." He reached his arm out as far as he could without moving, coming up a little over an inch short.

"Do it." Wren's voice brooked no arguments.

Grinning apprehensively, Jere stretched and twisted, as Wren held perfectly still. As Jere pulled away, Wren's hand didn't release on his cock any more, pulling it roughly, stretching it almost. As Jere twisted, he twisted around Wren's finger, rigid in his ass, and he cried out and tensed around it. Wren smiled, enjoying the control. He had been taken by surprise too many times in the past few days; it was time for him to call the shots.

With a lot of whimpers, Jere managed to grab the lube, and he offered it to Wren, who shook his head. "Pour it on. Let's see how good your aim is."

"Jesus!" Jere hissed as he sat up. The hands at his cock and ass were unrelenting. With shaking hands, he let a bit drip down, onto his cock, over Wren's hands.

Wren used his thumb to help move the lube onto his finger, and slid it in and out of Jere, more forcefully now that he was sure he wouldn't hurt him for real. Another finger joined a second later, and Jere was pumping up against him in earnest.

"Fuck, Wren!"

Wren smiled, slipping a third finger in to join the first two. "It would be in your best interest not to come just yet," he taunted, sliding his hand up and down Jere's cock as he did so.

Jere moaned, and his thrusts became a little calmer. His knuckles, Wren noticed, satisfied, were white as they clutched the sheets.

"Do you want to feel my lips right here?" Wren teased, squeezing the head of Jere's cock almost cruelly.

"Yes, yes, please, god, Wren please!"

Wren didn't respond for a moment, just shoved his fingers into his ass a few more times until he heard him keening in pleasure. He gripped the base of his cock and held him down, almost painfully, before wrapping his mouth around him.

Jere didn't move, freezing as he knew he was supposed to, but the way he tensed around Wren's fingers indicated how much of a struggle it was. Wren had come to love that struggle, and expertly worked his cock, running his tongue over and under and around it, sucking gently for a second, then ravenously, swallowing him whole, even grazing him oh-so-lightly with his teeth. The whole time his fingers were inside, thrusting, moving, pressing the spots that drove the man crazy.

It wasn't long before Jere was begging. "Please, Wren, please, I can't, I can't wait anymore, please, let me come, let me...." his voice trailed off, and Wren actually felt him pulling away, squirming down into the mattress as if he could escape.

Wren laughed, his mouth still around Jere's cock, causing him to moan desperately. *"Don't even think about it,"* he warned.

"Please, Wren!"

The sound of Jere begging him made him feel extra evil, and he pressed down harder, crushing any chances of escape while ramming into Jere with his fingers. *"I can go down further, too."*

"Wren, please, honestly, I won't be able to stop myself!" Jere managed, his hands desperately clinging to Wren's shoulders.

Wren slid back. "No," he said firmly, thrilled when Jere froze. Wren moved his mouth back into position, wrapped his lips around his teeth, and bit down carefully. He squeezed just below the head of Jere's cock, cutting his excitement short and forcing his orgasm back for a little longer.

Jere yelped and moaned. "Fuck. Fuck fuck fuck, Wren!"

He resumed sucking him.

Once Jere had again been driven to the point of helpless begging and whining, Wren pulled back, for real this time, and slid up, removing his fingers and immediately placing the head of his cock in their place.

"Yes, yes, please fuck me, please, fucking fuck me already!" Jere cried out.

Wren placed a hand over his mouth, leaning over him and loving the feeling. "Don't you think I'm going to do that already?" he challenged.

Silenced, Jere nodded helplessly, pressing closer and helping Wren to bury the tip of his cock inside of him.

For one second, maybe two, Wren was still, allowing Jere a moment to adjust to him inside. His body was taut with anticipation, and Wren enjoyed making him wait. He pulled back a fraction of an inch before slamming forward again, making Jere cry out under his hand and thrust back against him, clutching at his back, his legs, anything he could get a hold on.

The whimpers from Jere felt as good as the tight squeeze around his cock. Heedless of anything but his own pleasure, Wren kept thrusting, faster and faster, his speed gift aiding him in setting a brutal pace. He forced his way inside of Jere's body with the same insistence and brutality as those who used to fuck him and he enjoyed it. He felt Jere squirming and struggling underneath him, felt the burn where their skin was touching, and he enjoyed this, too. He had everything under control. Jere couldn't ask him uncomfortable questions, he didn't have to avoid or evade or give good answers. He didn't have to worry or think or care about anything but getting off.

A whimper, an actual pained whimper pulled him back to reality. He didn't know when he had closed his eyes, but he opened them to see Jere wincing a little as Wren kept thrusting into him. He took his hand off Jere's mouth and grabbed his cock instead, fisting it and pumping it as he thrust in and out of him. He felt so good, his cock deep inside of Jere, legs wrapped around his back, both of them moaning out their pleasure together. Neither of them lasted long, and both were soon gasping with their release.

Wren let himself collapse on top of Jere, heedless of the mess between them. Sliding out of him, he moved up to cup Jere's face in his hands, kissing him deeply for a few more minutes as they panted together. Finally, he rolled off, to lie next to him. Their arms and legs remained entwined.

"Jesus, Wren," Jere managed, finally. "I don't know whether to say 'fuck you' or 'thank you!'"

Wren grinned at him. "Well, then, how about if I just say 'you're welcome' and we call it even?"

Jere snuggled into him. "I like that plan," he mumbled, pressing close.

Wren grabbed the towel he had thought to bring along and had placed next to the bed, cleaning them up a bit before settling back in. The frantic excitement that had come along with the sex was fading, but he still felt high on the fact that Jere had gone along with it, had given Wren so much trust and freedom with his body. As many times as he said he trusted Jere, Wren was constantly redefining the word, scared by how close he was to really trusting the man. Jere always made the first move, opening himself up and allowing Wren to explore and test both their boundaries. There were so few barriers left between them. Wren almost felt safe.

"Jere?"

"Yeah?" Jere's voice was soft and sated and content.

"I, uh," Wren forced himself past his nervousness and pushed the words out all at once. "I think I want you to fuck me."

Jere was quiet for a moment, his hand stroking Wren's back lightly without interruption. "Yeah?" he said softly.

"Yeah." Wren didn't want to get rid of every barrier between them, he couldn't let himself, but he could get rid of this one. Jere let himself be tied down, ordered around, fucked raw tonight—Wren could think of no better way to repay him, to show Jere how much it meant. He knew how good it felt, how intimate it made him feel with Jere, and he had to make sure that Jere shared that feeling. The closer they were, the harder it would be for Jere to reject him later, no matter what might happen. Jere had been saying that he loved him for a while, now, but Wren felt safer taking this extra step. His memories of past experiences were awful, but he trusted Jere enough to believe that he would at least minimize the pain. Besides, it would be worth it to have that final bargaining chip.

Jere moved back, ever so slightly, and looked into Wren's eyes. "At the risk of looking a gift fuck in the mouth, I'm curious—you asked me this once—why?"

Wren shrugged. His main reasons were too private, too awful to explain. He looked away until a careful hand brushing his cheek brought him back. "I... I like doing it a lot. And I thought maybe you would, too."

"Mmm," Jere nodded, barely brushing his lips across Wren's. "I most certainly would, love. But, is there any other reason? Is it just about my pleasure?"

Wren felt himself going red. He felt stupid; of course Jere wouldn't just fuck him and appreciate it, he'd want to ask more questions and understand why and he would see through Wren's plans. He wished he had brought it up while they were already passionate and on top of each other. Maybe he never should have brought it up. He felt himself turning away.

"Hey, hey," Jere said softly, cupping his chin and bringing his face back up. "Wren, there's no right or wrong answer. I'm just curious."

"You seem to like it when I do it," Wren mumbled. "A lot. And I, I never liked it, but I never liked a lot of things before that I like with you now." Getting head, showering together, sleeping together—they were all things that had terrified him, that he had first done to some extent to please Jere, but he loved them all now. If things went as planned, not only would he ensure Jere's continued affections, but he had some hope that he might even come to like it. He had missed out on so much by being rigid and afraid. He just wanted to push past this final physical boundary between them. "So, I figured, why not try and see, and maybe, you know, maybe it would be good. Or something."

Jere smiled at him, kissing him again before going further. "Of course I like it. It feels great. *You* feel great. And I will do everything in my power to make it feel just as wonderful for you."

Wren considered this. "You mean it?"

"Of course."

"And it won't hurt?"

Jere was quiet for a moment, long enough for Wren to feel anxious about what his answer was going to be. "It won't hurt. I promise."

Wren hesitated. "How can you be sure?" he challenged. He had resigned himself to the pain, it had always hurt, and he could take it so they could get past this final obstacle. A part of him would have felt better if Jere hadn't made a promise like that.

"Because, kid, I am *that* good," Jere grinned at him, the cocky look back on his face.

Wren smiled in spite of himself. "But didn't it hurt the first time I...."

Jere smiled, sighing happily at the memory. "It did, but I didn't mind. As you seem quite aware, I'm okay with a little bit of pain. But I know you don't enjoy it, and so I'll make sure it doesn't happen, all right? You have my word. Besides, if I recall, I just wanted you to slam into me that night, but my plans for you would involve a lot more time and preparation."

Wren relaxed in his lover's arms. The plan was finalized. They would do it, and there wouldn't be any doubt in his or Jere's mind that this thing between them was real. They could have some sort of perfect love, and Jere would never leave him or reject him, no matter what happened or what he might find out. "Okay. I believe you. I trust you." Giving into the warmth, the closeness, the hands playing with his hair, he felt himself drifting off to sleep.

Jere's voice was almost sad, a half-dream as Wren dozed off. "Do you?"

Chapter 43
A Gift

When Jere awoke the next day, the brief, promising conversation he and Wren had the night before was the first thing on his mind. Looking over at his boy, surprised that he had woken up first, the only thing he wanted to do was take him right then and there.

As it was, he leaned over and placed a light, undemanding kiss on his lips. Wren was often displeased by overly forward advances when he hadn't quite woken up.

His eyes fluttered open, the bright blue peeking out first from the right side, then the left, then both. "Hi," he said with a smile.

"Hi, yourself," Jere responded, pulling him closer and kissing him a bit more deeply.

"You're up early," Wren said, grinning. While Wren usually woke up early of his own accord, left to his own devices, Jere slept late or until the alarm woke him up.

"Guess I slept well," Jere replied. *And I feel like a little kid at Christmas.* He figured it was wiser not to add that second thought.

"Mmm, did I tire you out last night or something?"

"You know you did!" Jere flashed him a smile before trailing his hand down his back, squeezing at his ass until he heard him draw a happy breath.

"You gonna tire me out tonight?" Wren challenged, a smirk on his face.

"I can think of nothing I'd like better. In fact, I'd take you, right here, right now...." He felt Wren shudder against him. "...But I really want to take my time with you."

They settled on thrusting against one another until they both came, leaving them just enough time to shower and get dressed for the workday. By lunchtime they were nearly on top of one another, and they just *might* have closed up the clinic a bit early in anticipation. Dinner was devoured more than eaten, and they all but raced into the bedroom, smiling wide and grabbing each other all over.

Lying in bed, Wren was straddling Jere, his knees spread to either side of Jere's hips as they kissed. "God, I want you!"

Jere felt his cock harden in response. "Me too, love, me too."

Wren slid down his neck, kissing and biting just the way Jere liked it, making him squirm and moan. Jere leaned into it, taking in the feeling, the excitement, the familiar weight on top of him. With reluctance and amazing self-control, he gently put a hand on Wren's shoulder as he dipped down lower.

"You first tonight, love," he stopped him, pulling him back up. "I want tonight to be about you."

Wren blushed a bit, smiling. "Okay," he agreed. "But I still get to undress you!"

Jere let himself go lax, a willing toy to be undressed at his lover's whim. It was a quick process, and he found himself naked underneath the younger man. "Better?" he asked as Wren looked over him appraisingly.

"Much," Wren agreed. His cocky demeanor cracked a bit. "And... and me?"

"It's up to you," Jere said. He knew the kid could get nervous about things like undressing, and he was never sure exactly what the best way to deal with that nervousness was going to be. Asking always worked.

"You can," Wren said shyly.

"Then come here," Jere beckoned him closer with one finger, and Wren leaned down.

Pulling him into a kiss, Jere started by running his hands across his back smoothly, calming him, then slipping his fingers up and underneath the thin cotton. Gently, he stroked across his back, feeling the muscles before working his way to the front. He moved over his stomach and chest before capturing the bottom of the garment and pulling it up, revealing the body he had grown so familiar with. Wren cooperated, lifting his arms as Jere slid it over his head.

Jere lifted his upper body a bit, pulling him closer to Wren's chest, tracing his lips across it ever so briefly before settling them back again. "Beautiful," he whispered, looking up at Wren, who blushed even as he smiled.

They kept kissing as Jere's hands trailed lower, dipping below Wren's waistband, cupping his ass and squeezing just a little, making him squirm. Jere held back his own moan. He slid his hands around Wren's hips and made quick work of the fastening. His hands moved inside the pants, around to the front, and he felt Wren's hips, his legs, and the barest hint of his cock.

Wren ground against him as he did, and he took a little longer before sliding his pants down, freeing up that very cock for him to play with a little more.

When Wren was moaning above him, Jere backed off for a moment. "Switch places with me," he suggested. "There's far more where this is coming from."

Wren lay down on his back, and Jere carefully removed his pants the rest of the way, leaving them both naked. Gently, he brushed his hands along Wren's inner thighs, which he had pressed together.

"Do I need a magic word?" he said lightly, only half-teasing.

"You'll be gentle?" Wren's face was open, trusting, hopeful.

Jere wanted to kill everyone who had ever hurt him. "I promise," he said sincerely, looking into his eyes.

Wren allowed his legs to relax and part, and Jere worked his way up them, kissing, touching, licking all the way up to his cock, which he took into his mouth very, very briefly.

"Jere…" Wren whined, needy.

He smiled, pulling back. "This is just the beginning, wait and see." He kept up the pattern, moving across and around his cock, playing with his balls, and dipping lower, tracing his tongue across his ass, dipping it in and out of his hole, something they had both come to enjoy quite a bit.

"Jere, god," Wren moaned.

"You feeling good, then?" Jere smirked. Wren was melting like butter under his hands and tongue. This was exactly what he wanted.

"Mmhmm," Wren stretched his legs out a bit, then parted them again.

Taking Wren's cock deep into his mouth for a few more seconds, Jere then pulled back. "Stay just like this," he said, standing up and going for the bottle of lube, returning quickly to where he had been. He was a little sad, but not at all surprised, to find Wren a little tense.

"Jere…" his voice held the edge of panic.

Jere ran his hand up and down the inside of his leg, soothing, calming. "It's okay, love, I swear, I know what I'm doing."

Wren's breath was still shallow, burdened.

Jere pressed his face to Wren's leg, kissing it slowly and softly, working his way up. "You can trust me, Wren, I wouldn't ever hurt you. And you're free to call this off whenever you want, all right? Doesn't matter what we're doing, just say the word and we will stop. I won't mind."

"But I—I want you to," Wren said, sounding only half-sure. "I want you to be able to."

Jere didn't bother arguing about Wren's motivations to do this. He wrapped his lips around Wren's cock, still half-hard. "*Just relax. Relax and trust me, I'll take care of everything else.*"

While he slowly continued working Wren's cock, he pressed his fingers against his ass, coated in lube, making the entire entrance slippery. He did nothing but apply pressure, swirling his tongue around the head of his cock as he did. After a few minutes, he felt Wren relax, and he pulled back a bit.

"I'm gonna put just one finger in, okay? Stay relaxed, and tell me if you want me to move it or go deeper or take it out." He spoke softly, and watched Wren as he nodded, eyes closed.

Ever so carefully, he pressed his finger in, pleased to see it slide in easily. He heard a sharp intake of breath and stopped, looking at Wren. With his free hand, he stroked his hip. "You okay?"

Wren nodded, then was silent for a moment. "Yeah, it, it feels fine."

Jere took Wren's cock in his mouth again, giving Wren a chance to figure out whether he really did like this or not. Wren didn't tell him otherwise, so he continued what he was doing, finger barely inside of him, and worked his cock for a while.

"It might feel good if you move a bit," he suggested, wishing Wren would take the lead.

A few seconds later, Wren did just that, sliding a bit further onto his finger, and sighing a bit in pleasure as he did. Jere kept his cock in his mouth, enjoying the feeling of Wren pumping in and out of his mouth as he moved experimentally over his finger. Finally, he needed a bit of a break, and pulled back again.

"You enjoying this?" he checked. Wren looked so nervous and serious, he wasn't sure.

"Mmhmm," Wren squirmed slowly against his finger.

"You ready for another?"

"I think so. If you want to." Wren stilled.

"Keep moving," Jere suggested, a knowing smile on his face as he squeezed some more lube out. "You can take me in when you're ready."

Wren nodded, continuing to move slowly, up and down, even as Jere slid another finger next to the first. Wren caught his eyes as he slid over the very tip, then a bit further, then all the way down on both fingers, causing him to moan unexpectedly.

"Still feeling good?" Jere checked.

"God, yes!" Wren let out a moan as he kept working himself on Jere's fingers.

Jere was relieved. Wren seemed to be enjoying this, physically, anyway, but he was so tense and serious. The clear answer helped convince Jere that Wren was just nervous. "Is it okay if I move them?"

"Yes," Wren said, slowing his thrusts down.

Jere worked his fingers carefully and slowly, twisting, caressing, sliding in and out, stretching ever so slightly before going to back to the soft strokes like Wren had been doing himself. He smiled encouragingly, knowing Wren was watching him, and brushed his fingers over his prostate.

Wren yelped. "What are you doing? Is it supposed to feel like that?"

Jere heard as much lust as he did fear in the questions, but he kept going. "Well, did it feel good?"

"That was… oh my god," Wren panted. "It felt really good."

"That's exactly how it's supposed to feel," Jere promised him. Wren continued to moan and rock against him, and Jere moved his fingers inside him, exploring and stretching until he was sure Wren had relaxed. He grabbed the lube again, making sure the passage was as slick as possible.

"Another one, it might be a little tight, but I'll go very slowly, and I want you to tell me if it doesn't feel right, okay?" Jere warned him, pressing his ring finger against the entrance.

Wren, mostly caught up in passion, just nodded, continuing to push against Jere. He slipped the third finger in, letting out a slight moan himself at the tight entrance, and eased it about halfway in when he heard Wren say "Stop!"

He froze, not moving in or out, and gently stroked Wren's leg with his free hand. "It's all right, just breathe," he said softly, holding still and trying to will his fingers to be thinner.

Wren drew in a few shuddering breaths before speaking. "S-sorry. It's just...."

"It's okay," Jere kissed his legs, up and down, still keeping his hand still. "Relax for me and take a deep breath."

Wren did as he was asked, and when he did, Jere slid his fingers out, immediately sliding them back in, but only barely. "How's this?"

Wren breathed a sigh of relief. "Good. Great. Thank you."

Jere said nothing, drew his tongue up the length of his cock. "When you're ready, slide down my fingers," he instructed. "I'll be busy down here."

With that, he took the length of Wren's cock into his mouth, working it up and down. Slowly but surely, he felt Wren starting to move to his rhythm, working himself further down onto Jere's fingers. Suddenly, his fingers were deep inside. Not wanting to spoil anything, Jere pulled back from his cock, grinning, and began to tease him.

"Jere, oh my god, this is good, this is so fucking good," Wren moaned, rocking on his hand. "Oh my god, I've never felt this way!"

Jere rested his head on Wren's knee, calming his own urge to ram into him immediately. "I keep my promises," he said with a smirk, Wren's dilated eyes catching his. "I wouldn't do it if you weren't enjoying it."

"Oh, god, I could come right now," Wren gasped, thrusting harder.

Jere smiled. He didn't pull back, but he didn't keep moving his fingers inside, either. "That's up to you, love. It's sometimes hard to keep going after you have, but if you want it, it's yours for the taking. We can keep trying after you've come, or we can try again tomorrow."

Wren slowed down his movements, though it was clearly a struggle. He shook his head. "No. If I wait, I might not want to do it again. I want you to fuck me. Tonight. Now. And I want you to make me come while you do."

Jere did his best not to lose it just thinking about it, reminding himself that this wasn't about him. He was ready for sex anytime, but for Wren, this was obviously a challenge.

"You're as ready as I'm going to get you," Jere said, his voice low and sultry. "So tell me when you want it, and I'm yours."

Wren grinned at him, his face shining. "I want you now."

Jere took Wren's cock in his mouth one last time as he slid his fingers out, then moved to slide up between his legs. Wren started twisting, and Jere put a light hand on his hip. "Where you going?"

"I thought, didn't you want...?" Wren looked uncertain.

Jere got it. "No, love, I want to see your face. I want you just like you are. Well, maybe a few pillows under you, like this...." He pulled a few down and slid them under his lover, supporting his back and lifting his ass up a bit.

He slid up between Wren's legs, gently using his knees to press them apart. "You comfortable?"

Wren closed his eyes for a minute, but nodded.

Jere felt Wren's nervousness through the mind connection, no matter how much he was trying to hide it. Every step seemed to be a new hurdle to cross, and as they came closer to the actual act, Wren was growing more nervous. Jere lubed up his cock and guided it toward Wren's entrance, stopping when he just barely touched skin.

Using his other hand, he traced patterns across Wren's stomach, dropping down occasionally and stroking his cock.

"I was going to have you on top," he explained softly, still teasing him with his hands. "But I know it's sometimes harder to relax that way. Let me do the work, you just concentrate on breathing and relaxing and thinking about how good you feel, all right? Tell me if it's not good, I'll do something different."

"Okay," Wren said, and Jere detected a trace of doubt in his voice.

"You can still tell me to stop, love," Jere reminded him, wishing that Wren would only believe such a thing.

Wren shook his head. "I want you to," he said again, although the look on his face suggested that he was more determined than anything else. "Do it, now, please?"

Jere continued to touch Wren's stomach, chest, legs, and cock, hoping to calm him down. Jere wanted this just as much, but he didn't want Wren to feel forced or pressured, not even by himself. As Wren started to respond more genuinely to his touch, Jere slowly increased the pressure of his cock against Wren's ass, trying not to think about how good it would feel to bury himself deep, deep inside. Finally, he felt Wren relaxing, opening to him a bit, and he slipped the head of his cock in.

For a second, he felt blissful joy, warmth, tightness... *fear, nervousness, panic!*

Reacting purely on instinct, Jere froze, and before he had a chance to think, his gift had taken over, and he realized he had blocked the pain that his lover was about to feel.

"Jere?" Wren's voice was alarmed.

"You're tensing up, kid," Jere said softly. He was almost afraid to move, afraid to even speak too loudly.

"Jere, what...?"

"You might feel a little numb," Jere said, with a bit of a wince. "I promised you it wouldn't hurt, and I didn't consider that it might hurt anyway if you tensed up while I was *inside* of you, and this was the best I could do."

"You're blocking the pain?" Wren asked in disbelief.

"Pain, pleasure. There's not much of a difference, biologically." Jere shook his head. Perhaps he had overreacted. "I know this is a big step for you, and I couldn't bear the thought of hurting you."

Wren reached up and touched his face. "Thank you. I never thought anyone would do something like this for me."

Jere felt himself blush. "I promised you," he said with a shrug.

"You can, you know, let me feel it," Wren offered.

"When I feel you relax, I will," Jere smiled back at him. He palmed Wren's cock. "If this is any indication, you're not turned off by this."

Wren leaned back and folded his arms behind his head. He breathed slowly, carefully, and Jere felt his body start to relax. As he did that, Jere continued stroking him, just as slowly, in time with his breaths, and soon he felt the painfully tight grip on his cock relax. He stopped blocking sensation for Wren, watching carefully to make sure he wasn't in pain again.

Wren drew in a sharp breath the second Jere pulled his gift back, arms flying up and clutching Jere's arms tightly, almost painfully.

"God, Wren, you feel so good!"

Wren said nothing, just whimpered in ecstasy.

Carefully, Jere slid in a little deeper, pausing to give Wren a few moments to adjust. He continued to stroke his cock as he did, very softly, not wanting this to end too soon. When he didn't hear or feel any complaints, he went deeper still, drawing a moan from Wren.

He stilled. "How is this?" he asked, praying for a good answer.

"It's…" Wren struggled with words. "It's good. It's a little… it burns a little but it doesn't hurt. I think — you're being so careful. I think I want you to move. Right? That would be better, right?"

Jere was perfectly aware that he was being careful, and actually a little surprised that Wren seemed so shocked. "I think we'll both enjoy it."

With painstaking slowness, he slid out a tiny bit, then back in, out, and in, working his hand up and down on Wren's cock as he did. Wren moaned underneath him, his face twisted on the very edge of pleasure as Jere coaxed his way deeper and deeper.

"Kiss me." Wren's face was dead serious, and left no room for argument.

Jere leaned forward, mindful of his cock, and Wren's cock, and his hand, and his legs, and as he let his weight rest on Wren's body, he felt a familiar rush of fear, and was reminded how much the boy hated being held down. He paused.

"Are you sure you—"

"Kiss me, damn you!" Wren snapped, his face set and determined.

Jere felt a hand coming up on the back of his head, and he was suddenly jerked down, meeting Wren's mouth before he had a chance to resist again. Not that he minded at all—Wren plundered his mouth like he owned it, and Jere was happy to let him. As he did, he felt Wren's slim legs coming up around him, and he allowed him to set the pace that way, slipping in and out, thrusting gently at first, then harder and faster as Wren writhed underneath of him the same way. Wren did always seem more comfortable having more control in bed. He felt Wren's cock pressed between them, hard and almost throbbing, and he knew how close he was to coming.

"Wanna feel you come inside me," Wren kept their mouths pressed together. Jere had rarely been so appreciative of mindspeak.

"When you do," he managed, words of any sort seeming like a foreign and unpleasant concept to him at the moment. He was almost painfully close to coming as it was.

Wren moaned under him, and Jere felt him tighten, squeezing around his cock until it almost hurt. As he felt the warm sensation of come on his stomach, he let himself go, thrusting once, then again, then finding that beautiful release of his own.

He kept moving, thrusting, and kissing for a few more seconds, riding the surge of his and Wren's orgasms until they were both shuddering. He started to pull out, but was stopped by legs pressed against his ass.

"Not yet," Wren muttered, his eyelids drooping even as he said it. "Don't go yet."

Jere smiled, resting on top of him. He lay his head on Wren's chest, feeling the warmth radiating from his body and listening to his racing heartbeat. "Not going anywhere," he promised, reaching up to run his hands through Wren's hair.

Wren leaned into the touch, moaning as he did. "That was so fucking good."

Jere smiled. "I'm glad I could make it good for you," he said. "I thought I might have lost you a few times."

"I was so fucking nervous," Wren shook his head. "God. I didn't think I'd be so scared!"

"You had reason to be," Jere said lightly. They didn't need to think of any of those reasons right now. "Thank you. For letting me show you something new."

"It was, I mean, it was good for you, right?" Wren took a deep, happy breath, letting his legs drop and stretching a bit. "I wanted it to be good for you."

"It was perfect," Jere reassured him. "What else would it be? Now I've had every part of you."

Wren closed his eyes. "You're right," he said quietly. "You have."

Jere slid out, moving to grab a towel, and cleaned them up. Within seconds, he had pulled Wren into his arms and onto the cleaner side of the bed, curling around him protectively as Wren gazed up at him with tired eyes.

"I love you," Jere whispered in his ear.

Wren pressed against him. "Thank you. This was the best gift anyone's ever given me."

Chapter 44
Burning Questions

Two weeks had passed since the first time Jere had taken Wren. It had happened a few more times, and each had been wonderful, in its own way, although nothing compared to that first time. Despite the awkward moments and the fear, that first time had been perfect, and Wren had enjoyed it enough to ask shyly that they do it again. In between, Jere was still begging to have his own ass pounded regularly, a request that Wren was happy to fill. While they liked it both ways, Wren topping seemed strangely more natural, more comfortable, and they filled most of their spare time with sex and touching.

Everything was perfect, right? Jere couldn't quite put a finger on it, but he felt burdened with some sense of unease. That was a lie; of course he could put his finger on it. It was what his mum had said to him, what she had told him that last night at the restaurant.

A firesetting gift.

Why did those three words come out of her mouth? Worse, why did his head automatically go to the most heinous place possible? He had asked Wren about it, here and there, subtle comments. Once he had even been daring enough to ask him about the fire, but the poor kid had started getting scared, trembling in his arms like he hadn't in months. Jere didn't like it. He didn't like questioning him, and he certainly didn't like doubting the sweet, soft boy who trusted him with everything else. Who was he to demand access to this particular memory? Just because his mum said he had a firesetting gift didn't mean anything. Maybe his mum was wrong.

But the signs were there. What he had explained away and ignored earlier all fit together now — the way Wren could broadcast his emotions so strongly, the way he was always so warm — especially his hands, especially when they were touching him, making his skin light up....

...But even the way that he worked the mind connection was unusual. Not quite that of someone with a physical gift, not quite that of someone who had a mental gift, either. And always guarded. Like he was trying to hide something.

Jere had always figured it was part of the kid's terrible trauma — the brief glimpses he had been allowed to access about his life at the training facility and with Matthias were enough to give anyone nightmares, and he had always assumed that Wren was just reluctant to think about those things, much less let Jere access them completely. Forcing Wren to think and talk about those things just seemed cruel. But some parts of the blocked areas didn't seem to match up with that, and despite the fact that Jere didn't want to pry, he found himself wondering more and more.

Did it matter, really, if Wren had secrets? Everyone had secrets, especially someone who had been through so much, like Wren had. Did it mean that Jere loved him any less, or that he didn't know him? He didn't think that anything he could hear could make him love him less, although he wondered how he could really say that if he had never been in a situation where he found out about one of those secrets. It wasn't in Jere's nature to pry — he had always been the type to accept and trust whatever he was told at face value, at least when it came to his loved ones. But the idea that Wren might be hiding something so damning had crept into his life, into his mind, and had sullied the perfect memories he and Wren were still making. Even more, he couldn't help but wonder why he hadn't mentioned a thing about it to Wren.

His mum had hounded him in her last letter about what Wren had said when Jere told him about the dual gift. He hadn't replied yet, because he hadn't yet mentioned it to Wren. A cynical part of him would have put money on the fact that his slave knew exactly what gifts he had, but didn't trust him enough to say so. That was the part that hurt — of everything they had been through, Wren didn't trust him enough for this. Jere couldn't help but think that maybe he was hiding other things as well, and that bothered him the most. He shared everything with Wren. Even the fact that he hadn't asked him about the gift yet made him uncomfortable, because Wren deserved to know.

Jere couldn't deal with the uncertainty anymore. If Wren knew, then why would he hide it, and if he didn't know, then why was he so secretive? Jere could only imagine that he must have felt guilty, that the accident that caused the fire must have scared him beyond belief. Perhaps it was the first time he realized he could do something like that? He would have been scared, if he had been in Wren's position. Or maybe he had known, and just hadn't realized how destructive it could be — certainly, the fire was destructive, nearly costing Wren his life. Maybe he was scared that he would be blamed. A darker part in Jere's head wondered if it was an accident at all, but of course it was. Of course that's what had happened. He just needed to find out the details.

They went to bed together, as they always did, and Wren slid over to his side of the bed, a smile on his face. This would be the time that they usually cuddled and more.

Jere pulled him close, cupping his face as he kissed him. When he felt Wren's hands start sliding down his stomach, Jere caught his wrist lightly, stopping him.

"Can we talk for a bit?" he smiled, trying to keep his voice bright.

"Sure," Wren smiled back at him, unguarded and careless. He arched his body against Jere, slow and seductive. "Maybe I can tell you all the things I'd like to do to you tonight."

Jere couldn't help being aroused at the touch, but he needed to figure out what was going on. He put his hands on Wren's shoulders, gently pushing him back. "Really, I want to talk with you about something."

Jere sat up, leaning against the headboard. Wren slinked up his body, capturing Jere's lips for a few seconds before he found the resolve to pull away.

"Ooh, a sitting-up talk," Wren grinned, his hands exploring now instead of his lips. "Must be important."

"Yes," Jere tried to keep the irritation out of his voice as he caught Wren's hands again. "Wren, seriously, I just want to talk with you."

"Can't you think of better things I could do with your mouth?" Wren asked, his voice taking on an insistent tone that Jere was unused to. It didn't fit with the underlying fear he could feel through the mind connection. Wren brought his leg up, rubbing it between Jere's, knowing exactly where to go with it.

"Wren, stop!" Jere protested. He twisted his body away.

Wren looked back at him, hurt. "What is there to talk about? I'm happy. You're happy."

"I just want to talk," Jere repeated, holding his arms out. He pulled Wren close and let him rest his head on his shoulder, hoping he was making a big deal out of nothing. He wasn't quite sure where to begin. "You told me, the other night, you said that you trust me."

Wren nodded. "Of course. I've trusted you for a while now."

Jere smiled back at him, hoping it didn't look as bittersweet as it felt. "Yeah, but often, before, you were selective about how you'd say it—you know, that you trusted me not to hurt you, or you trusted me to take care of you. This seemed, the other day, like a blanket statement."

Wren laughed, but the emotion didn't reach his eyes. He was suddenly guarded. "What's this about? Of course I trust you!"

"Then, if you trust me, you'll be truthful with me, right?"

"I trust you enough to kiss me," Wren offered, leaning in with a coy smile on his face.

Jere pulled away, shaking his head.

"You're the only one that I've ever trusted to fuck me and not hurt me," Wren tried, the smile starting to fade. "Is that it, do you want to—"

"Wren, all I want right now is to talk!" Jere felt a sense of dread. Nobody tried this hard to avoid talking about something, not unless something was wrong.

"Jere?" Wren's face started looking alarmed. "What's going on?"

"What is your gift, Wren?" Jere asked quietly, not wanting to hear the answer.

Wren's laugh was nervous now. "Jere, it's a speed gift, just like it's always been! Do you want me to demonstrate? There's that thing that I do that you really like...."

"What else?"

"I... people only have one gift."

Wren was stiff in his arms. Jere was starting to feel ill. "You know that's not true, don't you?"

"Jere...." Wren looked at him in fear, his eyes widening.

He couldn't do it, couldn't drag this out any longer. He deserved the truth. Wren deserved the truth. "Wren, my mum told me, when she was visiting. She knew. She picked up on it. And you... you had to know, this whole time, didn't you?"

Wren jerked away, violent and scared, and Jere let him. What else was he to do?

Curling up at the far end of the bed, Wren wrapped his arms around his knees, shaking, tears falling silently from his eyes. "No," he whispered, shaking. "This can't be happening!"

"Wren...." Jere's voice was pained. What the hell had he just done? Wren was so scared, like every hope he'd ever had was being taken away, like he was about to bolt out the door.

"This can't be happening!" Wren repeated. He looked at Jere, desperate. "Don't believe it! It's not true. It's a lie. She's lying!"

"Wren," Jere said softly. "I'm pretty sure you know she wouldn't lie about that."

"She did!" Wren insisted, but the defeated look on his face said otherwise. "Please don't believe it, Jere. Please!"

"You wouldn't be this upset if it wasn't true," Jere pointed out, wishing it wasn't.

"I tried so hard," Wren whimpered, wrapping his arms more tightly around himself. "I never deserved this life. I never deserved you!"

Jere couldn't say anything as his lover struggled. He winced as Wren dug his fingers into his upper arms, bruising himself.

"Wren, don't," he pleaded weakly. Of all the times he had seen Wren this upset, he had never seen him act like this. The mind connection was out of control with fear and guilt and panic.

"That's it, then," Wren muttered, rocking himself back and

forth, digging harder into his skin. "That's it. You know now. You know what I am, what I do. What I did?"

"What you—"

"Don't fucking play stupid, Jere, I know you put two and two together. Jesus," Wren had stopped rocking for a minute, settling on shaking violently instead. "I wondered, I wondered when you asked me about the fire, but then you let it go, and I, I...."

Jere couldn't stop himself from reaching out an arm to him. "Wren—"

"Don't touch me!" Wren snarled, jerking away and darting across the room. "I could hurt you! I could fucking kill you, I should fucking kill myself for real this time so that it just ends! I'd be better off dead, and so would you, don't you get it?"

"Wren, please calm down, it'll be okay!" Jere wanted it to be okay so badly. He didn't want to believe any of this.

"Don't you fucking get it?" Wren finally looked up at him, face contorted with pain and anger. "Nothing is okay. It won't ever be okay!" He turned and pressed himself against the wall, banging his body against it softly at first, then harder and harder.

"Wren, please stop!" Jere could feel the room shaking and it sickened him how much Wren must have been hurting himself.

Wren kept going, banging his body and his head harder against the wall until he collapsed, sliding down it and falling to his knees. "I'm a fucking freak, I'm wrong, I'm a fucking vandal and a terrible slave and... and a murderer."

The words hit Jere like a blow, a blow he hadn't wanted to expect, but did anyway. It hurt.

"I did it. Yes. I did. What you're thinking. And it wasn't an accident," Wren was forcing a smile now, a sick parody of happiness as tears continued to stream down his face. "I lit this fucking house on fire and I lit him on fire, and you know what else?"

Jere was silent. He didn't know if he wanted to know.

"I held him down and watched him burn," Wren continued, heedless of any response. "See, they all thought I was trying to drag him out, but no, I was keeping him inside. He was bigger and stronger than me, but I made the fire! And I had the speed! And I slowed him down enough that the fire got him, burned him, fucking took him out! I thought of every time he hit me, cut me, burned me, raped me, made me beg for death — I made sure that he could never, *ever* touch me again!"

Still sobbing, Wren wiped ineffectually at his eyes and nose with his hand. Jere could only watch, stunned and frozen. He couldn't respond, because Wren would know how ill he was at the very thought, and he still wanted to protect Wren from that reaction. He had seen hundreds of burn victims in his career, alive and dead, and he knew how horrible and painful the injuries were, even the smallest and most easily treated. The process of burning completely to death was unimaginably painful, and Jere was horrified that anyone could subject another human being to that, much less physically hold them down while the flames ate away at their skin, layer by layer.

This whole time, he had thought it had been accidental. He had considered the uncomfortable possibility that Wren's gift had caused it, but he never thought his lover was capable of doing such a thing intentionally. He had seen too many grotesque things in his medical career to be squeamish, but he couldn't deny or hide the fact that he had gone pale and cold at the thought.

"Do you know how much I hated him?" Wren asked with a voice holding no emotion, pressing himself back into the corner of the room. "I hated him so much, and I enjoyed killing him. I enjoyed knowing that he was suffering, that he was dying, that he was getting a *taste* of what he did to me… what's wrong with me?"

"Wren, nothing's wrong with you," Jere tried to contradict him, despite his own feelings of revulsion at the act Wren had committed. "He hurt you so much."

"I thought I was going to die, you know," Wren stared at him with dead eyes. "It was my plan, all along. Kill myself and take him out with me. So he couldn't… so he couldn't just get another boy after me. So I would be dead, so the pain would stop, so I could never hurt anyone again, because I was a fucking monster, too, just like him. But it didn't work. My fucking, my fucking gift, I can't control it very well, and as I lay there dying, I could feel the flames going out around me. I did what I could, I tried to stay in the fire, but all it did was burn and hurt and then go out. It never took me like it took him. And then, I—and then you came along, and I didn't have any fucking reason to kill you, and I knew you'd never let me get away with killing myself, and things started getting so good, and so I thought maybe, maybe it could just go away and I could forget about it and...."

"Wren...." Jere didn't know what else to say. His heart was breaking.

"Don't." Wren glared at him, failing to be intimidating through his tears. "Don't fucking pity me. I'm a cold-blooded killer. I did this. I chose to do it. It doesn't matter why. I need, I should be... I should be put down."

He hung his head, sobbing audibly for the first time since Jere had met him. The sound was chilling. Wren stood and walked slowly across the room, fists clenched tight, broken. He dropped into the bed, knees tucked beneath him, head pressed to the mattress, palms up and out in front of him.

"Please, sir, master," Wren whimpered, his voice muffled by the mattress. "Please, kill me. Don't turn me in. I know—I know you cared about the person you thought I was, so please, just make it fast. I won't fight you, I promise. Just please don't turn me in, don't have them do it. Please, sir."

Jere fought the urge to be sick. This was all a dream, all a very, very bad dream and he would wake up and none of this—

Another sob cut through his desperate attempt to ditch reality, and he could hear Wren whispering, "Please, please, please."

"Wren, come here." His voice was strained and gravelly. He bit back his own tears as the boy he loved crawled up to him, stopping next to him, still on his knees.

"Thank you for being humane about this...." Wren whimpered. "I'm so, so sorry."

Jere leaned forward and wrapped his arms around him, holding him while Wren tensed, while he drew in his breath, while he prepared to be killed. Throughout it all, Wren hadn't shut down the mind connection, and his emotions were stronger now than they had ever been.

And Jere kept holding him, whispering, "Shh, shh, it's okay," until Wren realized that he wasn't going to be killed, wasn't going to be "put down," wasn't even going to be let go. It was at this moment that he started to struggle, and for the first time, Jere didn't back down, didn't give him his space. He just held him tighter.

"Shh, love, you're not going anywhere. Nothing will happen to you. I promise. I will never let anything happen to you."

"No! Don't you get it, I killed my fucking master!" Wren sobbed. "It's wrong, it's *so* fucking wrong, because everything he did to me was okay, but it wasn't ever okay for me to retaliate!"

"That's the part that's wrong! You shouldn't be treated like that! He shouldn't have done that, and you're right to feel that way about him! You have every right to hate him!"

"No I don't!" Wren protested. "Because I can't just hate *him*. I hate being a slave, even if it's with someone kind, even if it's with someone as wonderful as you! I hate that I can be bought and sold and owned and I want to hurt people for letting it happen; I want to hurt *you* for letting it happen! I always have, because there's something wrong with me! So many people came in contact with my master for so many years and nobody ever saw him for the monster that he was! Why didn't they! Why didn't anybody stop him! You didn't stop him, and you can't stop other people, and I shouldn't expect anyone to help me because I'm a slave! Even *thinking* this way is wrong!"

Jere felt pain twist in his stomach. How responsible was he for Matthias's actions? How responsible was anyone? Jere hadn't known, but should he have worked to find out more? Should he be working more to help slaves, to stop the entire institution? "It's okay to be angry. You don't deserve to be hurt—no one does! There's nothing wrong with you."

"You don't even try to hurt me and sometimes I hate you too!" Wren screamed. "I hate you because you're free, and because you're happy, and what if I can't control it one day? What if I hurt you like I did him?"

Jere tried to consider it, but it was impossible. "Wren, I trust you with my life," he said quietly. "You might get angry and you might do or say something hurtful, but I can't see you as the type of person who would really hurt someone like that for no reason."

"Then why do I think about it? Why do I think about doing it again, about hurting people, about getting revenge? What if you did do something to hurt me one day?"

Jere chose his words carefully. "I think you have a lot of reasons to be angry, and that's okay. If you've been thinking about this since the fire, Wren, that's almost a year, and you haven't done anything. You haven't hurt anyone. It's okay to be angry. And I still trust that you wouldn't hurt me. I trust you."

"But, but I killed someone!" Wren was sobbing, struggling ineffectively. "I killed a free person, I killed my fucking master, and I lied to you, all this time, I lied to you!"

Jere pressed his head close to Wren's neck, whispering in his ear to be heard above his cries. "And I love you. Wren, honey, I love you, and you mean so much more to me than all that."

Finally, Wren stilled in his arms, going limp as he continued to sob.

"I could never harm you, Wren, my god." Jere realized he was crying too. To think that—no, it was all wrong, so wrong! Wren had actually thought that he would kill him!

"No, no, sir, master, Jere, please, don't let someone else do it!" Wren's cries were frantic again, and Jere found himself struggling to hold him again.

"Wren, no! Listen! I'm not going to tell anyone. Nobody is going to hurt you. This stays right here, between you and me!" Jere fought nausea again at the sight of his beautiful lover so upset, so regressed, like he was back when Jere had first arrived. Like Matthias had made him. "Please, Wren, I promise, you can trust me. Have I ever lied to you, ever?"

Wren drew a shuddering breath, shaking his head.

"Okay," Jere fought to keep his voice calm and soothing. "Then it won't start now. I promise. I will never tell anyone what you did, and I won't even tell anyone about your gift, if that's what you want. My mum knows, but she's more close-lipped about it than anyone, it's her job, remember."

Wren nodded, still trembling. Jere kissed him gently on his shoulder, resting his head there while he ran his fingers through the dark, sweaty hair. "Wren, honey, my god, did you really think I'd reject you for that?"

Wren's words were forced and clipped. "You don't get it. You're not from here. It's why people believe I tried to save him. Slaves are supposed to be loyal to their masters. Just a failure to help can be grounds for being put to death. Do you know… do you know what they do… if you… torture… for years… and then…."

"I don't know. And I don't want to." Jere was stroking his head again, rubbing his back, anything to try to soothe the boy — and himself. "All I know is, it won't happen to you."

"He was your friend," Wren managed, still shaky.

"He was a man I didn't know very well," Jere countered. He had never been able to reconcile the man he knew and enjoyed playing around with and the man who beat and tortured Wren for years.

"He drove you to that."

Wren tried to pull away again, but Jere held him tight. "Wren, this wasn't your fault. This wasn't something you did because you're evil, it's something you did because *he* was. He did everything in his power to hurt you, and you did the only thing you could to stop it. You used your gift and you stopped him."

"Let me go, you must be disgusted," he muttered, too tired to fight.

"No." Jere kept his hold. "I love you, and I've loved you for a fucking while, and that doesn't change because I know something new about you. You're still the same person you've always been, and goddamned if I'll let something like this change it!"

"But, I, I lied to you," Wren was whimpering again, shaking in Jere's arms. "I lied to you the whole time."

"You did," Jere said softly, pulling a hand back to caress his face and turn Wren to face him. "And I understand why you felt you needed to do it. And it's okay. And it doesn't change the way I feel about you. It just, it makes me understand how scared you must have been."

Wren said nothing, but nodded. "I've been scared for years," he muttered, but his tone sounded furious.

Jere pressed his lips to his forehead. "You don't have to be scared anymore, love. And it's okay if you're angry. At Matthias, at the world, at me — I've got you."

"You — you've had me since the first day you got here," Wren whispered, crying softly. "Taking care of me. Taking away the pain...."

"I won't ever stop," Jere whispered. "I promise, Wren."

They sat there for a few more minutes, Wren crying softly, Jere holding him, until they were both rather uncomfortable. Jere leaned back slowly, pulling Wren with him.

"Come on," he whispered, "lie with me."

Wren obeyed, although he lay with his back to Jere. Jere didn't push, and Wren didn't protest when Jere's arms went under his head and around his waist, pulling him close.

"I thought I'd be dead now," Wren mused, both of his hands suddenly clutching Jere's. "I thought I'd be dead if anyone ever knew."

"I'm sorry you had to live with that for so long."

"Even before... before the fire," Wren said, barely audible. "I always knew it would be bad if anyone found out about the other gift."

"It wouldn't have saved you from slavery?" Jere inquired. "I mean, it's so uncommon...."

"It would have saved me from slavery," Wren said quietly. "But I would have been taken for research instead. Tests. Experiments. You can imagine. The law is written that anyone *with* a physical gift is a slave. It says nothing about other gifts, or lack of."

Jere shook his head, squeezing Wren's hand with his own. "How old were you when you knew?"

"Thirteen, fourteen," Wren shrugged. "I was at the training facility. It was accidental, then, hard to control, just like my speed gift. One of the other kids saw it and warned me what would happen if I was ever caught."

"That must have been terrifying."

"He asked me to burn the facility down. With everyone in it." Wren shuddered. "I couldn't, though. Not then. I wasn't strong enough. I could barely heat up a cup of water, let alone burn down a training facility."

"You would have...." Jere tried not to feel sick at the realization. A building full of teenagers, and even the adult staff... it wouldn't have been a passionate way to save himself, it would have been planned mass murder.

"You don't get it," Wren shook his head. "You don't get how fucking miserable we were. All of us. Do you know how much it hurts to have your life ripped away from you? We were kids. The only reason we all didn't kill ourselves is because it was forbidden, because the punishment for failing suicide is weeks of torture. But plenty tried, anyway. I tried, and I failed, and I knew if I tried to burn it to the ground... what if I failed at that? They'd know about me. And I also thought, you know, maybe I would get a decent master. It didn't have to be someone great, or someone particularly kind, just someone fair, who only beat me when I disobeyed, who didn't try to hurt me too much when they raped me. I thought I could have a good life."

"Wren..." Jere didn't know what to say. As much as he could protect his love from further pain, there was no way to erase the past.

"I thought of him, that night," Wren laughed a little, a bitter, forced sound. "The boy who told me about my gift. The boy who tried to get me to kill us all. Jason. That was his name. They called him Jace, of course, but for some reason, he thought I should know his other name. I thought of him when I tried to die, and I hoped, somewhere out there, he had died, too. Death is the only peace I hoped for for years."

"You were begging me to let you die, that first day," Jere recalled, squeezing him tightly at the thought. "You've asked me so many times."

"It was the only way out I could imagine, the only way to keep myself safe and to keep everyone else around me safe. I've been wishing to die for the better part of my teenage years," Wren realized. "Until you."

"Until tonight," Jere said, almost regretfully.

"That was poor judgment," Wren declared, twisting in Jere's arms to face him. "You've given me the first reason to live I've ever had."

"I'm so glad," Jere whispered, kissing him ever so lightly, relieved when he didn't pull away. He lay there for a while longer, gently cupping Wren's face in the hand that wasn't still trapped beneath his head. "You've never told me your name, the other one you had, before Wren."

Wren was silent for a moment, shaking his head. "It's not important now. But it was Orrowen. It was going to be shortened to Owen, but another boy in the cohort already had that name, so they went with Wren. Orrowen the fourth. But don't ever call me that. It's... it would be shameful. To my family."

"I won't, love, I was just curious," Jere brushed a stray hair out of his face. "I figured you had a reason for never telling me."

"Aside from the fact that I'm a worthless fucking liar?" Wren looked up at him, as if expecting confirmation of this fact.

"Because sometimes it's not the right time to tell someone something," Jere said firmly. "And because sometimes, being safe is more important than being honest."

"I've always been safe with you," Wren muttered.

"But you didn't know that now, did you?" Jere teased a bit. "Wren, I don't hold it against you. I promise. I don't and I won't. Ever. And if you have more secrets, then I hope I get to hear them, but they're still yours to tell or not. Nothing you can tell me is gonna change how I think of you."

Wren didn't respond, but he buried his head against Jere's chest, still crying a little. Jere said nothing, holding him tightly, hands on his back, lips pressed down into his hair. Wren was safe with him, he realized, as much as he was safe with Wren. Eventually, he felt Wren's breathing even out, and he realized they were both going to fall asleep like this. He could think of nothing better.

He had almost drifted off when he heard a small voice, plaintive, uncertain, the vocal expression of tears.

"Jere?"

"What, love?" His eyes flew open to gaze into the red-rimmed, blue ones in front of him.

Wren sniffled for a moment before he spoke. "You, you told me you loved me a while back, and told me I didn't have to say anything in return."

"Yeah...."

"I just, I couldn't stand the thought of letting myself love you, knowing I was lying to you, knowing you would hate me when you found out...."

"I could never hate you, Wren."

"I know," Wren smiled at him, barely, but it was there. "I know that now."

They were silent again for a moment.

"Jere?"

"Yeah?"

"I... I love you, Jere."

"I love you too, Wren."

Chapter 45
Cooling Down

Jere woke the next day, still holding Wren tightly against his chest. He smiled, out of habit, then took a deep breath as last night's conversation came rushing back into his memory.

Why hadn't it all been a dream?

But it hadn't. Every bit of it had been real, too real, from Wren's sobbing confession to his pleas to be killed to the fact that he was a firesetter.

And a murderer.

Jere tried to reconcile the fact, tried to turn it over in his head. Did it change what he knew about him, how he thought about him? Did it make him a different person, or make Jere love him any less? His first instinct was to say no, of course not, but as he petted the hair of the person pressed to his chest, he couldn't help wondering whether that was the truth or not. He wondered, did he really know this person?

He tried to push the thoughts out of his head silently, subtly, like the way he slipped out from beneath the covers and out of bed, leaving Wren there, undisturbed. He looked so peaceful lying there, so innocent and fragile. Who would have thought that he was a powerful, dangerous weapon waiting to be set off?

Jere went out and made coffee, taking it and sitting outside in the early morning heat. It would still be a few hours before patients started coming in to the clinic, and Jere needed some time to think, to process what had happened last night.

He still loved him. That much he did know. He hadn't even considered the alternative, not when Wren had dumped that horrible news on him, and not now. Love didn't come with an on and off switch, and it certainly didn't disappear just like that. Jere had never spent a whole lot of time thinking about love; he wasn't a poet or a romantic or anything of the sort, but he had always held it as fact that true love was unconditional. And if it wasn't, then it just wasn't love, it was some lie told to win favor or get something out of the relationship. He was certain that whatever he had heard or might hear out of Wren's mouth, he would still love him. He might not agree with his actions, and he might even be a little put-off by him, but there was no changing the way he felt about him. It hadn't been planned, but it was strong, and he didn't have to think twice to determine how he really felt. Wren was still the same person he always was, and that was the person that Jere had fallen in love with.

That still didn't make the recent news any easier to take.

The longer he thought, the more conflicted he became, the more questions came up, the more he realized he needed to talk to Wren more. What he really wanted was to talk to his mum, and ask her a thousand different things and have her tell him what to do, but that wasn't an option. He wasn't a little boy anymore, and he didn't live in the same state, even. He envied his grandparents and the "telephones" that could so quickly put you in touch with your loved ones, letting you hear their voices, giving you instant access to their wisdom and advice and good sense.

There wasn't anyone he could talk to about this, not really, not without giving Wren away. Even if he hadn't promised that he would never tell anyone, who could he tell? Paltrek was out; while they were good enough friends, Jere still wouldn't trust him with something like this. They were too different, Paltrek was too embroiled in this culture, he would never understand. Kieran may or may not understand, but may or may not wasn't good enough for him. It certainly wasn't good enough for Wren's safety. Unsettled, he stirred his coffee.

There were so many thoughts in his head, thoughts that he had pushed back last night. Thoughts that he hadn't even allowed himself to have because Wren was breaking down, and the last thing he needed was for Jere to break down next to him, or to question him, or to do anything but support him. His old friend and mentor had tortured a young boy to the point of suicide. Jere was in love with that boy, but maybe Wren didn't return the feelings, and how could he, when Jere owned him? Jere wondered what to do with all that. What were you supposed to do after you found out your slave had killed your predecessor? Was it any different than what you were supposed to do after you found out your boyfriend had killed his torturer?

He supposed it was the fact that Wren had killed *anyone* that had him unsettled. Alone, safe, and knowing Wren was safe, his mind was free to race with implications and questions and doubts. What kind of person was his boyfriend?

He jumped, yelping as a hand touched his shoulder.

"S-sorry," Wren mumbled, backing away. "I didn't mean...."

Jere turned toward him and the thoughts he had just been entertaining vanished. His beautiful lover stood uncertainly, clad in nothing but sweatpants, hair a bit flattened from sleep. He looked so vulnerable, as if a harsh word would break him. It probably would.

"It's okay," Jere rushed to comfort him, opening his arms and beckoning him closer. "I just, I didn't realize you were up."

Wren came to him and squeezed next to him on the chair, all but sitting in his lap. Jere kissed him carefully, the taste of his skin so inviting and familiar. Everything could be perfect, if all he had to think about was Wren's skin.

"I woke up and you weren't there," Wren mumbled. "I couldn't find you."

Jere wrapped his arms around him protectively. "I'm not going anywhere," he promised. "Neither one of us is."

"Thank you," Wren whispered, nestling up as close as he could get.

They sat there for a while, neither of them speaking. They watched the sun rise higher and the dew dry off the grass. Everything was the same, except it wasn't.

"We should get ready for work," Jere observed, and they did.

He tried to ignore it, but something was off. Something about the way they worked together, the way that they moved around each other; it wasn't right, and Jere just couldn't manage to put a finger on it. They had been working together for almost a year, now, and up until today, Jere would have said that their coordination was flawless, their ability to act and react and predict what each other's intentions were was almost impeccable.

Today, they bumped into each other, they grabbed for the same tools, they misunderstood each other in both mindspeak and body language and even normal, out loud speech. Jere was only a little frustrated; more importantly, he was confused.

He finally realized, after the third time he bumped his leg on the edge of the exam table hard enough to bruise, that he was avoiding touching Wren. It made no sense, he loved him, he spent every night cuddling and fucking and kissing him, and he was shying away from his touch. But then again, he could swear that Wren was shying away from his as well.

They made it through the day, each making a few nervous jokes about being too tired or emotionally drained or whatever, and they settled down to eat the food that Wren had prepared. Jere couldn't have said what that food was, he was too busy thinking, too busy wondering. Had Wren heated it with the stove, or with his gift? Did he practice, when nobody was looking? When *he* wasn't looking? Had he practiced before he killed Matthias, and how had he gone undetected for so long? Who was this boy, previously so terrified and cowed, so fucking good at lying that he could do it for months while Jere had no idea?

It was unsettling. Jere thought he knew the person he shared everything with, but they didn't really share everything. Maybe he didn't really know Wren that well to begin with. What other secrets did he have? Jere tried to convince himself that it was pure self-preservation, but that was still hard to do. He couldn't tell, not this soon, if it made him feel different toward Wren or not. He was still trying to process the fact that he had been lied to all along.

After dinner, Jere smiled and asked if he could have a few minutes alone to write his mum a letter. She had, after all, been curious as to what Wren's reaction would be to learning he had a gift, and he figured he may as well tell her. Plus, every minute he spent writing a letter to his mum was a minute he could distract himself from his thoughts, from having to confront reality and Wren.

It wasn't a great plan. Wren looked hurt and rejected, although he encouraged Jere to write her in the most supportive way possible, given the situation. Jere couldn't help feeling anxious as he started to write, and soon he found himself pouring out page after page of anxiety and confusion and questions, more than half of which he realized he would never send, anyway. In addition to being more than he told Wren he would tell anyone, he would never trust the postal system with this most confidential information. It was just a way for him to get his ideas down, to process them outside of his head, to have at least an imaginary conversation since he couldn't have a real one. In the end, he tore up the pages he had written, then composed a short, lighthearted letter instead. He did ask one thing, though, and that was the only thing he hadn't really been able to answer for himself.

If someone has been lying to you for your whole relationship, how do you know they are who you think they are?

He didn't know whether his mum would have an answer for that or not, but at least it was something. Motherly advice sounded better than it ever had before.

After another cup of tea and a pointless check on something in the clinic, Jere finally caved and joined Wren in the bedroom. He looked so normal, lying in bed, reading a book. Maybe he could pretend that last night never happened? Maybe they both could.

Jere placed a quick kiss on Wren's head before taking a shower, intent on making this plan work. Forgetting couldn't be that difficult, could it? It was certainly less painful than talking.

He came out of the shower wearing only a towel and climbed into bed, just like they always did.

"Hey," Wren said, smiling tentatively. "Everything okay?"

"Yeah," Jere lied. Forgetting. "I just had to get back to my mum. She was curious. She wanted to know how you were."

"Oh." Wren looked at him, almost too intensely. A few moments passed. "Kiss me?" he asked, his voice uncertain.

Jere leaned in, pressing his lips against Wren's. God, he felt good. No matter what had happened, he still felt so wonderful and right and warm.

Oh.

Well, he didn't have to wonder why he was warm anymore, did he?

Jere tried to hide the fact that he had broken the kiss by moving down his throat, lightly biting and licking, until he felt Wren's arms come up around his back.

Was this how he did it? To Matthias? Did he seduce him into bed and get him relaxed and comfortable and put his arms around him and light him on fire?

He tried to focus. It wasn't like Wren would do that to him; he needed to stop worrying about it. Wren was his boyfriend, his lover, he liked having sex with him. He needed to stop thinking about scary, confusing things, to stop thinking about his friend being killed. Stop thinking about it all together.

He was mostly successful, caressing the body he knew so well, kissing him, pressing their bodies together. He was on top, for once, and Wren didn't seem to mind. He felt them both growing hard and he tossed the towel aside, smiling encouragingly and waiting for Wren to nod before undressing him as well. He leaned up and kissed him, the familiar rhythm and flow of their lovemaking taking over, and he looked into Wren's eyes as he asked, "You on top or me?" He liked to let Wren choose. Jere was perfectly happy with anything they did, so he liked to let Wren decide what he wanted so he could enjoy it as well. He waited, eagerly anticipating either answer.

"You can," Wren's response came out quiet and detached. He looked away as he spoke. "You deserve to do it."

Jere felt like a bucket of cold water had been splashed over him. He rolled away, quickly, sitting next to Wren and pulling him up to sit as well. "What?" he asked, shaking his head.

Wren gave a little half-shrug. "I put you through a lot last night. I lied to you. I killed someone. You have to deal with me being what I am. You deserve to fuck me. You can even... you can do it hard, if you want to. I don't mind. I won't fight you or anything."

Jere felt sick. "Wren, I have never fucked you because I thought I 'deserved' to, and I certainly hope that's not why you do it!"

Wren kept looking down, shaking his head. Jere could see him blinking back tears.

"Love," Jere reached out his hand, gently cupping Wren's face and bringing it up so he could look into his eyes. "Everything I do with you, I do because it feels good, and because it makes you feel good. That's all. Nothing else. There's nothing about anyone deserving or not deserving anything, and there never will be. I'm with you because I want to be with you, because I want you, because I thought... I thought you wanted me, too."

"I do," Wren mumbled, closing his eyes. He didn't turn away, though. "I shouldn't, and I don't deserve you, but I do."

"You *never* have to use sex to pay me, or bribe me, or reward me, or anything," Jere asserted. "I love you, and that isn't something that has to be earned. It's there, and I might also love fucking you, but they don't have anything to do with each other. I asked you because I want you to enjoy yourself as much as possible. That's what's important to me."

"It's okay," Wren said, his eyes still closed. "You can do it. I'll enjoy it. Or if you'd rather, I can top. I'd like that, too."

There was no passion there, no desire at all. Jere squirmed at the idea that he was being told what he wanted to hear, rather, what Wren *thought* he wanted to hear. "Babe, you know, you can say no," he said softly. "Not just if you're scared, like you have in the past, but you can say no for whatever reason. You don't have to, I mean, if you don't want to...."

Wren said nothing, but he did lean forward, pressing into Jere's chest. Jere pulled him close and held him there. How had they come to this misunderstanding again? He had no idea how Wren could worry about owing him sex; wasn't their relationship based on more than that?

"I do like it, and I do want to, just..." Wren drew in a shaky breath before he finished. "Something has felt off all day. I just want you to touch me, like you used to, but I can tell, you're disgusted with me, and you must be angry, and so maybe you could make it better. Just hurt me, like you want to, use me like I've used you. Then we'll be even."

"Whatever gave you the idea that I wouldn't enjoy a night of nothing but touching you?" Jere failed to keep the irritation out of his voice. He wasn't sure who to be more irritated with — Wren, for being so self-destructive, or himself, for doing exactly what Wren said he was doing and avoiding touching him all day.

"It's obviously not a big deal to you, if you didn't notice, so just — " Wren's voice cut off as his breath hitched and his eyes stung with bitter tears. He pulled away from Jere. "If you want to punish me, then just fucking hurt me, but don't pretend I don't exist! I can tell that you're angry and you probably should be but you'll feel better if you get off."

"Goddammit, Wren, of course I'm angry!" Jere snapped, moving away a few inches as well. Honestly, he wasn't sure how he felt, but angry was definitely a part of it. "I'm angry that you lied to me, and I'm angry that Matthias is dead, and I'm angry that he hurt you and that slavery exists and that you can't use your second gift without fear of being captured. I'm angry that this is fucking our relationship up, but I'm not all that angry with *you*, because I don't know what I would have done in your situation!"

"But wouldn't it make it better?" Wren choked out, still turned away. "Hurting me? You could let it out. You let me. You can use me, however you'd like."

"All I'd like to do is be with you," Jere said, defeated. "I know it might not seem like it, because I've had so much on my mind, but hurting you would make everything worse! I wouldn't do that!"

"You barely talked to me all day," Wren replied. "At least if you're hurting me, I know you see me."

Jere thought of how despondent Wren had been months ago, when Jere first came to Hojer and interacting with a slave had been so uncomfortable that he ignored the poor boy. He moved closer and wrapped his arms around Wren, pulling him close.

"Don't," Wren muttered.

"Do you really want me to stop?" Jere asked, picking up on his hesitation. "I'm *not* going to hurt you. Even if you want it, I don't. So, do you want me to stop touching you anyway?"

"I don't know," he mumbled. "I used sex, Jere. I used it all the time to get what I wanted, or to keep you close. If you're touching me, I know you won't leave. Are you still so sure you don't want to hurt me?"

The words hurt, but Jere forced himself to stay. "I'm very sure," he managed. "And I'm not leaving, either. You're not going to make me leave, no matter what horrible things you tell me. If it's the truth, I'd rather hear it."

"I just can't handle you finding out something else," Wren admitted. "I figure, eventually, you'll hear too much."

"At this point, I probably wouldn't even leave if you asked me to," Jere countered, scared by how true it was. "Was it all just a game?"

Wren shook his head. "I wanted it to be. But it wasn't. I loved it every time you touched me, and I still do, and I fell in love with you, even though I know better. But everything you did was honest, and everything I did was to survive."

There were worse things, Jere reflected, and even those worse things wouldn't make him want to hurt Wren. "We can get through this. We can just put it behind us."

"Is that what you want?" Wren asked, finally turning to look at him.

"Yes," Jere said, smiling. "And I don't have to hurt you to be here for you — I can touch you, or kiss you, or talk to you — whatever you want."

"You don't have to," Wren murmured, but he was already moving closer so Jere could reach him.

Jere kissed him, and for a second, it felt like the familiar kisses they had shared a thousand times before. "*I want to,*" he replied, resuming the touching he had started earlier.

Wren relaxed under Jere's hands, and soon after, under his mouth. They hadn't played like this in a while, so soft and tender and exploratory. For the past few weeks, they had fucked wildly, roughly, Wren pounding in to Jere until they both came and screamed and rocked the bed. Tonight was different, but Jere got just as much enjoyment out of using his hands to work a slow, steady orgasm out of Wren with practiced ease. Maybe what they both needed for a little while was just to cool down a bit.

Chapter 46
Not Enough

Something was still off and Wren could feel it.

Of course, something had been off for days. He knew what it was. He was wrong. Dangerous. It was nice of Jere to say otherwise, but it didn't change anything. It didn't change the way he felt about himself.

Jere was too nice, really. They hadn't talked about it again, and even that had seemed nice for a while. But nice wasn't what he needed, wanted even. Sure, he wanted things to go back to the way they were, but they wouldn't, not like this. He felt like he was growing paranoid — it was like Jere was avoiding him, still trying not to touch him. But that was ridiculous, Jere wouldn't do that. Besides, at night, when they went to bed, they touched.

Wren knew it wasn't exactly true. They had touched that first night, and that was nice, but still different, and then the next night they were tired, and then after that they would lie in bed together, sometimes, but sometimes Jere would stay up and read, or fall asleep while Wren was showering. Wren felt himself starting to panic more than once as he looked at the sleeping body next to him.

Wren winced, biting back a cry and blinking back tears. He was cleaning surgical equipment and he had somehow managed to slice his finger open with a scalpel. An idiot mistake, it showed just how little attention he was paying. It hurt. He so rarely felt pain anymore.

He bandaged it up as well as he could, continuing on with the evening cleanup, and then he finished dinner and laid it out, hoping Jere liked it. Jere hadn't commented on much that he had made lately, actually. He had said that he didn't have much of an appetite.

Jere didn't comment on much anymore, but then, neither did Wren, really.

"What happened to your finger?" Jere asked, the moment they sat down. "You're still bleeding, I can see it through the bandage."

Wren glanced down. He had forgotten he had even hurt himself. He certainly hadn't thought Jere would notice it. He didn't seem to notice much of anything, anymore. Then again, Jere had always noticed medical problems. "It's nothing," he dismissed. "Just a little scratch I got in the clinic whilst cleaning up."

"Well, it's not like you don't have a doctor for a boyfriend who might be able to heal you up," Jere teased, and for a second, Wren saw the old Jere shining through. For a second, they were back, nothing had changed, everything was fine and he should stop worrying.

"I'll go get something to clean off that tape with, and I'll be right back."

No, it wasn't fine, things had changed, and every time Jere went out of the room, Wren was almost paralyzed with the fear that he wouldn't come back.

"Please, don't go!" Wren begged, reaching out and clutching at Jere's hand, wincing when he pulled away. Why did he pull away? "I mean, we're in the middle of dinner," he tried to cover. *Don't leave me. Don't leave me.*

Jere sat down again, worry evident on his face. Wren didn't care. He felt like he had just staved off some sort of apocalypse in his life.

"Okay," Jere said. He spoke slowly, assessing the situation. Wren figured he was trying to determine how crazy he was. "I'll just heal it now, then, and we can go get supplies later."

Wren couldn't speak, so he nodded and tried to smile. It shouldn't be so goddamned hard, he was able to lie to the man for ten months, the least he should be able to do was smile!

Jere took his hand gently, healed it, and squeezed it lightly before placing it back on Wren's lap. "Is something the matter?" he asked, finally, cocking his head in that adorable way he had.

He didn't see it. Wren was panicking, and Jere didn't see anything the matter. He was content to just ignore it, maybe forever. Jere would go about his day, pretending everything was fine, pretending they weren't avoiding each other. Wren realized it might have been the brighter option, at least for him. As a slave, he faced terrible penalties for his actions, for murdering his master and lying and hiding his gift. They were both trying so hard to ignore these things, knowing it was for the best, but Wren still expected so much more from himself and from Jere. Something was the matter, and the worst part was that they couldn't talk about it.

"Can we talk?" he echoed Jere's words to him, days ago, the words that had started all this. "After dinner, can we talk about what happened? I feel like I'm losing my mind."

"Of course, love," Jere said, his brow furrowing. He reached out, almost touched Wren's arm, then pulled his hand back. "Whenever you'd like."

Wren forced himself to smile a little. Such a typical Jere response. Even... even now.

They finished dinner in near-silence. It wasn't much different from the past few days, but at least this time, Wren had something to think about *other* than the silence. He was trying to envision a conversation, trying to picture what he'd say, and what his master would say, and where they would come to after they had both spoken. Would it help, or would it just be more empty words? It was the emptiness that took its toll on Wren the most. They weren't strangers anymore, yet that's what they had been acting like. Jere wouldn't dare to yell at him, not even in the clinic, not even when Wren purposefully annoyed him. Jere seemed to be on his best behavior, polite to the point of insincerity. He didn't seem to dare to talk to him, either, and that was what was eating away at Wren.

After dinner, he cleaned up quickly, before Jere had even finished all the way, and he led Jere to the couch with no questions asked. He couldn't do this in their bedroom, it would only make it harder to do what he was planning to do, harder to stay focused and not get distracted by the touch of his hands or the smooth muscles on his back or the way his teeth grazed Wren's collarbone.

He sat at one end, as he had so many times, and Jere settled into the other end, looking entirely uncomfortable. Wren felt the same way.

"What's going on, love?" Jere asked, his face showing his concern.

Wren sighed. How did he even do this? "Ask me questions," he blurted out. "Ask me how I feel, or how I did it, or why I did it, or why I didn't tell you, or if I liked it, or if I want to do it again. Ask me anything, Jere, please, talk to me, because I don't know what to tell you if you don't, and I hate this silence between us."

"I didn't realize you wanted to talk about it," Jere said.

Wren thought it was obvious. Could something that big pass without any conversation? "When you act like it didn't happen, I can't help but think the worst!" he tried to explain. "You pull away from me and you don't talk to me and you act like nothing happened and so then I think you wish it didn't happen but it did and — am I just that horrible?"

Jere was quiet for a minute, shaking his head. "No," he said firmly, the tone that Wren always found calming. "No. You are not horrible. God, tell me I didn't really make you think that?"

Wren said nothing, he just waited. That wasn't the worst that he had been thinking about himself. He thought that and more every time Jere walked by him as though he wasn't there, or answered his questions in short, one-word sentences.

Jere sighed. "I'm just trying to deal with it, love. Something horrible *did* happen, but it happened over a year ago, and it started years before that. Someone that I thought I knew bought you and tortured you, and you finally caved and put a stop to it, and you almost died in the process. I still don't know what to make of it, especially that part where, well, I thought you were going to tell me the fire was accidental."

That was it, then. Jere could see what kind of person he was. The kind who killed people. The kind who tried to kill himself instead of dealing with problems. Why hadn't he said it was accidental, anyway? He could have pulled it off, could have lied just one more time. But he hadn't. It hadn't even occurred to him then.

"No, it was on purpose," Wren admitted, yet again. "It was the best suicide plan I had ever come up with, and then I thought to take my master down with me, and then I ended up living and he didn't."

"It started as a suicide plan?" Jere asked.

"Yeah. I just wanted it to end. The torture, the pain. I had planned it for weeks, how I would do it, which part of the house I would be in. I wanted to take down the part of the house that he tortured me in the most, the bedroom, so I could destroy all of his supplies," Wren explained. He remembered his own fuzzy thought process while he was making that decision, how carefully he had plotted and planned it for weeks, his joy at imagining the whips and the canes and restraints burning up along with him. "It wasn't until he mentioned getting another boy one day that I realized I couldn't just die and leave someone else to that. As it was, I had a hard time dealing with the thought that he might grow bored with me and move on to another fresh kid, but knowing that it was my selfishness that did it... I had to stop him, Jere. I did the only thing I knew how to do."

Jere looked at him then, his eyes wider. Wren was sure it was because he was appalled, disgusted that he would be so weak as take that road out.

"Do you think about it often?" Jere asked.

Wren shrugged. "I didn't, not for a while. At first, yes. I thought about it every day. Lately, it's been once every few days, and since... since we talked...."

Jere shook his head. "This must be so hard for you."

Wren nodded. "I had gotten really good at not thinking about it, you know? I mean, after the fire, then I was burned, and then you, and I had so much on my mind, so much more to think about than all that, and then, I guess I just tried to forget. I guess I did whatever I could to convince myself that it hadn't happened."

"And your gift? The firesetting, I mean."

"Don't worry, I don't use it," Wren rushed to explain. "I know it's dangerous. I can't control it, obviously, and the only thing I've ever intentionally done with it was the most horrible thing I can ever conceive of doing. I try to pretend it's not there."

"Matthias..." Jere started, looking confused. "He burned you, though. Didn't it show, then?"

"I tried *really hard* to pretend it wasn't there." Those had been some of the worst torture sessions, the brandings, the lit cigarettes put out on his skin. Knowing he could stop it, so easily, and fighting not to, to let it happen.

"You must have good control of it."

Good enough to kill someone. "I guess."

Jere was quiet, curled up in his spot at the end of the couch. He looked down for a while, and Wren forced himself to wait for whatever he had to say next. That he was finished. That he was disgusted by him. That he really wasn't going to stick around, despite what he had said the other night.

"This must have been so hard on you," he said, finally.

Wren nodded. The tears were starting in his eyes.

"What can I do to make it better?" Jere asked.

Of course he did. Of course that was what Jere would ask. Wren blinked hard, wiped at his eyes, and steadied himself. "I need some time, Jere. Time alone." God, this was hard.

"Like, now, you want me to go for a walk or something?"

More tears. Goddammit, why was he always so thick! "I want to move into the bedroom in the hall for a while. I need time to think."

Jere's face dropped from confused to devastated, and Wren felt the mirror emotions through the mind connection. Seconds later, he felt them blocked somewhat, and Jere carefully tried to school his face back to a neutral expression. He did a pretty bad job.

"It's not that I don't appreciate you, or that I don't love being with you, or that I'm ungrateful," Wren tried to explain. He didn't know what to explain; his idea to separate had been impulsive and he didn't really understand it himself. What he wanted was for Jere to ask him why, to help him figure out why he wanted it, to help convince him that he didn't really want it at all. "I just, it kills me the way things are now, and so, maybe, a little break...."

"Of course," Jere cut in, but his face was turned away. "Whatever you need."

"Jere, I still love you," Wren couldn't stop crying. "And I'm sorry."

"Don't apologize," Jere whispered, his jaw set to keep his face stoic. "If this is what you need...."

I need you! Wren wanted to scream, but he couldn't, because he didn't, not like this. He needed Jere like he was before. He needed Jere like he had been, just for a minute, when he told him about the fire, and he refused to let him go. He needed Jere to care more about what he needed that what he admitted to needing. He wanted so badly for Jere to say that they were going to sit right there and talk about what went wrong and fix it. "Maybe it is. Maybe love isn't enough. Maybe I just, I just need to figure some things out."

"I'll be here when you do."

Wren wasn't sure if that would be enough. "I know."

They sat there for a few moments, silent except for the denial-filled sniffles from both of them. Wren wasn't sure exactly what he had just done, except that he had done something, and something had to be better than nothing. Even a decision as painful as this had to be better than the limbo they had been in. Still, a part of him was waiting for Jere to say something, to utter the magic phrase or question that would halt this plan and bring them back together. It didn't come.

"It's not like we won't see each other," Wren mumbled, trying to make light of the situation. He had to, even if they both knew it was a lie. "I mean, I know where you work."

Jere forced a smile in return. "Yeah, and I know where you live."

Jere's attempt at joking only highlighted the pain that Wren felt. They used to be able to joke for real. "I'm sorry."

Jere smiled, but it was bittersweet. "You lead, and I'll follow," he promised. "Wherever you take me, I'll follow."

"I know," Wren said again. He did. He wouldn't have made this stupid move if he didn't. He didn't want to lead, not right now, but Jere had never been the one to take the lead. As hard as Jere tried, he had never been able to do that, and Wren wasn't sure if he knew how anymore.

"I guess I can help you get your things together," Jere said, looking miserable at the idea.

"Speed gift, Jere, I can get it." Wren didn't want to hear an offer to help move his things, he wanted to hear a plan for how to fix things.

"Right."

A few more minutes passed, and neither one of them looked at each other. Finally, Wren stood up, and Jere followed suit. They looked at each other for a minute before Wren caved and threw himself at Jere, wrapping his arms around his waist and burying his head into his chest. Was this the last time he would do this? He tried in vain to remember every part, every curve on his body, the way he smelled and how warm he was and the way his hands came up and stroked his head, moving through his hair and the way he felt so safe here.

After what was probably too long, he pulled away, not saying a word. He went to their bedroom and started collecting his things, speeding them from one room to another. Jere, thankfully, made himself scarce.

Chapter 47
All of You

Jere spent the next few days in a haze. Part of him didn't want to believe what had happened, and part of him simply couldn't keep up with all the changes. Since his mum had visited, his world had been turned upside down again, perhaps not as badly as it had been when he first moved here, but enough to throw him off balance. He wasn't even sure what it was that he and Wren were doing at first, and Wren kept giving him such mixed signals. One minute, he was avoiding him and acting like they were nothing more than coworkers, the next, he was running up and hugging him or kissing him, and for brief moments, Jere hoped that it could just go back to being the way it was.

It didn't, though. Wren kissed him goodnight every night, and more often than not he would come up behind him at the clinic and put his arms around him, like he used to. But it still wasn't the same. With no idea of what to do, Jere just stayed quiet, hiding his surprise and his sadness.

In the meantime, he evaluated his own life, finding he had an excess of time to take care of business he had never addressed before. As much as he hadn't wanted to admit it, Hojer was his new home, and it was time to start treating it as such. He dug up an old address book and found the contact information for people he hadn't talked to in months, sent letters and postcards telling them the news. He didn't explicitly mention that he would be stuck in Hojer forever, but he knew it. It seemed strange, doing it now, when he and Wren were having such a hard time, but the separation almost highlighted his commitment to the man he had grown to love.

Maybe there had always been some doubt when they were blissfully falling in love and oblivious to the world, some sort of unanswered question of "what if?" that left them both wondering. Now that the unpleasantness of separation was upon them, Jere realized just how strongly he felt about Wren. He could never leave him.

He was pondering this as he went to the post office to deliver some mail. In the weeks that had passed since Wren had asked for "time," he had started going out more, getting out of the house, putting less stress on Wren. As he handed the stack over to the woman behind the counter, she yelped, jerking her hand back.

"Paper cuts!" She exclaimed, shaking her finger. "So tiny, and they hurt so much!"

Jere smiled. He had gotten his fair share. "I'm a healer," he offered, feeling generous. "Would you like me to heal it?"

The woman raised an eyebrow. "Heavens no!" she protested. "The human body can heal itself perfectly well! I don't believe in medication and I don't believe in mind-healing! It's nice of you to offer, though."

Jere shrugged. Some people were touchy about the subject. He couldn't help but notice how jumpy she was as she took his money, though, careful to avoid touching his hand. Maybe she was concerned about bleeding on him?

He had made it maybe half a block down the road when he realized he had left his wallet in his hurry to get out of the post office. With a sigh, he went back in, finding the desk empty and unattended. He frowned, looking around for a bell to ring to call someone out, when he heard voices from the back of the office.

"Well, I don't! They're creepy!" That was the voice of the woman who had attended him.

"Oh, come on, who doesn't trust a healer?" another voice asked.

"They can heal, but they're dangerous! They can *kill* people if they want to, just by touching them! And probably all sorts of other things, too, with a gift like that!"

Feeling uncomfortable overhearing the conversation, Jere cleared his throat, relieved when an unfamiliar face appeared and returned his wallet. Could someone really consider him dangerous?

The first night had been the hardest. Wren lay sobbing in his room, a pillow over his head to drown out the sounds he knew he wasn't making anyway, and wondered whether he'd just thrown the best year of his life away. He couldn't find an answer. He wanted Jere back, but not the way it had been, and he didn't know if the damage between them could ever be repaired.

The next few weeks went better, and Wren started to think that he really had made the right decision. It was strange, they felt closer now with this artificial separation between them than they had in the days before it. Wren wasn't quite sure what to make of it, but he liked it, and he liked the way that they were slowly, *slowly* starting to talk to one another again. They weren't having sex, which was strange, because it hadn't been the sex that had been the problem, but then, neither had the cuddling, and they weren't doing much of that, either. They spent more time at the dining room table after dinner, lingering over their meal, or coffee, or dessert, or drinks. Sometimes they lingered well after the food and drinks were gone, and even though they didn't have too much to say, they were just with each other.

When they didn't, they went their separate ways. Wren spent most of his time lying bored in his bed, wishing he had something better to do than read and think about things that made him sad, so he got a journal, and he wrote, and some days he wrote words like "fire" and "murder" and "pain" on the pages and then tore them up and threw them away. He wished, now and again, that he hadn't moved to this bedroom, that he had stayed in the one Jere had first put him in. It was smaller and awkwardly located, but he had hidden out in there so many times when he and Jere first met each other, even when they first started dating. It might have felt more familiar, at least.

This was different, though. He didn't feel like he was hiding so much as he was working through things, trying to understand what had happened, what would be different now, and what he and Jere would continue to be to one another. He had wondered, ever so briefly, if Jere would call it off and head back to Sonova after all, but he showed no signs of that. From what Wren could tell, Jere was writing as well, writing more to his mum, more to Kieran, even a few letters to some friends and family back home. After nearly a year in Hojer, Jere was announcing that he had moved, and that he was staying, and that he probably wouldn't see most of the people in his life for a long time. Some, Wren realized, when he found out that one of Jere's closest childhood friends had a physical gift, would never see him again.

It was a big sacrifice for someone to make when the person they were making it for was halfway to breaking up with them.

But for once, Wren didn't feel guilty. Well, not more than he had that first night, which, granted, was a lot, but he didn't feel *more* guilty, and he actually started to feel comfortable with the way things were. He missed Jere, terribly in fact, but for now, this was an okay compromise.

He was debating the virtues of this compromise when he heard a knock on his door. It wasn't closed all the way, just cracked a little, but Jere had always knocked, even back when they first met.

"Hey," he said, smiling as Jere opened the door. Wren was struck by how much he missed him.

Jere smiled back at him, so wide and genuine. "Can I come in?"

"Sure," Wren nodded, sitting up. He had been lying face down in his bed, thinking about writing, but not writing. He sat up and swung his legs over the edge of the bed, making room for Jere. "Wanna sit?"

Jere nodded, sitting next to him. They weren't touching, but they could be, if they both just moved a few inches closer....

"What does it feel like, to light a fire with your mind?"

Wren was a bit startled. He never expected Jere to ask him about that! He assumed, hell, *he* didn't even like to think about it, so he assumed Jere would be just as disturbed.

But the look on his face wasn't disturbed, it was curious, open, friendly.

"It's weird, I guess. I mean, I don't do it much—I don't do it at all, now, but even when I did do it sometimes, it's different. It feels different than my speed gift, like, my speed gift is in my body, and

I'm so comfortable with it, and the firesetting, I don't really even understand it, I could just do it sometimes."

Jere smiled at him, seeming to want more.

"I used it sometimes when Burghe would put me in the cellar," Wren confessed. "In winter, it was so cold down there, and I'd heat myself up, just a little bit, just enough so that I didn't get sick. Or when he'd leave me for days, if he left water, and it froze, I'd thaw it. I don't know how he didn't know, or maybe he just didn't care."

"It's saved your life more than once, then," Jere observed.

"I usually used it in terrible situations," Wren agreed. "It's too dangerous to use, otherwise."

Jere smiled at him for a moment before reaching into his pocket. Wren couldn't help but peek to see what he was taking out, and he was a little surprised when Jere pulled out a tissue. Maybe he was planning on crying again.

He handed the tissue over to Wren. "Can I see you use it?" his voice was solemn, reverent almost, like the topic was too precious to discuss in normal tones. "Your gift?"

Wren dropped it. "I don't use it," he mumbled. "I could... it could get out of hand."

"How don't you use it, though?" Jere persisted. "I can't stand not using my gift, and you've told me the same thing about your speed gift, that it seems wrong if you don't use it, like you know you're neglecting a part of yourself."

"I don't want that to be a part of me."

"Wren, it's not a bad thing!" Jere was insistent, but he was smiling. "Look, it's kept you alive numerous times, and just think, if there was some sort of storm or something, and we had no heat, you could keep us warm!"

"I killed someone with it, and I had thought about it before." There. Was that what he wanted to hear?

Jere reached out and placed a hand on his leg, the first contact that he had initiated since Wren had moved out of their bedroom. He waited until Wren looked at him before he spoke.

"You say it's dangerous because you can kill with it, and that's true," Jere pointed out. "But what about my gift, Wren? I can hurt people just by touching them. I can, given enough time and motivation, kill them the same way. In less time than it would take you to burn the top layer of skin off of someone's body, I could induce a stroke in their brain that would kill them instantly."

He had never looked at it that way. He knew healers were dangerous, Burghe had taught him that firsthand, but he never considered Jere to be in that category.

"Wren, it's not the gift that's dangerous, it's the person who has the gift," Jere insisted.

Wren hadn't considered this. How could he, in a society where people with physical gifts were considered dangerous as a whole? How could he separate the two? His whole life, his identity and the identity of everyone around him was inextricably tied to their gifts, and only since meeting Jere had he started to question whether this was right or even true. And if it wasn't the gift, that only left him to blame.

"And what kind of person do you think I am?" Wren asked, intending for it to be rhetorical. "You know what I did!"

"Yeah, and I know what he did to you!" Jere replied. "It's easier, I think, to blame you, or to be afraid of you, because that lets Matthias off the hook. It's easier to think of you as out of control, or dangerous because of your gift, but the truth is, I spent years hooking up with someone so disturbed that he tortured you for years and I never knew what kind of person he was. I never thought that of him. As much as I wondered if *your* gift made you dangerous, I thought the whole time I knew him that *his* gift made him safe, because I spent so long in his shadow, wanting to be like him. But what he did to you pushed you too far, more than anyone could handle. Yes, you killed him, but he deserved to be killed. You don't. You were only doing what you had to do to survive."

"But doesn't it still scare you?" Wren asked. He scared himself, how could Jere not feel the same way?

"I think anyone could have responded the same way if they were treated like that. There is nothing that I fear from you," Jere said. "I never have, even... even right after you told me. I didn't know what to feel, but I was never really afraid of you. The only thing I've been afraid of from you is that I won't be good enough, that we won't work out, that you'll call it off and we'll never get to see where this goes."

"But, you pulled away every time I touched you. You wouldn't even talk about it."

"I guess." Jere squirmed, looking away a bit and blushing. "I guess I was a little hasty at first, and a little creeped out. I didn't want to think of you using it to hurt someone, so I tried not to think of it at all, but that's wrong, it's not a thing you have or don't have or use or don't use, it's a part of you, a part of who you are, and when I say I love you, that means all of you!"

Wren couldn't keep the smile off of his face. Would he keep smiling every time Jere said he loved him until they both grew old? That didn't sound so bad.

"You shouldn't have to hide any part of yourself, and if you'll let me, I'd love to explore it with you," Jere offered.

Wren picked the tissue up, considering the offer. Would he really? Did he really want to see this part of him? He toyed with the thin white paper.

"My mum said it would ignite and that the embers would float and go out before they burned anything," Jere confided. "And it shouldn't burn you, either. She's been, um, rather excited for you to explore."

Wren grinned. Of course, Janet would be excited about that. Seeing him reach his full, firesetting potential. After all, it was *her* gift that had brought this to their attention.

"I'm not sure if I can," Wren admitted. "I only actually set things on fire a few times, most were accidental, at the training facility, and then that last time, with Burghe, that just got out of control so quickly, I was so focused on being consumed by flames and consuming him as well...."

"I'd be impressed to just see you make it smoke," Jere grinned at him.

Wren felt supported as he explored his gift, something he hadn't had before, not with the firesetting, not with the speed gift. He held the tissue in his hands, thought about warmth and heat, tried to remember the focus he had when he had caused the fire. He imagined the little tissue catching and burning, not too fast, just from one edge, slowly spreading across the rest of the surface, until it was lit up completely. He didn't realize his eyes were closed until he smelled smoke, and he opened them to see the tiniest bit of fire starting on the tissue, exactly as he had imagined it. He focused a little more, tapping into that place in his mind that just felt like fire, and the flame grew, jumping to an inch high.

He panicked, clapping his hands together and putting it out, but even that couldn't stop his giddy laughter and smile.

Jere grabbed his hand, just as excited. "You did it! You made fire with your mind!"

"I know!" Wren beamed back at him. That was exciting, but even more, he had been able to control it and stop it. Sure, he hadn't lit up the whole tissue like Janet said he could, but he also hadn't burned down the house, and he hadn't hurt anybody, and Jere, well, Jere was pleased with him.

"That's wonderful, love!" Jere kissed his hands. "So much power here, so sexy."

Wren blushed. "I barely know how to use it! Besides, I'm better at just warming things, anyway. I've actually used that a few times."

"Really?" Jere asked, raising an eyebrow. He took Wren's hands, which he was still holding, and he pulled them up to either side of his face. "Show me?"

Wren's happiness was cut a bit short at the idea of doing such a thing! "Jere, I could burn you!" he protested.

"You won't." Jere's face was calm, open, even a little excited. "I trust you completely. That never changed."

Wren thought about it. He knew the difference, didn't he? He had warmed things often enough, warmed himself, warmed water, warmed synth food sometimes, just for practice. Jere was still holding his hands to his face, and Wren hadn't fought to pull them away. He bit his lower lip as he smiled, his eyes lighting up.

Carefully, much more carefully than he had done with the tissue, Wren focused on the part of his mind that made the heat, and he felt the temperature of his palms rise ever so slightly. He looked into Jere's eyes and was met with excitement and trust. How much had they trusted each other with? Everything. And yet, this still felt so intimate.

He brought the temperature up more, and he heard Jere draw in a breath, his mouth parting slightly.

"That is fucking amazing," he whispered. "I can feel my cheeks getting warm right now!"

Wren giggled, daring to bring it up a little bit more. "Imagine how it would feel somewhere else," he teased.

Jere's hands, which were still covering his, tightened on them. "You are so fucking sexy," he muttered.

Wren kept the temperature where it was, but looked his boyfriend in the eyes. "I'm sorry that I needed to be away from you to be able to do this," he said. "I wish I could say it was a mistake, but it was exactly what I needed."

Jere looked at him, confused.

"But I don't need it anymore," Wren smirked as he pulled Jere close, kissing him deep and hard and fast while his hands continued to stay warm on his cheeks, over his shoulders, down his back and then pushing him down, on his back, while he straddled his hips.

"I need *you*," Wren whispered, arching his body and pressing it close to Jere's.

Jere responded by reaching his arms up, wrapping them around Wren's waist, trailing his hands up and under his shirt. "I missed you so much."

"I missed you!" Wren felt like he could melt under Jere's hands, little sounds of pleasure escaping his lips before he pressed them to Jere's again. "*Thank you for waiting.*"

"*I told you I'd be here,*" Jere reminded him, kissing him back desperately.

Wren didn't break the contact between their lips as his hands went down to unzip his pants, jerking them down. He was so eager to feel more of his skin touching Jere's, he didn't care how or why or in what order, all he wanted to was to feel every part of him touching every part of Jere.

Jere helped a little in the frantic removal of his own pants, and soon they were both wearing only shirts. Wren was still reluctant to break the kiss, so he didn't, keeping them glued together as one hand trailed down, feeling up and down Jere's legs, between them, cupping his ass possessively, turning up the warmth down there as well.

He felt Jere jump as he did, and heard and felt his moans, muffled by Wren's mouth covering his. He kissed him harder, his tongue working in and out, his speed gift working so much more naturally and thoughtlessly than the firesetting gift.

Once his attention to Jere's ass had gotten them both thoroughly excited, Wren took his hand and worked his cock, extra careful to maintain a comfortable temperature, jerking him off slowly and tenderly, despite wanting to attack him and claim him and fuck him all night.

"Oh my fucking god, Wren," Jere spoke through the mind connection. *"This is absolutely the most amazing thing I have ever felt. Ever. Don't ever stop."*

Wren smiled, feeling quite proud of himself. *"But wouldn't you like me to fuck you sometime tonight?"*

Jere whimpered, and Wren could feel his cock twitch. Obviously, he would like that.

Finally, because shirts were irritating, and skin was better, Wren broke the kiss between them, thrilled when Jere stretched up for more, his eyes as desperate and longing as Wren felt. In seconds, he had stripped them both of their shirts and they lay there naked, not doing anything for the moment. Their bodies touched everywhere and the residual heat of Wren's gift and lovemaking radiated from both their bodies.

"Weren't you gonna fuck me?" Jere asked, his hands coming up to rub and press at Wren's ass.

Wren nodded. This felt so good! He took a few moments to reply, using that time to bite and lick along Jere's collarbone, tracing a full circle around and then back again before replying. "I want to fuck you until you scream," he growled, his mouth right next to Jere's ear. "But I want you to keep touching me for a while, just like this."

Jere seemed quite happy to fill that request, and Wren soon found himself moaning and squirming just as much as Jere was, as Jere's hands played around his ass, just barely teasing his entrance, creeping down to caress his cock and balls now and then.

After what seemed like an eternity, Wren reached over to the bedside drawer, infinitely glad that they had stocked this one with lube as well. He drew back, drawing his tongue down Jere's chest and stomach, and worked his way down to his cock, just barely trailing his tongue over the tip of it. As he did, he poured some lube into his hand and was working it into Jere along with his fingers, feeling him tighten and squeeze around him as he rocked his hips.

"God, Wren, you feel so good!" Jere was lifting up off the bed, trying to take Wren's fingers deeper. "Fuck me. Fuck me now!"

Wren smiled. He pulled his fingers out and slid himself up the length of Jere's body, his cock taunting him. He kissed him again, feeling Jere go pliant underneath him, and then he turned and whispered, "I'm fucking you in *our* bed tonight."

Jere's eyes revealed his excitement, but not nearly as much as they revealed his impatience. "You can!" he pleaded. "Next time. Later tonight! Right now, fuck me here, fuck me right here, please!"

Wren laughed. He had almost forgotten how adorable Jere was when he begged. He got up, his cock painfully hard, and got out of bed. He wrapped his hand around his cock and started stroking it, ever so slightly.

"If you want to get fucked right now, I suggest you get in that bedroom!"

Without waiting for Jere to protest, he darted across the hall, throwing himself onto the familiar sheets that he had missed so much, the ones that smelled not only like him, but like Jere.

Jere followed a few minutes later, looking a bit chagrined, but smiling when he saw Wren lying in bed, very hard cock still in hand.

"Front or back?" he asked, pausing by the end of the bed.

Wren resisted the urge to tackle him to the floor and fuck him there instead. That could wait. For later tonight. "Back," he ordered. "So I can kiss you while I fuck you!"

Jere scrambled on the bed a second later, lying on his back and spreading his legs wide. Wren knew it was one of his favorite positions, although there were a lot between the two of them. He moved himself between Jere's legs, positioning himself, feeling them wrap around him. He leaned forward, his face just inches away from

Jere's, and he thrust into him with no warning, gazing into his eyes as he gasped with pleasure, clung to his arms, and struggled for a just a moment to adjust to him. Wren loved seeing that look in his eyes, and it was only a few seconds before he was kissing him again, hard, matching the thrusts of his cock with the force of his kiss.

Jere rocked back against him, meeting him thrust for thrust, taking him deeper and holding him there with his legs. Wren didn't mind. He had long since ceased minding the feeling of Jere's legs wrapped around him. In fact, he found it sexy, the way the muscles in his calves tightened against his ass, the way his thighs pressed against his hips. He wanted to keep fucking all night.

Soon, Wren felt his own resolve starting to slip, and Jere had been begging him to make him come for probably ten minutes. Wren would work them both up, get them right at the edge, and then back off, slowing his strokes to almost nothing, relaxing his hold on Jere's cock as well. This time, though, he felt it building, and he felt Jere twitching and jerking underneath him, and he knew there was no chance of waiting any longer. He leaned down, biting Jere's earlobe and whispering "come" a second before he kissed him again, and thrust harder and faster into him, and stroked his cock a few more times. Jere came a fraction of a second before him; he felt him tighten around his cock, the warm pool of wetness between them, and Wren joined him, crying out as he exploded and rode Jere through the last vestiges of their orgasms.

They lay there panting, kissing softly, touching each other so lightly they barely felt it.

"You should use your firesetting gift more often," Jere mumbled, his face pressed against Wren and his eyes closed. "And not just in bed."

"You seemed to like it in bed," Wren pointed out, smiling at the memory. Yes, they would have to do that again.

"I like it everywhere. It's a part of you." Jere had turned his face up so he spoke clearly, but his eyes were still closed.

"I didn't think you'd ever accept that part of me."

Now Jere opened his eyes. "It was stupid of me to hesitate."

"I'm sorry we had to be apart," Wren muttered, pulling Jere close, unwilling to ever let him go.

"I needed it too, love," Jere reminded him. "I didn't ask, but I needed to think about all this. I realized I wasn't really seeing you. I'll try never to let that happen again. I love you too much to let something stupid like this get in the way again."

"I love you too," Wren agreed, cuddling up on Jere's chest. It was really the best place to be. "Thank you. For accepting me. For exploring with me."

"I want *so* much more of you," Jere insisted. "I want to explore all of you. Nothing I could ever find out would change that."

Wren settled in. "I agree," he stated, tracing yet another line of kisses across Jere's skin. "And in the future, let's find it out together. No more lies. No more doubt, just you and me, honest, together."

If you enjoyed this story, you can sign up for a free membership at ForbiddenFiction and discuss it with other readers and the author at the *Inherent Gifts* story page
at http://forbiddenfiction.com/library/story/AC2-1.000068

We do our best to proof all our work, but if you spot a text error we missed, please let us know via our website Contact Form
at http://forbiddenfiction.com/contact.

Author's Notes

Inherent Gifts started as a single image of a master and slave working side-by-side to heal people and save lives. It was December, and it seemed like everyone else I knew was posting the novels they had written during National Novel Writing Month, which I skipped, as usual, in favor of travel and concerts. The plot was left to simmer as I found myself trying to figure out who the master was, who the slave was, and what exactly had brought them to the point at which I saw them. The story filled itself out as quickly as it could be typed, spanning over forty chapters in the first draft. New characters joined the cast, plot and mystery settled comfortably into the storyline, and suddenly the world of Wren and Jere was as alive and vibrant as my own, if not more at times.

I posted it to the blogging community where I had been reading slave fiction for years, and was delighted to see that something I created received such positive responses. I instantly fell in love with the community and the feedback I received on my story, prompting me to make better edits and keep writing. I joined the team at Forbidden Fiction almost a year after the first inspiration for the story struck, and have been consistently thrilled to share my work with a wider audience. I look forward to writing more in this world and continuing to tell the stories of the characters that have grown so real to me.

About the Author

Alicia Cameron has been making up stories since before she can remember. After discovering erotica during a high school banned books project, she never really turned back. She lives in Denver, Colorado with a tiny dog and rabbit who conspire regularly to distract her from doing anything productive. By day she works in the mental health field and is passionate about youth rights and welfare. In her spare time, she enjoys traveling, glitter, and punk rock concerts.

About the Publisher

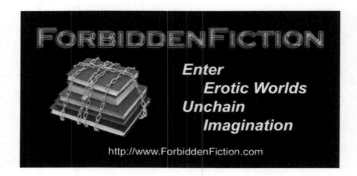

ForbiddenFiction.com is a publisher devoted to writing that breaks the boundaries of original erotic fiction. Our stories combine intense sexuality with quality writing. Stories at Forbidden Fiction.com not only arouse readers through sensations, but also engage them emotionally and mentally through storytelling as well-crafted as the sex is hot.

ForbiddenFiction.com is also designed to be a social reading environment. You'll have fun even if just reading the latest post each day, yet you will have the chance for so much more. Readers and authors can be part of ongoing discussions of specific works and individual authors as well as more general topics.

Sign up for a FREE Membership today at ForbiddenFiction. com